THE HERO'S RIGHT HAND

Bhav Das-Romain

Cover art by Joseph Idoko
Cover design by Inorai
Back cover art by Robyn Das-Romain

ISBNs: 979-8-9907000-0-0 (paperback), 979-8-9907000-1-7 (ebook)

To the friends who made me the hero of my own story.

CHAPTER ONE

As Legend Foretold

The town of Neves never got attacked. Being built around the legendary Hero's sword, *Valefor*, gave it magical protection. Kharim's blessing would stand forever. But the old story was little more than a fairytale. Since no one could pull the weapon from its obsidian slab, it only stood as a landmark of the settlement that was beset upon.

A red-haired guard stood with his back to a merchant stall. Heavy metal armor encumbered his movements. Blocking an incoming swipe caused his blade to shatter. Kargon had little energy left and couldn't find an opening. He looked to his closest ally, both in proximity and relation. The purple horned woman, Aisha, was in equally dire straits. Maybe worse as her weapon was nowhere to be seen and blood dripped from a large cut across her right eye.

Whether it was Aisha's lack of depth perception, a stroke of luck, or desperation, she stumbled next to the legendary sword. Without hesitation, she gripped the leather wrapped hilt. In a swift motion, she rended the blade from stone, bisecting her assailant. Blood slid off along with years of rust and debris.

All froze as they took in the sight of the shining silver blade. Kargon took the opportunity to toss aside his useless weapon then pummel a bandit into submission while Aisha tore through the remaining bandits with ease. Unmatched bladework only improved with *Valefor* in her grasp.

The aftermath of the attack left the duo dumbfounded. For the first time in twenty two years, people took notice of the soft spoken woman. Even those affected had more interest in Aisha than their own wellbeing.

The town elder, Niko, pulled Aisha from her guard post and moved her to a secure hut near the guard tower. Swordmasters and mages traveled from all over the continent of Tetria to train her. Even a world renowned healer visited to heal Aisha's right eye. At least, that's what she told others.

"It's fake. I can't even see through it, Kargon. It's a conduit," Aisha said while stirring her third cup of tea.

Spellcasting wasn't possible for most humanoids without use of a conduit. Few races could access their mana without one. A half-elf like Aisha was no different.

"Isn't *Valefor* already a conduit?" Kargon gulped down his own boiling hot beverage.

"I'm not strong enough to use it like that. Not yet, at least. Though the prosthetic does let me use some vision based spells and I can literally see mana," Aisha bragged. "But it's gonna take some getting used to if you don't wanna get sick every time.

A woman many years her elder rubbed Aisha's head softly and said, "You'll do great, hun."

Marniese, Aisha's mother, was full blooded tiefling. Purple skin with long horns and a slender tail adorned her slender form. Business at her cafe was steady with rumors that the Hero stopped by. The home they shared felt barren since Aisha began training for her quest. As a result, Kargon made a point to often check in on his godmother. A guard's schedule, while packed, was nowhere near as busy as the chosen one.

"You always say that, Mom," Aisha replied with an assuring soft smile.

"I ain't been wrong before, have I?" Marniese looked at Kargon.

He smirked. "Not once."

Aisha rolled her eyes then finished her drink. Habits told them it was time to part. She quickly hugged the others before stepping into the night.

Breaks were few and far between with all the necessary training. Hundreds of years worth of sword techniques were drilled into her.

Manipulation of mana and conduit control took forever to understand. Loneliness was unavoidable as she went weeks without seeing anyone except the rotating mentors. Some were friendly while others only sought to garner fame from training the future Hero. It took eight years of constant pressure and focus for her skill to reach an acceptable level.

Meanwhile, Kargon's free time was spent caring for all the things Aisha held dear about Neves. Foods she liked were brought to each hangout. Small gifts were sprinkled throughout Marniese's home. He even trained in secret in hopes of understanding what his best friend was going through.

"You can rest, firecracker," Velana, Kargon's mother, said as she nervously braided her pristine black hair between thin fingers. "You run yourself ragged."

"Aisha can't... so, I can't," Kargon panted. "I need to get stronger."

"Why?"

"It's the way of the warrior, my love." A large, red haired man said as he placed a warm hand on his wife's shoulder. Zigon towered over most with his muscular frame. Many referred to him as a gentle giant. "Strength is a means to protect the person he loves."

Kargon rolled his eyes at the words. Friendship was the sole purpose behind his hard work. But explaining that to the lovebirds that were his parents was pointless.

Guards were expected to fight complimentary to Aisha. Not that the commander or town elder asked her. Kargon didn't bother telling Aisha something she likely deduced. Everyone needed to reach a new standard. There was no more freedom in combat styles. The best soldiers received conduits and magic training. Kargon never so much as tested one. His swordsmanship lacked and he was unworthy of the front lines. Standing alongside Aisha was a pipe dream.

News of the Hero spread across the continent, followed by rumors of calamity. Most were overjoyed that someone appeared to face the oncoming cataclysm. Others were frustrated that the Hero didn't hail from their region. Even some cursed that a woman had drawn *Valefor*. If any of it bothered Aisha, she did well to hide it.

Old friends distanced themselves without a reason. Kargon had his own assumptions. It took every fiber of his being not to say something on the off chance they crossed paths with Aisha.

The chance of awkward encounters ended abruptly. Elder Niko announced Aisha's departure a year in advance. The decade of training would soon end and her quest would begin.

Preparations started for a grand party. Visitors arrived from every corner of the globe. Every single week had some event to aid in preparation yet Kargon remained uninvolved. It all passed in a blur until only a week was left before Aisha's departure and the town was abuzz with guests.

Kargon kept busy. It was the only thing distracting him from losing his best friend. For the first time in his life, he kept quiet. But, he couldn't stay that way when he was called to the guard commander's office. Kargon was prepared to be fired. Instead, he found the commander and town elder arguing with Aisha while a dozen armored adventurers stood by.

"He really doesn't exude reliability," Elder Niko sighed while looking pointedly at the fiery hair atop Kargon's lean form. "Aisha, you can't be serious about this."

"I am," she replied.

Bystanders immediately shouted refusals and barked insults at Kargon.

"What's going on?" he asked.

Commander Ivana sighed. "Aisha wants you to be her guardian."

Elder Niko threw up his hands. "After we went to the trouble of gathering trained warriors who've traveled the world! Fought countless battles! Some even came out of retirement for this opportunity! And she wants a simple town guard to go with her. Not only that but the WORST soldier in Neves!"

Aisha glared at them ferociously. Each stood at least a head taller than her, yet still cowered.

"He was never meant to be a soldier," Aisha replied calmly. "No amount of training would allow him to unlearn the ways of a monk."

"Five years of his youth is not enough time for him to be a formidable monk," Commander Ivana said.

"I agree. But he's been training on his own since he was 21. For each hour he trains as a soldier, he does twice as much as a monk. He's even in contact with his old master!"

Commander Ivana counted in her head and replied, "Fourteen

years of training is commendable. Have you truly been doing so, Kargon?"

Aisha didn't answer and turned to Kargon. His quizzical look didn't soften her gaze. How she knew he still trained was a mystery. He'd made a point not to mention it.

Aisha cleared her throat and tilted her head towards the others.

"Yes, ma'am. My master drilled the importance of continued practice into me," Kargon answered. "Whenever I felt I was stagnating, I would send him a letter. He'd provide cryp— guidance."

Commander Ivana nodded and said, "Your most successful defenses have involved loss of your weapon. Not to say anything of your grit and effort."

"But that's still not enough to be your guardian," Elder Niko complained.

"I want a traveling companion — not a guardian," Aisha said angrily. "I haven't even hit my first half century and we lead lives spanning a few hundred years. I don't want it ruined by someone's 'experiences'. If the quest takes longer than you assume, I want an ally who will be around for the whole of it."

Elder Niko grumbled, "He doesn't even have a conduit."

Surprisingly, Commander Ivana responded to the childish statement. "We will provide him with one. That is, if he accepts."

Kargon stared up at his best friend. "Aisha. Why me?"

She shook her head and sighed. "For years you've said people would bend over backwards wanting to help me. Are you really gonna say no when I'm personally asking for it?"

"Of course not—"

"Then say yes!"

With a deep breath, Kargon studied his friend's inquisitive face. In a flash, his mind returned to the dozens of times they talked about adventuring as children. When that dream vanished was beyond him. It should have been a given that the path back would be led by Aisha.

A smile cracked as Kargon left his reverie. "Absolutely. The Hero asked for me, after all."

Few people were excited about Kargon being the Hero's first party member. None could deduce her true motives. Even Kargon gave up trying and just prepared to travel. The following week went by quickly.

"So, you got your armor?" Aisha asked as they stood over a table in his family's home.

"Came in with Master Avant's blessing," Zigon said as he looked over his son's ensemble.

Kargon wore a skintight sleeveless black tunic with a rigid collar that covered half his neck. White threads trailed down the center where it was bound together. Loose black pants ended near his ankles which were bound by white wraps. Similar wraps covered his arms, caramel skin peeking through. A sturdy dark red sash was tied tightly around his waist with thick ends hanging off his hip down to his knees. Simple black flats slipped over his feet.

"Left quite an impression on that old bird," his father stated.

Velana rubbed her son's head and chuckled. "It is rather shocking considering how you were when you got there."

"Don't remind me," Kargon groaned. "I'm just glad he remembered not to include sleeves."

"They got here right on time," Aisha chortled, hoping no one saw the rising glow on her copper cheeks. "How'd you swing such a fast delivery?"

Elder Niko covered the costs. He likely hated every moment of it but with every passing day there were less opportunities to complain. Maybe that was why only Commander Ivana was around when it came time for Kargon to receive his conduit.

"You know how this works, right?" Commander Ivana had asked while welding the links of a bracelet tightly around the monk's wrist. A small ruby shimmered at the center of the chain.

"Yes, ma'am," Kargon replied. "We tested them in school."

"What kind of magic do you have?"

"Self-immolation."

Commander Ivana wore the same face everyone else did when Kargon answered this question. Shock with a twinge of concern. She looked at the bracelet, seemingly ready to rip it off the man's arm.

"Kargon, explain," Aisha groaned.

"Right, sorry. I can wreath myself in fire and burn things on contact.. It doesn't affect me but I need special clothes." His eyes wandered with his thoughts. "My attacks get an explosive impact. Oh!

I can snuff out other flames by touching them. More fire requires more effort."

"That doesn't seem versatile enough for this journey," the commander said.

"It'll be fine," Aisha said. "Come on, let's get the last of our stuff ready before we head out."

She dragged Kargon out before they could be stopped. Locals and tourists tried to get their attention but the duo ignored them.

Behind closed doors, the constant attention annoyed Aisha. Over the last week, she'd given Kargon a crash course in what to expect from the general public. No amount of warnings could have prepared him. Shaking hands and kissing babies was the easiest part of the job. Some asked the duo to do menial favors in hopes of mention in Aisha's future legend. She mastered the art of turning them down.

Standing outside Kargon's home, Aisha smiled softly. There wouldn't be time for goodbyes after the celebration. It had to be now.

Zigon and Velana waited inside with their son's bag packed, his mother's face streaked with tears. With silent footsteps Kargon stepped forward and bowed to his parents. Velana hugged her boy tightly then stepped back. A silent stare passed between Kargon and his father. Something small was hidden in Zigon's large hands. He raised them up and Kargon intuitively shut his eyes. Normally the firm hand would ruffle his hair. Instead he felt something slip over his head and land on his neck. Upon opening his eyes, the adventurer saw a pair of goggles resting on him.

Blue lenses reflected the image of his father. Small gold wingtips protruded from both sides.

"It's an heirloom from my family. A reminder for you that we're still here," Zigon explained. "It'll empower your flames as it did mine."

"Pops." Kargon searched for words but nothing felt right. "Thanks. I'll take care of them."

"I'm sorry for asking him to come with me," Aisha said.

Velana shook her head furiously. "Don't dare apologize for inviting our son to join you. Not you of all people."

"Go with our blessing," Zigon said and placed a hand on both children's shoulders.

As they left, Aisha avoided the growing crowd in the town. She dreaded the upcoming celebration. Just the idea of the party was exhausting. Hiding in her hut until it was time was the best option.

Aisha landed heavily on her bed and stared at the ceiling while Kargon sat at the table nearby. Long groans and heavy sighs was the only conversation for many minutes. It reminded Kargon of their youth when he did all the talking.

"Why don't we just leave?" he asked.

"And what, get to the party early?" Aisha scoffed.

"No. I mean, we're all packed. Why don't we leave?"

"We'd get caught," the Hero said readily, though the confidence on her face wasn't reflected in her voice. "Wouldn't we?"

"There are routes out only you and I know, remember?" Kargon replied.

"And some of the people we grew up with," Aisha amended with a somber look.

"Do you think they'd give us away?"

Aisha shook her head as she looked down. Her right index finger and thumb pressed against her horns, slowly rubbing upwards before moving her hand away then repeating the motion. A habit from their childhood that predicated a successful plan

"Any idea where we'd go?" Kargon asked.

"Balur," Aisha answered dryly. "The home of the first Hero. The elves said they'd help me find my way."

"How would we get there?"

"Carriage on the outskirts of town. One of us would need to drive."

"Easy enough. I'm guessing the carriage has all our supplies."

"Yes. And my equipment is here," Aisha said as she stood up from her chair.

Meticulously, she donned her armor. A silver chestplate reflected the dim candlelight of the room. Peeking out of the top was a long black scarf with a tail that hung down to her shins. Matching pauldrons with simple joints covered her shoulders. Underneath, black padded leather hugged Aisha's form. Gloves made of the same material adorned her hands. Metallic skirt pieces and boots completed the suit. Kargon couldn't take his eyes off her mesmerizing form. Every part of him screamed to say something. Instead he silently focused on *Valefor,* sheathed on Aisha's hip.

Pulling her hair into a messy bun, she said, "This is your last chance to turn back."

Kargon's mind calmed and he smiled. "People will bend over backwards to help the Hero, right?"

Aisha grinned back. "Right."

Both stood at the window until a declaration was made. One Aisha used to guide the duo since childhood.

"With me."

CHAPTER TWO

Diverging Paths

Sneaking through Neves was easier said than done. The streets were beyond bustling as the celebration neared. Decorations adorned every corner and streamers covered the sky, spreading a rainbow of light below. Citizens occupied most every gathering place. Navigating through most familiar locations was impossible.

Staying hidden in shadows wasn't difficult with their overwhelmingly dark ensembles. But light easily reflected off Aisha's platemail. Bright sheens immediately garnered attention. If someone so much as shuffled in the duo's general direction, they ducked into a different path. Thankfully, the armor wasn't as loud as it was eye-catching. Sigils etched into each piece kept them silent.

"You know, I didn't think about how much bigger we are now," Kargon whispered.

"What are you talking about?" Aisha said while leading them to a small alcove.

"Are we gonna fit?"

A wall of tightly packed oaks grew on this side of town. One large trunk bolstered the foundation of nearby buildings, with a small opening beneath. Luckily, a loose plank could be moved aside for access.

Much to their chagrin, there were people loitering a few buildings away from their perfect escape. The duo paused near another alley. There were only a few routes left.

"We could always try the bakery," Aisha said and nodded to the building next to them.

"I'm not avoiding it to be petty," Kargon replied. "The place is crawling with people even when Neves isn't filled with tourists. What about the rooftops?"

"I'll stick out like a sore thumb."

By a stroke of bad luck, eyes wandered towards the alley where they hid. Aisha pushed Kargon further into the corner and squeezed close in hopes they weren't caught. Her hand felt soft against his chest. Aisha noted how toned the monk's muscles were.

Encroaching footsteps pulled them to their senses. Voices grew louder. Just as the civilians turned the corner, the shop door burst open and blocked their view. A cart covered in decadent pastries rolled out and a plump, elephant-headed man stepped outside. He tapped his foot against Kargon, who pulled Aisha swiftly into the store.

"Whoa, there. Plenty of goodies to go around," the man said jovially. "No reason to knock down my employee entrance."

"Bennett, did you see the Hero? She was right there!" someone said.

The baker turned in a circle slowly then shrugged. "What would she be doing here?" Bennett put his hand beneath the cover of his cart and fished out three cookies. "Take a load off, on me."

Bennett watched the group leave. When the coast was clear, he dashed inside and slammed the door shut. Only Kargon, Aisha, and Bennett stood in the dimly lit kitchen, surrounded by baked goods. A smile stretched across the baker's face as he took in the sight of old friends. It quickly changed to a pained expression and he turned away. Before anyone could speak, he retrieved a bag set aside from everything else.

"I wanted to give this to you before you left. It's some pastries you both liked. I practiced so I could..." Bennett's eyes grew teary as he spoke. "I'm sorry I didn't stick around. There was so much happening and I can't do much for the Hero. I'm really happy for both of you though! I know you'll be great. I'm sorry..."

Aisha pulled the man into a hug. A soft kiss on the cheek calmed him. Confusion was all he could manage while looking at Aisha then Kargon. The monk hopped up to slap Bennett's shoulder.

"She gets it. You know that means I do, too," Kargon said while snatching the bag of pastries.

Tears flowed nonstop even as Bennett tried to wipe them away. A fervent nod was all he could muster before pulling both adventurers into a hug. After a few moments, he led them to a loose board at the other side of the kitchen.

"Ever since you found this thing we've been using it to feed some strays.," Bennett said. "Use the break. And take care of each other."

"You too, Benji," Aisha said softly. She dashed through the exit with Kargon hot on her heels. The hidden path they had originally planned to use was clearly occupied by the overwhelming citizens. One other simple path existed that they would have avoided if not for Bennett's assistance. Aisha didn't want to face the people who'd left her. But it was unbecoming of a Hero to flee from confrontation.

The local armory's backdoor could only be opened by a few people. A nearby decorative piece of metal needed to be pushed a specific way for the door to give. Aisha kept watch while Kargon crept through to make sure the coast was clear. There weren't any customers in the closed shop. However, the armorer's family were relaxing around one of the tables. They stared at him.

"Um, can we cut through here?" Kargon asked.

All of them were shocked to see the man who'd avoided the shop for a decade. The most surprised was the leatherworker who caused his avoidance. With a deep gulp, Petla invited Kargon inside and in turn, he signaled Aisha. Shock turned to excitement as the Hero made her presence known.

"Aisha!" Petla squealed and rushed over before staring intently at the leather armor and scarf worn by her old friend. "Oh, it fits perfectly! I was so worried. How's it feel?"

"Good?" Aisha replied hesitantly, shooting a look of concern at Kargon..

"Petla, did you make those?" Kargon asked.

The leatherer regained her composure. With a slow nod she answered, "Yes. I hope that's okay. When the order came in I demanded that I craft Aisha's inner armor. I'm still learning how to work with steel so..." Petla looked at Aisha and huffed. "I'm in the wrong, I know. I'm sorry for not getting in touch while you were training. I didn't want to be a distraction. If you got hurt or messed up because of me I'd never forgive myself. So I focused on something I—"

Aisha tightly hugged the frantic woman. "You've done amazingly, Petla. No need to apologize."

It took some time for Petla to calm down and reciprocate the gesture. They hadn't embraced in years. Both knew it was possibly the last time. Even Kargon couldn't know what was shared in that silent embrace, only that Aisha seemed a little lighter afterwards.

There were a few exits from the armory that connected to the path out of town. The side of the armory had a path into the forest that split either onto the main road or back towards the stables. Going directly for the carriage was the only option. As the celebration grew closer, foot traffic would die down.

"We can wrap around the outside of town," Kargon said. "It's risky but we need the carriage."

Aisha nodded. "Less risky than running past the market."

Instead of going on the path, the duo cut through the trees to get back to town. From the foliage it was possible to see a row of wagons parked in stalls with horses resting across from them.

"Is that one ours?" Kargon asked as he nodded to a pristine white wagon with gold embellishments.

Aisha's mouth was agape. "You've got to be kidding me."

"Why don't we take one of the other rentals?"

"Moving our supplies would take too long."

"It's a good thing you don't have to," a voice said from behind them. A haughty aura wafted off Quintin as it had since their youth. "Such a vehicle doesn't suit the needs of an adventurer, does it?"

"It just needs a horse," Kargon replied defensively.

"Hm, yes. And then it will garner the attention of every bandit in a ten mile radius. Wonderful idea, Kargon. Please, allow Aisha to be the brains of your operation."

The Hero stared intently at the confident aristocrat, a practiced gaze that put Quintin at unease. They cleared their throat and gestured for the duo to follow. Kargon rolled his eyes. However, Aisha readily went after their old acquaintance which convinced her best friend to follow.

They arrived at a secluded alcove, hidden yet easily accessible from the main road. A suited butler awaited the group next to a prepared carriage saddled to two black horses. Contrary to Quintin's own immaculate clothes, the vehicle was very plain.

"Bennett contacted me after your encounter," Quintin explained. "I pulled some strings to examine your carriage and Jonah moved your supplies to a more inconspicuous vehicle."

"Why?" Kargon asked curiously.

"It may surprise you but I hope for your success."

They squirmed under Aisha's intense gaze until she finally spoke. "What changed?"

"I... I thought you believed you were above all of us. It didn't occur to me until a few years ago that you were forced into a position and doing your best with what was handed to you. I know a little about that," Quintin admitted. "When news spread that you chose Kargon to join your quest... You're the same child who used him as a messenger. Though, significantly stronger now."

"That's the first time you haven't sounded like a complete ass since we were teenagers," Kargon chided then slapped his old friend's back. It was the closest thing he was willing to give in the form of acceptance.

Aisha looked at the usually confident Quintin as they hung their head in shame. With a smile, Aisha kissed their cheek and thanked them.

"We'll take it from here, Jonah. Thanks, Quin," Kargon said over his shoulder while hopping into the driver's seat.

As the duo distanced themselves from their home, years of doubts melted away. Future concerns occupied their mind, but neither could hide the smiles only known to adventurers.

CHAPTER THREE

Between a Rock

Guiding horses to pull a carriage was much harder than Kargon anticipated. The hundreds of pounds in the wagon slowed the beasts. Unpaved roads made relaxation nearly impossible as everything vibrated while passing over pebbles. Not to mention, Aisha was fiercely pouting at her friend and refused to let him relax.

"You seriously left a note?" she complained.

"Yes. So no one would think we ran away," Kargon answered.

"They didn't need to know!"

"Knowing Elder Niko, he'll spin this into some story that it was planned all along," Kargon replied. "The town should party and send us off with a bang regardless of where we are."

"If you're so worried about them, we shouldn't have snuck out," Aisha argued.

"I was worried about you."

Aisha's frustration masked her blush well. She shook her head.

Kargon continued, "Sneaking out was the best option but there's the chance they'd assume the worst and I wanted to avoid that."

Aisha sighed. "At least it's not like when we were kids and you'd tell our parents we were going to the secret tunnel."

"I was nine! I'm shocked we didn't get lost with you leading," Kargon retaliated.

"That only happened once!" Aisha whined. "Not to mention, I was still the only one willing to lead after that."

She had relaxed since leaving, like years of pent up stress began to fade. It enticed Kargon to tease his best friend.

"Do you know which way we're going now?"

Aisha hesitated before reaching into their bags. She retrieved a rolled up map and unfurled it, murmuring while examining the path forward. The road from their hometown ran parallel to a river that ran east before depositing into the southern sea. Centuries ago, the island of Balur floated far from the land but had turned invisible following Kharim's passing.

Kargon started, "You mentioned the elves said they'd help you—"

"They didn't give me a way to contact or reach them," Aisha interrupted.

"How exactly do you expect us to get there?"

The Hero huffed. "I don't know, Kargon. But they made their presence known so someone should know how to get there."

"Do you think anyone in Wolden would know?" he asked, referring to the nearest village along the river.

"It's our best option."

It didn't sit well with Kargon to work off Aisha's impulses. She usually had a plan and left risk-taking to the monk. Regardless, the best option was to follow the path and hopefully arrive at their destination in a few days. It meant they'd need to camp like they'd dreamed about as kids. Though, neither had actually camped out since then.

The duo hoped the trip to Balur wouldn't be long. Every passing moment raised the chance of encountering other people. Travelers were a big concern as they might recognize the intrepid Hero. Aisha grew accustomed to quickly stowing away in the wagon when others approached. Luckily, Kargon was unknown outside of Neves. Some quick wit and general knowledge of the area allowed him to point people in the right direction before making a quick getaway. Unfortunately, roads weren't only occupied by innocent travelers.

After hours, the road cleared and Aisha sat on high alert. She could normally point out oddities from hundreds of feet away. Something must have distracted her as they were beset upon. Loud neighing echoed for mere seconds before being abruptly silenced. The familiar sensation of Aisha's kick kept Kargon awake for mere seconds. Pain pounded in his head as he struggled to move or keep his eyes open.

Neither adventurer understood when they lost consciousness.

***

The sun had long set by the time Kargon awoke. Surrounding him was a large stone room with metal bars grafted onto one side. It made for uncomfortable sleeping quarters. Kargon could see in the dark, albeit with little color distinction. Even so, he instantly noticed Aisha angrily staring at the bandits. Yet, for all her fury, the cage still stood.

"How come you haven't broken out?" he whispered.

"There's a magical seal surrounding this thing. I can't do a thing," Aisha said. "They took my sword. I can't cut through the rocks."

The ability to detect magic escaped Kargon. Nevertheless, he attempted to produce a flame to no avail. An inactive conduit remained equipped to his wrist. In a panic, he examined his neck and found Zigon's goggles had been taken. Before he could look for it, another voice in the cage drew his attention.

"It is a powerful seal considering it was created by weaklings," a person said from the opposite corner of the cage. "I am unsure if they are overconfident or foolish for trusting it."

Sandy brown hair peeked out of a dark cloak and hood that covered the elf's smooth cream skin. Grey and brown leather armor adorned their body. Draconic scales jutting out of the entire left side of the elf required openings across their clothing. Whatever accursed thing caused such a wound had mutated the left side of their face to resemble a dragon's; down to the pupil. Their left arm resembled a full length bracer but moved with no impediments. Sharp golden eyes boring into Kargon made him realize he'd been staring for too long.

"Ah, sorry. How do you know about the seal?" he asked.

"It is rather obvious when you consider that your conduit has remained equipped. I planned to break out when they opened the cell to move me. Unfortunately, they magically lifted the entire cage instead," the elf replied gruffly.

"One of them has to be a geomancer," Aisha said quietly.

Kargon pressed his face against the metal bars and peered through. Their carriage and horses stood on the other side of the small forest opening. Stone muzzles sealed the creature's mouths. Another horse drawn wagon sat close by that looked large enough to carry the stone prison. A campfire surrounded by five bandits blocked the way. Within their grasp were a handful of goods, including the goggles and *Valefor*.

Kargon turned quickly and whispered to Aisha, "You let go of the sword?"

"They knocked me out too, idiot," she rebutted. "They can't draw it from the sheath. Only I can."

"A magic sword?" the stranger's eyes narrowed while studying the other prisoners. "Black clothing adorned by travelers from the west. Nevesi believe the color is auspicious."

"What about it?" Kargon asked.

"For you to have a magic sword means it is likely *Valefor*? Am I correct?"

A silent gaze passed between the adventuring duo. The elf's intrigued look changed to disappointment.

"Assuming that is *Valefor*, that means you are the chosen one," they said. "How could you allow yourself to be captured by these fools?"

"You're trapped in here too," Aisha replied.

"I don't owe an explanation to amateurs who failed to cast a ward on their carriage. It is common practice when leaving on a journey."

"I'm blaming Quintin for that," Kargon said.

Aisha turned to him. "No. We should've known to check."

"Dammit," Kargon grunted. "That's in the past. We need to get out of here if we're going to reach Wolden."

The elf's ears perked. "Why are you traveling to Wolden?"

Kargon silently stared at Aisha. A roll of her eyes and nod were her response.

"We are trying to reach Balur," Kargon said.

The other prisoner chuckled, sighed and leaned against the wall. "I'm interested in seeing you try while trapped in this magic box. I am incapable of breaking the metal."

Aisha's eyes widened and she shoved Kargon into the bars. With her friend blocking the view, it was possible to study the cage without wandering eyes. Light taps confirmed a suspicion before Aisha pulled her friend back to the center of the cage.

"You can judge us and all but if we break out of here, will you help us?" Aisha asked their cellmate. "Just with the bandits. Then we can go our separate ways."

The elf eyed Aisha then Kargon before nodding. "How will we escape?"

"They aren't maintaining concentration on the spell that's binding the stones. We just need a strong force to knock the bars out," Aisha explained. "One shot only. If we're heard, they'll reinforce the cell."

"I am not the kind to use brute strength to muscle through obstacles," the elf said.

"Neither am I. My strength is pretty average but I have speed," Aisha said. "Kargon, on the other hand, should be able to break us out no problem."

From where Kargon stood, it was possible to strike the center of the bars. A focused strike should work. Aisha's confidence was as close to a guarantee there was. Kargon focused his mind. With a sharp breath, he launched his fist forward and blasted the metal bars off the cell.

He rushed to the campfire as some of the bandits rose from their seats. One with its back turned had his neck snapped instantly. Two of the captors turned their attention to the monk with weapons drawn while the others looked towards the broken jail cell. Aisha magically dashed past Kargon and his opponents, the cover of night obscuring her movement. A powerful strike knocked her sword away from the bandit holding it. From midair, Aisha grabbed the hilt and with a fluid motion unsheathed *Valefor* before decapitating the bandit. Swift kicking to the falling sheath propelled it into the other bandit's face. While he was blinded, Aisha pierced his chest.

Taking Aisha's lead, Kargon retrieved his goggles and awkwardly strapped them to his face while ducking under a sword swing. The long tails at the back of the eyewear whipped in the wind. A forceful pull tightened them around the monk's eyes. With a deep breath, he ignited his fists to obscure the attackers' vision. To Kargon's surprise, the wraps on his arms didn't burn. Even more shocking was that he could see them within the flames. Thanks were quickly whispered to his father before taking the offensive.

Dirt shifted as Kargon stomped his left foot forward, his right arm cocked back. The attack was often frowned upon for all its openings but Kargon swore by its reliability. With one punch, he left a burning imprint on the enemy's chest as his fist dug in. Boiling blood burst outward. Even though the wound cauterized, there was no way to survive a blazing heart.

Long preparation allowed the final bandit to get behind the monk. Instincts roared that a sword would cut through him. But the feeling vanished as suddenly as it appeared. Two arrows were jammed through the bandit's ears and blood poured from the wounds. The elf used them as grips to violently throw the corpse aside.

"Thank you," Kargon said.

"Likewise," the elf replied. "Are there any others?"

"If there were, they're long dead," Kargon replied while nodding towards Aisha who already walked to the carriage.

"Confident," the elf said as they approached.

Aisha passed a rucksack over. "Thank you for your assistance. I take it this is yours."

"Yes," the elf said and checked inside. "What are you seeking in Balur?"

"We have questions for the conclave."

"Shall we travel together then? Until Balur?"

Aisha narrowed her gaze then tilted her head towards Kargon. "I'll leave it to him."

Both sets of eyes laid on the monk. With the dim light of the campfire he could now see the elf more clearly. There was a chip on their shoulder and inexplicable anger in their eyes. It reminded Kargon of his youth.

"My name is Kargon, the chosen one's first ally." He put out a hand.

"Sariel," the elf replied and shook it.

Aisha introduced herself then pulled open the curtain of the covered wagon.

"Now that I know we're in this together; do you know what this is?"

Almost everything in the carriage was as they'd left it, if a little out of place. But that wasn't what Aisha inquired about. An intricate cobalt chest lined with gold embellishments demanded their attention. No one recognized it. Aisha had checked their supplies earlier and guaranteed this wasn't from Neves.

The chest was warm to the touch but didn't burn. A metal lock hung on the front and Sariel offered to unlock it. Vines grew from dexterous fingers which fooled the lock into opening. Afterwards, they stepped back and nodded to Aisha who in turn nodded to Kargon.

"Why me?" he asked. "You're the Hero."

"Are you serious? It's hot!" Aisha replied.

"No, it's not! I barely feel it!"

"Are you completely unaware of your magic's passive traits?" Sariel grunted.

The monk huffed. "What do you — Oh."

He shuffled forward quickly to hide his reddening cheeks. Ornaments on the chest made it obvious a wealthy patron had owned whatever was locked inside. Regardless of the form it took, the value had to be high. Shaky hands hovered over the latch. With trepidation, Kargon opened the chest.

CHAPTER FOUR

First Stop

"Who would purchase an egg?" Sariel asked while watching the chest. "Is this some form of long cooking?"

"I think it's an incubator," Kargon replied from the driver's seat. "Though I'm not sure why someone would travel with it."

Aisha didn't look up from studying the map and nonchalantly said, "Bandits attack towns. They probably thought there was treasure inside."

"Warm treasure?" Sariel snorted. "Ignoramuses."

"Yet somehow they captured us," Kargon sighed. "Thanks for putting a ward on the carriage, Sariel."

"Consider the scroll recompense for allowing me to join you."

"Don't mention it," Aisha said. "Now, can we please focus on finding Wolden? It should be nearby... Unless I'm misreading the map."

"Allow me," Sariel said and held out their hand. It took a second of study before they stated, "Another two hours traveling east will get us to farmland. On the opposite side, Wolden."

As predicted, nearly two hours later they arrived. A large wooden barn connected to a stable towered over a small fenced garden. Livestock grazed lazily on vast farmland. Opposite the farm was a house. The group pulled their carriage off-road before making for the building. Kargon led with Aisha following closely and Sariel at their backs.

A middle-aged human woman dressed in common clothing answered the door. "Oh, dear. I believe the festival is already over. You're too late."

"Festival?" Kargon asked.

"In Neves. You are traveling there, aren't you?" the woman asked while looking between the group.

"Margaret, their carriage is facing our town. Must've just arrived," a gruff voice said from inside. "Invite them in."

With a slight bow, the party was welcomed into the humble abode. Squeezed into a cushioned chair, a hulking orc read the national newspaper. Wiry glasses rested on his angular green nose and softened the gaze of battle hardened eyes. Damaged canines jutted out of his underbite. If not for the surprisingly domestic outfit and warm smile on his face, the party might have mistaken him for an enemy.

"Of course the Hero's party already has a new member," the orc said.

Aisha blinked. "News travels quickly."

"Quite right. Not to mention, images of you have traveled around the world over the last decade," he explained while getting out of the seat to shake Aisha's hand. "My name is Pavrin Tenrok, Wolden's welcoming committee. You've already met my wife, Margaret."

The familiar aura of a gentle giant emanated off him. It helped calm any nerves Aisha had while introducing her party. With the Tenrok's help, the party stowed the carriage, stabled their horses, and retrieved their rucksacks. Kargon opted to hide the warm chest in his relatively empty bag.

Margaret treated the party to a warm meal. It had only been a few days but the comfort of a home felt alien. Graciously, the hosts offered to have someone help the adventurers on their search in the village. The welcoming committee had clearly practiced approaching this subject. As if on queue, their teenage daughter burst out of her room and introduced herself as Melinda. The blank stare on her face made it clear she hadn't realized who the guests were. It took until she caught sight of Aisha for the young girl's eyes to sparkle with delight.

Melinda rushed to sit next to the Hero before asking, "Is it true you were only twenty when you drew *Valefor*?"

"Twenty two, actually. Though not on purpose... The papers were exaggerated," Aisha answered.

"Sure. But you couldn't have fought them without practice! That's all you!"

Aisha smirked. "I've heard that before." Before Melinda could titter off more questions, Aisha asked, "Is there anywhere we can conduct research in Wolden?"

"The library," Melinda replied. "Oh! Father Vofric! He's the guy to go to for any info."

"Priests are rarely forthcoming with outsiders," Sariel said.

"He's no ordinary priest! Trust me. He's helped me deal with… some stuff that happened."

Calling Wolden a town was an understatement even compared to Neves. From the center square, the village only stretched for about a mile in every direction. The library north of the square was of negligible size but that didn't diminish the importance of research found there.

Excited villagers approached the party. Though, they avoided Aisha and instead directed their conversations at the others. Sariel was cold and dismissed the rabble. Kargon, however, expected to handle conversations the moment Aisha invited him on the quest. Fielding a party's worth of questions was more difficult than he anticipated. Aisha and Sariel entered the library to continue the search, leaving the Hero's companion to entertain the villagers' curiosity.

The faint idea of what to search for allowed Aisha to quickly gather reading material before sitting at an empty table. Meanwhile, Sariel sauntered between the shelves with little interest in actual research. It took a few minutes before Kargon joined with Melinda in tow. Even less time passed before her feigned interest was no more. A long heavy sigh made it clear what she wanted.

Kargon muffled a sigh, tapped her shoulder, and asked, "Where is Father Vofric?"

The answer was so quick that he didn't actually catch the words. Upon exiting the library, Melinda dashed to what appeared to be a large house. Inside were only rows of pews with a single chair at the front facing them. Not a single idol or podium rested in the house of worship.

"Melinda, what brings you here?" a gruff voice asked from behind one of the pews.

A dwarf stepped around the corner, spinning a small hammer in his worn hand. Grey dreadlocks clung to a sweaty black forehead. A thick, well-kept beard covered almost half of his torso. Instead of robes, the man wore a buttoned flannel shirt and khaki pants. Wise orange eyes from someone half Kargon's height demanded respect with a single calm glance.

Melinda smiled. "Father Vofric, good afternoon. This is Kargon, he's a companion of the Hero!"

The monk stepped forward and bowed slightly. "Pleasure to meet you, Father. Melinda speaks very highly of you."

"You may address me as Vofric," he said and shook hands with his visitor. Splinters fell from his beard as he brushed through it and sighed. "I had heard the Hero's party was visiting our humble town but was not expecting to make your acquaintance. What brings you here?"

"We are searching for a means to reach Balur," Kargon replied.

"The first Hero's home. A good starting place to embark on your quest," Vofric said then frowned. "Unfortunately, our village is of no use. Better you head to Sespik. It is a port town to the southeast."

Immediate dismissal caused Kargon to push for information. "Wolden may be far from Balur but there is the library where the Hero is sure she's found something of note. And you seem well informed."

"You misunderstand, Kargon. We are unable to help due to current events." A raised eyebrow and nod from his guest invited Vofric to continue. He sighed and looked at Melinda who was staring quietly at the ground. "Villagers have gone missing over the past months. Melinda's friend, Erlav, suffered a similar fate," Vofric said. "The village watch and I are preoccupied with the search for our people."

"Why haven't you contacted adventurers for help?" Kargon asked.

"We have. None have returned. I am unsure whether they failed or fled but I hope for the latter."

"Do you have any clues?"

Vofric took a breath and turned to Melinda. "It's getting dark, dear. Be safe on your way home."

"I still need to show them to the inn," Melinda argued.

"I will take care of that. Please, go."

Vofric's stern, caring tone convinced the stubborn girl. Moments after her departure, he led Kargon to the back of the church. An open door revealed papers stacked high on a small table. It took effort to sift through them before retrieving a raggedy sheet with scattered markings.

"This is my most recent discovery. Its words are indecipherable with my magic. I have sought notes on the language and await information from contacts outside Wolden," Vofric explained. "Gatherings have stopped due to the frequency of missing person cases."

"What about the village watch? Where are they?" Kargon asked.

"Their weekly meetings occur at the tavern beneath our local inn. You will need to pay for a room if you wish to gain access."

The idea of a hidden tavern nagged at Kargon. It was bad for business. Even if the inn was a popular establishment, it was unlikely that patrons cared for an underground bar. Something about using it for village watch meetings rubbed the adventurer the wrong way.

"When is the next meeting?"

Vofric paused to think and replied, "In a few days time."

Kargon examined the paper and it felt like the marks moved. For the briefest of seconds they were legible. Moments later, they changed to a different language.

"Aisha can probably read this," he said.

"It's odd hearing someone say the Hero's name with such familiarity," Vofric replied.

"To everyone else she's the Hero first. For me, she's a friend. Can I take this to her?"

"I'd like to keep it safe here. But bring her and I'll happily let the Hero try her hand at deciphering it."

It didn't take any more convincing for Kargon to beeline to the library. There wasn't a doubt in his mind that Aisha could decipher the paper. The problem was he needed to convince her to put their journey on hold. Not just to decipher but to stay in town and learn more about the disappearances. With a little more information, he was sure their party could solve the case.

The crowd outside the library had worked up the courage to speak with the Hero. She was confidently replying to them and delegating to Sariel when the questions were overwhelming. If not for the apparent concern on Kargon's face, they may have stayed to answer more. With a slick maneuver Aisha pulled Sariel away from the crowd.

Kargon remained silent until the villagers dispersed. A strong memory helped in giving a clear recollection of Vofric's words. While the information was prudent, Aisha would have followed simply from seeing the distress on her friend's face.

"Hold on," Sariel demanded before the party could move a step. "How does this open the path to Balur?"

"It doesn't, but Wolden needs help," Kargon replied.

"As does every town across the world. Will you stop to help each one?"

Aisha was saddened by the question. "Yes. When someone needs help, the Hero's party helps. Even temporary members. If you don't like it, you can go."

"Though, trying to reach Balur alone may not be the best idea," Kargon added.

Sariel let out a deep sigh. "People are lucky to have such a gracious Hero." They were the first to head in the direction of the church. "Let's hope this Vofric fellow has information about Balur."

Night time made the church feel far less welcoming. Lit torches illuminated the walls, but it only made the shabby building feel like a crypt. Anxiety emanated from Vofric's very being yet he still properly greeted the guests.

"Pleasure. You can call me Aisha," the Hero said.

"Am I correct in believing Kargon informed you of Wolden's predicament?" Vofric asked.

Sariel grunted. "Predicament is quite an understatement."

"He did," Aisha replied. "Though I'd appreciate it if you could go over it again for me."

Vofric sighed, the exhaustion from reliving the past weighing on his small form. A practiced recital of the events was repeated before Aisha received the coded paper. Sharp eyes peered at it as though threatening it to reveal its secrets. When she began magically deciphering the sheet her fake eye's iris glowed a brilliant purple. Seemingly nonsensical words passed through her muttering lips.

"Are you sure it says 'Caelum?'" Vofric asked suddenly.

"Yes," Aisha responded. "For our lord, Caelum. We bleed."

Vofric's hairs stood on end and he let out a growl. "They are trampling over Yuna's name for a devil!"

"Yuna… Starcaller? One of Kharim's allies?" Aisha asked in a surprisingly excited tone.

"Turned goddess, yes."

Sariel hummed softly. "I see you are one of her worshipers."

Vofric shook his head. A silence passed as he carefully considered his response. "I follow her teachings. She did not want to be worshiped but for others to learn from her."

"Who is Caelum?" Kargon asked.

"Yuna's brother. A jealous man who could not bear to be ignored by the first Hero. He sided with the forces of evil. Though he never reached godhood, he left a permanent impression on this world in the form of his cult."

"For a cult of Caelum to rise after *Valefor* was drawn is no coincidence."

"Indeed," Vofric agreed.

"He had cults during the first Hero's time, correct?" Sariel asked. "How was he worshiped? What were the rituals? There may be a connection to the disappearances."

Vofric's shoulders sank. "I do not know. Outside Yuna's teachings, my godly knowledge is lacking."

"Sacrifices," Aisha said with a thousand yard stare. "I had to learn about them during my training."

"Why would they do this?" Kargon insisted.

"Does a good reason excuse the villagers being kidnapped?!" Vofric barked.

Sariel put their hand in front of Vofric and said, "No one is suggesting such a thing."

"There's no point trying to figure out devil worshipers," Aisha said. "What matters is our next step."

Vofric agreed. "We must tell the village watch. With their help, we can bring an end to this."

Aisha had a look on her face only Kargon recognized. Every word Vofric said drowned her mind in a sea of ideas, each getting lost as more flooded forward.

"We haven't rested since getting here," Kargon stated. "The inn isn't far from here."

Sariel caught on quickly and added. "There is little we can do late into the night."

Vofric nodded slowly. "Of course, allow me to guide you."

"No, we'll be okay." Aisha's head lilted as she stepped away from the group. "Good night, Father Vofric."

He tried to protest but words fell on deaf ears. Silently, the party shut the church doors.

CHAPTER FIVE

Finding Divinity

Fresh breakfast and panicked dwarven screams welcomed the new day. Vofric's incoherent yelling echoed outside the inn as the sun barely rose over the horizon.

"We must go!" he barked.

"What are you saying, little man?" Sariel replied, staring down their nose at the dwarf.

"Vofric, explain yourself," Aisha said.

"No time!" he huffed and dashed away.

Aisha signaled for the party to follow. All of them quickly deduced where they were being led. A heavy weight pressed on the Tenrok's home. It was a far cry from the warm place that welcomed the party. Inside, Pavrin and Margaret meekly stared at their daughter's empty room.

Sorrow was evident on Margaret as she slumped on the couch. Wispy strands of hair riddled her puffy face. Thick lines marked where tears had flowed. Even Pavrin's stoic demeanor was gone. Exhaustion weighed on his shoulders. Kargon did his best to comfort them while his party entered Melinda's room.

The bandits had been kinder to the carriage than whoever ransacked this place. Glass and cloth scraps littered the floor. Splintered wood from a broken desk riddled the room. Vofric's heartbroken gaze became focused when examined the scene. Oddly, Sariel began sniffing the air while Aisha examined anything undisturbed.

Having spent years teaching in the village, Vofric had specific knowledge that aided their cause. Between his fingers were cloth scraps that he swore weren't from Melinda's wardrobe. Slowly, he tilted his head to the closet where Aisha was looking through the clothes.

"Are there any damaged pieces of clothing?" Vofric asked.

Aisha had been meticulously checking and replied with a shake of her head. As she moved away to shut the door something caught Sariel's attention. A mirror hanging on the frame was marked by a bloody symbol of Caelum's cult. Such an obvious sign sent a chill down everyone's spines.

A knock at the front door pulled attention away from the mark. Pavrin answered while the party stepped out of Melinda's room. Silently, he led a man and woman inside. The Hero's party was greeted by a goliath who stared at them stiffly and called himself Mason. Guiding him was a small gnome named Nila. Vofric immediately introduced them as members of the village watch.

"Daphal told us you'd come screaming bloody murder this morning. Took a bit of tracking until we found out what happened," Nila said.

"Sent Roc to tell others." His gaze trained on Aisha, Kargon, and Sariel. "New adventurers. When did they come?"

A quizzical look appeared on Vofric's face as he looked at the party. "Yesterday. I planned to make an introduction later today."

"Now's a good a time as any." Nila brushed past Aisha and gazed intently at the cult symbol. "What is this? Was Melinda involved with dark magic?"

"No!" Vofric protested. "It is the symbol I previously mentioned to you. A drawing was provided, as well."

"Yes, it is in records," Mason replied. "Please step out. We will search room... Alone."

Vofric hesitantly nodded and looked to Aisha whose eyes never left the shut door. There was no reason they could not stay to comfort the family. Even so, they remained silent while waiting for Nila and Mason to return.

The village watch didn't stay in the room long. Without

acknowledging the scene, Nila demanded the party's attention. "Melinda may have been hurt. We're having an emergency meeting at the tavern."

"You all come." Mason added.

Aisha flicked her wrist. "We'll be there shortly. Go ahead, Vofric."

"I will wait and direct you," Vofric said soberly while Pavrin guided the watch out of the house. As soon as the guests were out of earshot, the dwarf whispered, "Something is amiss."

Sariel snorted. "The blood in the room does not share Melinda's scent." A long silent stare caused them to explain. "My senses are sharper than others'. Melinda smells of vegetation and dirt. This blood smells like a dank cave."

"We'll keep that to ourselves. I don't care for this village watch but even incompetent eyes can assist in finding Melinda," Aisha said.

The sun hung high overhead as Vofric led the group back to their inn. Kargon had never felt so downtrodden while basking in sunlight. Warmth did nothing to remedy his goosebumped skin. Every blind corner and alley entrance was under scrutiny. Suddenly, the small village felt like a threat.

The door to the basement tavern was shut tight. Daphal, the innkeeper, told the group to wait for the village watch to allow entrance. Vofric almost knocked but Aisha stopped him. Silent hand gestures signaled to listen carefully. Everyone spread out and pressed against the wall.

"Who in the hell drew the mark?" Nila yelled. "That was the stupidest stunt I've ever seen!"

"Mark is for ritual. Not calling card," Mason added.

"And you're saying adventurers are looking into it?" another voice asked.

"Yes."

"Vofric says they arrived yesterday. What happened to the days of him sending them to us immediately?" Nila groaned.

Mason grunted. "Made job easier."

"We'll deal with the girl, the adventurers and then that stupid priest."

Color drained from Vofric's face as he stumbled back from the wall. A swift grab from Kargon stopped the dwarf from falling and making a sound.

The stout man fought back tears. "I must go."

No one tried to stop him. Unease was evident on Aisha's face but she just pressed her ear harder against the wall.

"Where are the adventurers? You said you invited them here," someone said.

"Must think we beneath them," Mason said. "Or looking for ritual site."

"We should go. If they do come here, it's better that they have to wait."

Aisha gestured for the party to leave immediately. Never had the soft croaks of wood flooring felt like a worse nuisance. Daphal furrowed a brow but otherwise paid the party no mind. The moment they stepped out of the inn, they looked to Aisha.

"Hide and wait. Follow the last to leave. It's the sixth person," she commanded.

How Aisha deduced the number of people was beyond Kargon. Pre-solved mysteries weren't Sariel's concern. They looked for a lookout point then leapt onto a nearby rooftop. While Kargon stared at his swift elvish ally, Aisha looked for a place to hide. It didn't take long before she pulled Kargon into a nearby alley. No matter how the light hit it, certain areas remained in shadow. The angle was perfect to keep an eye on the inn.

"I'll focus on listening. You keep an eye out," she whispered.

Kargon trained his eyes on the doorway of the inn. Heartbeats thrummed in his ears with Aisha pressed so close. It was a blessing he wasn't meant to listen for anything.

Within a minute the first village watch members exited. Mason and two others headed towards the city gate. A few minutes later, another person left with Nila. Minutes passed with no other exits. Kargon's eyes were trained on the door the entire time. If he'd missed someone Sariel would have moved from their perch. But no one needed to confirm that Aisha was right about the sixth member. Exactly fifteen minutes passed before a halfling crept out of the inn. The party's target, and by the looks of it, she expected to be tracked.

From atop the building Sariel nodded to Kargon and Aisha. Adept, silent movements made it clear they were an expert of rooftop traversal. The hidden duo waited for the halfling to get further away before stepping out of the shadows. Walls provided cover as they followed at a safe distance out of Wolden.

Moments after exiting the village, the halfling dashed into the forest. Kargon and Aisha couldn't give chase without surrendering their location. Fortunately, the treetops provided cover and a perfect traversal route for Sariel to follow the target.

"I can keep track of them," Aisha said as she watched the trees.

Trees rustled overhead as Sariel dashed between them to keep track of the target. Aisha kept her eyes on the elf while Kargon watched the ground to make sure they didn't misstep. Nearly ten minutes of cautious hunting brought them to the edge of the forest. Across the flat land was a large cliff face with an overhang. It perfectly obscured an opening where the halfling disappeared. Sariel dropped to the ground and joined their allies near the clearing.

"The chance of combat increases exponentially once we get inside," Aisha stated and looked at Sariel. "You don't even have arrows. Will you be okay?"

Sariel silently held out their dragon scarred left arm. Branches slowly grew out of the claw and twisted into the shape of a bow. A thin vine between both ends functioned as a bowstring.

They smirked and said, "I can similarly create ammunition."

Aisha's eyes twinkled with amazement at the summoning but her face remained stoic. "Good. Get in formation."

The party crossed the threshold and stumbled into what resembled the maw of a stony beast. Jagged formations jutted from every direction. The smell of rot and blood hung in the air. Echoes bounced through the tunnel. It felt impossible to mask their steps and Kargon was sure they would be caught. That fear only compounded when he heard voices.

The party couldn't discern the murmurs but any person of the cloth would be familiar with the cadence. Prayers were being sung in a foreign language. Words of divinity invited the party further into the cavern.

What sat at the end of the cavern was a perversion of Vofric's church. Craggy stone benches built into the ground were occupied by cultists with heads hung low. Bloody hands reached for the wall as they chanted. Engraved into it was Caelum's crest, which cast an imposing image over a large, flat stone slab on the ground. Dried blood caked the rock in layers of brown rust that clung to an unconscious Melinda.

Above her stood a man in a torn shirt with small cuts across his arms. Veins bulged out of his head from tightly shut eyes. He bellowed deep guttural prayers while fiddling with a dagger aimed at the sacrifice.

Aisha couldn't remain still while facing the horrendous sight. The faint sound of a bow being pulled taut made clear that Sariel was prepared. With a practiced motion, Kargon pulled up his goggles and fastened them. Embers crept along his fingers while awaiting the Hero's signal.

"Attack!" she commanded.

Sparks burst into wild flames along the monk's arms as he rushed in and grabbed the nearest cultist. They stared back with bloodshot eyes. Only now did Kargon notice a bloody sigil carved into their torso. Similarly, the cultist was surprised by the ignited hand of their assailant. Fanatical excitement appeared in their eyes until they conflagrated. Horrified screams stopped the other cultists' prayers.

The silence was broken by unseen arrows flying zipping through the air. Precise shots immediately killed another cultist. Under the cover of the projectiles, Aisha dashed in and cut down two more. Only five cultists remained, including Mason and Nila.

The villainous duo roared at the sight of their fallen comrades. With maddening fervor, they tore off chunks of skin. Bones twisted and ripped through muscle. Grotesque squelches and cracks echoed through the room as the humanoids morphed. Jagged horns burst out of their foreheads, eclipsing Aisha's in size. A barbed tail sprouted at the base of their spines as haunting yellow eyes leered at the adventurers.

"No fear!" Mason barked. "Not first time!"

"Sacrifice the girl to resurrect the others!" Nila commanded. "They will gain our very same blessing."

The cultist standing above Melinda complied with the order. As his blade plummeted towards its target a bright light blinded everyone in the room. Stone collided with metal. Not even a second later was a loud scream which abruptly ended with a crack. As the light dimmed, Kargon was able to make out the shape of the cultist, dead with a small hammer crushing his torso. The dagger laid harmlessly on the floor. There was no plausible way such a devastating attack could come from such a weapon without magic being involved.

"My foolishness allowed adventurers to be driven into your clutches. I have spouted empty words. Such actions are unbecoming of one who seeks justice," an ironclad Vofric said as he entered the room.

Pristine white armor with gold embellishments commanded reverence. Previously loose dreadlocks were pulled back into a bun that revealed furious eyes. He recalled his light hammer and smoothly hooked it to his belt before unsheathing a war-hammer from his back. The marble headed weapon was twice its wielder's size yet handled with ease.

Aisha was the first to regain her composure and attacked. The sound of a moving blade pulled Sariel's attention. More arrows zipped through the other villagers. Only the demons stood between the party and Melinda.

Mason readied himself to attack Aisha while Nila moved for the dagger. Even though Kargon doubted his success, he rushed forward to intercept the monster. Suddenly, the world around him blurred. His body moved faster than ever before as golden energy wreathed him. Serene eyes stared at Kargon as Vofric blessed him to protect Melinda.

"Sariel, help Aisha!" the monk commanded.

They grunted. "Understood."

Two more arrows fired into Mason's arm. He scoffed and tugged at them but the arrows didn't budge. The hesitation allowed Aisha to get close and kick the shafts. Barbed arrowheads pushed completely through the demon's arm. The awkward angle sent them into his torso, locking his limb in place.

"You're not used to that form," Aisha said.

"I am powerful!" Mason cried like a child throwing a tantrum.

Wild flailing was all the demon could manage with his free hand. It didn't matter as a blade easily weaved between his fingers. Aisha cut along the length of his arm. Bones posed no issue as she tore the *Valefor* through the cultist's shoulder. A bloody chunk of meat fell to the floor and all Mason could manage was an animalistic screech.

Nila was too stunned to move from being outpaced by a humanoid. The break in combat allowed Kargon to think about his training.

Memories of multi-limbed attacks raced through his mind. With his right leg he kicked away the knife and simultaneously delivered a left handed punch to his opponent's chest. Fire didn't make the demon hesitate like the other cultists. But raw power left an impression. It was possible to overpower the demon if given another chance. None came, however.

A glowing sigil appeared on Vofric's war-hammer as he menacingly approached the devil. The massive bludgeon would have crushed anyone with a simple swing. Instead, the dwarf swung his weapon horizontally into Nila's spine, shattering it. He followed with a spin that carried her body through the air before slamming it to the ground. The force of the strike and holy magic disintegrated the demon. All that remained were a blob of partially mutated organs and viscera.

Mason's face dropped at the sight. The passable defense he'd been stalling with fell away with a blood curdling scream. Crimson ichor poured from his eyes and he blindly clawed at Aisha. Slight movements and changes in momentum kept Aisha safe. The loss of blood was catching up to the demon and both fighters could feel the vast gap in skill between them. The Hero summoned lightning to the fingers of her free hand. A flick of the wrist sent it into Mason's chest, forcing him back. It was enough of an opening for Aisha to rear back and decapitate the demon.

"Are there others?" she asked.

Vofric scanned the room and shook his head. "Is Melinda hurt?"

Kargon approached the girl and was happy to see her unscathed. "Not physically."

"Good. Take her home and await my return."

Sariel was hesitant to take command from the priest until they noticed the others depart. With Melinda in hand, their party entered the jagged hall and shortly left the cave. A painful scream accompanied sorrowful weeps that echoed from the chamber. None dared turn back. The people Vofric trusted for so long had betrayed him. Pain from such an experience was unimaginable. Melinda began to stir and Kargon could only hope she wouldn't remember what happened.

The adventurers' return to the Tenrok home was met with elation. The sight of her daughter brought light to Margaret's eyes. Questions about what happened started immediately but Aisha refused to elaborate. It was dealt with and wouldn't happen again. Joy lessened when the powerful scent of blood neared. Vofric returned covered in copious amounts of the red liquid. Margaret's shock at the sight of the bloody paladin was less surprising than Pavrin's lack of a reaction.

"It seems you are once again needed," he said.

"It was bound to happen based on my proximity to Neves," Vofric replied then turned to the Hero. "Meet me at the church within the hour." It was more an order than a request.

The sun was approaching the horizon as the weary party made its way to the church. Kargon could finally appreciate the warmth engulfing him. The building was lit in a way that gave it new life. This was the place Melinda wanted to show the party.

Vofric sat on one of the many pews and without looking at his guests murmured, "Thank you."

"We couldn't turn a blind eye to what was happening. No adventurer would," Aisha replied. "I take it you were one too."

Vofric slowly leaned back and stared at the ceiling. "Centuries have passed since then. My grandmother was a well-known adventurer and imparted her wisdom to me."

"Who was she?" Kargon asked.

"Yuna Starcaller."

Even Aisha couldn't hide her astonishment. If not for the somber air around the conversation, it would feel like Vofric was bragging. A youthful expression appeared on his face while reminiscing about his grandmother.

"Her stories were like fables. Always a lesson to be learned. I was the first to hear them. Directly from the source, no less." He smiled softly as tears welled in his eyes. "Others only know the goddess, Yuna. Thus, her stories became lessons and a storyteller, a priest. I cannot accept the title of 'father' since I do not believe myself a preacher. I simply find joy in sharing my grandmother's stories."

"I'd love to hear them," Kargon said.

Anyone else would think they were empty words but Vofric could feel the half-elf's genuine curiosity. Aisha gave her friend a warm smile. A slight upward curl appeared on the side of Sariel's lips but was gone before anyone noticed.

"What of the cave?" they asked to change the subject.

"It is no more. The entrance has been destroyed. The village watch had no remaining family, thus their deaths will be simple to excuse," Vofric replied.

"Peculiar coincidence."

The dwarf exhaled slowly, fighting back tears. "They had family in the past. Some went missing while others departed Wolden. It dawns on me that each was likely sacrificed. Caelum's followers see no value in family regardless of their affiliation with the bastard."

"I will speak with Pavrin about moving the last residents from here," he said while kneading the bridge of his nose. "The last cultists will be weeded out."

"What about you? Couldn't you help?" Kargon asked. "What if Caelum comes back?"

Vofric shook his head. "Caelum never achieved godhood. He cannot resurrect. But the presence of his cultist's raises alarming concerns. It must be related—"

"To me," Aisha interjected. "We're not even sure why a chosen one appeared but something must be wrong in our realm. Caelum last lived during a similar crisis."

"Exactly," Vofric confirmed. "I believe the elves of Balur may have information. I will accompany you to their enclave. Based on what we learn, I may stay by your side. If you'll have me."

Aisha furrowed her brow and said, "Are you sure the villagers will be safe without you?"

"They were unsafe with my presence. We failed because we were complacent," Vofric explained. "Pavrin is an experienced guard captain. The villagers are under his watch."

"You might never see them again," Kargon said.

Vofric smiled softly, "If that is a sacrifice that must be made for their safety, I will happily accept it."

Aisha rose from her seat and shook Vofric's hand. "Sacrifices are a given on any journey. Facing them will be easier with a strong ally by our side."

"Pack any supplies you require," Sariel said. "There is no need to dally here. We shall meet at Pavrin's and make for Sespik in one hour."

No one had a chance to respond before the elf departed. Aisha thanked the dwarf and was hot on the heels of her ally. There was no hurry for Kargon with his minimal supplies. A firm handshake welcomed Vofric to the party.

"Looks like we'll have plenty of time for those stories."

CHAPTER SIX

Warm Welcome

The carriage rocked less with four riders. Wind whistled by as the horses trotted along the road. Years of natural flattening made the road to Sespik relatively smooth. Unfortunately, stepping off the pavement was even more jarring. Setting camp in open areas was the norm. With a proper party, it was possible to sleep in shifts so someone was always on watch. It didn't take long to figure out a system of unpacking and packing the carriage. Including tools for their various pastimes. Aisha was adamant that the party get moments to relax during the days they'd be between destinations.

She would spend the time as she had since childhood — in an empty area, laying down to watch the sky. There were times when Kargon would join her but sometimes he left her to enjoy the serenity alone. Hidden in a pouch under Sariel's waist cape was a small notebook. Documented inside were notes about flora, fauna, and even monsters with detailed drawings. It wasn't something Sariel shared and no one pestered them to do so. Especially since the elf readily provided any useful information if the need arose.

The person Kargon spent the most time with was Vofric. Camp was often set by a body of water and the dwarf was a master fisherman. He recounted his grandmother's stories while the monk meditated nearby. Flowing water accompanied by Vofric's smooth voice put Kargon's mind at ease. It never took long for him to drift into a state of complete calm.

"Sariel, what is it?" Vofric asked suddenly, pulling Kargon from his trance.

"There's been an incident," they declared loudly while rushing towards the men. "Kargon! Your egg is cracking."

The information took a moment to process for the younger adventurer. Vofric, on the other hand, jumped up instantly and patted the stupefied monk. It helped him get composure and run back to camp with his allies.

Aisha stood over the opened chest with an intense stare. Something was clearly amiss. The egg had a crack running along its side that widened as Kargon approached. Faint growling permeated from within, weakly asking for help. The heat of the chest was no longer present. As it diminished, so too did the movement of the dark figure inside.

"Kargon, heat it up," Aisha said.

"I burn too hot," he replied.

"You are only capable of one temperature?" Sariel asked incredulously.

"I told you before. I haven't had a conduit for long."

Vofric grabbed his ally's wrist and turned him so they faced each other. "Shut your eyes, ignite your arms and meditate. You can do that much, correct?"

"Y-yes." Kargon replied and ignited without a second thought. The dirt shifted as Sariel and Aisha stepped back. Vofric quickly released the half-elf's arm but remained close enough to make his presence known.

"Imagine a raging fire in a sealed room. Do not think of anything but how hot it burns," Vofric instructed.

Kargon kneaded his fingers uncomfortably. Meditation relied on calm thoughts and feelings. On the other hand, his ignition relied on raw emotions. But hesitation was never an option. Especially when life was in the balance. The monk let out a slow, steady breath and put on his goggles to ease his mind.

"Force the flames to shrink." Vofric continued. "Do not wait for it to happen naturally. Force it to the size of a candle flame. Recognize the warmth it provides."

In his mind, Kargon stood by a flaming torrent that threatened to break out of containment. With outstretched arms, he strained to hold it back. Crackling blazes slowly drained into embers. Within seconds, the raging fire diminished significantly.

"It's almost nothing," he said softly.

Vofric grunted affirmatively. "Yes. But a dozen candles-"

"Can provide warmth."

The flame in Kargon's mind grew steadily until a few candles worth hovered in front of him.

"Good. Open your eyes," Vofric instructed.

Weak flames permeated off the monk's palms. Surprisingly, the temperature of his entire body rose. Soft embers that burned nothing followed every move.

"Remember this feeling," Vofric said. "Recognize the difference from your combative flame."

Kargon nodded.

"Now, lift the egg. It needs you."

The young adventurer wavered, briefly burning brighter. A few steady breaths calmed him before carefully lifting the egg. It was heavier than he remembered. Or maybe the chest was enchanted to be lighter. It was possible he was misremembering.

"Focus, Kargon," Aisha said calmly, doing her best to match Vofric's tone.

"It moves again," Sariel added in kind.

Cracks widened as the figure inside shifted. Light taps were expected when a creature searched for freedom outside of its egg. Instead, Kargon braced against forceful strikes of a beast being held in a cage. His flame gave it the energy needed to fight with full strength.

"Can someone help it break the shell?" he asked.

"No," Sariel grunted. "This is the first test of any beast. You are providing ample assistance. Do not make it complacent."

From within the egg, the beast growled in agreement. It was heartier than before. Another fierce attack broke part of the shell and revealed a beak surrounded by wet fur. The mass tore through the opening using a small paw with unrefined claws.

"Put it down gently," Sariel commanded.

Kargon did as he was told and remained close. With intense focus he raised his temperature slightly in order for it to reach the egg. The beast let out a sound similar to a laugh. Aggressive rocking sent the egg to and fro. Sounds of furious scratching eked out. Pieces rapidly broke and in no time, the egg fell apart..

Light brown fur caught on pieces of shell as the creature stepped out. Awkward motions helped balance while rising to its feet. Four stubby legs carried surprising strength, holding up a body that looked too large for a cub. Soft white fur covered the beast's underbelly. Large blue eyes warily stared at the party from a tilted gaze. The owlbear cub growled softly as its feathers bristled.

Vofric quietly passed Kargon a fish he caught and gestured to offer it. It took several seconds before the monk understood. Cautiously, Kargon kneeled in front of the cub with fish in hand. The beast approached warily while keeping everyone in its field of vision. Sariel and Aisha stood as still as possible at Kargon's side with Vofric on the other.

The newborn slowly gripped the fish in its beak and pulled it to the ground. A simple lick of the morsel eased the cub's tension. Excited yips escaped its beak as it devoured the meal. It let out a cheery growl and approached Kargon. The young man tightened up as the creature rubbed against his leg. Owlbear fur was softer than anything he'd ever felt but was too scared to engage directly.

"He trusts you," Sariel said and crouched to the cub's level. "We have earned it via proxy."

"How do you know it's a he?" Kargon asked.

Sariel stared back, dumbfounded by the question too stupid to dignify with a response.

"How can you understand him?" Aisha asked.

"Bestial vocalization is clear to me. It has been as long as I can remember," Sariel explained.

Kargon nodded, finally leaving his frozen state. He reached to pull down his goggles but hesitated. The wing tips resembled an owl's eyes that possibly comforted the little beast. Based on how calmly it accepted a pat on the head, Kargon had to be right. He extinguished his flame and ruffled the cub's fur. It chirped softly, playfully pushing against the half-elf's flaming palm.

"You may remove your goggles. I'm sure he will recognize you without them," Vofric said.

The monk wasn't sure but he'd never hatched an egg before either.

None of this would have been possible without his allies. The cub didn't care as Kargon's face was revealed. It was more interested in pawing at its new master's palm with retracted claws. Overwhelming emotion hit Kargon.

"What's his name?" he asked while holding back tears.

"Do you have a habit of asking newborns what their name is?" Sariel snorted.

Vofric chuckled, "He just gave birth. He's not thinking straight."

Aisha lightly sighed, "We have our work cut out for us."

The owlbear growled in a way that mimicked a laugh. It reminded Kargon of the head of his monastery, Master Avant. The hue of the cub's fur and his feathery features were also similar to the old master.

"Sariel, I figure he can understand me so translate what he says, okay?" Kargon asked, then turned to the cub. "I'll call you Avant, how's that sound?"

The cub grunted.

"Powerful," Sariel stated.

"We've got a long road ahead of us, will you travel with us?" Kargon asked.

Avant replied with another grunt followed by high pitched whine.

"It is a fish. River trout to be exact," Sariel said to the owlbear before replying to Kargon. "He inquires about our fish stock."

Vofric laughed and petted the cub. "I will make sure there is plenty."

Avant growled and nodded.

Kargon gestured to the carriage. "Sariel, Vofric. Can you please go pack up the rest of the carriage? I need to talk to Aisha."

Normally they took direction from Aisha but could tell this was important. Avant stared at the half-elf with wide eyes. The best option for him was to plop down by his caretaker's legs. A smile crept across Kargon's face at the innocent gesture.

With a turn to Aisha, he asked, "Is this okay?"

She smiled softly and nodded. "All this journey guarantees is unexpected encounters." She knelt down and poked Avant's beak, causing him to let out a soft trill. "At least with you by my side, this'll be fun." She scooped the cub into her arms before moving towards the carriage to hide flushed cheeks. "Come on, we should get back on the road."

Driving was far more enjoyable with Avant perched next to Kargon. Everything intrigued the cub. Fluttering leaves painted glorious pictures. Some crunched in his grasp as he learned their scent. He was like a mage trying to solve the realms' secrets. Only naps and pets outweighed the mysteries of his expanding universe. If Kargon was too focused, Avant would hop into the covered wagon and spend time with the party.

Aisha opted to lift him to get around the moving carriage. Though it never happened, she worried he'd fall and hurt himself. Much time was spent learning about owlbear capabilities from Sariel. Meanwhile, Vofric educated himself on what snacks Avant preferred. While the cub ate a morsel, the dwarf settled down next to Kargon.

"I have been meaning to ask, were you a student of the Sanctuary of Spiritual Combustion?" he inquired.

Kargon's ears perked at the name. "Yeah. How'd you know?"

"About one hundred years ago, I traveled with an owlminn. He had a taste for berries like our little friend here. Often he mentioned starting a monastery in Mount Iana. He—"

"Liked how close it was to the sky!" Kargon exclaimed. "Master Avant was an adventurer! He tried to deny it but I knew!"

Vofric chuckled, "I am surprised your monastic training only lasted five years. He always said people needed at least ten years to grasp astral projection."

"I mean, Master Avant might've been strict but understood I left to take care of my sick father."

"I'm so sorry."

"He's fine now," Kargon replied hastily. "Mom panicked and asked me to come home. It was a rough few months. Once everything settled down they saw no reason to send me back."

"Why did they initially?"

Aisha poked her head out of the carriage and answered, "As punishment for bad behavior. The combination of monastic training and taking care of his parents really calmed Kargon down."

The monk blushed and nodded. "I didn't tell my parents I was being trained to control my magic. But If I can lessen the intensity, I'm sure I can increase it as well. There's not much else to learn."

Vofric looked at Kargon quizzically and asked, "Avant had to approve of you being his disciple, correct? He swore to only teach individuals capable of astral magics."

"I guess."

Kargon's attention was pulled away by the sound of roaring waves in the distance. Long shadows from stone buildings stretched onto the road. Groups walked through the bustling streets of Sespik. Ships of every size floated calmly at the dock. Workers rushed between with crates full of unknown goods. The distinct smell of fish carried through the air. It was impossible to take in everything happening. Kargon never turned back to Vofric but his words rattled in the young adventurer's head.

"Kargon, I believe there is more to your magic than you know."

CHAPTER SEVEN

Open Seas

Sespik smelled of salt water and fish. It was especially pungent on the docks. Aisha and Kargon briefly debated if leaving their carriage with local lenders was a good idea. In the long run, it probably didn't matter and they had other priorities. Supplies were depleted so each adventurer just carried a rucksack.

Avant stayed near his master while warily watching passersby. The busy streets reminded Kargon of home. Merchants shouted for his attention to sell their wares. Residents passed judgment on the merry band but none approached. Aisha was thankful not to entertain civilians and focused on getting to the port.

Large wooden planks bound together to create a massive platform. It stretched further than Kargon could see with all the ships blocking view. Workers yelled to sailors as they handled cargo. Aisha examined every large vessel she passed. No one in the party was experienced enough to sail and even if they were, four people wasn't enough to man a ship. They needed a crew.

"We're looking for passage to Balur," Aisha said as she engaged another sailor.

"Already got a job to do," the captain replied abruptly.

"If gold is what you seek, we can offer a substantial amount in order for you to divert your route," Vofric said persuasively.

The captain sneered. "Don't matter. I've got a route and our ship is full."

"It looks rather unfilled. Not a single crate has been loaded onto it," Sariel said while looking at the crew on the ship.

They stared back, whispering amongst themselves.

"I said it's full!" the captain barked. "Go pester someone else! I ain't got time to waste with you!"

Before the group could reply, she walked away. Aisha swore under breath. Another ship nearby was the next target.

"The sailor's won't help ya," a person said from the railing dividing the port and town. They wore an ironed deep blue uniform and shining boat shoes. Salty black hair was tucked into a cap with the sigil of the Vethyean world government.

"Why would a marine be bothered by adventurers seeking passage?" Aisha asked.

"It's a local branch's duty to check anything out of the ordinary at their location," the marine explained. "The chosen one and her party fall into that criteria, wouldn't ya say?"

"Just Aisha is fine."

"Bailey Lakelet. Please follow me." They pointed behind Kargon. "Ya should stop your familiar from stealing or it could cause problems."

He quickly turned to see Avant with his head in an open crate of fish. A panicked young sailor was carefully stepping away from the beast. Few things could have prepared him for an owlbear. Kargon apologized while tossing over a few silver coins then tucked Avant under his arm as the cub feasted on ill gotten gains. An apology was given to Aisha but she didn't accept.

"I was getting frustrated with the sailors. Avant's antics gave me a second to calm down," Aisha whispered.

The port entrance to the marine base sat at the south end of Sespik. Their dock was covered by a rocky overhang. Multiple small ships lined the dock but most of the crew cleaned a large vessel. None openly acknowledged the party as they moved to the courtyard, a large field connecting the port to a guard tower.

Only upon entering did people take notice of the Hero's party. Some ogled, while others saluted. For her part, Aisha walked with her head held high and exuded confidence. Kargon followed behind her looking as competent as one could with a baby owlbear under their arm. The natural air of arrogance permeating off Sariel matched the high ranking officials. Without trying, Vofric fit in perfectly in his shining armor and stoic demeanor.

On the highest floor of the building, Officer Lakelet guided the party into an office and shut the door. A woman with long curly ombre hair covered by a captain's hat sat inside. Adorned in regalia, she firmly planted elbows on the desk and interlocked her fingers at eye level. Sharp eyes examined each adventurer that approached.

"I heard only two of you left Neves. It hasn't been more than a week yet you have a sizable party," she said. "I am Captain Julian Stormclaw of the Vethyean Marines."

Aisha had grown accustomed to introducing the party. She followed up with, "I thought Sespik sailors were talented. Why do they all refuse to help us?"

"Pride is an unfortunate trait and the sailors here are drowning in it. They refuse to admit they can't sail the seas around Balur," Captain Julian explained.

"What makes the Balur Sea so treacherous?" Kargon asked.

"Whatever spell the conclave used to hide their city also enchanted the surrounding area. The few ships that return from there are heavily damaged. Whatever happened between entering and exiting the Balur Sea is forgotten."

"Are you saying we can't go there?"

Aisha shook her head and answered, "The captain is saying only the marines are willing to take us."

"If you're willing to travel with us," Captain Julian amended.

"What do you gain from this?" Sariel asked.

Vofric nodded, "I am unsure we can compensate you at a rate befitting Vethyean marines."

Captain Julian stood up and walked to a map on her wall. Dated pins across the board marked when bodies of water were discovered. The waters surrounding most of the connected continents were heavily explored. All except for the Balur Sea.

"My crew is judged harshly for choosing to join me in Sespik. Defending a tiny town on the smallest continent of Vethyea doesn't garner respect," the captain huffed. "But let me tell you, they're some of the best marines I've seen in my century-long tenure. They deserve recognition and sailing the Balur Sea will get them just that. Having the Hero's party on board would be a blessing."

"I didn't know sailors were so superstitious," Aisha replied.

Kargon scoffed. "Shows what you know."

Aisha rolled her eyes and approached the captain with an outstretched hand. "When do we set sail?"

The captain smiled and shook the Hero's hand heartily. "Dawn."

Cheers erupted in the hall. Officer Lakelet peeked outside to see half a dozen marines excitedly congratulating each other. They smiled back, unashamed of their antics. While Aisha handled logistics with Captain Julian and the others, she requested Kargon join the marines. Someone from the party should help deliver the news. No one was better than the friendliest of her companions.

The joyful eavesdroppers patted the monk's back and welcomed him. Kargon was surprised that all were half-breeds. Like children, they ran through the halls calling for attention. Some others joined as they descended the building, ran across the field and back to the ships.

"The expedition for the Balur Sea sails at dawn!" someone yelled.

Roars from everyone on the dock shook Kargon to his core. Avant's fur stood on end and he trilled happily. Some officers cheerfully gave the cub a snack. Others gave Kargon a tight hug and lifted him in the air. After a dozen embraces he could barely feel his arms but it didn't let up. There was no reason to dampen the mood so he went to great efforts to reciprocate the action.

Throughout the next few hours the large ship's final preparations were completed. The party's bags laid in a room that could easily fit all of them with the captain's quarters across the hall. Other high ranking officers' surrounded them. As soon as the ship was ready to sail, marines were out celebrating. Curiously, Vofric saw it as a ritual and insisted the party join them. Sariel and Aisha agreed but Kargon's nerves were catching up to him. He opted to rest on the docked ship to get accustomed to the water. Avant had eaten double his weight in gifted fish and laid on his stomach. The ship rocked lightly and quickly put them to sleep.

***

* * *

Sunlight reflected on the surface of the water. Captain Julian warned it would be blinding but the party was still ill prepared for it. Tears flowed for longer than any one would ever admit. Once they regained vision, it was apparent why people lived to explore the seas. Aquatic life of all shapes and sizes could be seen through the clear waters. The sound of soft waves calmed nerves. Even the scent of fresh salt water was distinct from what was in the air of Sespik.

Kargon wasn't meant for sea exploration. Salt air and soft waves quickly lost their beauty on him. After two days of sailing, he was antsy to do something. It wasn't possible to steer the boat and the crew was so efficient they didn't need extra hands. The only option was to meditate. He'd learned to lower his temperature without much effort but couldn't understand how to burn more fiercely. Attempting to do so would likely set the ship ablaze.

Words spoken during the trip to Sespik nagged at the back of Kargon's mind. The assumption that he didn't know his magic was infuriating. Immolation was incredibly straightforward. Not to mention the lack of manifesting astral projections that Vofric suggested. Then again, the dwarf had expanded horizons before.

With frustration, Kargon put on his goggles and held out a hand. Master Avant said magic was about the ability to create a vivid image in one's mind. Kargon thought about a hand floating in front of his own. Muscular fingers and worn palms levitating a few feet above ground. There should be no body, only the strong pressure from disciplined hands. He sat — arm outstretched — for what felt like an hour. Pain shot through his physical joints but he fought to keep them aloft. Until the boat rocked violently.

"We're entering the Balur Sea!" Captain Julian's voice boomed throughout the ship.

It was like the calm seas from earlier were a lie. Waters roared like an untamed beast under the bright sun. The clear skies became a mesmerizing reflection that stretched and warped endlessly. Logically the ship was still moving forward, yet everyone on board felt it spinning uncontrollably.

"—OFF THE PORT BOW!" someone screamed.

"Man the cannons!"

Kargon rushed to the deck, frantically searching for what needed to be defended against. Aisha grabbed him and pointed towards the front of the ship. Scales protruded from the water, trailing along a massive serpentine body. Towering waves rippled off the leviathan as it slithered toward them. The sea shook when the beast leapt out and landed heavily. Its gargantuan head alone was nearly the size of the marine ship. With an ear-piercing screech it shook the hull.

Cannonballs collided into the beast's scales, revealing a soft underbelly. A wild flail of the head brought it down on the deck. The grotesque sound of crushed bones alerted everyone of marines getting caught in the impact. Aisha barked a spell and a jolt of lighting blasted the creature's revealed muscle. It opened its mouth and lunged at her. While she easily leapt out of the way, nearby marines were swallowed whole.

"Stay back and focus your fire!" Aisha ordered.

It was easiest for Sariel as they ran along the masts and fired an array of arrows into precise points. In a similar vein, Vofric threw his light hammer with divine blessings that erupted on impact, shattering scales and flinging the hammer back to its wielder. Meanwhile, Kargon helped load the cannons for another volley.

He tried to keep track of Avant but the cub dashed between everyone and centered himself. Fear was prevalent in everyone's minds. An unfamiliar roar from the owlbear summoned faint blue energy that expanded outward to wreath all his allies. Their minds were clear. No one dared question it, instead focusing on continuing the attacks.

It wasn't enough. The leviathan snapped its jaws, catching marines with every bite. Bloody corpses lined its jagged maw. Officer Lakelet tried to turn the ship around to no avail. The beast coiled its body around the vessel. It hunted for another snack and zeroed in on Sariel. They were fast but the beast's size allowed it to encompass the main mast within its jaw. It clamped down but the elf survived. A moment before the attack, Vofric used his war-hammer to break the structure. Sariel plummeted to the floor and continued to fight. Marines' numbers quickly dwindled with every second.

The leviathan slowed its attacks and sneered at the thinning group. Kargon assisted the few remaining marines with firing cannons. Even with Avant's blessing they were running ragged. As the last cannonball erupted against the beast's face, it roared. No one else seemed to matter, it was focused on Aisha and her party. The voracious maw lunged towards them. The Hero sliced into the bottom of the creature's mouth. It hesitated enough for everyone to widen the gap.

The monster reared back and lunged again. Vofric followed Aisha's lead and cracked one of the beast's teeth. Again, the group stepped aside before attacking. Soon enough, they found themselves with Kargon and the last standing marines. But unfamiliar terrain provided the leviathan an advantage. The humanoids had no way to escape. Violent waters below were no better than the beast. It opened its maw and lunged again.

Master Avant's voice whispered in Kargon's mind.

"The mind's eye is most clear when one's senses are heightened,"

Muscular fingers wrapped around jagged teeth. Worn palms held back monstrous force. Dozens of feet separated the monk from astral hands keeping the leviathan's maw open around them. Kargon could feel the pressure in his own limbs, quaking under the weight. Sweat dripped from his forehead as he pushed back. But a sudden revelation didn't guarantee power. The astral hands were fading fast. He needed the others to move. The beast roared as it overpowered the monk's hands.

He screamed, "Fall back! I can't—"

CHAPTER EIGHT

Finding the Way

Kargon felt the overwhelming urge to vomit as he awoke with a cruel headache. Water rushed nearby and the ground shook beneath him. For a hopeful moment, he thought the ship was intact. Until he felt the dirt beneath his hands. Bruises covered his body but there were no lacerations. Misaligned goggles hung on his face. He straightened them then turned to the rhythmic pressure pushing on his arm.

Soft whines escaped Avant's beak while he lightly nudged his master. He was relatively unscathed barring a small cut on his side. Kargon lifted him into a hug and rose to his feet.

To one side of them was a cliff overlooking the ocean. The other was a dense forest with foliage easily eclipsing Avant in size. Birds chirped overhead and animals hunted in the canopy. No one else from the ship was around. Taking a step, Kargon felt a shock travel up his body. A floating hand flashed into existence in front of him then vanished instantly. Avant looked at Kargon curiously.

"Not the time," he muttered while shaking his head. "We have to find the others."

Kargon tucked the owlbear under his arm and trekked inland. Walking through the plants proved difficult as it shifted just like the sky's above the marine ship. Branches appeared randomly and obscured paths. Upon examination, they didn't actually exist. Kargon removed his goggles and squinted. Eyesight was unreliable and the odd sounds of the forest made average hearing useless. Sometimes animals would sound close but were never seen. The half-elf couldn't tell if the forest was to blame or his concussion.

"You've got better ears than me, right?" Kargon asked Avant.

He grunted an affirmative.

"Do you think we're going the right way?"

Avant pushed his master towards the right.

The further they walked, the harder it became to identify the forest's tricks. Thankfully, Avant could reliably navigate. Urgent movements directed Kargon. Sounds became more distinct further into the forest. Figures could be seen moving in the distance. Kargon was sure it wasn't a trick since he felt the frenetic energy of battle throughout his body. Approaching the alcove, he signaled Avant to stay quiet.

Arrows flew through the sky as Sariel leapt between branches while battling a large panther. Lunges from the beast were easily dodged. Even with swift movements, it was obvious Sariel was struggling. They were hindered by large wounds on their legs and torso. Labored breathing accompanied each arrow.

It was possible to focus on the panther's movements in the unshifting clearing. Still, there was no way Kargon could take the beast head on. But he had the chance to assist from afar. Closed fists pulled back like he'd throw a punch. Aiming at the panther, he swung forward.

A flaming fist appeared in the clearing and slammed into the beast. When it stumbled, Kargon swung his arm up before bringing it back down. The flaming projection connected with the creature's spine. Sturdy bones were clear against the monk's weary knuckles.

Avant let out a soft hoot and Kargon was surrounded in a faint blue glow that stretched to Sariel. Three arrows launched from their bow, piercing the panther's eyes and a leg. It couldn't fight back against the burning fist that set its fur ablaze. Bones cracked and blood spurted from the beast's mouth. It collapsed seconds before the astral hand vanished.

Sariel dropped from the tree and approached the tired duo.

"You're both alive," they said and awkwardly ruffled the tuft of fur on Avant's head. "I'm pleased."

It was the kindest tone Sariel could muster. Kargon didn't want to bring attention to it and simply replied, "Me too. But we're all a little worse for wear."

Sariel noted his wounds and sighed. "Do you know where we are?"

"I think the leviathan's mouth was a portal," Kargon answered.

"It seems Aisha isn't the only one capable of deduction between you two. Have you thought of how to find her?"

"I planned to do the same thing that led me to you. Avant listened for sounds and I followed his lead."

Sariel stared at their furry compatriot relaxing in the monk's grasp. "Enterprising."

Avant started wiggling and pushing to go left. Branches once again twisted in maddening patterns. Illusory tree trunks made it impossible to chart a path without assistance. Thankfully, Sariel's heightened hearing provided aid.

"Do you hear that?" they asked.

While Kargon didn't, it was obvious Avant knew what the elf spoke of. They directed the group forward and within minutes it was possible to hear people chattering. Figures moved slowly in the brush towards an unknown goal. Upon further inspection, Kargon recognized the marines trying to navigate the forest. Tensions were high as they accused each other of lying about where to go.

"You said there was a path!" one yelled.

"I did! I don't know where it went!" the other replied.

"Ain't no wonder the captain kept y'all from navigatin'," a third said.

Officer Lakelet walked silently amidst them with a mixture of shame and rage on their face.

Vofric let out a low growl and barked, "Enough! Is this how Vethyean marines conduct themselves in an emergency? Have you lost all professionalism now that we're stranded on land?"

"Vofric!" Kargon yelled excitedly and hesitated. "Avant, is it safe to head that way?"

Sariel scoffed and walked forward, the half-elf following closely before giving Vofric a hug.

He sighed and petted Avant's head. "It is good that you three are safe. Did you land together?"

"That was the case for Kargon and Avant. We only recently joined together," Sariel answered. "Have you encountered Aisha?"

"I have only found marines. We were making our way towards that beacon."

Vofric pointed at a shining light. Blue swirling particles became a single beam as it stretched skyward. The base was out of view but trees parted to provide a clear path. There was no reason Kargon shouldn't have seen it prior. Even from the ship, it should've been visible. So, should have the island for that matter.

"Wait, did anyone see this island when we were on the ship?" Kargon inquired.

"I was distracted by the giant sea serpent ripping our boat apart!" a marine said while staring daggers at the man.

"Right, sorry."

Sariel grunted. "Hold. Kargon is correct. This island should have been visible from the ship but was not. It is likely enchanted by Balur."

A collective sigh of disdain passed through everyone's lips as they tired of Balur's use of magic. Swirling patterns seemed to speed up the longer the group remained still. A psychological attack from a landmass was an unexpected encounter. Kargon shut his eyes and tried to fight past throbbing head pain. Avant wriggled and brought the monk back to his senses; whatever good that was.

"We need to move," Kargon commanded.

"Where exactly?" someone groaned.

"Away from here. This place is messing with us and I'd rather not stay still."

Without another word, he walked out of the opening. Even with their complaints, no one stayed behind. It was apparent Kargon didn't need to blindly follow Avant's lead. Within minutes he had some idea of their destination. Not because of the beacon; obviously that was their ultimate goal. Rather, there was a break in the pattern of the trees. It was being forcefully broken. Powerful magic was countering the enchanted island. The monk deviated from Avant's path but wasn't challenged as everyone noticed the singularity.

A silver blade shone through the canopy. Air itself molded around *Valefor* while held to the skies by a wounded Aisha. Slight movements caused reality to twist around the weapon. Interlocked vines opened to allow the adventurer through.

"Aisha!" Kargon ran to her and hugged her tightly. Both felt a twinge of pain as they embraced but didn't part for a few moments. Only did a meek chirp cause them to part.

"Sorry about that, Avant," Aisha said while pulling away.

Kargon apologized to his familiar then asked, "Where did you land? Are you alone?"

"It's difficult to say where. I've been walking for a while. You're the first people I've seen. I figured we'd regroup at that light."

"It is good fortune that our plans aligned," Vofric said. "Everyone, please come close." He made a fist with his right hand and held it in front of him. With his left palm placed firmly on top he prayed. "By the grace of Yuna."

A golden glow surrounded everyone as their wounds healed. Kargon had never experienced the rapid effects of such a spell. It walked the line of uncomfortable and painful but growing accustomed was necessary.

"Why did you wait to do that?" Sariel asked.

"Battle depleted much of my mana. I wanted to heal as many people as possible with a single spell," Vofric explained.

"And wanted to make sure our party was part of it. Appreciated."

Some of the marines muttered complaints but the deed was done and they were better off for it. Aisha slowly looked herself over and without a word walked away.

The party readily followed her with the marines close behind. However, something was off about the Hero's usually radiant demeanor. Quietness was a normal occurrence to Kargon but this was different. But there was no time to focus on such concerns.

The forest was still teeming with danger. With *Valefor* creating a bubble of normalcy, people's senses sharpened. It was like the magic of the island paid respect to Aisha. Raw power deterred the creatures in the shadows until they finally reached the beacon.

It stemmed from a massive obelisk resting at the center of a decrepit courtyard. Husks of old constructs surrounded the single intact feature. The hypnotic enchantment around the island was nonexistent here. Aisha sheathed her weapon and slowly crossed the threshold.

Magic circles were known to create a soft hum when activated.

Kargon had only heard it a few times when protected by spellcasters as a soldier. The sound grew to an unprecedented volume that shook the very ground it emanated from.

The beacon split into five downward arching lines. Each beam moved along etched patterns in the courtyard, unimpeded by debris. Everyone scrambled to find a way to stop it but the circle was completed before they could act.

The cacophonous hum vanished as debris rose from the ground to reveal humanoid and bestial constructs. Their size was more surprising than their existence. None of the five golems were taller than Sariel. Past the creatures was something far more interesting. A portal revealed itself within the base of the obelisk. Beyond it was a glowing treescape paradise resembling ancient images of Balur.

"We need to get through the portal," Kargon said while putting Avant down. "Get ready for a fight."

He wasn't confident enough to summon astral hands but still ignited his fists. Others drew their weapons in kind. Even Avant let out a growl as his fur bristled. Aisha didn't draw her blade but stepped in front of her party and signaled them to stay back. Arm outstretched, she produced a marble of lightning. Powerful vibrations made it difficult to hold back as it grew larger with every passing second. No one could track when it launched from her palm, only when it stopped in the middle of the golems. Jagged lines of electricity violently burst out and instantly shattered the stone monsters.

One tattered golem tried to remain standing but met its end by a swift strike from Aisha's blade. She kept a straight face but Kargon noticed pain in her gaze. Something gnawed at her conscience. A long breath exhaled from her barely open lips. Kargon was sure no one else noticed by the awe in their voices. The party, however, all wore looks of concern, garnering Kargon's respect.

Even so, he brushed aside any concern and cheerfully said, "Nice one, dude!"

Aisha snapped out of her trance and replied, "I'm glad I still had the mana for that."

"I believe—" Sariel hesitated, knowing not to bring attention to Aisha's wild actions. "We should go through the portal. It is time for answers regarding our quests."

Aisha nodded and led them through the portal. Kargon waited for the last of the marines before exiting the hellish island.

On the other side was a completely different world — as though detached from the party's home plane. Tropical birds and beasts perched on massive verdant vines. Decoratively molded marble paths connected large platforms with various buildings. Thick stalks weaved alongside the roads. The enclave's many buildings were obscured by its vertical construction. Trees stretched from a deep abyss upwards past the visible skyline. Even the mysterious fog that hung over lower parts of the city felt inviting.

An elf clad in shining garments demanded the group's attention. His regal air was oft unseen. He asked each marine to separate from the party as they stepped forward.

"You have done well to overcome the tests in your path, young Hero." His soft voice carried on the air, demanding attention from surrounding elves. "It is with great honor I, Hastios, welcome you to Balur."

CHAPTER NINE

The Elven Enclave

Walking the streets of Balur was like a dream. Scents of unknown foods wafted through the air. Soft humming emanated from every direction like a song on the wind. Each step taken felt light and airy on roads that felt soft to the touch. The city eased the tension among the Hero's party. The marines, on the other hand, grew angrier with each new experience.

Officer Lakelet finally broke their silence. "What was the point of that serpent? My comrades died! Others are still missing! And you want us to believe Balur is peaceful?!"

Hastios stopped and gestured for something. Another elf approached the group.

"We understand your frustrations but rest assured, the Vethyean marines who arrived before you are in good health," the elf said. "We can provide your meal at a later time if you would like to see your crewmates first."

There was some grumbling but no marine dared question Officer Lakelet.

"Please lead the way," they replied and thanked Aisha.

"We'll see each other again," she said then turned to Hastios. "We have questions regarding our quests.

Hastios smiled. "Of course, but the mind functions better once the body is fed. And let us not forget the many wounds you've all suffered." As he spoke, two similarly dressed elven women approached us. "We've prepared a place where your party can relax with a meal. I'm sure you agree it is necessary after the test that was thrust upon you."

"Violence of that scale was a horrid vessel for your portal," Sariel groaned.

"I cannot ask you to understand our ways. Simply believe you did well. Now, you may enjoy the fruits of your labor."

With a wave of his hand, the thick wooden doors of a nearby building opened. Around it were circular flourishes that mimicked golden flowers budding from the marble wall. Ornamentation continued to every corner of the building.

Inside, scents of food overwhelmed everyone's senses. A table that stretched for dozens of feet was filled with delicacies of all kinds. Meats dripped with juices that glowed under the chandeliers. Fruits were cut into intricate shapes. Drinks flowed endlessly from enchanted bottles into silverware few could afford in a lifetime.

The prospect of a warm meal was mouth watering. It had been just over a week since they left Wolden but the memory of Margaret's cooking was fresh in mind. Even Nevesi soldiers had more access to proper meals. Kargon couldn't help but find joy in the infrequent indulgence. Especially upon seeing it spread in front of him.

Aisha sat at the head of the table with Sariel and Vofric on one side and Kargon on the other. Avant occupied the floor next to his master with a bowl. Whatever food or drink was asked for, the elves provided. Unsure who else would be partaking, Kargon hesitated at first.

"There is no need to restrain yourself," Hastios said. "This is our gift to your party. Please indulge yourselves. When you are ready, you will each have a room to rest. We can discuss everything you wish to learn afterwards."

Aisha sighed and shook her head. "No, this is good. It gives me time to get my thoughts in order."

Hastios stepped out and the party finally breathed easy for the first time.

"What about you, Sariel?" Kargon asked. "You never told us what you needed from Balur."

They took a deep breath, then answered. "I fail to recall anything prior to fifty years ago."

The implication befuddled Kargon. "Wait, how old are you?"

Sariel gave a patented dumbfounded look. "I have appeared as I do in front of you for as long as I can remember. The scales... look fine; disgusting but tolerable. However, when I use magic it feels uneasy. I don't..." They leaned close and whispered. "I don't require a conduit. While it's an appreciated ability, I dislike the unknown."

"Elves are well known for their arcane knowledge," Vofric said assuredly. "Seeking answers from Balur is a logical choice."

Sariel nodded and took an aggressive bite of the meat placed on their plate. Based on every meal the group shared with the elf, it was clear little else would be said. Kargon followed their lead and focused on his meal.

The tenderness of the mouth melting boar meat was extraordinary. A single sip of elven wine drowned him in indescribable flavors. It took every fiber of being to eat in a polite manner. Avant excitedly dug in and left a mess all over himself. The jealousy everyone felt was evident. Conversation became more scarce. Even Aisha focused on her meal and its divine tastes. It was hard not to stare at the content smile on her face. Warmth flourished in Kargon's chest at the sight.

Unfortunately, the time came when no one could eat another bite. They had to forego the remaining mountain of delicacies. Silent attendants gestured for the party to follow. Avant was swaying back and forth near his bowl, eyes barely staying open. Though it was difficult after the meal, Kargon carried the owlbear. Their path led deeper into the magnificent inn.

Kargon didn't process his party being split up or where everyone else went. The room had a painted ceiling that mesmerized him. Childlike wonder washed over as he stared at the mattress resting atop a golden bed frame. Silk sheets brushed away any worldly cares. The moment Avant laid down, he let out a loud snore. It was all the convincing needed for the monk to do the same.

***

Cold stone pressed against Kargon's back. No amount of movement made him comfortable. Avant's presence was nearby and Kargon reached for the owlbear. His hand was met with a powerful strike.

Kargon awoke with a jolt. Pristine marble stared down at him from the ceiling. It was no longer painted and dozens of feet high. There was no furniture in the significantly smaller room, only the flat walls. Even the gold embellishments were gone. Instead of the stone door of the bedroom, there was a barred metal one with magic symbols etched into it. Once Kargon's eyes were less bleary he recognized Sariel and Vofric in the darkness.

"Narcotization," Sariel grumbled as the monk sat up.

Vofric kneaded the bridge of his nose and said, "We have been stripped of our weapons."

Kargon furrowed his brow when he noticed the dwarf's necklace. A thin golden chain with a star shaped pendant. The sight of his own silver bracelet confirmed suspicions.

"They left our conduits."

"The cell dispels magic," Sariel sighed. "This brings back memories I do not seek."

Kargon's mind was hazy from whatever concoction was used. "Any idea who did this?"

"The Balurians."

"But, why? We're the Hero's party. She'd never be okay with this."

Vofric sighed. "They did not make a request. She is likely trapped as well."

Sariel studied the cell door. "This is well built. Our previous escape plan will fail."

Vofric checked the back walls while Kargon joined the elf. The craftsmanship of the cell was exquisite. Metal melded directly into the wall, kept together by high level magic. Kargon tried to pry two bars apart but felt the strength drain from his body. Within seconds he was fighting just to keep his footing. Shaky legs dropped him away from the beams. The metal was directly enchanted to deter physically strong prisoners.

Sariel helped Kargon to his feet and they continued studying the walls. Well constructed prisons still had weaknesses. If it wasn't physically present, it was in the minds of the guards. Realization hit like a truck and Kargon rushed Avant to the gate. Without effort, he could pass through the bars.

"Little guy, go look for a key to the gate. It'll look something like this," Kargon said while tracing a shape in the air. "Don't get caught or we're out of luck. Sariel, please translate anything he didn't get."

They shook their head. "He understands you."

Kargon nodded and ruffled Avant's head. "We'll wait for you. Go!"

Avant crept to the corner of the bars and waited for a patrol to pass. Several minutes passed without sign of one. The owlbear was outside and vanished from sight immediately. and ran out of sight. Kargon involuntarily let out a shaky breath.

"He shows far greater intelligence than the average cub." Sariel patted the worrisome caretaker's back.

"Let us not forget his unique abilities." Vofric added. "Trust him."

Worry was unavoidable. A small beast was at a disadvantage in a massive unknown dungeon. Avant's spells remained a mystery. Based on past uses they were blessings similar to Vofric's. Then again, the beast might have access to magic but not know how to cast it. Maybe a dangerous mission was the perfect time for him to learn. Or he'd been set on a path towards his death.

Kargon's heartbeat quickened and he forced himself to stop thinking. Shutting his eyes and imagining a dim flame put him in a meditative state. But it felt different this time. There was something tugging at the corners of his mind. Flames fluctuated with little effort but something else was trying to emerge. With great focus Kargon was able to discern something moving within the pyre.

"CATCH THAT BEAST!" someone roared and forced Kargon back to reality.

Jingling keys flew into the air in front of the prisoners' cell. With catlike reflexes, Sariel grabbed them and quickly jammed one into the door lock. Their lanky arms were perfect for avoiding the metal bars. Vofric aided with aiming the key. Unfortunately, the first one didn't work. It took a few seconds to awkwardly switch to another with one hand.

Kargon watched the hall as a glowing furball approached with armor clambering behind it. Magic bolstered Avant but his small build was a hindrance. It took everything Kargon had not to rush Sariel. They were already under pressure with the imminent capture of their ally. Stones and arrows clattered on the floor inches from the owlbear's tail. He was nearly in front of the others when a guard lobbed a sword. It was the perfect arc to bisect the cub.

Then there was a loud click.

A persistent hum dissipated around the cell. Kargon leapt through the door and knocked the blade away. It clattered against the wall and Avant slid to a stop, panting. The two guards targeting him glared at the monk blocking their way. Kargon took a deep breath, remembering the sensation he felt during meditation. Igniting his fists summoned two flaming astral hands nearby. With a push, the hands flew forward. Curled fingers were mirrored by the projections as they gripped the guards' heads. Anger flared in Kargon's eyes as he smashed his opponents into adjacent walls. Before they could retaliate he viciously pummeled them. The astral hands were only slightly larger than his own fists yet moved significantly faster. Only a few attacks were needed to incapacitate the Balurian elves. As they fell to the floor, Kargon dispelled his astral creations.

"Good job, Avant," he said and petted the beast.

"The Balurians should have anticipated something like this." Sariel tossed the keys to Avant and stepped out of the cell.

Vofric shook his head. "Hubris. They left Avant in an escapable cage. Our conduits were not taken. They even fed and healed us. We are not seen as a threat."

Kargon shook his head and looked towards the end of the hall. "They'll figure it out."

CHAPTER TEN

The Right Hand's Role

Fierce drive didn't help with directions. Marble walls stretched in every direction like a maze. Halls were lined with gratuitous gold embellishments surrounded by empty well-lit cells. Corridors stretched to lengths that Balurian platforms couldn't match. Stalks outside might be hollow but they lacked this depth. Lack of discernible features was dizzying and Kargon was sure the building was enchanted. Thankfully, Avant readily guided the party with a confidence that made it clear he found Aisha.

The most distinguishing hallway had an intricate wooden door at the center. Two guards on high alert flanked either side of it. Platemail that looked heavier than it was covered them entirely. At the corner, each member of Kargon's party took turns peering around to work on a plan. Sneaking past wasn't possible even without Vofric's clattering armor. An inquisitive look passed Sariel's face and they told everyone to stand back.

Their back was pressed against the wall as a shortbow emerged from their draconic palm. Two needle-like arrowheads atop thin shafts grew from their wrist and needed to be pulled free. Knocked on their bow, Sariel gave a nod. Before anyone could react, they leapt out of the corner and loosed the sedating arrows. Precision shots easily found small openings in the guards' armor. Kargon shuddered at the potency of the drugged arrows as the guards collapsed. The expected clattering of metal never came.

"A silencing spell," Vofric whispered, glowing golden eyes peering down the hall. "Whoever occupies the room does not wish to be disturbed."

The bubble only covered a small portion of the hall. Footsteps were masked completely upon stepping into the zone of silence. That and curiosity were what caused Kargon to act rashly. He had to know what was so important that guard's couldn't make a sound outside the very room they defended.

"—sword in that stupid forest. Neves was never meant to exist!" an overconfident Balurian barked.

"Had *Valefor* never been taken from Balur, the new Hero would be one of ours. An elf is meant to take a grand role," another said. "If Kharim didn't betray us this wouldn't be happening."

The first Hero's name caught everyone else's attention and they inched closer to the door. It stung to hear Kharim be denounced for founding a half-elf haven. His reclusive cabin built near *Valefor* became surrounded by homes and over the course of a decade, Neves developed. With the town's connection to Balur, Kargon always assumed the elves would appreciate a Hero from his village.

"Agreed, Tenyorel," said Hastios's familiar voice. "With the capture of that foolish Hero and her party, the next blessed one will hail from the correct domain."

An unknown voice scoffed. "Did you see that dwarf sympathizing with the half-breeds? I never knew his kind to be so unintelligent. He is not only traveling with them but following orders!"

Stoicism failed to hide sadness in Vofric's eyes as the elves laughed. Insults wouldn't cause him to lose focus on the task at hand.

"I'm rather intrigued by the dragon scarred elf," another Balurian chimed in. "How idiotic must she be to challenge a dragon? Or worse, fallen into the clutches of a biomancer? It's unbecoming of a pureblood."

For the first time, Sariel's confidence visibly wavered with an eye twitch. It was clear in that moment that these people knew nothing of Sariel's draconic plight.

"How do we plan to deal with the failed Hero?" Tenyorel asked.

Hastios hummed and replied, "She has received the full mana capacity from both her tiefling and elvish heritage. We'll siphon that and when she's no longer of use, we will show mercy."

"The others?" someone asked.

"They are of no importance. Use them as you please," Hastios answered.

Gross snickers carried through the room as Kargon wordlessly walked away. Avant was the first to notice his master's departure and quickly gathered the others to follow.

Kargon's mind raced and he couldn't meditate to calm down. Escaping Balur was the priority and Aisha was nowhere to be found. Empty cells were so prominent that Kargon completely forgot about them. Thankfully, he wasn't working alone. Vofric grabbed the younger man's arm and pulled him back to the only cell housing prisoners.

"If it isn't our intrepid heroes," said Captain Julian with a mirthless smirk. "Good on ya for bringing them back, Avant."

He tossed the keys to Sariel and they quickly cycled through to let out the prisoners; every marine that survived the ship attack. Most looked the same as when they arrived on Balur.

"You remain unfed," Vofric said.

"I don't think we were worth wining and dining," Officer Lakelet replied haggardly

The paladin let out a sad sigh while healing the marines' wounds. Nothing could be done about their empty stomachs. Without thinking, Kargon started to walk towards the next hall leading deeper into the prison. A quick command from Sariel instructed everyone to follow.

"I was wondering where Miss Hero was," Captain Julian said as she briskly walked to Kargon's side. "Don't worry, she's a tough one."

Words would do nothing to silence the elves' conversation that repeated in his mind. Their refusal to understand others was likely why Balur was hidden, not for protection but superiority. A complex so twisted it excused killing without cause. Neves was no better than a cattle farm in their eyes. The only reason Aisha mattered was because they viewed her as a thief. And yet they were able to hide it long enough to fool a party of half-breeds and their dwarven "sympathizer."

Spiraling thoughts felt like an assault on Kargon even as he pressed forward toward their goal. Close behind were Vofric and Avant, primarily focused on keeping everyone hidden. Sariel was at the back with sharp eyes watching for anything out of place. The unarmed marines' hungered for revenge and they would pounce at the first signal from their captain.

Even so, Kargon couldn't ease his mind for not noticing something amiss in Balur. Complacency and exhaustion clouded their judgment —got them trapped. Self loathing continued even when the group arrived at a hall with a single intricate door at the opposite end. Two guards standing watch took notice of the group but were taken out by swift arrows.

Kargon didn't bother with trepidation and rushed through the door into a room housing various weapons. Loads of armor piled up in a messy stack like forgotten garments. A six foot high metal arch was bolted into the center of the room with Aisha bound to it—arms spread wide.

Long curls clung to her sweaty forehead and blocked vision. Pain and exhaustion weighed on drooping shoulders. By some miracle she was able to stay standing in a slowly expanding crimson pool at her feet that soaked into the dark scarf limply hanging to the floor. Tattered leather with deep cuts was all that covered her—metal armor likely in the nearby pile.

Rocks loudly scraping together pulled Kargon's focus toward a nearby elf. A familiar war-hammer was within the torturer's grasp and dragged to the prisoner. Grunting effortfully, the torturer hoisted the weapon and prepared to shatter Aisha's leg.

"Come now, Hero. This is a conversation. Stay quiet and I may do something we might both regret," the woman cackled.

Kargon stomped over and she turned slightly before laughing at the new audience. Words spoken fell on deaf ears as the monk tightly gripped her shoulder. Instant combustion unlike anything he'd used before torched the elf. A blood curdling scream and thunderous drop of stone echoed into the halls. The marines scrambled to shut the door and barricade it with anything.

Bursting flames pulled Aisha's tired eyes from the floor to the man in front of her. "Been a long time since you've had that look on your face," she choked out.

Expressionless eyes with constricted pupils stared back. Kargon's blank stare could be considered dumbfounded if his rage wasn't so obvious. A cold air emanated from his jaw, clenched so tightly his teeth might shatter. Mindlessly, he released the burnt husk losing shape in his grasp. The corpse collapsed near his friend's war-hammer and Kargon let out a breath he'd been holding.

"We need to go," he said, trying to calm down.

"What's the point?" Aisha replied.

Sariel brushed past the monk and grabbed Aisha's collar. "What are you saying?"

Avant whined with concern but stopped short of the bloody pool.

"I doubt something like this will stop her," Vofric said while pulling Sariel back. He made eye contact with Kargon and nodded towards the door where approaching footsteps grew louder. "We will prepare ourselves." He effortlessly picked up his hammer before going to the armor pile.

Kargon turned back to Aisha and asked, "What happened?"

"Captain Julian's saber," she said dryly. "Well-maintained."

"That's not what I meant. Why are you hesitating to leave?"

Aisha strained to lift her head further and met Kargon's eyes. It was, unfortunately, a familiar gaze—one she wore at her father's funeral. The man in front of her didn't block her from seeing a distant hidden landscape.

"You don't know what they think of me," she muttered.

"We overheard," Kargon replied through gritted teeth.

"Are they wrong? I got cocky against the leviathan and people died!" Aisha yelled. "I thought people would help the Hero, no questions asked. I've done nothing! I was chosen for this. That doesn't make me a Hero. I'm a naive idiot. A failure..."

Tears muddied with blood on her cheeks but eye contact never broke. Shaky screams didn't overpower fierce determination and some part of her was still willing to fight. It was a familiar one that Kargon had relied on before and he'd readily do so again. Shuffling through thousands of ideas proved difficult with loud banging against the door. Everyone armed themselves with whatever they could find, luckily some of it their own armor. Avant retrieved Aisha's armor and stubbornly dragged it over. *Valefor* remained strapped to the metal skirt.

"Is it so wrong to make mistakes when we just started? There's been successes, too," Kargon said while looking at their allies. "Take it as a lesson. Let people prove they deserve our trust. Don't hold back and work on getting stronger."

"All my strength comes from *Valefor.*" Aisha spat a wad of blood on the floor.

Kargon shook his head. "*Valefor* bolsters you physically but you've always been good with a sword. Your control of magic is unrelated, too. Even the elves know your mana comes from Devlin and Marniese. *Valefor* may help you, but it'd be impossible to wield without the strength you've always had."

Words were Kargon's specialty and he hoped something would pull the Hero out of her rut. It was hard to read Aisha's puffy and wounded face. Fluttering eyes could be related to her parents or memories of training. Chains and exhaustion made understanding body language difficult.

Whatever was outside the room was heavily bombarding it in hopes of breaking through. Memories of the Balur Sea storms sent a collective shudder down the marines' spines. But it bolstered Kargon with the memory of his astral abilities. Aisha was right, they wouldn't ever hold back again.

"Do you remember when we first met?" Kargon asked softly.

"No," Aisha grumbled.

"Well, I do. You've always been determined. It was grating when you wouldn't give up a lost schoolyard game. Everything's a hard fought victory with you. I wasn't ever allowed to give up if you thought I could succeed." The monk sighed heavily and stared at his bare hands. "I understand falling—never suited me to stay down. Doesn't suit you either. Fighting to prove people wrong suits you. Being the smart one who figures out plans suits you. So tell me how to free you so I can stop thinking so hard!"

It felt dumber than anything else he'd said but Kargon knew that it reached Aisha. Clear eyes met his own and for a moment he lost himself in the violet galaxies. Until the racket outside grew more violent—weakening beams holding the door in place. Marines' readied weapons but Sariel and Vofric stood back near an unmoving Kargon and Aisha. Avant guarded the Hero's tools silently. He'd already learned his master's stubbornness. No adventurer would move until given direction by their leader.

"I need my sword."

Aisha's quiet words rang in her party member's ears. A powerful kick from Avant sent *Valefor* towards Sariel who in turn whipped it to Kargon. He only gripped the enchanted sheath, knowing nothing would allow anyone to draw the blade. Aisha's fingers curled tightly around the hilt, releasing the seal seconds before Kargon stepped back to assist in unsheathing the Hero's sword.

"Vofric, please heal my wounds," Aisha commanded.

A glow surrounded her and wounds closed as the smiling dwarf placed a hand on her arm. Tightly pulled chains easily broke from a single strike of the blade. Once free, Aisha donned her armor as the last wounds healed. A portion of her scarf was torn off to tie her hair into its usual messy bun while studying the exit. The barricade fell and the door would soon follow.

Aisha remained calm, almost nonchalant while commanding the forces. "Sariel, the door's wooden. Think you can create vines and bolster it? Just for a few more seconds."

Sariel smiled their usual cocky grin. "Undoubtedly."

Thick stalks burst from the splintered wood and quickly wrapped around the damaged door frame. Non-stop attacks did nothing against Sariel's grit teeth as they held back the onslaught. White knuckles gripped their bow as every bit of effort focused on keeping the vines intact.

"Avant, let's get some fire in everyone's eyes."

The beast roared, sending a wave of blue energy through every weary marine.

"The only way out is through this door," Aisha said boisterously. "We don't stop until we reach the city portal station. Any portal will do but we must escape together. Am I clear?"

"Yes, Hero!" marines barked. Even Captain Julian and Officer Lakelet joined in.

"Good." Aisha walked in front of everyone with Sariel, Vofric, and Avant. A spot was deliberately left at her unarmed right. "Kargon! You better back up all that talk with that astral magic I saw on the ship. Burn this wall down and show them Nevesi can't be messed with!"

He stood by the Hero's side as she had requested many times before, tightly strapping on his goggles. Embers around his arms turned to brilliant flames while taking a fighting stance. Glowing astral arms made of fire easily manifested in the air ahead of him. They mimicked pulling back his right arm and burned hotter than ever before. He didn't wait for Aisha to give a signal, her command assigned him the role. Full ignition empowered the Hero's right hand as he blasted open the walls that bound them.

CHAPTER ELEVEN

Half-Breed Bloodbath

Flaming wooden planks and burning vines rained into the hall, plummeting towards the closest elves. Marines rushed past the Hero's party to take advantage of the surprise. Captain Julian and Officer Lakelet stood with the adventurers. Aisha studied the elves—most were guards with standard armor and weapons. At the end of the hall, behind the large group, stood the Balurian figureheads in pristine robes that glowed in the embers' light. They sneered at the half-breeds making no attempt to defend themselves.

Some elves foolishly tried to push past the marines but were met with a surprising defense. There was no leviathan here to overpower the raging crew. Equal footing invigorated them as adrenaline drowned out any pangs of hunger. Elven guards were separated to opposite walls to create a path for the adventurers. Aisha charged through with Kargon, Vofric, Avant, and Captain Julian while Sariel and Officer Lakelet stayed behind the marines to provide cover fire.

"I'm low on arrows," Officer Lakelet swore, removing a large magazine from their automatic crossbow.

Green light emitted from Sariel's claw as they grabbed the empty cartridge and packed it full of ammunition. They wordlessly tossed it back and the officer opened fire. It was surprising to see someone match Sariel's accuracy. If a guard didn't fall immediately, they were cut down by another marine.

Aisha kept her fury focused on the Balurian leaders but couldn't bypass the innumerable guards firing magic blindly. Each spell was negated by a swift strike from *Valefor*.

"Still underestimating us, huh?" she growled, reaching for one of the elves.

They stumbled back in fear, blind to Captain Julian's advance. A powerful cut bisected the guard before she moved onto another.

"They ain't good at working together," she said.

A cool wind emitted from her next target's hands before a jagged icicle shot out. Kargon swung his left arm and the astral copy blocked the chilling attack. Captain Julian leapt off the floating knuckle and plunged her sword through the elf.

"Good cover, Kargon," she said with a smirk.

Hastios sneered with disgust and left with the other leaders in tow. No one else might have noticed if not for Aisha's rage-filled scream. Where others heard frustration, Kargon heard the Hero's goal. Nothing would stop him from getting her there.

"We need to clear the fodder," he shouted.

Aisha sighed aggressively. "Vofric, make a path. Everyone else, occupy them. We're not wasting time."

Golden light erupted from the paladin's war-hammer with a stern prayer. He raised the weapon's momentum by spinning his whole body. Such a wild attack was inaccurate but that was Vofric's intent. Striking the ground forced nearby enemies off their feet. Light poured out of the cracked marble, creating a shockwave that pushed back all the airborne guards. Marines rushed forward to assault the scrambling elves.

"Glory." Vofric released his war-hammer and roared a blessing. "In the name of the Starcaller!"

The glow burst from his hammer to nearby allies. Following his lead, Avant engulfed everyone in a blue glow. Fresh wounds quickly healed before an animalistic energy overwhelmed the marines' senses. Frenzied attacks easily took out any elves who dared cross them.

The glow persisted even as Vofric lifted his weapon. "They carry our strength. Aisha, is it time?"

Not a word was uttered by the Hero—her presence made clear that everyone should prepare themselves. Purple light from her prosthetic pupil burst out like lightning which trailed in the air as Aisha slowly crouched. Electricity traveled through her hair, pulling it skyward. The walls shook as small bursts of lightning erupted from the gathering storm in the palm of her hand.

As the Hero opened her mouth, electricity bounced between her lips. "Kargon, help me up." Grit teeth were all she could do to keep the attack contained.

With an astral hand he gripped the front of Aisha's armor. Even without physical contact Kargon could feel sparks against his palm. It took more focus than expected to move her. Instincts screamed for Kargon to avoid the danger but years of experience silenced them. There was no safer place to be than by Aisha's side when she was letting loose. Kargon roared as he launched the Hero above the largest clump of elven guards. A ball of lightning in half-elf form hovered above them.

Aisha thrust her palm forward so fast it produced a thunder clap after the lightning burst out. Searing light blinded everyone for a split second, enough to hide the attack. Electricity effortlessly tore through the guards, showering the marble walls with crimson gore as they cracked under pressure. Armor clattered to the floor in a wave as whatever vigor remained vanished. The only remaining guards attempted to run but it was pointless. Fear and hesitation overcame any autonomy as marines cut them down, trampling corpses in their advance. Vofric and Avant focused on bolstering their allies while Captain Julian and Kargon dashed past Aisha to eradicate the furthest living guards. Arrows flew overhead, killing any guard who might escape impending doom.

Over fifty Balurian guards were wiped out in minutes, their blood coating the ground and walls. It was finally possible for the prisoners to press forward. A few marines led with Captain Julian and Kargon. Aisha and Avant followed closely behind with Sariel and Officer Lakelet watching their backs. At the rear were the last of the marines and Vofric keeping an eye out for any stragglers.

The disappointing marble repeated endlessly through every hall. Not a single ambush awaited them from unknown corners and allowed the group to reach the highest floor with ease. It was the first time any of them saw a window in the entire building. Outside were the Balurian leaders—expressions of shock and disgust on their faces. Before they could act, Aisha ran through the door and swung at the nearest one. Finally recognizing her capabilities, the elf had summoned a magic shield that propelled him out of reach.

The rest of her allies joined her on the large platform held in the clouds. Kargon focused on not getting lightheaded with the hard to breath air. Dizzying heights made the surrounding oceans clear. Even the faintest shape of Tetria's shores visible to the north. Thick stalks connected dozens of platforms throughout Balur in a webbed pattern that could be mistaken for beautiful not for all the enemies standing atop them.

"We are grossly outnumbered," Sariel whispered. "And we lack the advantage of enclosed space."

Vofric nodded. "Magic permeates from all directions. They are far more capable than the guards."

"We need to get out of here," Kargon said.

Aisha grumbled and nodded, "We're done here. Everyone, make for the portal station!"

The elders chuckled, causing the surrounding elves to erupt into laughter. One standing in the center wore a robe similar to Elder Niko's, though this one was golden and white instead of black and gray. Hastios stood with a condescending smirk as his subjects looked on in awe. Why he had taken the time to change while the prisoners escaped was beyond logic. Possibly because the garb demanded reverence; something that wouldn't come from the escapees.

Hastios watched intently, contemplating the half-breeds' next action. "You won't escape after bringing carnage to our home," he said eerily. As if on command, the elves spat and swore at the adventurers.

The elder needed only to hold up a hand to stop the commotion. "This is the fault of our brethren and other purebloods. Half-breeds have spread like a plague over five centuries due to their mercy. That is why one foolishly wields *Valefor* against its rightful owners. That cannot stand!"

He raised his arm ceremoniously, pulling in a stream of red energy that even Kargon could see. Embers appeared out of nowhere and quickly gathered into a fireball that eclipsed the platform in size and exuded unimaginable pressure.

"I can't stop that," Kargon admitted.

"If this is where we fall, we're taking some of these bastards with us," Captain Julian said.

"No," Aisha commanded. "Everyone spread out."

Hastios scoffed, "It will do no good against my engulfing blaze."

The threat was pointless after Aisha had already spoken. In dire straits everyone put faith in the Hero. Kargon grabbed Avant as the group cautiously separated under the slowly moving orb of flames. It was possibly the fastest it could move and the elf was simply hiding the fact. Regardless, it brought sweat to every brow except the monk's. Rising temperatures all felt the same to Kargon but he was surprised to see Aisha remain unphased. Then he noticed the faint glow in her right hand, hidden from Hastios's view. Tightly packed between her thumb and index finger was a ball of lightning

"You know the problem with concentrated spells like that, Hastios?" Aisha asked. "One little thing out of place and they explode."

"The only thing out of place here is you," Hastios retorted.

The fireball grew closer until it was only an arms length away. She raised her hand, lightning arcing off and destabilizing the flaming orb. It stopped for mere seconds—enough time for the Hero to throw her spell at the empty space on the platform. A large hole erupted in the marble platform and broke several vine support beams underneath.

"With me!" Aisha commanded to a group that was already diving.

As soon as the last marine jumped, Hastios's destabilized spell exploded into a massive firestorm. The initial blast accelerated everyone's descent through Balur. Burning meteors endlessly rained from the sky from a spell packing more mana than Kargon could imagine. That didn't matter with an army of pissed off elves targeting everyone while they searched for the portal station.

Verticality made the openings between platforms, paths, and plant stalks stand out. It wasn't necessary to land until reaching the portal station but it did help with dodging when cover was scarce. Hundreds of elemental spells chased the escapees without regard for collateral damage. Giant stalks that held the city aloft blazed as structures crumbled under the power of elven magic. Hastios roared commands, the half-breeds falling further from his reach.

They were wise to split up and find individual paths. Sariel shot arrows with vines into nearby walls that some marines grabbed to swing through incoming blasts. Unfortunately, attacks grazed them but nothing made full contact. Healing was a matter for later. It seemed Vofric had his work cut out for him but right now he had the easiest time escaping. His size allowed him to weave through attacks as they collided with wreckage. Kargon desperately searched for Aisha but she vanished from sight faster than anyone else.

"She'll be okay," he muttered unconvinced and focused on getting through a nearby opening. "Hold on tight, Avant."

Claws extended, the cub wrapped around Kargon's arm. It stung but wasn't a problem compared to everything else going on. Jagged edges from broken rubble cut his bare skin while searching for flat surfaces to change trajectory. Smoke and rubble clung to his goggles as he plummeted through the collapsing city. He could just barely see the portals below but turned his attention to Sariel who was stuck in battle. Three armed elves cornered the ranger on a crumbling platform. Two of them were held back but one approached from behind.

Kargon skidded against a burning stalk and leapt off, arriving in time to kick the assailant aside. The attack wasn't incapacitating but created an opening for Kargon to interject in Sariel's fight. Their bow was bending under the pressure of blocking two maces. By tackling one assailant, Kargon allowed Sariel to retaliate against the other. Before they could attack again the adventurers dashed off the platform. Thin vines made for decent cover as they weaved through then separated via a cracked building.

By now some of their allies had made it to the portals but carried fear in their eyes. A quick look around revealed a large cage of ice between Vofric and the station. He uncontrollably dropped towards it, racking his brain for a way to bypass safely. Since Kargon was safe he turned his attention to saving his ally. It was slightly outside his astral hand's reach but Vofric was quick-witted enough to grab the flaming projection. With a swift pull, he was out of harm's way and falling towards the station. Turning back, he opened his arms wide and stared at the monk. Without a thought, Kargon threw Avant who curled into a ball before landing in Vofric's grasp.

There was plenty of room at the portal station where Sariel and marines guarded a single portal. An involuntary groan escaped Kargon when he realized Aisha was missing. She was definitely up to something.

A nearly unscathed platform off Kargon's path drew his attention. Standing atop it were Hastios and Aisha, each exuding killing intent.

Another vine nearby pulled Kargon to the battle.

"This wasn't very heroic of you. Only a monster would retaliate like this," Hastios growled.

Aisha scoffed. "You admit we retaliated yet refuse any blame in what's happened here. They'll be better off without you."

"There will always be more Balurians to support my cause. They will find you no matter where you escape to."

"So, you'll take all that half-breed hate and focus it on me? I can live with that."

"Not for long!" Hastios roared and lunged at the Hero.

Magic wreathed around him but the spell was too slow to stop Aisha from cutting his arm. She pierced his leg before ripping the sword out, slashing the other leg.

"It's not easy to survive empty-handed near me," the Hero taunted.

The elf swore and clapped his hands, conjuring a blast that launched each fighter backwards. Nails scratched against stone as Hastios scribbled something into the bloodied floor. Aisha was only a step away when he slammed the marks. A hum erupted around the platform and fire traced the perimeter before expanding vertically into a sphere.

"Now there's nowhere to run!" Blood dripped from the elder's mouth. "I don't have to survive! My people will avenge me! Your useless half-breeds can do nothing to save you!"

Aisha looked at Kargon and guided him without a word. An ignited hand was all he produced while approaching the wall of fire. Dousing a natural flame was child's play but he'd never fought against someone else's creation. Hastios had a stronger grasp of his magic than the half-elf he needed to be brought down to size. Aisha wasn't the only half-breed that could overpower him. Fire met flame as Kargon planted his palm against the wall and felt the area weaken.

Hastios finally realized someone was behind him in time to see the monk fail. Laughter wasn't enough to shake Kargon. With a strike of his knuckle, embers burst forth and opened a hole in the structure.

"Looks like my allies can save me." Aisha sauntered towards Hastios. "I can't say the same for you."

Before the elf could utter any vitriol, she slit his throat. Blood poured from the wound as life escaped the collapsing Balur elder. The opening Kargon created grew wide enough for the elves to clearly see their fallen leader. Magic rained like a torrential downpour with fury that cracked even the sturdiest structures. Aisha dashed to Kargon, grabbed his hand, and leapt toward their goal.

The Balurians seemingly stopped caring for their city as tattered constructs plummeted from the sky. Giant boulders destroyed platforms which indiscriminately crushed elves. The portal station was in shambles with half a dozen gates destroyed. Kargon's allies stood their ground against heavily armed elves, their backs to a single arch with Officer Lakelet on the other side.

"This is it!" they yelled.

It was all the marines needed to rush through. Captain Julian stood her ground with the rest of the Hero's party. Time quickly dwindled as a heavy greatclub cracked the arch, weakening the portal. Vofric tackled the elf away and released Avant through the portal before physically holding the stones in place.

"Go!"

Captain Julian ran through with Sariel in tow. They quickly tied a rope around Vofric's wrist before teleporting. The moment Kargon and Aisha arrived, they grabbed the rope before passing through the portal. As the magic vanished from existence, their dwarven ally burst through, aided by his lifeline.

"Is that everyone?" Aisha frantically looked at the group.

Scattered acknowledgments came in waves and the sensation of relief knocked the energy out of her. With a deep sigh, she fell to the ground and invited others to do the same. Marines wept for fallen comrades and comforted each other. Hollow laughter echoed from Vofric's gut while Sariel stared soberly into the distance. Large tears poured from Avant's eyes as he curled into his master's lap who was too stunned to act. Kargon simply removed his goggles and sat by Aisha as she stared blankly at the afternoon sky, unsure where to go next.

CHAPTER TWELVE

Much Needed Rest

Every pyromancer knew the dangers of setting the wrong thing ablaze. It was a fear Kargon carried since childhood and yet he'd never done something like causing the collapse of an ancient city. Obviously there was blood on his hands but that was a given for Vethyean adventurers. Even combusting the torturer was understandable given the circumstances. Yet he couldn't fathom how far gone Hastios was to justify burning down his own home.

All the survivors ruminated on Balur as they recovered from separate breakdowns. According to Captain Julian, another portal could be created as long as it stood. It was just a fortuitous coincidence that everyone needed an outlet for their rage. The scent of fire finally dissipated as the last stone was smashed.

"Even if the portal's gone, won't the elves come after us?" a marine asked.

Another chimed in. "Yeah, aren't we wanted now?"

"It's unlikely," Aisha answered. "They're secretive... and too proud for their own good. They had every advantage against us and still lost. If word got out, they'd be admitting we proved their very ideology wrong."

"If you ask me, they cared more about mistreating half-breeds than their own city." Kargon added.

"Exactly, so it's up to us what we tell people." Aisha turned to Captain Julian. "Your crew are the most likely to be questioned. I trust you know what to say."

The captain nodded. "Aye. First we have to find a settlement. Lakelet, I assume you recognize the area."

Officer Lakelet sighed. "Of course, I do. You should too."

Everyone grabbed their few belongings and followed the officer out of the clearing. A normal forest was appreciated after trekking through the illusory nightmare. Avant happily crunched leaves with jovial hops, only pausing to eat loose berries. Watching the cub saunter calmed any lasting nerves. Brief respite demanded appreciation while it lasted. Whatever came next was guaranteed to be more stressful.

Getting out of the thicket landed everyone onto a developed road, inlaid with cobblestone that invited travelers towards a massive metropolis in the distance. Within the city stood a giant structure that immediately identified the location; one that could be seen from the top of Neves' guard tower. Aisha had dreamt of one day visiting the capital of the Tetria—home of the ruler and city of light.

"Dawncaster!" she exclaimed happily. "We can get info and rest for a bit."

"It'll be a good place to restock our lost supplies," Kargon said.

"We need to get in first," Captain Julian interjected.

The main gate of the city was blocked by a long line of carriages and vehicles awaiting entry. Silver chestplates engraved with a cobalt moon weighed on soldiers inspecting travelers based on documents they presented. Stacked chevrons on left pauldrons identified the Kingsguards' ranks while enchanted ridge helmets concealed their faces. One of them was adorned with a cobalt cape that identified him as the commander; Captain Julian's target.

"There's blood on your garb, Stormclaw," the commander said.

"Ain't there always, Rusty?" Captain Julian replied.

"How'd you know it was — My voice." Rusty laughed, ignoring his identifiable cape. "Last time you said blood stains were the sign of adventure. But what brings you here?"

"We had some problems on our last voyage. Why else would we be at the main gate?"

"Sorry to hear that. I don't have a problem letting you in but what about them?" Rusty nodded at Aisha. "That one looks familiar."

Captain Julian waved her hand dismissively. "Don't mind 'em. We had similar goals and these fine adventurers assisted us. Mind looking the other way this one time? They ain't even got supplies."

The guard captain looked the party over. "If anyone asks, Commander Telos wasn't the one who helped you. And keep an eye on your familiar."

"Understood, sir." Aisha replied. "Thank you."

Kargon looked at Avant and whispered, "Stay close."

Textbook information did no justice to Dawncaster's magnificence. Its well-known districts were each nearly the size of a town. Buildings spread through the city put Neves' guard tower to shame. Most impressive was the castle housed in the central district, home to the royal family. Every visible corner, and some not so, had a guard keeping watch. According to Captain Julian, the docks were located on the southwest side of the Dawncaster.

"We'll part ways with ya here," she said. "I've gotta report... something to my commander."

"Should we be worried about being branded criminals?" Kargon asked.

"No. Forget other elves — no one had seen them since the land vanished 500 years ago. Aside from our little group, no one is aware we sailed for Balur yet. I'll handle what's shared." Captain Julian held out her hand towards Aisha. "You've got a journey to get back on track."

Aisha shook the captain's hand. "Thank you."

"Don't mention it. If you're ever in need of a ship, send for us."

With the marines' departure, the party was left in the middle of the road with nothing but bloody garments and dirt. Bustling city streets didn't suit battered warriors. Aside from guards, no one wore armor and even fewer carried a weapon.

"We look suspicious," Aisha said. "A change of clothes would do us good."

"With what coin?" Kargon asked.

Sariel grunted. "Adventurers cross the city often. It is common for them to remain stained for one day."

"One day to get clean clothes. Again, with what coin?"

Vofric silently looked at the surrounding streets pivoting only enough to center himself. Unknown allies and paths made the city more daunting than Kargon would willingly admit. However, the dwarf seemed at ease looking through the crowds. One nearby corner grabbed his attention and he nearly jumped with joy.

Waving his companions over, Vofric said, "We needn't worry. Follow me."

Naturally small stature naturally allowed him to weave through crowds but there was a familiarity with how he traversed the side streets. Some citizens noticed the group but paid no mind to the dried blood on their garments. Discoloration was a minor issue—the pungent odor that would develop in a day was a different matter.

Nothing particularly distinct separated the districts aside from signs on street poles. Ashborne housed the main gate and Vofric led everyone into Bamborough where buildings were packed together with any empty space occupied by market stalls. Stores invited customers with bombastic decorations. Merchants yelled about sales ending within the day. Neither Kargon nor Aisha could hide their excitement at the differences from Neves. Avant was equally surprised by the busy city. Fortunately, Sariel remained undistracted and kept the young adventurers on track. If not for their guidance, Vofric would vanish completely.

Banners hung high above a wide street dubbed Greycastle Market. Stores were even larger with brighter lights and no space between them. People were packed tightly into the wide street. Kargon quickly picked up Avant, pushing through the crowd to catch Vofric. It was almost impossible to track him here. Thankfully, he stopped at the center of the street near a low rock wall encircling smaller merchant stalls. Between two at the back was a wide, two story building.

A line waited to enter the miniature market, kept orderly by a young man at the entrance. Silver hair rested messily atop his innocent pale face. Lightweight gray armor complimented his lean form which exuded a surprisingly powerful aura. Vofric approached slowly, a wide grin plastered on his face.

"Sorry, you'll have to get to the back—" the guard hesitated as he noticed Aisha further away than expected. He looked down to see the dwarf between them. "Uncle Vof?!"

"You've grown quite a bit, Albert," Vofric replied, arms spread out.

Albert dropped to his knee for a hug. "I've been taller than you since

I was seven!"

"Apologies, then. I haven't returned since you were a toddler."

"Don't worry about it, Mom and Mama will be happy to see you! And I assume your party?"

Vofric nodded as he left the embrace.

Albert turned towards the crowd and shouted, "Rolan, come take over. We have a guest."

A man slightly older than swapped positions as the boy led his guests into the large shop behind the stalls. Potions, tools—really anything a traveler could need—lined the shelves. Jewelry and accessories were locked behind a glass case and radiated unique properties. Enamoring wooden figures sat on any number of selves, advertising commissioned pieces for sale.

Kargon pointed it out to Aisha and whispered, "We could get some of us."

"Later!" She did her best to hide how much she wanted a souvenir.

"Mom, look who's here!" Albert yelled to a human woman stowing coins in a safe.

Chin length hair rested over the collar of an unbuttoned flannel hanging loosely around her. "Blood," she muttered, reaching for a dagger strapped to her denim clad leg. Then she saw the party and stopped. "Vofric? What a surprise, old man. Thought you'd retired."

"Circumstances demanded otherwise," he replied. "May we talk elsewhere, Mia?"

"Of course."

Mia said something inaudible to a nearby employee before heading to the back. A crafting room filled with equipment made it clear that everything in the store was handmade. Further questions couldn't be asked before they arrived at a locked door to the second floor; the shopowners' home.

"Before I let you up; confirm who you are to Vofric," Mia said. "I'm guessing Al's working on an assumption or Vofric's word. I want to be sure."

Nonchalant words did little to lighten her scrutinizing gaze. Sariel exuded a threatening aura, but that was normal for some adventurers. Kargon's natural confusion was a benefit in times like these. Aisha, however, stared back seriously.

"We're Vofric's adventuring party, ma'am," she insisted.

Mia raised an eyebrow, studying the wounded fighter with more bloodstains than wounds. Only a great healer could cause such a peculiar image and she knew how powerful Vofric was. "Good enough," she said.

Reaching the top of the stairs, the group was hit with overwhelming scents of meat and stew that drowned their concerns. For a brief second, Balur was a bad dream. But scars and exhaustion quickly dashed the fantasy..

"Dinner's not ready yet, hun. What brought you up early?" a woman asked with large horns, waving a slender tail with each hummed word. Silky silver hair was braided past the shawl on her back. A long skirt and apron complimented her skin; the color almost a match for the dried marks on the adventurer's clothes.

Mia smirked. "Louise, there's an old man here. Wanted to have a word with us."

Louise was beaming before she'd turned. "Vofric! How are you? What brings you here? Is that blood? Did you get hurt? Are you adventuring again? Who are your friends?"

Vofric held up his hands and calmly replied, "I'll explain everything. May we sit?"

The party was led to covered chairs surrounding a coffee table where Albert and his mothers got settled. It wasn't right to avoid the topic at hand with how suddenly the guests appeared. Carefully, Vofric broached the subject of the Hero, how they crossed paths, why he left—and then he paused.

"How much can I tell them?" he asked Aisha.

She hesitated. "They don't seem like strangers to you."

"They are as close to family as I have left"

"Go for it."

The dwarf went on to explain how their party sailed to Balur, what they did to escape, even how many elves might have been affected. Finally, he arrived at their predicament in Dawncaster.

Kargon hadn't realized how much had already happened since he left home but Mia's quiet contemplation made it clear. The furtive tension was challenged by excited glances from Albert. The silence lasted long enough to be awkward—a feeling Louise didn't care for.

"It makes sense the Hero could bring you out of retirement after you were so adamant about it," she said. Without looking away from Vofric, she grabbed a cookie out of the tray of snacks and held it in front of Avant long enough to convince the cub to cuddle. She pet the owlbear softly, turned to Aisha and continued, "The rumors of Balur painted them viciously. It sounds like you're not too much at fault for their downfall so don't let it weigh on you. "

Her manner of speech was much like Marniese's and easily broke Aisha's guard, calming her. She relaxed ever so slightly at the familiar feelings.

"Sariel, was it? Why are you still with them? Balur was your original goal." Louise pointed out. "If you simply need a change of clothes, we can provide it."

The elf slowly looked over the party before landing on Aisha. "Balur did not provide the information I sought. But I could not have reached it, nor escaped, without all of you. I would like to seek answers while traveling alongside you."

A brief flicker in Aisha's eye made it obvious to Kargon that she'd forgotten why Sariel joined in the first place. "What about after you get your answers? What if our quest is incomplete?" she asked.

"I will stay. If you will have me."

Aisha smiled and nodded to Kargon. "What do you think?"

He pretended to contemplate, as if their party would be complete without the sharp tongued elf. "I was going to ask them to stay if talk of leaving came up," he admitted. "It's our party. That includes you."

Sariel gave the briefest smile."Wonderful."

"Wonderful." Louise repeated with a beaming smile. "Mia, what would you like to do?"

She eyed the group over. "The Balur situation ain't a problem. Not to mention, how much we owe old Vof. We've got some extra rooms in this place so feel free to use them." Mia looked out the back window and continued, "We've got a business to run so whatever help we provide has to be lawful. And I gotta ask you not to lead trouble back here." She turned to Aisha and Kargon. "You two got your first taste of the real world. People won't jump to help the Hero, okay? You have to show them you're worth believing in. Don't just blindly trust folks either. Balur should've put a chip on that shoulder. Don't forget it."

"We've realized that for some time," Aisha replied. Kargon nodded in agreement.

"Good. Vofric seems to believe in you so we'll do the same. Feel free to use Al here if you need. Kid's got a knack for finding things and you've got a lot of searching to do."

"I'm not sure where to start. Dawncaster is massive."

"Don't worry about it for tonight. Enjoy a meal and rest." Louise chimed in. "We'll get you some clothes for your stay while your armor is fixed up."

Aisha shook her head. "You letting us stay is more than enough."

"Nonsense! We have means to help you, so let us. Consider it repayment for Vofric's help."

Kargon looked at the dwarf, who glanced back with a shrug that made it clear he'd given up the argument long ago. "What did he do?" he asked.

Mia sighed, clearly having explained enough for a lifetime. "We were traveling merchants. Al got into some trouble as a toddler. Vofric saved our lives. Got us to Dawncaster. We wouldn't be where we are now if not for him and Adrian,."

Kargon furrowed my brow and inquired further. "Who's Adrian?"

"Adrian Greycastle was Al's grandfather. Circumstances brought us together and he accepted us as his own," Louise explained. "This market, this home, wouldn't exist without his help. Let us pay it forward to you."

The conversation continued into the night through tea and dinner. Avant roamed the halls with a doting Louise steps behind. Chatter echoed through the house as Albert and Vofric discussed goings on about town. Mia went back to the shop to assist the last shift with Sariel as they wanted to learn about the market. Exhaustion finally caught up to Kargon and he retired to his borrowed room. It didn't take long for it to open and Aisha to join him donned in clothes borrowed from their generous hosts.

"You look like a mom," Kargon joked, doing his best not to stare.

"Shut up, Kargon. I know," she replied while laying down and pulling up the covers.

Kargon laid down next to her and asked, "What's on your mind?"

"A lot. Don't immediately trust people. Not everyone will help us. Be smart. Be cautious. Don't immediately trust people..."

She repeated in a trance while the exhausted monk searched for words of comfort. "Don't change too much," he said. "We'll assess the next situation better."

"What if we repeat the same mistakes as yesterday? Or the day before?"

"Up until now, every mistake we've made was different than the last. Improvement doesn't mean we need to fundamentally change."

Aisha scoffed. "You're saying we'll make more mistakes."

"Yes," Kargon replied. "But they'll be less severe. We'll recover faster. And we'll get further in our journey each time."

"Spoken like a true monk." Aisha snickered in a way that put Kargon at ease. "Thanks."

Kargon's surety that made Aisha feel unstoppable. "Of course, Hero."

CHAPTER THIRTEEN

Filling in the Gaps

Dawncaster enticed Aisha to explore and indulge like a tourist but it wasn't possible. Research needed to be done and her mind was clear for the first time in days. Kargon accompanied the Hero to check any records about Kharim that might be in the city library. Local contacts allowed Vofric to tackle the problem from a social angle. With no connections to speak of, Sariel opted to run errands with Albert's assistance.

It was hard to leave Avant behind when he wanted to join Kargon. The infrastructure of Dawncaster accommodated even the largest familiars. But, certain concessions had to be made for the safety of rare tomes. The stubborn owlbear refused to join anyone else and stayed back to be pampered.

Aisha studied a messy map provided by Albert, having trouble deciphering the crude trail drawn on it. Urban areas were much easier to navigate for her than forest trails. Thus Kargon opted to follow quietly as they weaved through streets towards the central Dicoris district. Passages to other districts had watchful eyes guarding them. According to Aisha, it was best to avoid long interactions with the Kingsguard since they might know about Balur or have ill will towards the Hero. Maybe they didn't even know who Aisha was and would find her questions suspicious. Either way, it was best not to linger for long.

From the castle district, the duo went to Zeffari where they entered

Library Raebkayd. Engraved legends decorated gargantuan walls with doors wide enough to accommodate multiple carriages. The path remained open during all operational hours as a quick way to cross from Zeffari to the Ramshorn district. The scent of leather and fresh paper permeated past the doors and invited guests to enter. One step inside made the smell even more potent, almost bowling Kargon over.

Books lined five stories of floor to ceiling shelves filled with centuries of written word. Gigantic chandeliers emitted light which magically snaked through dark corners and brightened the entire building. Floating platforms with railing carried guests quickly between floors when they were in too much of a hurry to climb spiral staircases wrapped around multiple support pillars.

"Where do we even start?" Kargon asked, mouth agape.

The attempt at bringing the duo out of their stupor worked surprisingly well. They turned towards a large circular table at the center of the ground floor housing two librarians. Glowing eyes stared skyward, scanning for information, even when addressing guests.

"How may I help you?" One asked slowly as Aisha approached.

"Information on the first Hero, Kharim," she replied.

The librarian's eyes flashed. "All information regarding historical legends can be found in section six of the second floor. Stairs near the west wall will place you eight hundred feet from your destination."

Aisha was off while Kargon scrambled to thank the librarians and keep up. Steps echoed through the upper floors where guests were quieter. Pages flipped softly in all directions as hushed voices discussed myriad topics without regard for who might overhear. Quick glances passed over the Nevesi duo, people recognizing Aisha. Kargon said a silent thanks that no one bothered her while she was focused on the quest.

On the second floor sat one-sided shelves pressed together to form a small alcove labeled with a large number "6". The perimeter was marked by glowing letters that produced an invisible wall which could only be crossed at a break near the entrance of the section. A single Dawncaster guard kept watch of the empty area.

"Are we allowed to go in?" Kargon asked.

"The librarian wouldn't have sent us this way if we weren't," Aisha replied and approached the entrance. "I'm guessing the books can't be taken from here."

A grunt was the only answer the guard gave before stepping aside to allow Aisha through.

Contrary to the physical shelves, books were significantly spaced out with most covers facing outward. Titles—or attempts—were scrawled across records that were painstakingly recovered, never to be reproduced. A myriad of emotions could be felt from every written piece almost lost to time. Aisha brushed aside her theories and began her search, focusing on one half of the enclosure while Kargon went to the other.

Records were organized chronologically with multiple thousand year gaps. Older books relating to worldly discoveries were similar to Sariel's notes—exploratory with theories in the margins. Original authors presented unproven claims that were erased as facts became common knowledge. Anything relating to the first hero was hidden amongst these hundreds of tomes. The duo only found two related to Kharim's journey.

"I'll check one, you check the other," Aisha said.

Skills of the Hero was heavy-handedly written across the front of her book and Kargon's didn't have one. A loose note on top explained that it recollected notes of Kharim's travels.

Notes were scarce prior to the creation of *Valefor*, forged from adamantium and dragon scales midway through the first Hero's quest. He was nothing more than an average adventurer doing odd jobs for nearly a decade. Members of his party joined by proving themselves and left of their own volition. Some stuck with him through the end while others passed away during battle. Few notes acknowledged them as more than peons of the first Hero.

Valefor changed Kharim's life, introducing the threat of demons and otherworldly beings. Their motives and abilities were barely mentioned. Non-permanent wounds received by the Hero were understated as long as he was victorious. No matter the number or strength of his enemies, Kharim remained steadfast. Nothing could stand in his way. The exact skills he employed were relegated to the other book.

Kharim often ended fights in a draw—specifically against a single demon. No name was provided but certain details came up repeatedly —specifically its transforming weapon. Their final battle resulted in many of Kharim's comrades giving their lives. It was a decisive victory over the unnamed demon. Then half a page was torn out with only a few words remaining.

"The fate of the land rests in their hand."

There were no other notes, even regarding planting *Valefor*. The first Hero lived long after the end of his journey yet it was deemed unimportant. Kargon ran to the shelves in search of more records about Kharim or Neves but even the next chronological book was unrelated. For good measure, Kargon leafed through the pages but found nothing. With a long sigh, he sat back at the table before slowly going over the notebook again. There was no information about Kharim's nemesis or what plagued the realm. Nothing about what changed Kharim from an adventurer to a legend. Battles weren't all that molded the first Hero but the book proved useless in learning more.

"He was strong," Aisha said in awe, shutting her book. "The way this is written... It's speculative instructions on how Kharim fought. His fighting style has no name or history beyond himself. When things got tough, he learned a new trick to face the hardship. When his enemy used a new weapon, Kharim countered in kind. He was so skilled that he didn't rely solely on *Valefor*..." There was a twinge of pain in her voice but pushed past it. "Anything interesting on your side?"

Kargon shrugged. "It's all interesting but there's nothing about what threat he faced. If I had to guess, it's related to the hells. And I think this is some incomplete prophecy."

He passed the book to Aisha with it turned to the torn page. Upon reading the passage, she searched for more pages. Finding nothing, Aisha leaned back in her chair and let out a long sigh.

"That's a Hero," she muttered. "Kharim did stuff that deserved the title. What have I done?"

"Saved an elf, a small town, some marines, and defended half-breeds," Kargon replied. He had a hunch Aisha wasn't okay and experience dictated he have words ready to help. "Your story isn't finished like Kharim's. You can call him a legend but you're no less of a Hero. You know what I mean?"

"Yeah... Do you really believe it?" Aisha asked.

"Is the sky blue?"

"Not when it's cloudy."

Kargon smirked. "You're a Hero then, too."

"Alright." Aisha drew out the word and rolled her eyes, recognizing Kargon dug his heels in and wouldn't relent. "We still need to figure out what the prophecy means. Clearly someone needs to protect some place."

"It's possible the enemy wasn't originally related to Kharim."

Kargon stood up and slowly scanned the shelves, approaching the oldest, dustiest text. It might crumble if not handled delicately. Leafing through gave him a passing idea what it was about; battles between gods and how they shaped the planet. Nothing obviously related to Kharim. Aisha grumbled, realizing what her friend was doing, and grabbed a different book. The next book Kargon found was a foreign language so he moved on to one about other continents—interesting but useless.

Slowly, they scanned through every book's drawl on their exhaustive search. Dull book covers blended into muted shelves while letters turned hazy. Handwritten notes scrawled by mad historians weren't meant for scouring. A pulsating rhythm pounded in Kargon's head and he pressed his palms against his eyes.

"What if the notes are purposely hidden?" he said absentmindedly.

Aisha let out a gasp, carefully returned her book to the shelf and grabbed Kargon's hand. Soft words repeated under her breath as she quickly guided them back to the librarians. With each approaching step, the words got louder until they arrived.

"Where can I find the full prophecy that contains the phrase: The fate of the land rests in their hand?"

The librarians blinked, light disappearing from their eyes as they turned to each other. Then they studied the two half-elves, one with a fiery determination and the other very confused. Finally, one spoke. "Information regarding the history of Kharim the First Hero is protected by the Dicoris family."

The name carried weight that Kargon wished to avoid but knew he'd have to face. Dawncaster's central district carried history that stemmed from the discovery of Tetria. Nasim Dicoris was the current ruler, highly regarded by his congregation. It was why the high number of guards in the central district wasn't surprising—they watched over Dicoris castle. Frustration in Aisha's eyes made clear she knew what to do next.

"Thank you," she said as kindly as possible while pulling Kargon to the exit.

"We need to talk to the royal family, don't we?" he asked.

"I think the librarian mentioned them because he recognized me. A small hint towards the right direction but also a test for the Hero. We need to figure out how to actually reach the Dicoris's."

"Why not just ask for an audience?"

"It won't work. One of my swordmasters is part of their family and I tried to meet them during our training. They said no."

"Did you ask why?"

"Master Victor said it was likely because I hadn't proven myself yet. And I still haven't," Aisha grumbled. "If you've got any ideas I'd love to hear them."

They stepped out into the evening breeze, lights slowly coming to life in magical street lamps. Losing time within the library was simple with the lack of windows and persistent illumination. By now, the sun approached toward the western horizon and long shadows covered the street.

Several minutes passed getting from Zeffari to Bamborough and Aisha spent the entirety silently contemplating next steps. That was impossible for Kargon as his eyes were transfixed on their clasped palms. Free hands were needed to think straight, so as naturally as possible, he slipped his hand away and Aisha finally realized how long they'd walked together. There was a twitch on her face Kargon didn't catch as she nearly ran away.

"Do you think the Greycastles have ever met the Dicoris's?" Kargon asked loudly, stopping Aisha in her tracks. "I mean, they're probably bringing a lot of people to the city."

After a slow exhale, she replied, "We'd be asking for quite a bit."

"Did you think of anything else?"

"Nothing that doesn't involve us coming back years from now."

"You're already leaving?" Albert asked sadly, as he approached from behind. "I wanted to learn more from you."

Sariel patted the boy's back and looked at their leader with a furrowed brow. "Have you found what we seek?"

Aisha shook her head. "I'll explain once we get inside."

No one questioned the group skipping the line to the Greycastle's shop. Mia and Vofric worked in tandem to sell goods while checking over large purchases. A small group of customers obsessed over a well-behaved Avant as he quietly ate a cookie out of someone's hand. It wasn't more enticing than seeing his master return, however. Before Avant made it all the way, Aisha scooped him into a hug and retreated upstairs. Kargon's group followed while Vofric continued to assist Mia.

Louise waited while sipping tea with snacks preset so everyone could share their findings. Everyone joined her, giving space for Aisha to start her explanation. Instead, she paced through the hall at dizzying speed with Avant in hand. Whenever she wanted to ask others for a favor her legs carried her in a loop until the right words came. Only requests from Kargon didn't cause the stressful habit to occur. Mia and Vofric's entrance did nothing to stop the cycle of muttered words. He had an announcement but remained silent at the sight of Aisha. Scattered glances turned to the hall every time she got near the exit.

Finally, Aisha entered the living room and huffed. "Kargon, how would you ask?"

All eyes turned to him and the monk suddenly understood the pressure the Hero was under. He turned to Mia and Louise. "Do you two have a way to contact the Dicoris family?"

Louise looked stunned but her wife remained nonplussed. "We need you to elaborate before jumping into a question like that," Mia said.

Everything that was revealed in the library would've taken far too long to explain. Instead, Kargon started reporting what wasn't within the records. Lack of information about allies clearly struck a nerve. When Aisha chimed in it was clear she was also displeased with what was deemed worth reporting. Both emphasized how vague the records about crucial battles were and why they latched onto the torn page.

"The librarian specifically told you the Dicoris's have more information?" Mia asked.

"They said the information is 'protected by the Dicoris family.' I assume that means yes," Aisha replied.

Mia contemplated something and responded to an unasked question. "But we can't invite additional people."

Albert understood and asked, "Are you talking about the gala?"

Mia nodded then addressed the adventurers. "Galas are often thrown by prominent figures of Dawncaster to collect charity for various city projects. As community leaders in Bamborough, we are expected to attend. Unfortunately, we are unable to bring additional guests on such short notice."

"I can assist with that." Vofric chimed in. "An old colleague mentioned the Ramshorn Gala. I was offered entry for myself and any party members."

Wide-eyed adventurers stared at the dwarf's nonchalant declaration. Contrary to his party, the Greycastles were accustomed to such an occurrence. Clearly the paladin had led a life that demanded others' respect but it was stunning how easily high society accepted him.

Aisha let out a sigh of relief. "Yes, Vofric. Thank you."

A concerning look flashed across Louise's face at a speed few would notice.

"Is there something we should be concerned about?" Kargon asked.

Sariel grumbled, "The royal family may not attend, correct?"

"No, not that. In fact, it's one of the only times they mingle openly," Louise explained. "The issue is your goal of speaking about something not only important but likely private. It's not unheard of to use galas as a way to schedule meetings. The Dicoris family is very discerning in whom they humor with their time. To get their attention you'll need to prove yourselves. It's the very reason it took us many years of owning Greycastle Market before we were invited to such events. Vofric must know someone the family is close with to get an invite so soon before the event."

Every passing moment made it harder not to question Vofric and his connection. Thankfully, Aisha had self control and remained focused on the topic at hand. "So even if we don't learn anything at the gala, we can talk to the Dicoris's later," she said.

"If they permit, yes," Mia answered.

"It wouldn't be the first time you've had to impress someone on a clock," Kargon retorted.

"Not just her, however. We must prove to the royal family that her party is worth their time," Sariel stated. "I would like not to be remembered as fodder. This is an opportunity to prove the Hero has selected reliable allies."

Albert hopped up and said, "I think I can help with that. Lemme do some legwork the next couple days."

"Are you sure, Albert?" Aisha asked. "You're all doing so much already."

"Mom and Mama are. I haven't done anything yet. I wanna be able to say I helped the Hero's party."

Aisha smiled. "I'll leave it to you, then."

Louise clapped her hands and said, "Looks like you have a plan. Am I correct in assuming you don't have anything to wear?" There was no need to answer the rhetorical question. "That just won't do. Let's make sure you receive the right kind of attention." Sweet words came from a smile that sent shivers down everyone's spines.

CHAPTER FOURTEEN

Where a Hero is Needed

"Thought you weren't a priest," Kargon said, eying Vofric's outfit.

"I had certain duties in the past." Vofric buttoned his high collar behind his braided beard. "It was the only formal clothing I'd left with Louise." The white suit accentuated his muscular form and dazzled just like his armor. An ironed orange shawl draped over his shoulders, flattening against his broad chest. Kargon imagined this was the person Melinda always imagined when speaking of Father Vofric.

"You look good," Kargon complimented.

"Thank you. How do you like your suit?"

It was itchy. Three piece suits had two too many layers for Kargon's liking. A crisp black suit bound his arms from comfortable movement. The crimson vest was alright but the matching tie was suffocating compared to his goggles—which had to be left behind. At least his silver bracelet passed for a fashion accessory on the undeniably pristine suit. That didn't stop Kargon from desperately wanting to tear the sleeves off.

"I don't think I can fight in this," he groaned. "One ignition and it'll go up in flames."

"It's not meant for fighting. And you don't rely on fire for a good punch." Vofric chuckled.

"Let us avoid violence at all costs." Sariel grunted, folding back the left sleeve of their green button down past their jagged draconic elbow. A suit looked far better on the elf and Kargon readily admitted it. The emerald ensemble along with a half-cape over their shoulder hid every mutation perfectly. Without a hood, Sariel revealed sharp features across their angular face. With slicked back hair they resembled an aristocratic elf—scornful glare and all.

"I'm just glad it fit," Mia said, joining the trio in a strapless sapphire dress that ended asymmetrically below her knees. Scars and muscles along her shoulders spoke of a colorful past no one dared broach.

Albert followed his mother in a navy three-piece suit—apparently purchased with Kargon's for a steal. Though his dignified aura made clear how comfortable the boy felt in such garments. At the Greycastle's feet was a bow-tie clad Avant with a slicked back tuft of fur that kept his eyes clear.

"You're sure he'll be allowed?" Kargon asked.

Mia nodded. "Familiars are permitted at this event. But the bow tie is unnecessary."

"It makes him look dapper!" Louise yelled as she burst out of her room in a dazzling silver chiffon dress. A thin cape hugged her shoulders and wrapped around her arms.

While everyone was passing quick compliments, Kargon remained silent. Louise looked between him and the room at the end of the hall. There was an obvious air of excitement through the waiting group that Kargon equated to the upcoming gala. Everyone deserved a night of decadence after the ordeal they'd been through in Balur, especially the Hero.

He was lost in thought when Aisha entered the hallway, reminding everyone she was more than her responsibilities. A black satin dress fit tightly around her, flaring at the hips into a flowing skirt that ended at her knees. Smooth skin could be seen under sheer fabric at her neck and arms. She tugged at the sleeves which ended at the edge of her palms. Kargon couldn't remember the last time he saw her curly hair loosely hanging to her shoulders.

Mia whistled and said, "Love, I'm sorry but I think that dress was made for Aisha."

"Don't apologize for being right." Louise chuckled.

"You look wonderful," Vofric said.

Others agreed but Kargon didn't process it, enamored by Aisha. She lifted Avant into her arms and looked back at her best friend silently.

In their entire life he'd never complimented her in any capacity unrelated to combat.

"No one's ever looked so good." Kargon's words spilled out uncontrollably and his face flushed. It was a rare occurrence he would never be fond of.

Aisha smiled softly. "That means Louise already got us part way through the plan. As did Albert, if I do say so myself. Now we just impress the royal family."

Kargon silently thanked his friend for moving the conversation forward. "What's the plan to do that?" he asked.

"You're the talker. Talk to people. Get as much information as you can." Clothes didn't take the leader out of Aisha. "Sariel, listen in for any information that might help us. I'll go with Vofric to meet his old friends and hopefully leave an impression that spreads to the royal family. Avant, you keep an eye out for anything out of the ordinary. Got it?"

The owlbear chirped affirmatively.

"Good."

***

Ramshorn's famed docks caused many to assume it was a small district when in reality it was one of the largest. The mountainous portion could only be reached by following the path from Bamborough. Mansions occupied massive plots of land separated by wide roads. All of them were magnificent but none compared to the gala location which illuminated most of the area on its own. The building was no larger than the others but its visitors skewed the value. Hundreds of the most prominent figures mingled in the grand halls, lined with souvenirs the world over. Instead of hired help, magic armors from different continents and eras served guests while masterfully staying out of the way.

Boisterous laughs and lively conversation poured out of the walls by the time Kargon's group arrived. The Greycastles entered separately to avoid any undue suspicion. Drinks were Sariel's first target, along with an hors d'oeuvre they threw to Avant which was all the signal he needed to stick to the elf. Treasures throughout the home naturally gathered groups that whispered conversation too loudly for Sariel to ignore. With eyes on the relics they garnered no attention.

Vofric was immediately found by some important looking person—possibly a government official based on their badges. There was brief hesitation when Aisha caught his eye and she couldn't be invited along fast enough.

For once, Kargon hesitated on how to approach anyone here. Thinking about what to say was a foreign concept and thinking about thinking was nauseating. Words literally poured out of his mouth after years of understanding the minutiae of interaction. Unfortunately, that included never getting along with overly posh people like Elder Niko and Quintin and now they were everywhere.

A man approached with more familiarity than expected. Warm brown eyes studied the half-elf as if they knew exactly what he was thinking. A smile spread appeared as Kargon got more visibly confused.

"You're the adventurer that was traveling with Stormclaw, right?" he asked.

The adventurer scoured his mind for anyone with cornrows and black skin that traveled with Captain Julian. But this man was no half-breed—in fact he was completely human. There was only one person Kargon wouldn't recognize related to the captain.

"Are you the commander?" he asked.

The man laughed and they shook hands. "Apologies. I forget about the illusory helmets. Rowen Telos. Commander of the Kingsguard. Call me Rusty."

"Pleasure. Kargon," the monk replied. Rusty stared expectantly and the ex-soldier awkwardly continued, "Meliamne. Sorry, I never was good at introductions."

"Where were you stationed?"

"Neves. Born and raised."

Rusty looked over the adventurer. "What made you start adventuring?"

"I wanted to travel the world of my own volition," Kargon replied readily, avoiding any chance of revealing Aisha's identity. To avoid any delving further, he asked, "Are you working as security for the gala?"

Rusty chuckled. "It's an understandable assumption but no. This is my home."

"I'm so sorry!" Kargon blurted out.

"For my home? Is it not to your liking?"

"No! Oh my gods, no. It's wonderful—"

Rusty grinned widely and exclaimed, "I'm joking, Kargon. You're a fun one."

With a sigh he replied, "I've been told. Do you mind telling me about your collection?"

Rusty gave a practiced tour of his home, making sure to stop at unique weapons most adventurers fancied. The articles were enamoring but Kargon made sure to keep his focus on the surroundings. A city of mixed beings might not trap the adventurers but he'd be damned to let his guard down after everything that happened in Balur.

Confidence exuded from Sariel as they sauntered through groups, stopping only for quick chats. A keen eye could catch the smallest twitches of their ears while listening to whispers in the crowd. However, that looked to be the norm for other elves so Sariel looked like they belonged in the regal crowd. With a nonchalant greeting they passed Aisha and Vofric who spoke with a metal man; a forgeminn.

It was surprising to see how lively the robotic man was during conversation. Equally mind-boggling was how easily Vofric and Aisha played off each other—as though they hadn't met within the month. Quick nods and handshakes came from dozens of people upon seeing Vofric. Many paused at the sight of his half-elf companion who always acknowledged them with a quick wave. Aisha's usually mischievous smirk transformed into the gorgeous smile of an aristocrat.

Rusty followed Kargon's eyes and said, "She fits in here more than most adventurers. Did that scar drive her to quest?"

"No, the scar is just that. There's just no one better at adventuring than her," Kargon replied. "She's just taking advantage of our first real break."

"My subordinates could learn a thing from her." Rusty nodded towards two guards awkwardly hovering near a hallway. "How well can they guard on the outskirts of the crowd? They should be intermingling."

With their unseen faces and heavy armor it wasn't clear how that was supposed to happen but Kargon wasn't about to point it out. Though he was intrigued to see they carried any choice of weapons. Clearly Commander Ivana and Elder Niko exaggerated how many people wanted to mimic the Hero in combat.

"I can understand being uneasy on duty," Kargon said. "Guests weren't allowed to bring weapons so everything is in the soldier's hands."

"True, but nothing will. The royal family is only invited when we're sure a gala will be safe," Rusty said. "Speaking of which, it seems they've noticed your friend."

The Dicoris family exuded an aura that could only be described as holy. Air djinnai controlled wind with ease, flowing through their wild white hair to reveal light blue skin glimmering like jewels. Navy robes flowed like an ocean current in the magical breeze. King Nasim stood tall and smiled warmly at other guests but there was a glassy look in his eyes. Holding his arm was Queen Lyra, hovering a foot in the air to match her husband's height. Her smile was what drew people towards the royal's without hesitation. Unlike his parents, Prince Makani was nearly silent with intermittent greetings. Boredom would be obvious if anyone looked at him for more than a second.

They drifted towards Aisha, Vofric, and the forgeminn. Hearing them from afar was impossible but it never hurt to keep watch. Clearly Sariel had the same idea as they examined display cases nearby with Avant on their shoulder, facing the Hero.

"Your group's bigger than I remember," Rusty said coldly. "It's ballsy to try something now."

"What are you talking about?" Kargon asked.

Rusty stepped closer with a deadly glare. "No need to play dumb, Kargon. The scarred elf and owlbear are watching the king. He's distracted by your half-elf friend and the dwarf. The gnome is sneaking closer and don't think I haven't noticed your felminn along the walls." The point of a blade slowly pressed against Kargon's back. "A glance alone tells me they're getting ready to pounce on the Dicoris's. Call them off."

With an expanded view it was obvious the commander was right but the adventurers got too caught up in their own plan. Not only innocent eyes watched Aisha or the royal family. A thick air of bloodlust hung over the party.

"Rusty, I think there's a problem with your guards," Kargon said.

"Openly threatening me now, huh?" Rusty pushed his dagger through Kargon's blazer.

"No! I realize you've been watching me since we entered. That's fine! But for one moment look at your subordinates!"

They stood still throughout the house; more rigid than the magic armor. It was possible whatever affected them was widespread.

Rusty groaned. "Paralysis. Cowardly tactics."

"No, that's almost a textbook assassination tactic," the monk foolishly said.

A gnome stepped out of the crowd behind the royal family, ripping extra fabric stitched into her gown. Metal shimmered underneath as a dagger fell to her palm. Shadows shifted along the ceiling as something left the corner. No one noticed either assailant.

"Aisha!" Kargon screamed over the crowd.

She didn't turn but her jovial demeanor vanished. Pain struck Kargon, cold steel sending a jolt up his spine as Rusty plunged a blade into his back.

"You're not going anywhere," he spat.

"Neither... will they," Kargon choked.

Aisha commanded the room with one shout. "Sword!"

The sudden roar of an owlbear stunned everyone, including the would-be assassin. Vines shot out of Sariel's palm and shaped into a sturdy wooden blade that they threw over the crowd to the Hero. The gnome assassin lunged at King Nasim but got blocked by Aisha's blade, magically refined to overpower mundane weapons. Deflecting the dagger, Aisha pushed forward and kicked the gnome hard in her chest. Something cracked and blood spurted from her mouth as she collapsed to the floor.

During the fight, the hidden assailant leapt from the, revealing a cat-like humanoid armed with jagged claws aimed for the queen's throat. But the speed of a falling beast was predetermined, something a sharpshooter was well aware of. Two arrows collided with the assassin's arms—blunt and with enough force to throw off his trajectory. Once the queen was out of harm's way, a volley of arrows rained down on the failed assassin and knocked him out.

Unparalyzed guards rushed into the room while attendees evacuated. Even though they were too slow to stop the assassination, they drew weapons on the adventurers. Sariel and Avant were shoved towards Aisha and Vofric before getting encircled. The forgeminn looked heartbroken as he joined the royal family. No amount of straining let Kargon speak as he helplessly watched his friends get cornered.

"Cease!" Prince Makani demanded, a powerful breeze rushing through the home.

While people finally looked towards him, he stared intently at his father. There was no telling what was said in their silent conversation. Eventually, the king nodded and a strong wind pressed every remaining person in the room to their knees. King Nasim walked around the adventuring party, examining them carefully, before turning to his wife who stood with the prince. Another silent conversation occurred then the queen vanished. Moments later she reappeared next to the king, whispering something while staring at Aisha.

"We will grant you one opportunity for explanation. Bring them to the Grand Hall," King Nasim said assuredly. "Commander Telos; that includes the firebrand."

CHAPTER FIFTEEN

The Dicoris's Quest

White pillars embellished with cobalt lining held a tower ceiling aloft where murals of air djinnai leered down. Thick walls held small windows just below the ceiling allowing moonlight to shine through. It landed directly on the adventurers as they looked up at the Dicoris's, sitting in a row of raised thrones while scrutinizing the party silently. Kingsguard soldiers lined the walls while Rusty and the forgeminn flanked the adventurers.

It was no surprise that the gala ended the instant of the attack. Getting here was another ordeal as Rusty hid Kargon's wound from citizens while shoving him to the castle. The pain was gone but he was still stiff, like something was forcing his body to remain still.

"Commander Telos, has it been a challenge?" King Nasim asked.

"No, sir," Rusty replied.

"You may unbind him."

Suddenly, Kargon's back flared in pain even though the dagger was long gone. He quickly turned to see a stream of blood coagulate into an orb above the commander's hand before getting snapped out of existence.

"Eyes forward," Rusty stated dryly.

Kargon turned back, noticeably less stiff.

"Are these individuals your party members?" King Nasim asked, his eyes hovering on Aisha.

"Yes, your majesty," she responded.

"I presume *Valefor* is secure and you did not abandon it for a celebration."

"Correct, your majesty."

Queen Lyra hummed softly. "I heard you arrived with no supplies and covered in blood. You must have compatriots in Dawncaster to have attended the gala. Let alone know of it."

Aisha remained silent and turned towards Vofric who nodded then answered. "Yes, your highness. I have acquaintances throughout the city," he explained. "They kindly lent us room and board."

Before the king or queen could speak, Prince Makani interjected. "Anyone can say they have connections or they possess a magic sword. People even lie about being the Hero. I'd like proof. If we were to send someone, could they retrieve the weapon?"

Aisha hesitated then nodded. "Yes, the sword is retrievable."

The idea of retrieving the sword brought life to the forgeminn's eyes. A metallic, direct voice emitted from his mouth. "I shall go, Master Makani. I know who was housing them."

Prince Makani looked to his father, who was already nodding in response. Turning back to the retainer, he said, "With haste, Victor."

Victor's cane glowed before he vanished from sight. While everyone else stood in silence, Kargon's curiosity got the best of him. Aisha mentioned the name before and it seemed Vofric knew the man separately.

Kargon stammered. "Was-"

"Not now," Aisha whispered.

"Speak." Queen Lyra commanded sternly. "You may address anyone. Choose your words wisely."

Aisha stared at Kargon and mouthed, "Wisely."

"Was that Master Victor?" he asked. "You mentioned him wanting to bring you here years back."

"Yes, but we didn't get an audience."

Queen Lyra chimed in, "Victor is family but we needn't indulge his student, even if she is the Hero. There is merit in traveling here yourself."

Undeserved scrutiny made Aisha's blood boil, yet she nodded politely as if the queen hadn't accused her of being a fraud.

The large stone doors of the grand hall creaked open as heavy metal footsteps carried Victor inside. It was obvious why he hadn't teleported back when he crossed the adventurers. Behind him was a confused, slightly scared Albert who fell in line next to Kargon.

"The Greycastle's boy," King Nasim said.

Albert bowed. "Apologies. I wanted to make sure Sir Victor wasn't lying about his identity and he allowed me to follow him as proof."

"Understandable," King Nasim said dismissively. "Victor, draw the sword."

The forgeminn made a show of placing down his cane before gripping *Valefor's* hilt. Robotic grunts echoed through the chamber for an uncomfortable minute before he dramatically threw his head back in forfeit. A smile briefly crossed his metallic visage but was gone when he looked back at the king.

"The sheath is lined with the obsidian Kharim enchanted," Victor said. "It can only be drawn by the Hero."

King Nasim commanded Aisha, "Prove your identity."

She stepped forward and gave a curt bow to Victor. Only *Valefor's* hilt was allowed in Aisha's grasp but that was enough to draw the weapon. The silver glow triggered instincts to focus mana into her prosthetic eye, causing a brilliant aura to emit off her. It was doubtful she expected to ever wield the sword while dressed for high society, especially under suspicion of attacking the royal family.

"Good," King Nasim said. "Why did you approach my family at the gala? I'd like to believe that you aren't assassins but too many adventurers have strayed from the path of heroism for wealth."

"No, your majesty. We really just wanted an audience with you," Aisha explained. "We need information about the first Hero. Specifically his nemesis. It might pertain to my quest."

King Nasim shut his eyes and nodded. "It seems you learned nothing in Balur."

Silence fell over the party. Aisha nearly said something but Kargon stepped forward to stop her. There was a twinkle in the king's eye that was waiting for them to say too much.

"Captain Julian was a great help," Kargon said.

"She mentioned needing to protect you," the king replied. "What else have you done before arriving here?"

It hadn't registered how much closer Kargon was to the royal family now. Aisha patted his shoulder and signaled to continue. "We have crossed towns… and seas while helping anyone in need."

The queen gave an approving nod. "I commend your understanding of the Hero's role within a few weeks."

"Not only do you have a decently sized party but also connections outside your corner of Tetria." Prince Makani added, staring at Albert; a boy his age standing with the Hero.

Albert checked if anyone else would respond before speaking up. "My family owes a debt and offered to assist them."

King Nasim was about to respond but was stopped by the prince who sat up and asked, "What about once the debt is repaid? Is your connection only temporary?"

"I don't see why it should be. You can't ever have too many friends." Albert smiled.

Prince Makani scoffed and leaned back, a response that surprised his parents. It was the most casual response given by any of the royals and seemed to jostle the king and queen out of their stoic facade. Foggy eyes cleared as they warmly looked at Albert before looking at each adventurer.

"The Greycastles are a trusted pillar of this great city and Victor has been by my side a lifetime," King Nasim said. "I'm convinced to give you a quest. Succeed and we will share the secrets of Kharim's journey." He contemplated something while staring at the ceiling, only speaking after looking down again. "There are many secrets hidden in Dawncaster; such as the goal of whatever mastermind was behind the attempted assassination. I would like you to uncover their identity and motive."

"We are not so cruel as to leave you with a small network of help," Queen Lyra explained and waved towards her son. "Makani and Victor will provide aid you need from the Dicoris family. If matters escalate, they can reach us."

Prince Makani shook his head and said, "They require a starting point. Blindly stumbling onto the right path presents too much danger. To them and our city. There must be something we can tell them."

"I can help with that," Rusty exclaimed. "My subordinates have been gathering intel from the assassins we captured. I can provide it if his majesty approves."

"I have no qualms," King Nasim said. "That is, if the Hero will accept this quest."

Aisha tilted her head in confusion. "Are you saying we can walk away?"

"Yes. 'Hero' is a meaningless four letter word until given meaning through deeds. Leaving here will tell Dawncaster, and in turn Tetria, what Hero means when referring to you. By all means, seek information elsewhere. I cannot speak to how you will be regarded for doing so."

It was like the king could see into Aisha's mind and knew exactly what being the Hero meant to her. Not only that, but he'd offered a rare reward as well. Information about the first Hero's quest was almost nonexistent. The quest wasn't just the best option for research; it was the only one.

"It's a way forward," Aisha said, recovering from her brief stupor. "Assassinations are a means to an end. We'll uncover the motives endangering your lives."

Kargon gave a quick thumbs up at his friend's declaration while Vofric and Sariel quietly nodded. The usual chirp of approval never came as Avant had fallen asleep at their feet.

"Good." King Nasim faced Albert. "Your family is permitted to assist them by any legal means. Don't abuse your freedom."

Albert was taken aback and stuttered out a meek, "Okay. Sir... Your Majesty!"

The royal family rose from their seats and wind billowed through the hall as King Nasim said, "Commander Telos, send them on their way. Report to us at a later time."

Rusty put his fists together, bowed, then turned to the exit. "Follow me."

Kargon lifted Avant and joined his party. They were a few steps out the door when Rusty sighed deeply, as if the Dicoris's wind gave him strength.

He turned to Kargon and said, "I'm sorry for stabbing you in the back. Literally. You seemed like a threat."

The wound stung at the mention of it but Kargon wasn't angry. If adventurers randomly showed up in Neves and surrounded the Elder, even he would've been protective. Not to mention, the first time Rusty saw everyone, they were blood-soaked.

"It happens," Kargon replied.

"What did you learn from the assassins?" Aisha asked.

Rusty avoided the question. "We can meet tomorrow morning and discuss it."

Now that they had a clear goal, Aisha was ready to face anything. Either she got information from him or found it herself. "What. Did. You. Learn?" Aisha asked deliberately.

Sariel scoffed. "It is likely very little, thus he is stalling."

"I'd appreciate you not taking your frustrations out on me, alright?" Rusty groaned. "If I got a chance to investigate, I'd have more answers."

"Forgive my friends. It's been a long night," Vofric said.

The commander sighed, nodded, took a deep breath, then sighed again "Give me eight hours—until noon tomorrow. It's a lot to ask but I want to help fix my mistake."

Aisha studied the man who'd recently stabbed her best friend, still infuriated. But taking out her anger was unheroic and foolish. Kindness here would most definitely pay off later. "We'll meet you at Greycastle Market at twelve. On the dot," she said and put her hand out.

Rusty shook it and nodded firmly. Without another word he dashed away from the castle with an unspoken plan in mind. Everyone else left in the opposite direction, stepping onto lamp lit streets bustling with nocturnal residents. Many were confused to see the diurnal adventurers but made no issue of it.

Dizziness and exhaustion weighed on Kargon until a firm hand tapped his back. Familiar pains and uncomfortable stitching signaled that his wound was forcibly closed as cells rapidly repopulated his bloodstream.

"Apologies, it slipped my mind," Vofric said with a groggy smile which Kargon responded to in kind.

"What's the plan?" Albert asked.

"Tomorrow," Aisha answered.

"But couldn't we—"

"We made a deal with Rusty." Aisha replied sternly. "We wait until tomorrow."

CHAPTER SIXTEEN

Tag Team

Rowen Telos adored being the commander of the Dawncaster Kingsguard. Protecting others came as naturally as breathing and garnered respect. But the man darting through the dark streets of Dicoris received no such attention. The magical helmet that concealed his identity allowed Rusty to move freely outside his armor.

Eight hours was ample time for many things—definitely not a proper investigation. Culprits had more opportunities to escape as time passed. Guards would interrogate the assassins but it was clear they were simple mercenaries. They'd have few answers from whatever mastermind concocted the assassination. But someone else with Dawncaster might know what led to the incident. Rusty hated that shady characters remained in the city but they were the perfect people to question as an unrecognizable detective. Sticking to the quiet streets of Ramshorn, he cemented the plan. Forcing answers out of people would work but going alone was foolish and endangering a subordinate's identity was reckless. Thankfully, the perfect candidate was in town.

He arrived at a packed tavern reeking of saltwater and sadness. All the circular tables lined with empty mugs were surrounded by depressed half-breeds demanding ale. Bar stools remained mostly unoccupied as everyone focused on lifting their comrades' spirits. Sitting barside was a woman with a leather jacket and long mohawk. Even without medals or a captain's hat, she radiated ferocity—

slightly diminished by her slumped shoulders.

"I don't think I've ever seen you this dower, Stormclaw," Rusty said, sliding into the stool next to Julian. "Then again, few people deal with what you're going through. I'm sorry about what happened."

"Don't be. I'd have been dishonorably discharged if not for you," she replied, taking another swig of her drink. "Instead, I was just forced to resign."

"It was a given after everything you said about Balur. Was telling the Dicoris's necessary?"

"They would've found out eventually. Aisha and her crew didn't need to take the fall for the elves' bullshit."

"And you did? Even though it cost you everything?"

Julian looked at her old friend then tilted her head towards the drunk half-breeds crowding the bar. "I didn't lose my crew," she said, grinning.

"You're not a captain anymore, though," Rusty replied.

"Don't you dare disrespect Captain Julian like that!" Bailey Lakelet yelled from their table. The crew roared in approval, ready to clobber the commander. With a wave, Julian stopped them from acting.

"He meant nothing by it," she said then turned to Rusty. "I don't need a ship to be a captain."

"My mistake," Rusty said with a smile. "Them sticking with you will make operating your next vessel easier."

"Appreciate the sentiment but no one's hiring an ex-marine. How's a pirate supposed to get a ship?"

"I can get you one."

Julian squinted at the man. "For what cost?"

"Nothing major. I just need some help," Rusty replied nonchalantly.

"The only time you need help is for an investigation. And based on the timing, it has to do with that mess at the gala."

"News travels fast."

For a moment, Julian simply stared at her associate as he tried to feign serenity. At some point Rusty had discarded his suit jacket and openly presented his wrinkly vest and messy pocket square. Worn sleeves stuck to his dewy skin as he nervously cracked his knuckles. It was a habit he picked up in training.

"What do we need to do?" Julian asked, finishing off her drink.

"Put on a show," Rusty said.

"I hate it when you say that."

"But you'll still do it."

"Ship's is an enticing offer. Where's the audience?"

"Zeffari district. There's a lounge—"

"Kora's Cavern." Julian hated that name. "I know the place." She walked towards the exit and stopped her crew from humoring the idea of helping. They knew how powerful their captain was and hindering her personal business wouldn't bode well for anyone. It was impressive how easily she kept such a rowdy group in line— exactly what Rusty needed from his investigation partner.

"I should return home and change," Rusty said as the duo stepped outside.

"Not a chance, Red. You're going to look like that if my plan's going to work," Julian replied. With each step her natural saunter turned more aggressive and brutish.

With a single word, Rusty knew to don a relaxed demeanor and force out every bit of swagger he could manage. Red was a practiced role that had made appearances in Dawncaster's dark corners when necessary. "I'm going in as a failed assassin?" Rusty whispered. "You sure that'll work?"

"What's my track record when it comes to putting on a show?" Julian asked.

"Standing ovations only."

"Then drop the pointless questions. You've been putting me in this position for years. Trust that I know what I'm doing."

Rusty sighed. "I guess it has been every time you're in Dawncaster."

"Forget Dawncaster. You've been doing it since we met in Ulcarn."

"It was a rowdy place. And you had a knack for tricking folks."

"I still do. Now shut up, Red. We're here," Julian said forcefully, nodding at the door of an unmarked establishment.

"Lead the way, Blue."

Three seconds was all the time Rusty had to process Julian's plan as she sauntered to the metal door and thrust a heavy boot at it.

"Hey! Watch it!" The bouncer nearby glowered at Julian and Rusty but couldn't match their intense stares.

Before he could speak up, Julian barked, "Shut the fuck up! I don't wanna hear your voice. Got enough trouble after the shit down south."

The demand left the bouncer stunned long enough for Julian and Rusty to stomp into the lounge. No pair of seats were left empty; exactly what the duo needed.

Rusty approached the bartop and slammed his fist on it between two occupants. An icy stare was all he needed to move them aside before he and Julian sat down.

"Another fuckin' coward! This place is just full of 'em, I swear," Julian rambled, signaling for a drink.

"Can't believe they got the damn job," Rusty grumbled, his voice a few octaves deeper. "Didn't even land a scratch…"

"Fuckin' amateurs should've left the job to the experts."

A nearby denizen pointed a finger at the duo and said, "You act like you could've done better but didn't even get the job."

"That's because trash lowered their price to take on something they couldn't handle," Rusty replied.

"No one could've expected the Hero to be there," another patron complained.

"Kill could've been secured regardless."

Another drunken criminal rose from his seat and stepped toward Rusty.

"Then why didn't you do it?" she asked.

Julian guffawed and sneered at the woman. "What? Give your buddies credit? They couldn't even get close without getting seen."

The first bar occupant turned quickly, spilling most of his ale onto Julian's jacket. "You dunno wha'ish like to get stuck ina crowd," he slurred.

"If there's a crowd you fuckin' thin it out," Julian replied coldly.

"Big wors from a… wannabe."

The drunk shot up with his last word to reveal he was several heads taller than Julian. Other patrons followed his lead, arming themselves with weapons and bottles.

Julian furrowed a brow. "You bringin' swords to this?"

"Ish'a lil girl scared now?" the drunk asked.

Rusty rose from his seat, cracking his knuckles. "We just wanna make sure you've accepted the consequences."

The giant man stepped closer to Julian but she didn't bother getting up. A powerful kick shattered his shin and when he curled in pain, Julian brought his head down on a glass mug. Shards pierced through before he crumpled to the floor in a heap. Before anyone could react, Rusty snatched a bottle from the bartop and shattered it against a nearby thug's temple.

Dozens of mercenaries riddled the duo with attacks but failed to do any real damage. On the other hand, Julian and Rusty needed only a few strikes to knock out their opponents. Within minutes, unconscious criminals littered the ground—bloody and battered. Not a single one had died, though some might wish they had. Bruises covered Julian and Rusty as they stepped out of Kora's Cavern. They'd need healing from their respective group members.

"So much for getting clues," Rusty groaned. "Where to next?"

Julian nonchalantly fished a piece of paper from her pocket and held it up. "Someone slipped this to me during the fight. Says there's a meeting tomorrow night in Ramshorn."

"What? Why didn't you grab them?"

"Same reason we didn't arrest anyone we beat. There's no point. What good would catching the messenger do?"

Rusty sighed. "They wouldn't have information either. Dammit, the Hero is expecting news in a few hours. I don't have until tomorrow night."

"You don't need it. Let Aisha and her crew handle the meeting," Julian said.

"Okay..." Rusty reached for the slip of paper but Julian pulled it away.

"How about I hand this to them and you work on getting my ship? Or whatever else you guards do. Maybe get some rest."

"I could say the same to you, Stormclaw."

"There's no job stopping me from resting," Julian taunted and turned towards Bamborough. "I expect that ship by the end of the week, got it? I want to get on the Balurian's radar as soon as I can."

With those words, Rusty was left alone in the middle of Zeffari. Questions flooded his head about his friend's last words but asking her to elaborate had always been a fruitless endeavor. He would help without an explanation but the Kingsguard commander had more pressing matters to attend to. Pain from the fight gnawed at him but it was preferable to the restless feelings from before.

CHAPTER SEVENTEEN

Rendezvous at Ramshorn

Aisha was already waiting by the door at noon but was stunned to receive news from Julian Stormclaw, especially in casual clothes and covered in bruises.

"What happened?" Aisha asked.

"Don't worry about it. You've got bigger fish," Julian replied and passed a slip of paper to the adventurer. "That's what Rusty and I found."

"Thank you, Captain—"

"Just Julian. Bane of Balur," she replied with a smirk. "Good luck, Aisha."

The Hero wondered if Julian made a habit of short goodbyes as she returned upstairs to her waiting party. A small coffee table surrounded by armor clad warriors momentarily took her back to the day they arrived. Though the only one talking was Sariel as they noted down rumors they'd heard at the party.

That was until Aisha tossed the paper onto the table, marked with an nondescript location and time. Silently, everyone thought up hundreds of solutions to tackle the situation. It must have looked insane to see four people intently staring at a piece of scrap on the table. None of it bothered Albert as he sat down and patiently waited.

Once everyone fell silent, Aisha said, "Let's leave the interrogation completely to Rusty and focus on the meeting. We know for sure that the meeting place is somewhere in Ramshorn. Unfortunately, the district is massive."

"Not to mention it's happening today. There's not much time for deduction," Kargon added.

Vofric let out a groan that shook the room. "Criminals were not so honorbound in my time. It is possible they are cursed to silence."

With a loud thud, Sariel purposefully placed their notebook on the table for all to see. "The note says 'night.' Our timeline is between dusk and midnight. There are half a dozen meeting places in Ramshorn that I know of though there could be more."

A surprisingly detailed map of the district was sketched across two pages. Enclosures spread throughout were circled with details written neatly in the margins. Flipping the page revealed even more of the massive locale, specifically docks, the marine base, and taverns and inns. Based on the age of the sketches, Kargon assumed Sariel had visited this area in the past.

"Some of this is speculation," they explained. "It is rather surprising how willingly people discuss their illegal dealings at an event with their peers."

Avant wiggled out of Kargon's grasp and hopped onto the table. With a chirp, he lightly patted one part of the page.

Sariel circled it and said, "You're correct. I had forgotten the rumors about the fish markets. Are there any others you think I missed?"

Nudging the corner of one page with his beak awkwardly flipped it back before he used both front paws to tap along a route.

"How could I forget?" Sariel said while tracing the path. "This route is often used to evade guards but none have deduced where it leads."

"You're saying they just disappear?" Aisha asked.

"Likely using magical means," Vofric interjected. "Why else would a criminal use a publicly known route?"

Albert hummed. "The 'mastermind', as King Nasim said, might know how to use it. Our biggest hurdle is figuring out where the meeting spot is."

Everyone's eyes fell on the notebook as Aisha leaned in and began flipping through the map. Marked locations were examined with extreme scrutiny—finger tapping them as she muttered. Sariel silently handed over a pen, permitting the Hero to mark new areas. After Aisha was satisfied, she leaned back and quietly rubbed her right index finger and thumb against her horns. She'd hit a wall. Asking the right questions fell to Kargon but he was too uninformed to help her press forward.

His eyes fell to the new marks. "If one person goes to each vantage point, we should be able to see every potential meeting spot. One of us can pretend we know the assassins and meet the mastermind."

"If the mastermind—" Aisha groaned. "—was at the gala, they'll recognize us."

"Not me. Rusty had me stuck in the crowd."

"So, one of us would signal you to go where the mastermind is."

Albert chimed in. "But he'll be late."

"That should not be an issue. Paranoia causes an expectation of lateness in the criminal world," Vofric assured. It was peculiar how confident he was. Clearly, his past involved some things unbecoming of a paladin but instead of elaborating, he moved on. "How good is Kargon at lying?"

"Decent," the half-elf replied.

Vofric sighed. "I asked Aisha because you have a history of failing to gage your abilities."

"He's good," Aisha answered. "The issue is how easily the mastermind will read him."

"If they catch on, I can always fight them," Kargon said readily.

"You win and then what?" Aisha asked. "We can't just interrogate them in public."

"Couldn't we take them to the prison?"

"Regardless of who gave us this quest, I don't want to undermine the guards."

Albert perked up. "I can check with Mom if we can bring them here."

"No!" Vofric barked, furiously shaking his head. "I am uncomfortable with allowing you to join us. Putting your family in further danger is unfathomable. Do I make myself clear?"

"Right," Albert replied dejectedly. "Sorry, Uncle Vof."

Sariel reviewed the map and asked, "What if we gave chase? We can place ourselves along the escape route during the meeting. With our numbers it is possible to deduce the path's end."

Aisha nodded slowly and looked at the map again. "They can still get away but it's our best bet. We need to go scout the area. Albert, you've got the most knowledge of Ramshorn so I want you on this apartment rooftop," she said, pointing to a circle on the map. "It overlooks the escape route and two rumored meeting spots. Sariel, take this spot. It's the highest and will allow you to provide cover fire if we need it. Once Kargon meets the target, move here." Aisha traced a thin point of interest and explained, "Avant, this alley is the only one that sees this meeting spot and you can call Sariel for backup. Afterwards, go here." The owlbear nuzzled Aisha's hand and she petted him before moving on. "Vofric, you go to this street corner. Hide in a tavern or something and watch these spots. During the meeting, shift to this position. Kargon, I want you to go here. The building is centralized and the rooftops are close enough for you to get across. Keep your eyes open for a signal from us to get moving."

One thing bothered Kargon and he asked, "What if there's multiple meetings happening?"

"I don't know! We hope we get the right one?"

Aisha's frustration wasn't because of Kargon's question but the general uncertainty of the situation. With a soft chuckle, Vofric patted the woman's arm and calmed her."

"It will be okay," he said confidently. "Rumors of a failed assassination are likely spreading. Groups will avoid meeting spots in fear of increased patrols. The only reason we know the mastermind will be present is due to the note."

"You speak as though you have experience with similar situations," Sariel said.

"Similar, yes."

Aisha sighed and rose to her feet. "I hope you're right. We should go separately to avoid suspicion. At least more than adventurers already get."

There were no protests as she exited the home. There were hours left until the sunset and it was clear Aisha wanted a lot of time to pass between departures. The first to leave was Vofric—over an hour later. Albert waited even longer so he could study the map. When Sariel left they took Avant and the book since only a couple hours remained until the plan began.

Sitting silently in the Greycastles' living room, it dawned on Kargon how much responsibility was on him. Talking to people was one of the only skills he took pride in but few of them were adversaries. Challenging people verbally didn't suit Kargon; he preferred action over debates. If talks ever soured to the point of conflict, violence was close behind. Chasing someone after being caught in a lie was annoying.

Anxiety and anticipation flooded Kargon as he walked towards Ramshorn. The district eclipsed the hill of mansions in size even though it looked tiny from on high. Several random turns and a little luck got him to a recognizable street from Sariel's map. Looking at his surroundings, Kargon realized there was no obvious path to the rooftops. Knowledge of the city allowed Albert to find a perch while powerful jumps carried Sariel and Aisha. Vofric and Avant didn't even need rooftops. But the sun was setting fast and a signal could come soon.

The central building of Ramshorn was a three story inn with well-lit occupied rooms that lit the darkened surroundings of the building. Hugging the shadows, Kargon circled to the back where there were fewer occupants. A few feet off the ground was the bottom rung of a ladder to the roof. With a jump, Kargon grabbed it and scrambled up.

Only a few buildings in the district were taller, the most noticeable a lighthouse to the west with a peculiar silhouette hidden near the light. It was hard to distinguish Sariel's waves from afar and Kargon realized he didn't know what signals to look for. The loss of direction and sunlight compounded into an overwhelming paranoia. Darkvision was pointless if he didn't know what to look for.

Nearly an hour passed as his worries spiraled uncontrollably. What kept him sane was remembering who relied on him. It didn't matter if he didn't know the signals, his friends would make them clear without getting undue attention. Like the broken street lamp flickering at ground level a few blocks away. There was no snapped neck making it hang low and the flashing was too rhythmic for a normal flame. Within the light was the shape of a familiar hammer, reflecting its light off Vofric's bushy white beard. Based on his location, the meeting spot was clear. Kargon snapped his fingers and emitted a large spark to signal his ally who immediately disabled his light.

The monk walked to one side of the roof before pivoting and dashing to the other edge then leaping off. Gaps between buildings were smaller in this area and Kargon broke into a sprint upon landing. He stuck to the rooftops to confirm which meeting spot was his destination. The presence of the others moving along the rooftops was clear but he was too focused to check their locations.

The roof above Vofric's original vantage point overlooked two enclosed areas. One was the backlot of a shop and currently sat empty. Hundreds of feet away, in the empty space created by four buildings, was a smaller spot. It could be accessed from a few tight alleys but a proper view was only possible from above and the opening Vofric was at—otherwise it remained hidden. Looking past the myriad signs and awnings hanging over the alcove, Kargon noticed a cloaked figure waiting in the shadows.

Without hesitation, he jumped to the other side of one of the alleys and shimmied towards the opening. The tight squeeze made his exit less graceful and he tripped out, drawing the attention of the shadow. Their face was covered but the distinct snout of a crimson dragominn, a draconic humanoid, stuck out. They didn't move, silently watching Kargon.

It occurred to him how much information was lacking about the captured assassins, something the mastermind may not know. "Are you the one who hired a gnome to take out the royal family?" he asked.

The cloaked figure looked Kargon over then replied in biting tone, "Who's asking?"

"A subordinate who got away. She told me to come here no matter what happened."

The dragominn smirked, jagged teeth shining in the moonlight. "Course she failed. Needed more bodies."

"How did you know? We paralyzed enough guards and got close easily."

"Rumors are core to our business. Folks have been saying the Hero's in town. Not surprised she was with all the Dawncaster bigwigs." Smoke and embers ascended from flared nostrils, illuminating maroon pupils. There was no attempt to hide deep hatred for the aristocrats.

"Why didn't you warn us?" Kargon asked.

"Not my job. You wanted a test, you got a test. Not my problem that you failed," the figure scoffed.

"You're saying the targets didn't even matter?"

"Only an amateur would say that."

"You're the one who said it was a test!"

The dragominn was enjoying how infuriated Kargon felt. "Who ever said a test can't have real importance? Say you had some easy no-name targets. You'd succeed and then what? We'd have weak newbies and guards on high alert."

Kargon's ears perked up at the dragominn's use of "we." He allowed his emotions to show a little in hopes of getting more information. "By failing, you don't take us on. But who says the guards aren't on high alert after what happened? My comrades are locked up!"

"Won't get a chance to snitch, though. Guards will be on high alert in Dicoris. Rest of Dawncaster is the same as before," the dragominn said. Their surety in the guards' reaction time made it obvious they had insider information.

Kargon sighed. "If your target is the Dicoris's, isn't having more guards a bad thing?"

"No. More opportunities to sneak in. More folks to use. More fear to force on the royal family. See how they act with daggers at their throats!" Smoke billowed fiercely from the dragominn's nostrils, embers slowly manifesting. "If anything, we can eradicate the guards. Leave Dawncaster defenseless."

"If the city fell Tetria would fall apart," Kargon replied, not thinking about if a criminal would care.

"Who ever said anything about the city falling?" The figure smirked. "Just gotta topple the royal family."

Kargon took a breath and asked an admittedly risky question. "How will you do that?"

Surprisingly, the dragominn was feeling generous with information. "We push the timeline."

The words were like darts that pierced through Kargon as his mind flooded with connections. A timeline meant this possibly well-laid plan was already in motion. "Is it because of the failed assassination or the Hero?"

"Little bit of both." The dragominn smirked. "Why do you ask? Your job's done."

"Let's say I'm looking for new employment," Kargon said as convincingly as he could manage.

"So much for loyalty."

"I did my job and came to meet with you."

"Goes to show how inexperienced you are. Or maybe you call it courageous," the dragominn said, shrugging open their cloak to reveal a magic pistol.

Kargon had heard about their rise during Aisha's training. Pulling a small lever on the side broke its binding seal and ignited something inside. The flames of the fired projectiles might not harm the monk but their impact was said to be devastating.

"Either way you're foolish," the shadow continued. "Ain't gonna hire you and can't leave you around with all that info."

"Isn't that your fault?" Kargon said tauntingly.

The dragominn scoffed and held up their weapon, breaking the seal. It needed time to fire so the wielder stalled. "You're interesting. Might've been friends if not for our work."

"We still can be. No reason this needs to get violent."

"No can do. Part of my job."

Heat emanated from the barrel of the pistol as it got within seconds of firing.

Kargon steeled himself. "Okay."

He kicked the hand holding the gun, enough force in the attack to disarm his opponent. Upon landing, Kargon attempted a backhand. The shadow dodged before breathing a plume of fire that singed their surroundings. While Kargon was unscathed, he paused in surprise that his clothes were intact. The dragominn snapped their fingers and a hum came from the gun seconds before it exploded. There was just enough time for Kargon to ignite and put up his arms to shield himself from shrapnel. Unfortunately, without his goggles equipped, he was blinded. The dragominn used the opportunity to get through an alley. Kargon glimpsed the cloak as it turned a corner and gave chase while strapping on his eyewear.

The dragominn expertly weaved through the darkened streets, easily breaking line of sight with Kargon. Only straight roads allowed him to close the gap and get accustomed to maneuvering through the messy corridors. It was ample time for the dragominn to reach the magical escape route. If not for the rumors, Kargon would've thought the upcoming dead end would stop his target. A silver shimmer on the wall rippled into a portal surrounded by a circle drawn in chalk.

With every approaching step the portal lost potency. The dragominn was attempting to dive through without followers. No one in the party had portal magic and Traveler's Dust was rare. They needed something to work with if no one could get through—there was still more information.

Kargon reached for the cloak fluttering a few feet ahead of him. Astral magic called to him as a burning ethereal hand appeared near the cape. A tight grip tore it off the dragominn, causing them to stumble. They threw off the cloak and lunged into the disappearing portal. As much as Kargon hoped they'd hit a wall, it didn't happen. The mastermind vanished into a shimmering pool of silver.

Aisha dropped to street level and walked over while scanning the wall with her magical eye. "Was that—"

"Traveler's dust," Kargon confirmed.

"I seriously hope they don't have more."

"Yeah," Kargon sighed while picking up the cloak. "See anything?"

Aisha shook her head and replied, "Nothing that'll tell me where they went."

"I did not hear a portal's hum anywhere else nearby," Sariel said as they joined, Avant resting in their arms.

Albert landed with them and ran a finger over the building's graffiti. "This is plain chalk. We sell the same stuff."

"Either we debrief now or give chase." Vofric grunted, stepping out of an alley

"Better we go after them," Aisha said. "But I have no idea how."

"I do." Grabbing the cloak from Kargon, the dwarf tossed it to Albert. Only Avant seemed to have any idea what was going on as he gave a hoot of approval.

"But Mama says—" Albert tried to contest.

"I'm not a fool." Vofric raised his hand and looked skyward. "It's a beautiful night."

Everyone reactively looked upward at the beautiful white marble overhead. Its magnificent presence illuminated the dim alleys and chilled the air. A faint cloud emitted from Albert's deep sigh before tilted his head skyward. Under the moonlight, his dark green eyes shone like emeralds.

CHAPTER EIGHTEEN

Midnight Stroll

It was inconceivable that someone could enjoy a mutation but Albert smiled while he transformed. Fur burst from every part of his body and fused with his armor as bones bent inhumanely. Teeth sharpened in his elongated muzzle as the boy grew taller than Sariel. Relaxed demeanor and calm eyes both turned bestial and a blood curdling howl erupted from his maw.

Avant happily approached the werewolf—still the excitable boy who wanted to impress the adventurers. With retracted claws, he gently petted the owlbear.

"Please don't be scared," Albert said with a deep, innate growl. "I'll answer any questions later. All that matters is I've got full control of this form."

Not completely out of her stupor, Aisha said, "Uh, yeah. Lead on."

A sniff of the cloak made Albert's fur bristle and eyes dilate. "Sariel, mark me, please."

An innocuous branch was bound into Albert's silk hide. "Run as wildly as you please. We will find you," Sariel instructed.

The only response was howling wind as the lycanthrope leapt skyward in a blur. Aisha and Sariel followed, albeit with slower jumps, with Avant in hand. With Vofric's permission, Kargon grabbed the front of his armor and launched him to the rooftops. With that much strength, the half-elf didn't need a ladder. But he wasn't confident in his jumping ability and instead looked for a foothold.

Random bricks had small nicks to plant his feet on. Kicking off those led to a pipe further up followed by planks and cables. Kargon was slower than the others but didn't feel like a hindrance.

"Albert is going toward Zeffari district," Sariel said when Kargon arrived.

The party sprinted before Aisha asked, "How long have you known about Albert?"

Vofric—a few steps behind with Avant—replied, "Since the day we met. His bloodline is all shapechangers."

It took a second for Kargon to realize what he meant. "Adrian."

"The man was the largest werebear I ever encountered. I expect something similar from Albert," Vofric confirmed.

Aisha hummed. "Do Mia and Louise know?"

"Of course. They are family."

"Are they aware of the rumors?" Sariel asked as they crossed from Ramshorn to Dicoris, avoiding Library Raebkayd. "I disregarded them during the gala but now realize they referred to Albert. A vigilante donned in silver fur roams the night hunting criminals known only as Palehound."

"If a rumor has spread, I'm sure his mothers are aware," Vofric said with a smirk.

Albert slowed down in Zeffari, both so the others could catch up and to pinpoint his prey. Jittery movements led his snout while honing in on the scent and led the group to the edge of the district. A wide street separated buildings from the city wall and northwestern Dawncaster gate. Late shift guards continued to check civilians and patrol the top of the wall.

Albert hid behind a rooftop ledge and let out a long steady breath, transforming into human form with ease. "The smell leads to an alchemy lab near the wall over there," he said with a nod.

"Secret paths are common in Zeffari—repurposed for criminal activity," Vofric explained. "They may be common knowledge but remain uncharted."

"That's because they're buried."

Sariel grunted. "Anything buried can be rediscovered. Our collective efforts can uncover whatever may be hidden."

The rooftops provided an easy path to the laboratory with plenty of space to hide if guards noticed the party. It was clear Albert's sense remained heightened in human form as even while diverting from the path, he never lost track of his prey. They arrived at the roof overlooking the back of the unassuming lab and descended into it. Faded diagrams of a confusing doorway were scribbled on the wall, inviting Kargon and Aisha to study them. To avoid unnecessary interruptions, Vofric and Avant kept watch of the single ground level exit. Albert was sure the trail continued and Sariel began to hear a peculiar click.

"Gears," they said while slowly pacing the length of the alley. Three loops with a lilting stride and concentrated listening brought them to a stop a quarter of the way up the alley. They knelt, bringing their head close to the patchwork cobblestone. Albert confirmed the scent was strongest underneath.

Aisha hummed in acknowledgment then squinted at Vofric. "Look carefully at the opening to the alley. There's no actual entrance."

The dwarf looked at his leader quizzically then cautiously walked to the entrance but stopped short. Muscular fingers reached out and landed on an invisible barrier. "Someone has crafted an optical illusion and bolstered it with illusory magic," he said. "Come, Avant. There is no need to guard here."

A familiar look on Aisha's face made it clear something had bloomed in her mind. Her eyes jittered, searching for a clue on the walk from the wall to the hidden passage. Within a second of activating her conduit, she smiled. Mana gathered near her foot—appearing like violet electricity—and she stomped on six specific stones. Something clicked near imperceptibly.

"If people could get to this alley, everyone would find this door," she scoffed.

Stones inlaid in a circular pattern shifted upwards, separated in a spiral pattern via mechanical arms. Layers of molded rock revealed themselves deeper in the ground, opening and locking into place one after the other. A single large stone remained each time—a single stair. Clicking and shifting continued for much longer than expected but once complete, it was possible to descend.

"According to the diagram, there should be a way to close it inside," Kargon said and turned to Aisha. "Right?"

She nodded and took the first step. "With me."

Having seen how the stairs appeared, no one dared close the doorway until everyone reached the bottom. Clearly the machines had been slow as the stairwell wasn't deep. Light from deeper in the tunnel illuminated the spiral. Kargon stayed back to make sure everything closed as the others delved further.

The tunnel wasn't as well crafted as the stairs, with just enough space carved out for a single file line. Patches of jagged stone jutted out at random angles making it difficult to maneuver. The rooms it led to, however, were as well-built as ones above ground. Flattened stone clicked underfoot and walls housed shelves and tables. On either side of the main room were smaller ones—one with abandoned weapon racks and ratty bed mats in the other. At the opposite end of the main room was another hall with no end in sight.

Kargon's attention was drawn to a brazier built into the floor of the main room. Every passing day it became easier to identify the properties of fire even without ignition. There wasn't the smallest glow on the coals but he could feel the remnants of a once burning pyre. "Someone was here. Within the day," he said assuredly.

"If they just abandoned the place, it's because of the gala." Aisha added. "Kargon and Vofric, look for any clues left behind. Albert, try to find that dragominn. Take Sariel and Avant."

Sariel nodded and summoned their bow, taking the lead into the further tunnel. The others looked over the barren room. Even in a hurry, the original occupants left as little as possible. All that remained were unimportant pieces of a large puzzle. Incomplete notes were scattered throughout the few notebooks left in the main room. Pages were torn out, leaving broken sketches in their place. The only intact books were well-known stories that could be found in any bookstore. Aisha seemed enamored by the possibilities they presented. Kargon opted to help Vofric piece together whatever clues they could from the damaged notes.

Whoever was planning to harm the Dicoris's could be as ragtag as Aisha's party. The damaged writings resembled records from Library Raebkayd—wild and untested. Margins were filled to the brim and surrounded torn apart magic circles. Even notes regarding early steps of the plan were shredded only leaving some mention of the gala intact.

"This symbol appears repeatedly." Vofric motioned to a pile of drawings he'd torn out of the books.

Crude circles filled with a web of messy lines that connected to a scepter. Foreign letters encircled the diagram—sometimes drawn intricately and other times made of simple shapes. Either the scepter drew power from the magic circle or empowered it instead. All Kargon and Vofric could do was speculate.

Aisha approached with pages she ripped out of the bargain books. "Is there any mention of daylight or daybreak in there?"

There was no need to check again but Kargon did so nonetheless. "No, but your hunches are usually right, which means it's something important," he replied. "It's a given that those notes are gone, then."

Vofric nodded. "How often is daylight mentioned in those books?"

"Every single one. It has to mean something in Dawncaster," Aisha said. "Vofric, you've been here before. Anything of note in the city's history?"

"Nothing that is available to the public. And as I'm sure you are aware, Victor is bound by a vow of silence."

"The dragominn did mention wanting to take over Dawncaster." Kargon recalled.

Footsteps fast approached and Avant burst into the room, roaring for attention. Bristled fur from the solitary owlbear made everyone aware that something was wrong. Aisha soared over him without dictating any sort of plan. Quickly stowing all the notes, Vofric followed.

Kargon was only last because he almost picked up Avant. It dawned on him that the beast had kept up on his own all evening; not counting traversing vertically. He was as capable as anyone else in the party, especially as he seemed larger than before.

"Let's go," Kargon said, running with his familiar by his side.

The hall exiting the main room was much longer than any other they'd experienced. It crudely snaked around stones that couldn't be dug out while leading downward. With every passing moment more dirt shifted and gravel fell from the ceiling. It ended at a loose wall that had been moved to reveal a door where Albert and Sariel prepared to battle a dozen Kingsguards.

"Wait!" Aisha roared, bursting into the room.

Cell walls were unfortunately familiar to the party. Its metal door was unlatched with guards inside and out ready to skewer them.

"Why are you here?" one yelled.

"We're on a mission from the royal family!" Aisha barked.

"A likely story," another replied.

It hadn't even been a day since the party received their instructions. These were likely the guards who missed an announcement due to an awkward shift change.

"Call Victor!" Kargon demanded as he arrived to Aisha's right.

A guard, wearing a captain's mark, stepped forward with her spear drawn. Without hesitation, Vofric walked in front of her with a warm smile and shaking head. Faint gold radiated from his chest and eased tension throughout the room.

"There is no need for violence. If Victor is not available you may contact Captain Telos. Tell him the Hero requests his presence," Vofric instructed.

The guard captain studied Vofric then the group of intruders before finally commanding someone to get Victor and Rusty. "Both of 'em better trust y'all," she growled.

No one moved a muscle while awaiting the contact's return. Aisha's hand hovered inches from her blade while Kargon was a second from combusting the room. Mana accumulated near Sariel, her entire left arm shining. Avant bristled with every heavy breath. Even Albert looked like he'd gouge someone's eyes out. The guards were no different—ready to lunge if they didn't receive an order to stand down. Only Vofric stood with no intent for violence, fully aware his party would protect him if things went awry.

For the first time in a while, nothing did. Where the party expected a confirmation of their declaration, they were met with Victor and Rusty's presence. More surprising was Prince Makani, following his family retainer. The commander immediately went about calming his subordinates while the prince and Victor approached Aisha. In response she signaled the party to stand down.

"How did you get access to my family's dungeon?" Prince Makani asked while staring at the broken wall.

Victor explained, "This dungeon is meant for criminals who specifically threaten the royal family. There should be no way to access it without their express permission."

"There haven't been prisoners for months. Years when it comes to this cell."

"We entered through the other side of this tunnel. I'll show you," Aisha replied then turned to Kargon. "Tell Rusty about the mastermind. He and the guards might be able to find them."

Albert and Avant stayed with the monk while everyone else accompanied Aisha to the bunker. Some guards apologized as they departed and Kargon readily accepted the understandable mistake.

Once everyone dispersed, Rusty approached and asked,"Any idea who you met?"

"Not really, they had this cloak on the whole time," Kargon replied and gestured for Albert to hand it over. "Are there records of any dragominn prisoners? Or ones in the city?"

Rusty examined the cloak and said, "You know how many dragominn there are in Dawncaster? Did you catch their color? Or element?"

It hadn't been long but with everything going on Kargon found himself having trouble remembering the figure in the alley. With closed eyes he entered a meditative state, pulling his mind back to the rooftops of Ramshorn. He recalled Vofric's flashing light hammer and jumping through the district. Large buildings spaced out by tiny alleys to create the perfect alcove blocked by ropes and signs. Finally, in the corner of the meeting spot, Kargon saw a creature with deep hatred for the aristocrats of Dawncaster.

"Red scales and pupils," Kargon muttered. "They hissed whenever high society was mentioned. Fire came out of their mouth and nostrils. Tried to shoot me. I'd never seen a pistol up close."

"What?!" Rusty asked and pulled the monk from his trance. The face covering helmet did little to hide the commander's shock. "The gun. Was it mechanical or magical?"

"Magical. Do you know the criminal?"

Rusty looked at the cell door's lock, quickly identifying unnoticeable damage. With minimal effort anyone could enter. Panicked mutters echoed in Rusty's helmet—something Kargon had grown accustomed to hearing from Aisha. The commander grew sullen as the identity of the dragominn cemented in his mind.

CHAPTER NINETEEN

Artifact

A meeting room normally meant for foreign delegates now housed Prince Makani, Victor, Rusty, the Hero's party, Albert and palpable tension. Memories of Balur and the exquisite meal were clear in the party's minds, though this table was covered in notes instead of food. Victor read each one thoroughly while the party relayed everything they'd learned. Finally, Rusty explained what he'd discovered after Kargon talked about the alleyway meeting.

"What do you mean the mastermind is one of your subordinates?" Prince Makani yelled, causing a powerful gust of wind to blow through the room. "Call them here!"

"They took some time off," Rusty said meekly, clearly wishing he hadn't removed his helmet. "It's been years since Elmud voluntarily offered to work in the Dicoris dungeon. It rarely sees prisoners so we used to rotate the guards. That way no one... gets bored." The captain awkwardly looked at the prince before averting his gaze. "They used to complain about the royal family and other pillars of the city but turned over a new leaf. According to others, they were similarly displeased with the Hero."

"You allowed someone like this close to the Dicoris family?" Victor asked angrily.

Rusty shook his head. "No! Victor, you know I'd never do that. Elmud's behavior and demeanor improved over the last seven years. The person who requested to work the dungeon was a model

Kingsguard. No acceptable reason existed to decline and you know how I feel about second chances."

The commander hung his head in shame when no one said anything. To be fair, it was an understandable mistake after seeing how much depended on the commander. More than a few people in the room could relate.

"I'm very sorry and understand if you want me to step down," he offered.

"No," Prince Makani replied immediately. "To take responsibility you must continue to work in your position. I do not know how I would have acted in similar circumstances." He didn't bother waiting for a response before addressing the party. "What do you make of this?"

Aisha answered, "You know the motive and identity of the mastermind." Then she debated her next words while looking at her party members. By all intents, their quest was complete and requesting information about their quest was well within their rights. This mystery didn't involve the party but it couldn't be left alone. Letting a criminal get away didn't sit well with Sariel and justice was one of Vofric's core beliefs. Avant would follow Kargon who was waiting on Aisha's decision. Then he realized her eyes were squarely on him, asking for help.

Continuing the journey brought them closer to the end but that was still in the distance. The Greycastles would get pulled into whatever came next and that didn't sit right. More than anything, Kargon wanted to punch Elmud. Not to mention Aisha clearly wanted to press forward. A simple nod was all the monk provided.

"We want to help stop Elmud," Aisha stated.

"Spoken like a Hero," Prince Makani said with a smile. "Victor, is there anything recognizable in the notes?"

Victor passed the notes with drawings to the prince and held up Aisha's findings about the sun. "Aisha, you did well in connecting the dots regarding light in the books. Master Makani, you will recognize the centerpiece in each of the drawings. I leave the decision of sharing further information in your hands."

The prince looked quizzically between the forgeminn and notes, his eyes growing wide with realization. Quick fingers wildly flipped through the pages before slowly placing them down. Prince Makani placed his head in his hands and slowly ran his fingers through his hair.

"Rusty, tell the guards to look for Elmud," he said dryly, staring at the table. "Be on high alert and contact me if you learn anything."

"Yes, your majesty," Rusty replied with a salute then departed.

Nothing else was said for many minutes. It seemed the forgeminn was accustomed to his majesty's silent contemplation. No one dared move or speak while the prince deliberated. He was still just a boy forced into an unenviable situation. Familial secrets were created by elders and shared only at their discretion. The room grew colder with each stressed breath.

"Hey, dude, are you okay?" Albert asked, breaking the silence.

The prince slowly looked up and stared at the subject who dared speak to him so casually. "I must make a decision that could affect Dawncaster forever. There is no way for me to know if it will be for better or worse," he said. "I find it difficult to be 'okay' at this time."

"The decision itself doesn't affect what'll happen. It's how everyone deals with the decision," Albert replied.

Prince Makani furrowed a brow. "How do you mean?"

"Like." Albert hummed. "I have an affliction that could ruin my life. But instead of letting it get out of control, I studied it. I found people to teach me. Now it's something I can use to help people."

"It's rather odd for an affliction to be useful. Can you share what it is?"

"I don't mind telling you if you'll share what's on your mind," Albert grinned.

The prince cracked a smile, for once appearing as a boy—not royalty. A soft groan of concern came from Vofric; unease with his nephew's nonchalance about his secret. But it was Albert's choice who to tell and the prince seemed trustworthy.

"I have lycanthropy." Albert said then hurriedly explained, "Please don't be scared. I have learned to control it."

"Is that true?" Victor asked the boy's temporary guardians.

Aisha answered, "He led us to the underground lab by scent alone. I doubt any citizens even saw him."

"It's rare for someone so young to be disciplined enough to control a bestial form. I'm impressed." Victor turned to the prince. "Young master?"

Prince Makani hummed and rose from his seat. "Follow me."

He patted Albert's shoulder, signaling him to stay close. Victor stood slightly behind them and the others followed. They traveled further into Dicoris Castle—a humble abode compared to the buildings in Balur. Meticulously carved stone walls looked plain with no embellishments. Family portraits of past generations smiling and laughing lined the walls.

Two guards stood by a thick steel door and saluted Prince Makani. A sphere was carved out of the center that he covered with both hands. Unlike elves, faint light emitted from djinnai when casting magic. As the prince began to levitate, his skin shimmered like the sky. A heavy gust of wind passed through the halls before swirling around him then redirecting into the door. The hum of a magic circle rang out accompanied by clicking mechanical gears. The steel slabs shifted open to reveal stairs descending at a sharp angle towards an illuminated platform. Once the group got inside, the door clamped shut behind them. Floating orbs of light appeared around them with each bit of progress. Steep steps made it a necessity for Kargon to carry Avant—frustrated by his size but happily settling into his master's arms.

"The Dicoris bloodline is tasked with protecting an Artifact of Arcana," Prince Makani said, his voice amplified to grandeur. "Many were destroyed or lost but not the one in our care. *Lightbringer* is a staff meant to fight back against darkness and we wouldn't see it fall into the wrong hands."

"Your findings suggest it would have been used as some sort of controller," Victor explained.

"Silence!" Sariel said abruptly with ears strained. "There are sounds of struggle below. We must hurry."

Makani flew down as the others struggled to keep up with the awkward angle of steps. Fortunately, they didn't encounter any enemies. Queen Lyra stood on the platform, examining the scepter installed in the center. White cloth bindings wrapped around the crooked wooden staff. A large hook—the head of the weapon—looked empty with no orb within. King Nasim's hand was planted on it as he struggled to move the staff.

"Makani," he grumbled upon noticing his son hovering nearby. It was frustration at his task that quickly changed targets upon seeing the approaching outsiders. He released the staff and stood upright, glaring at his son. "You dare bring outsiders here?!"

The prince shuddered and froze, all composure lost with his father's roar.

Without hesitation, Albert walked closer and lightly bumped a fist against the prince's back. "You've got this."

Prince Makani nodded. "The He— Aisha and her party found the mastermind and Rusty is currently leading a search."

"You have yet to explain the connection to the Artifact." Queen Lyra said calmly.

"Apologies. Notes were hidden in a bunker that was connected to our dungeon," the prince explained and handed the papers over. "Victor immediately recognized the centerpiece of the magic circles. There were also many books with stories regarding light."

Scrutinous eyes poured over the notes as the king and queen whispered amongst themselves. Anger was evident on the king's face but no longer turned towards his son. He placed a hand softly on Makani's head. "I apologize. You did well to bring them here."

"Well done, Makani." Queen Lyra added, then turned to the adventurers. "I believe you are willing to help us if you are here."

Aisha bowed and said, "If you permit, your majesty."

With a deep bow, Nasim accepted, then said, "We expected something to threaten the safety of Dawncaster when you drew *Valefor*. Through no fault of your own, mind you. It is simply a curse that comes with your role. Kharim dealt with similar hardships. His assistance allowed us to turn *Lightbringer* into a perpetual source of protection for the city."

"If it's passively protecting the city, why are you trying to move it?" Kargon asked.

"No one willing to openly attack the royal family will be stopped by a passive defense. I would not be surprised if they could bypass *Lightbringer's* defenses. We must be ready to use it when the time comes."

Queen Lyra hummed. "Unfortunately, we are unable to move it from its post."

"Is there possibly a mechanism holding it in place?" Victor asked, crouching near the base of the staff and waving Aisha over. "Do you see anything that may hinder the king?"

Aisha's eye glowed as she circled *Lightbringer*. It looked plain until she unconsciously hovered her hand over *Valefor's* hilt. With a gasp, she shut her eyes and turned away. "Bright," she muttered. "There's no mechanical parts."

"But I must be able to move it. Dicoris blood is needed to do so," the king demanded.

"You're not the only ones here, though." Albert said obviously then pushed Prince Makani forward.

Queen Lyra stepped between the staff and her son. "Wait! We considered it may be Makani but wielding this staff is a daunting task. You will not only be a ruler of Dawncaster but must learn the arts bound to *Lightbringer*."

"I can already cast spells, Mother," Prince Makani replied.

"That's not what she means, my boy." King Nasim explained, "Your natural connection to magic is of little help when wielding the staff. It controls the element of light and like any conduit, you must channel mana through it. You have never done so."

Prince Makani hesitated at the reminder of his lack of experience. It was important to consider every possibility before the next step. Slowly, he looked at Victor and Aisha, warriors whose experience with magic eclipsed his lifetime. Even Kargon had more practice with his conduit. Vofric kept as stoic a face as possible while pitying the unfortunate decision. When Prince Makani's eyes met Sariel's they shared a moment as the only individuals with no knowledge of conduits. It wasn't like Albert who had no magical abilities to speak of.

The young Greycastle never bothered to look at the prince—focused entirely on *Lightbringer*. "The outcome is decided by your decision."

"Were you scared the first time you purposely transformed?" Prince Makani asked.

Albert nodded as their eyes met. "And every time since. Mom says fear is a driving force. Mama says that's only if you push past it. Ask the Hero or anyone else. They probably deal with it, too."

No one knew how many years of vigilantism caused the young boy to mature so rapidly. Maybe it happened when he decided to control his lycanthropy and protect Dawncaster. It reminded Kargon of the days he pushed himself to meet Aisha even when shamefully failing training. Of nights spent meditating and destroying his knuckles for the day he might be needed.

"No one can stop you if you choose this for yourself," Aisha said, resting her hand on her sword.

The prince took a deep breath, nodded, and stepped forward. His parents each placed a hand on their son's shoulders in support. There was no resistance—no challenge— from *Lightbringer* as he pulled it from the platform. Loose bindings unraveled further and floated perpetually around the conduit. Winds shifted throughout the room but nothing else happened.

"I have much training ahead of me," Prince Makani scoffed.

There was no opportunity to celebrate as a heavy bell rang through the chamber. Victor teleported out of the room in an instant while Vofric and Albert dashed to the stairs. Without question or understanding, the rest of the party followed but found themselves levitating. Even Vofric and Albert were pulled from the ground as King Nasim's body glowed like sapphire. Everyone shot upwards past the steel door and towards the high ceiling as magical words passed from the queen's lips. Moments before collision, the group turned ethereal and passed through the walls. It was impossible to understand what was happening until they arrived in the observation deck of Dicoris Castle.

A small room surrounded by glass walls overlooked the entire city. From Zeffari's busy streets to Ramshorn hilltop mansions, everything was visible. For the first time, Kargon became aware of Library Raebkayd's rooftop gardens. Bamborough's shops looked manageable from here. The massive city was within reach.

Bells grafted into large structures on the city walls rang continually as gates shook under outside attacks. Panicked masses fled through packed streets from an unknown threat. Guards moved to defensive positions, attempting to retaliate, but weren't fast enough. Almost simultaneously, every gate shattered as an undead horde burst through.

A crimson winged dragominn, Elmud, hovered over them near the main gate to the city and barked orders at their underlings. Their eyes settled on Dicoris castle before garbled roars from endless undead shook the ground.

"We will support the troops from the castle entrance," King Nasim stated as a powerful gust of wind forced all the glass windows open. No one could challenge the battle hardened king, ready to leap out of the observation deck. "Makani, are you ready?"

"I'll do my best," he said, clearly overwhelmed.

"I have to check on my moms!" Albert shifted to werewolf form and jumped out of the room. "I'll be back!"

With seconds to go, Aisha assigned jobs to her party members. The sheer number of residents in Ramshorn needed a protector and Vofric was perfect with his ability to heal and bolster them. Meanwhile, Sariel would go to the city walls to support the Kingsguard while also getting more angles of attack for a sharpshooter.

"Avant, can you keep up?" Aisha asked.

The owlbear's affirmative growl was deeper than usual.

"Good. You and Kargon, with me."

CHAPTER TWENTY

Castle Defense

Shambling corpses were no match for Vofric's war-hammer—carrying him forward with each swing. Bodies were crushed and sent flying as he carved a path through the city. He could've thinned out the horde all the way to the southern gate if he didn't care for innocent lives. Monsters fell over each other as they attempted to break into a home with unarmed civilians. Smashing his hammer into the ground, Vofric shot massive shards of pavement through his targets and left their lifeless corpses as a blockade.

"You are safe!" he yelled inside. "Find cover and remain still!"

Panicked noncombatants led more enemies towards the dwarf with every passing moment and he easily clobbered them. The civilians didn't dare step away from Vofric which only made fighting harder. Mana was pouring into his war-hammer at a staggering rate. Golden shockwaves ripped through the streets, launching undead into the sky. The horrifying sound of bones crunching on impact froze the very people Vofric vowed to protect. They wouldn't move anywhere except towards obvious shelter.

Buildings were starting to fill with undead as they broke through meek defenses. Streets that were cleared minutes ago were once again overrun. Vofric knew it was wishful thinking that the shelter he first saved might still be standing but he attempted to reach it nonetheless, finding it easily thanks to the pile of corpses he'd left behind. Its presence was the only reason the door remained standing.

Unfortunately, the unending horde shattered windows and damaged some of the outer walls. Distinct blood stains marked the walls and pained breathing could be heard inside. Vofric didn't bother calling out for anyone. With a powerful swing he shifted the entire pile of dead then forced himself through the door and was met with a shriek.

"Hold! We seek shelter!" he yelled as he saw the culprit.

A small family of four cowered in the corner while pressing rags to a myriad of wounds. Vofric signaled the outsiders to come in before he rushed to the youngest child with a gash in her arm. The dwarf was a giant presence as warmth radiated from his as sturdy hands quickly healed them. Uncomfortable aches were far more manageable than gaping wounds.

"Thank you," one of the fathers said.

"Worry not. Please barricade the door once I depart. I cannot return here without endangering this group," Vofric replied.

Scattered words of gratitude followed him out of the door. In the brief moment he spent inside, more undead flooded the streets. Most Kingsguards were at the walls or in Dicoris and Vofric groaned at his lack of aid. Not a single moment passed when he wasn't surrounded but he did well to keep them far enough away to maneuver his war-hammer.

It had been many years since he found himself in such a situation. Maybe that was why mindless creatures were able to corner him. However, dwarves were not known to give up in the face of adversary —always fighting until their last breath. The size of his war-hammer had always been a benefit but as more undead encroached, it became more difficult to fight back.

"This ain't the place for a last stand!" yelled a familiar voice; its origin dropping from a nearby building. Multiple monsters were swiftly cut down by a woman wielding two cutlasses adorned with a customized black captain's hat.

"Captain!" Vofric said joyfully, finally catching his breath. "You regained your post!"

"Something like that," Julian said with a smirk.

Rowdy half-breeds leapt off rooftops and engaged the undead. Metal pounded against stone as they violently tore through the monsters; not bothering to wait for one monster to fall before engaging another. It would almost be terrifying if not for the control they displayed when fighting near civilians. A large group cowered behind the pirates, pointing out shelter and shifting the group's attention towards it.

Julian looked at the dwarf and tilted her head. "You need a break, old man?"

Vofric flourished his war-hammer. "Starcallers rest when the job is done."

***

Projectiles rained from the sky, tearing through demons and undead alike. Mages and archers occupied the wall and rooftops of the city while bringing down any enemy within sight. While one shot getting a kill was normally impressive, it was causing problems in terms of ammunition. Mana was dwindling for spellcasters who'd been fighting nonstop. Some gargled down potions like madmen while chanting spells. Others picked up any melee weapon in reach with no regard for personal safety.

Sariel commended the warriors but knew their inexperience would only be a detriment to all. Stories from Kargon's failed training rang in their ears and they found themself thankful he avoided weaponry. Unlike everyone else, Sariel could take out multiple enemies with a single modified arrow. The heavy arrowhead allowed the powerful bolt to pierce all the way through a single monster's body before ripping through more enemies.

At first some guards thought the elf was firing randomly, not worried about hitting a civilian with such devastating arrows. Only after watching Sariel's sharp eyes did they understand how far ahead the elf was thinking. They operated at a level few understood when it came to landing shots. But the longer they battled, the clearer it became that a single archer wouldn't be enough.

"Cover me!" Sariel yelled to a nearby duo.

They each only had a few arrows but obliged, hesitantly reaching back to grab what should have been the last of their ammo. Instead they felt a quiver filled to the brim and saw Sariel dash away with an emerald arm. Arrows were stuffed into any holster within reach, allowing people to fight at their best for just a bit longer.

When guards were disarmed or shattered their weapons—wooden

weapons of unequal caliber appeared in hand. Vines erupted from the hilts and allowed Sariel to control the flow of battle. Fighters who misstepped off the high structures were able to be saved. It wasn't perfect, though, and deaths weighed heavily when safety was a possibility. But such thoughts were a detriment no one could afford.

Minutes passed and Sariel finally stopped at one of the many ballistas lining the wall. Guards had stopped using them, assumedly because they lacked ammo. Only upon closer inspection did Sariel realize they had fallen apart from monster attacks. The light never dimmed from their scales as a gamble came to mind. Slamming their hand against the wooden structure, they focused with every shred of will. Splinters extended into vines that wreathed around fallen pieces and reconnected them properly. As more parts were set, the verdant magic hardened. No one could understand if it was their imagination or Sariel's intent but the front of each ballista appeared like the open mouth of a dragon. With a quick swipe, every massive ballistic arrow grew sharper and sturdier.

"Guide me to the other ballistas!" Sariel yelled without looking at anyone. A Kingsguard captain rushed over with a wooden sword and quiver full of arrows. The look on her face was one of gratitude but there was no time for words. Each of them nodded as the guard dashed through the crowd with a draconic god watching over her.

***

Undead creatures were known to detest fire. A warrior with four flaming fists felt no fear when facing them. Kargon's punches ripped through the monsters, a single swing sending two explosive punches that eviscerated more enemies. There were no astral projections of his flaming legs but they were equally devastating with the power to throw monsters tens of feet back. Protecting civilians was easiest when flames were doused and the moment they were out of harm's way, he reignited.

Lightning tore through streets and danced around civilians without pause. Aisha blitzed through crowds of undead, a blur bisecting monsters in her path. Flying imps had no chance to approach as electricity arched towards them in violent jolts.

Avant stayed close to his master but only bolstered himself. Mana manifested in the form of a blue shell of energy that sharpened his feathers. A single roar was the only warning before he barrelled towards groups of monsters. One leap sent him hurtling through their chests. Even with powerful tactics, he remained near Kargon.

"Avant, you don't have to follow me! Go wild!" the monk ordered.

The owlbear roared happily before biting another monster. That wasn't necessarily what his master meant and the cub's health would need to be checked later, but that wouldn't be anytime soon.

The center of the city was the eye of a storm as cutting winds tore through monsters around the castle. King Nasim and Queen Lyra's control of air was masterful, weaving between their subjects and the undead without harming the undeserving. It reminded Kargon of the flowing attacks his master used. But when Kargon tried it, they were incapable of quickly killing the undead. His aggressive attacks were difficult to balance with monastic teachings.

"Kargon!" Aisha yelled from a nearby rooftop. "Stop focusing on what you learned. Your stances suck! Just do what feels right!"

Normally the man wouldn't question his best friend. But what felt right was garbage; at least according to Master Avant. It was apparently wrong to rush at someone and drill a fist into them without preparing. Then again, he never had a way to prepare his attacks before. When he first learned to ignite, it only set things ablaze. Now he could strengthen himself—prepare himself.

An undead shambled towards him and flailed an arm. Kargon ducked underneath while simultaneously igniting his fist. With a grunt he sent a flaming punch up through the monster's chin and knocked its head clean off. Another monster approached and Kargon lunged at it with his other hand to slam it to the ground. Without realizing, he yelled and ripped its head from its body. More monsters rushed in but nothing could stop him. Astral hands floating nearby conflagarated any monsters that were foolish enough to get close. Some innate part of Kargon kept the flames controlled and civilians safe.

"That's more like it!" Aisha yelled happily as she cut down another imp.

Unlike almost everyone else, she wasn't stationary. Dead demons plummeted from the sky as the Hero leapt between and killed them. The monsters' uncoordinated attacks were useless against her maneuvers. Like a dancer she weaved through wild strikes while retaliating in kind. Where Kargon put all his strength behind each attack, Aisha could nonchalantly cut down hordes.

Meanwhile, Prince Makani struggled to utilize *Lightbringer*. Anytime he tried to cast a spell, a gust of wind manifested and pushed back the enemy. Thankfully, his parents stood by his side and helped fight from the top of the steps leading into the castle. But as the fight persisted, they became further outnumbered. Avant was the first to fall back towards the castle; clearly the right call as Aisha followed using her monstrous platforms. A dozen fell by the time she arrived near the royal family. Kargon summoned his astral hands to open a path as he retreated.

Victor and Rusty defended the royal family as others joined. The forgeminn's cane handle detached from the base and revealed a thin metal blade that easily felled his enemies. Its sheath acted as a weapon that could crush enemies in his off hand. Rusty stiffly swung a longsword with all his weight behind it, assisted by the heavy greatsword on his back. It looked like a wasteful accessory with its spiked hilt. Dozens of guards lined the bottom of the steps outside the castle, fighting ferociously with their commander.

Unfortunately, the monsters were gradually getting stronger. Citizens' dying screams filled the air. Guards were overpowered and slaughtered. Blood and decay layered the streets. Horrifyingly, living beings who fell rose to attack past comrades. The line near the castle stumbled for a second and a single guard fell. Like dominoes, others succumbed to the horde. Kargon finally reached the center of the city, sure he would have been ripped apart a second later.

Suddenly, a silver light flew past his head and burned through ten undead. Only seconds passed before it exploded spectacularly, eradicating a large clump of monsters. Prince Makani held *Lightbringer* aggressively in front of him with a white knuckle grip. A glowing orb hovered in the once empty hooked head of the staff. A swing of the weapon sent the sphere through the nearby crowd. Unfortunately, it fizzled out before exploding.

"My mistake... was assuming... daylight," the prince panted. "The moon shines... just as brightly."

"How much time do you need to cast the spell again?" King Nasim asked.

"I don't know … Hard to control."

Victor commanded the group. "We must buy Prince Makani time! Captain Telos, inform the troops!"

It was clear the commander was awaiting such a signal as he ferociously threw away his longsword. Tightly gripping the greatsword dug the spikes deep into his palm and poured blood into the sheath as he drew the weapon. As the crimson ichor wrapped the blade it grew sharper, cutting through six undead with a single swing. Leftover blood erupted from within and eradicated other nearby monsters. Rusty slammed the blade to the ground, summoning a wall of blood that stretched hundreds of feet high.

"Guards! Stay strong!" Rusty's helmet glowed with every word. "We must buy time for the prince! We fight for dawn!"

A cacophonous roar from remaining guards rang throughout the city. "We fight for dawn!"

Aisha leapt into the horde and attacked wildly with Avant in tow. Alongside them was Victor with glowing cane in hand. He teleported while swinging his blade and vanished, reappearing in random spots around the castle perimeter. Kargon stayed back and focused on the openings between the guards, killing any undead that broke through. Waves of blood from Rusty's sword created momentary walls that redirected monsters towards the monk's fists.

"Makani! Don't hesitate!" Aisha yelled, forgetting her decorum.

"It's unruly. I cannot control my mana output," Prince Makani yelled back.

A pale blur brushed past the prince and collided with nearby monsters. Guards nearly turned on it until Palehound spoke. "Why are you trying to control it?" Albert asked. "Give it everything you've got. The more of these things you take out the less work for the rest of us."

The prince looked at the werewolf in stunned silence then smiled. The staff glowed brightly, as did his body, and a gust of wind carried his voice through the city. "Hold them off."

It was likely the first command Prince Makani had given in his life. Citizens who had no business fighting raised arms to defend their home. Familiar half-breeds appeared from Ramshorn with Julian leading them. By her side was Vofric who skillfully threw his light hammer forward, ripping through enemies in his path. A volley of explosive arrows rained from the city walls. All ballistas looked into the city like guardian dragons, providing cover for Sariel as they rushed to the castle. Any imps who dared block the path were quickly disposed of. A familiar roar erupted from Avant in a deeper tone than ever before. Cobalt energy cascaded over the Dicoris district and empowered every warrior in its reach. With newfound energy, the owlbear tore through the undead like children's playthings. Silent understanding passed between Aisha and Albert as they swapped spots so the former could get near the castle. Seeing the werewolf eviscerate humanoids made everyone thankful he was in control of his abilities.

Feeling invigorated, Kargon prepared to rush into the crowd but felt a familiar hand stop him. Aisha nodded toward the main gate. Amongst the carnage, the monk had almost forgotten Elmud was still commanding their troops from above. The best course of action was to carve a path and make room for the Hero to defeat the enemy leader. Unfortunately, the main entrance to the city was filled with monsters. Every citizen had fled or died trying. Living corpses lined the street, forced to march by their new master.

An inferno encompassed Kargon's limbs in preparation to engage the horde. Astral hands weren't enough and this was no time to waste mana on them. Physical combat with a fiery passion was the best course of action. He tightened his goggles and took a step back to accommodate a long jump. Aisha pulled him back again.

"I'll carve a path for you," Kargon said.

Aisha pointed *Valefor* at the street leading to the main gate. "Look at that crowd. Which is better at handling combat while outnumbered, a sword or fists?"

"But what about Elmud?"

"The Kargon I know doesn't shy away from a fist fight." Aisha smirked.

She was right. Kargon wanted nothing more than to beat Elmud. But that wasn't his role. But there was no chance to argue with his best friend.

"I didn't just pick you to stay on the sidelines. I wanted an equal," Aisha insisted and nodded towards Elmud.

Kargon made a point to face the dragominn. They sneered while an army of undead did all the work for them. It was aggravating. Though the monk's fire was likely to be ineffective in the fight, it didn't matter. Aisha had surely thought of it yet still demanded that her right hand engage the enemy leader.

"What do you need from me?" Kargon asked.

The Hero took a fighting stance, ready to carve a path. "Finish this."

CHAPTER TWENTY-ONE

Repelling Darkness

Leather crunched as Aisha's left grip tightened around *Valefor's* hilt and electricity fought to erupt from her other hand. She leapt over the guards, firing a chain of lightning from the sky to open space in the crowd of undead. Control of the element posed no issue for the Hero.

The spell dissipated as Aisha landed and Kargon ran past the guards to join her. Creatures began stumbling over each other in hopes of making contact but stood no chance against Aisha's advance. Though her express instructions were for Kargon to conserve energy, he refused to stand idly by. It was possible to defeat the undead without igniting. When any inevitably got close, the monk dodged and threw the monster into the path of the Hero's swift blade.

The street near the main gate was packed with undead clambering over each other to attack. One powerful slice of *Valefor* killed five targets. More took their place but the hindrance of corpses allowed the duo to gain ground. It was obvious Kargon couldn't hold back from fighting but he kept his word and didn't ignite.

Furious punches shattered brittle bones and devastating kicks tore through the decrepit bodies. The most difficult opponents were fresh corpses turned monstrous and demons. Thankfully, Aisha handled those with ease. However, the waves of monsters only got more restless as the gate grew closer.

"You don't seem like an assassin!" Elmud yelled, hovering near the gate.

"You don't seem like a guard!" the half-elf replied without breaking stride.

Kargon couldn't stop fighting to talk with the wall of monsters coagulating into a mass of limbs that blocked the path. Rotted extremities came from every direction in hopes of tearing the duo apart. Aisha quickly slashed at crucial supports in the crowd and sent lightning through the openings to crumple the structure. Few monsters remained intact and Kargon handled them with an aggression that would disgust his master. After punching an opponent, Kargon lifted himself to kick another before grabbing the head of one more and crushing it in his grasp. A less trained eye would see wild flailing—the monk couldn't be more aware of every action.

"You're doing good but I'll be staying up here until you collapse," Elmud taunted.

"Bold of you to assume I won't bring you down," Aisha replied through grit teeth.

The dragominn scoffed at Kargon. "Are you so unreliable that the chosen one must do everything?"

The monk ignited a hand and chopped it through the collar of a monster. Simultaneously, an astral hand appeared above Elmud and caught them off guard. While the attack didn't cut through them, it forced the dragominn to the ground. They landed feet first, unbothered, then rolled their shoulders to hide their wings.

"Aisha won't be wasting time with you," Kargon said with as intimidating a voice as he could muster. Smoke billowed out with the threat as flames danced along his tongue. A brief uncomfortable sensation was the most defenseless part of his body becoming familiar with flames. He didn't have time to process why flames appeared somewhere new while Elmud stared him down.

"Looks like I hit a nerve." the dragominn smirked. "Now, tell me. How will you fight within my army?"

The undead gathered around their master and blocked Kargon's path. Even if he took them down, more would interfere with the fight and Elmud could win via cowardice.

"I'll be damned if you won't offer a fair fight," Aisha grunted as she mowed through the crowd.

A marble of lightning launched from her fingertips and flew

between Elmud and Kargon. When it erupted against one of the undead a ring of electricity expanded outward, stretching farther than either fighter expected. They moved in an uncomfortably similar way to flip over the expanding ring. Monsters weren't smart enough to do so and disintegrated as the spell expanded. After a few seconds, the ring became stagnant, providing an empty arena for the fiery brawlers. An endless stream of undead ran at the lightning but died on contact. Though Aisha was putting on a good show of holding her own, even her strength would run out eventually.

"She's needed after—" Elmud tried to speak but was stopped by a swift kick to the jaw.

They didn't bother trying to dodge the once Kargon. Being underestimated was par for the course when traveling with the Hero. She was the one who knew what he could really do—smirking in the midst of battle at the result of Kargon's attack. Scales cracked on Elmud's lower muzzle as they were pushed back. Slowly, they reached up to touch their bleeding jaw and Kargon lunged again. The dragominn retaliated with a swipe of their claw. Kargon's fist met his opponent's palm, canceling both attacks.

"You really aren't an assassin," Elmud scoffed. "And you're not the only one proficient in hand-to-hand combat."

"I don't see anyone else here who is." Kargon pulled back for a second then dashed into arms reach, sending a flurry of blows towards Elmud's chest.

Arms raised to guard against the onslaught but Kargon didn't slow down in hopes of breaking through. Focus of such a high degree was easy to capitalize on and Elmud whipped their tail into Kargon's left forearm. Bones cracked from the impact and sent a jolt through his body. Pulling back, he noticed cuts all over from the dragominn's scales that compounded with his severe pain.

"Fewer extremities are a weakness for your kind. You lack augments. Did you fail to wield a weapon and fall back on your fists?' Elmud asked.

Unphased, Kargon rushed forward again. Attempting to block the dragonminn's tail was foolish but dodging would work. It moved slowly thanks to its size and position, allowing the monk to weave around and attack. Elmud slowly found Kargon's rhythm and fought back. Moments when his guard broke were met with savage claw strikes. For each punch that cracked scales, small blades cut through half-elf skin. Blood and shrapnel sprayed across the small arena as damage became more visible and wounds appeared after each attack.

Flecks of crimson liquid blinded the dragominn while Projectile shards dug into Kargon's skin. But he refused to let up. Bloody knuckles met the very blades tearing through them yet Kargon knew he was stronger. Natural evolution had gone to Elmud's head. Untrained claws were painful but not devastating. The impact from refined fists visibly shook the dragominn. It was clear they were plotting something.

The fighters' arms crossed and Elmud skillfully locked them in place. Instead of a tail swipe, they used it for support while breathing a plume of fire. Kargon prepared for burns but was met with a warm breeze. Cautiously, he looked at his undamaged skin within the flames. Fire resistance was common in pyromancers—few had fire immunity.

Kargon wondered if Elmud could say the same, especially with his undefended muscle inviting attacks. The flames that erupted from Kargon's arms were incomparable. A hair raising screech was all Elmud managed before shoving the monk away. Wild flailing was their initial solution to stopping the flames until it dawned that dousing it would be easier.

A large charred wound lay across the dragominn's arm. Before Elmud had a chance to speak, Kargon dashed forward. Repeated punches made him easy to predict and Elmud's defense was strong enough to stall. However, that wasn't Kargon's intent. With a strong grip, he pushed the dragominn directly into the electric ring. While plenty of undead had collided with the outside and disintegrated, none broke through. With the force of two warriors it was bound to. Thunderous magic plunged into the villain's spine like hundreds of daggers. Kargon used Elmud to protect himself from the massive electric pulse that thinned the horde as well.

A pained scream accompanied Elmud's efforts to break free of Kargon's grasp. The moment they separated, wings sprouted on the mastermind's back. Kargon leapt forward and summoned astral hands at the base of each wing. As soon as Elmud tried to fly, the monk stopped it, forcing the dragominn to their knees.

"You may stop me, but what of the army?" Elmud stared hatefully at Kargon. "Think this is the only place they were summoned? Our plan is global! You're not strong enough. Not you or the Hero!"

Aisha backed away from the crowd of monsters and approached their master. "Strong enough for what?" She placed *Valefor* at Elmud's neck.

"To protect any of them. Master is far more powerful than a few adventurers in over their heads. What will Tetria do against overwhelming odds?"

The duo had further questions but the monsters encroached on them. Kargon couldn't move without releasing Elmud and Aisha was clearly exhausted. Adrenaline was quickly depleting as the sea of darkness grew closer.

That was until a flash of silver light burst from Dicoris Castle.

A beam emerged from *Lightbringer*, flying past the clouds. It expanded steadily and engulfed those at its origin before completely encompassing the city. Monsters that came into contact with it disintegrated instantly. The light stretched past the gates and shattered unseen stones that were endlessly summoning the creatures. In the blink of an eye, the Nevesi duo were no longer surrounded. A howl of victory erupted from the other districts but Kargon refused to turn away from Elmud.

They sighed and stared at the ground. "What is your name?"

"Aisha. Don't presume knowing my name makes us equals," she said.

"Not you, Hero," Elmud replied and stared daggers at the monk. "You."

He retaliated with daggers of his own. "Kargon."

"Kargon. Name's Elmud," they replied then lunged forward. Aisha was unprepared to stop the dragominn from slitting their own neck. Scales cracked violently as blood poured over Elmud and their lifeless body was held up by Kargon. Within seconds, their body disintegrated and only empty astral hands remained unable to catch the charred embers that flew away.

"That's not normal," Kargon said.

"A contingency plan. We'll report it to King Nasim," Aisha replied and patted him on the back. "You did well."

It didn't take long for the man to notice the myriad wounds across his best friend's body. Kargon's unmoving gaze caused Aisha to examine herself. She let out a heavy sigh and gestured for him to lend her a shoulder. Her right hand man obliged and they walked towards Dicoris Castle, basking in the cheers of Dawncaster.

CHAPTER TWENTY-TWO

Moonlit

Several days passed while Dawncaster recovered from the monster attack. On the off chance that any survived, every corner of the city was searched. It didn't take long to confirm that Makani eradicated them all. Missing persons were accounted for and any who turned monstrous were identified—whatever peace that brought their loved ones. A ceremony honoring the dead would be held after the King was informed of what happened by the Hero's Party. It was surprisingly casual—none of them wearing armor and Albert in attendance. Even so, Aisha kept decorum and handled discussing the party's findings.

"Elmud mentioned that their plan is continent-wide. Undead were summoned everywhere," she explained.

King Nasim nodded silently as his gaze turned to Kargon. "Is it true Elmud turned to embers?" he asked.

"Yes, your majesty."

The king turned to his wife and son, then turned back to the party as he let out a slow breath. All three rose from their thrones and stepped forward.

"An onslaught of undead creatures on Tetria makes it clear this is related to the prophecy," King Nasim explained. "It was perpetrated by an unknown cabal and their leader is spoken of with no name."

Queen Lyra nodded. "Furthermore, the embers left behind by Elmud were common during the demon king's uprising. It is important you learn who Kharim faced."

Victor retrieved a magically sealed scroll and handed it to Aisha. The royal family's voices melded together as they spoke. The scroll unfurled in the Hero's hands.

"Aeraza, once vanquished, shall rise from depths below,
    To claim dominion again and leave the world hollow
    From humble origins, a Hero shall emerge,
    Alongside, allies of like will converge
    Born of mortal blood, yet touched by powers divine
    Each trial overcome, fates intertwine
    Against almighty darkness, heroes makes a stand
    The fate of the land rest in their hand"

Aisha's intense stare could've bore a hole into the scroll. "A random disaster wasn't why *Valefor* woke up. It was because Aeraza came back."

"Yes," King Nasim said. "That is why many are wary of you. They are unsure if you are deserving or overly fortunate."

The light dulled in Aisha's eyes. "Right."

Queen Lyra huffed at her husband. "Dear, you will sadden our savior." She turned to Aisha. "You have proven, without a shadow of a doubt, to be not only worthy of *Valefor* but our respect. We will make an effort to diminish the doubts of naysayers. I cannot guarantee it will help but such fears should not hinder us."

"Though, I still think it was foolish no one mentioned Aeraza to you before," Makani grumbled.

"Allow me to explain," King Nasim said. "Those present during Aeraza's defeat were bound to secrecy. Information can only be shared to preserve history. By revealing it, you may now speak and hear Aeraza's name within specific magic circles; one of which is beneath this castle and a replica is sketched on your scroll."

The villain's name was whispered by everyone who learned it.

Sariel's eyes flashed and they grabbed their arm. Only Kargon could see how tight the grip really was. The two adventurers looked at each other and Sariel faintly shook their head. With a nod, Kargon promised not to pry.

"He's probably the 'Master' Elmud mentioned," Aisha said.

"The dragominn is our first step towards stopping Aeraza," Sariel grunted.

"He's been active at least eight years if we consider when Aisha was chosen." Kargon added.

Every gaze in the room fell on the Hero as she slowly rolled up the scroll and stowed it in a pouch on her hip. " Retracing steps would help us get closer to Aeraza's group. Elmud's hometown might have people that know something," she explained.

Vofric nodded in agreement. "Our time in Dawncaster is over."

Albert frowned. "You're gonna need to prep before you go, right?"

"According to Captain Telos, Elmud comes from Gromsev," Queen Lyra said. "Reaching the town will take weeks, maybe a month. Not only will you need supplies but we would like to request your presence at the honoring ceremony."

Makani awkwardly cleared his throat to grab everyone's attention. "This is unrelated, but Albert; will you be leaving with Aisha's party?"

The boy absentmindedly rubbed a wound on his arm and looked at Aisha. In truth, she didn't expect his presence after everything that happened.

But, before either of them could say anything, Queen Lyra interjected. "Before you make a decision, we have an offer for you. It is rare to see a warrior who is so adept at a young age. You have even overpowered your lycanthropic gene," she exclaimed. "Taking this into account, we would like to offer you a position as Makani's retainer. You would be given time to help your family but your primary role would be similar to Victor's. We do not expect an immediate response—"

"Wait!" Albert interrupted. Doubt turned to annoyance and he glared at Makani. "I'm sorry but I didn't help the queen or king. I helped you. What do you want?"

Aisha quickly covered her mouth to hide a smirk. The rest of her party didn't bother to hide theirs. Ignoring decorum in hopes of helping his new friend suited Albert. What mattered most was if Makani could act similarly. Much to the prince's surprise, his parents wore expectant smiles.

"I..." Makani's slow gaze passed over the party, stopping on Aisha and Kargon. Something clicked. "I don't want a retainer. I don't want to be a king who's handed a throne. I want to train my new abilities and adventure!" He turned to Albert and said, "I don't want a retainer but a friend and companion, Albert. Is that acceptable?"

"You're not going to give me time to think like the queen?" he asked.

Makani stammered, "Oh, of course. If you need—"

"I'm joking!" Albert laughed. "You're too gullible, Makani. Of course, I'll have your back."

King Nasim cleared his throat. While he enjoyed the display of friendship—the boys didn't know what preparation entailed. "That is all well and good, but we must discuss logistics. We can do so at a later time with all the Greycastles. It must be kept secret from the citizenry as a security measure." He turned his attention to Aisha and said, "I apologize that my son has taken one of the members of your party."

"Everyone in our party chose to join me," Aisha replied. "If Albert is choosing to join Makani, who am I to stop him?"

"Thank you, He— Aisha." Queen Lyra shared a look with her husband then continued, "I believe that is everything for today. The celebration honoring the fallen and your send-off is in three days. Please enjoy your remaining time here."

The party collectively bowed before following Victor out of the castle. Without the forgeminn's help it would have been easy to get lost. "Kargon is the man you spoke of during training, am I correct?" he asked Aisha.

"Yes, sir."

"Elder Niko misjudged his reliability." Victor chuckled. "Not even djinnai's elemental affinity provides immunity."

Kargon almost asked for more information but Aisha lightly punched him to stop it. Now wasn't the time to pry for information no matter how curious he was about his rare ability. They stepped out of the main gate and faced the stairs to the city.

Victor stopped them one last time. "I have served the Dicoris's for decades and am sure they expect much from each of you. Do not let them down."

"We won't, sir." Aisha replied as the door shut.

Bustling city streets never looked so inviting as citizens greeted them with warmth. Soldiers spoke to Sariel with the same reverence they carried for their commander. Ramshorn residents greeted Vofric excitedly with hugs and handshakes. Some half-breeds nodded with a fist out which the dwarf bumped familiarly. Shopkeepers tossed food in Avant's path which he caught midair. Trilled chirps brought smiles to his friends and fans. Brief transformations to human form garnered Albert a fan club who openly referred to him as Palehound.

Aisha was approached by citizens with the same frequency but these ones openly thanked their savior. Being met as an equal brought a warm glow to the Hero's face and tears welled in her eyes. Nods, hugs, handshakes; everything was met in kind by the warrior. Suddenly, she looked back and pointed at him.

"He took down the dragominn," she said.

The small crowd turned to him and a child wiggled through. She stared at Kargon intensely then yelled, "YOU DIDN'T GET BURNED!"

He looked at his arms and chuckled. "You're right."

Looking back, he saw Aisha grin widely—unabashed joy she hadn't shown in years. Neither shied away from the other's intoxicating glow. But as the growing crowd split the party, the Nevesi duo's eye contact broke. How long everyone answered questions, they couldn't say. It was the adventurers' first experience with well-deserved recognition yet Kargon found himself wanting nothing more than to spend time with his best friend.

***

Stalls lined every street of the Dicoris district and many others, offering goods to help in the revitalization of Dawncaster. Citizens and tourists from across the continent awaited the opening ceremony and send-off of the Hero's party. A massive crowd gathered near Dicoris Castle chatting with guards behind a barricade of shields.

Victor led the royal family and adventuring party to the platform outside the castle. A balcony had never been built for announcements; King Nasim preferred being close to his people. No one knew why he and the queen were carrying weapons but they were mesmerizing. The king held a jeweled sheath that housed a magnificent longsword. Queen Lyra, on the other hand, gripped a wooden quarterstaff bound together by molded metal.

The doors of the castle slowly opened and Kargon whispered to Aisha. "We're not running this time?"

"Neves was celebrating me before I'd done anything. The Dicoris's are thanking us for protecting the city," Aisha explained. "I don't feel ashamed for accepting it."

As the party stepped outside, horns blared from flanking towers of the castle. Spellcasters manipulated lights overhead that reflected everything below. The king and queen approached the front of the platform; with each step the citizens' cheers growing louder. Stalls paused operation while everyone turned to face the royals. Rusty and Julian stood with their respective subordinates. When they shouted for attention, the dichotomy of their positions was clear. Guards slammed their shields against the ground and fell silent. Julian's crew, however, roared collectively in a way that silenced the crowd. King Nasim cleared his throat and wind carried through the city to amplify his voice.

"Citizens, travelers, and all others, I am King Nasim of Dawncaster," he announced. "I thank you for joining us after our fair city faced a devastating attack. We know little of who threatened our home or why. But today, that is not what matters. We come together to honor those who are no longer with us. In order to defend us they gave their lives."

Whispers spread across the crowd as fresh wounds were acknowledged.

"To honor those who protected Dawncaster, we have erected pillars throughout the city," Queen Lyra said. "Each district's saviors will be carved into the very stone that bolsters us. May we never forget their names and bravery."

The crowd cheered as the starry image overhead turned into a city map. Specific points glowed to represent each pillar and beams of light launched upward throughout the city. Seven stone pillars stood ten feet high with silver embellishments along the edge. Cheers persisted as each pillar flashed on the screen until it returned to the king and queen.

With a deep breath, King Nasim explained, "I have never experienced something like this in my centuries of life. Attacks of this scale are rare and often predicate important moments."

With a simple gesture Makani knew to join his father. The boy stared wide-eyed at the king while he continued.

"While the undead left quite an impact on us, so did the future king. Prince Makani's light shone brighter than the sun. A power that not only eradicated the threat but spread throughout the world. Moonlight now flows within the very air we breathe. It empowers us. Brings us hope."

The king choked up and shut his eyes tightly, disregarding the murmurs as pride swelled in his chest. Tears welled in the queen's eyes as she glanced at the man her boy was turning into. Makani breathed slowly as he looked between his parents.

With a soft smile Queen Lyra announced, "The prince has decided to go on a journey to learn of this world. To gain perspective on the continent he has given a moonlit blessing. So we may all feel at ease the day he becomes King Makani."

Makani was nudged forward and the queen nodded to *Lightbringer*, still gripped tightly in the boy's hand. Stunned by the overwhelming cheers of the crowd, he hesitated. That was until he saw a familiar face past the barricade. A silver haired boy; the prince's first friend. Albert stood with his mothers and made eye contact. A tight fist to his chest and nod signaled confidence.

The prince gripped his staff tightly and thrust it upward. A ball of light launched forth and exploded like a firework. Thunderous chants drowned out any words attempted to be spoken. As long as the staff was held, the cheers continued. Makani used the chance to think carefully about what to say. When he found the words, he lowered his weapon, waited the few seconds it took for cheers to end, then spoke.

"I am honored by your praise. But, I could not have wielded this weapon nor found my path without help," Makani said. "The Hero and her party fought for our city. They took to the frontlines when I needed aid. The blessing we have would not be possible without them!"

Aisha guided her party forward, clearly having rehearsed with the prince beforehand. Lights overhead expanded to fit the entire group. The adventurer's took one step down from the platform as the royal family approached from behind. Aisha stood at the center with the others spreading out on either side, anxiously staring back at the crowd below.

"You will collect many titles during your journey," King Nasim said. "Let us honor you with our own before you depart."

A hallowed sound rang out as he unsheathed his sword. Radiance and pressure emanated from the blade and shook Kargon to the core. A tightly closed fist kept him calm but it was impossible to hide his nervousness.

"Ramshorn would have fallen if not for the guidance of the Emissary of the Starcaller," King Nasim said as he placed the flat of his blade on each of Vofric's shoulders. The dwarf took one more step down the stairs then stood at attention.

King Nasim continued, "Dawncaster could not have battled with newfound might if not for the Sylvan Dragon."

Sariel followed Vofric's lead. Kargon readied himself but didn't sense the king's approach. Soft chuckles from the crowd made clear who would be titled.

"Unexpected power bolstered those blessed by the Guardian Beast," King Nasim announced.

Avant stepped forward and roared. Children happily cheered until they were instructed to stop. It was a calming distraction for Kargon just before a powerful presence appeared behind him. Though he'd stood near the king before, it was never so daunting. But King Nasim did not garner fear, only reverence.

"Few can say they have withstood the flames of a dragon like the Firebrand," he said pridefully.

Feeling the weight of the blade made clear how heavy the duty of a king was. Kargon's spine tingled as his relationship with fire was brought up again. But this was no place to ask questions. Instead he quietly stepped forward and joined the crowd in waiting to hear the Hero's title. She stood with her head high, exuding a mighty aura.

"When the opportunity came for the Hero to leave, she refused and aided us. She led not only her allies but our guards. At every encounter, she found a solution." King Nasim paused, studying the eyes of the waiting crowd. " This city will never forget what you did for us. Thank you, Champion of Dawncaster."

The crowd cheered and Kargon couldn't stop himself from joining them. He turned slightly to look at Aisha and noticed the entire party doing the same. A smirk appeared on Sariel's face as they clapped. Gruff cheers erupted from Vofric that matched Avant's hoots of excitement. Rusty and Julian ignored decorum and roared joyously. Howls that drowned out the crowd erupted from the Greycastles.

Queen Lyra joined King Nasim in holding the sword as they blessed the Hero. Tears flowed from Aisha's good eye as she stepped forward and the city cheered for her humility. It only stopped after King Nasim slowly sheathed the sword. He had little else to say and gestured for his son to speak.

"Aisha, our champion, brought attention to a mistake made by our ancestors that I will remedy. Kharim was indeed a Hero but those who stood alongside him were no less. However, they have been lost to time. That shall not happen again. Aisha is not a lone Hero." Makani didn't bother hiding a smile as he looked between the adventurers in front of him. "These heroes strengthened Dawncaster. Let us honor their deeds with proper reverence!"

Kargon didn't think it was possible for the crowd to cheer any louder than they already had. And not only for Aisha but the whole party. They persisted as the barricade opened and Aisha led her allies forward. Albert, Mia, and Louise signaled the party forward towards the middle of the street where a carriage awaited, surrounded by guards. Kargon and Aisha quickly thanked the gods that it looked plain.

Makani, however, revealed there was more to it. "Sariel provided us with a strong base for the carriage but that alone wouldn't be enough for your journey. The artificers of Zeffari crafted an engine and steering system so you may travel without need for a horse."

"I shall pilot the vehicle first," Sariel said readily.

"You're the only one trained to," Kargon replied as he looked at the driver seat, completely unaware how to operate the engine and lever.

Vofric cleared his throat. "I expect us all to learn the intricacies of the carriage."

The party was showered in gifts and gratitude while slowly preparing the carriage. Kargon couldn't imagine how much it would cost to commission such a vehicle.

"Looks like you gave my kid some ideas," Mia said to the party as she checked the last of the supplies.

Vofric laughed. "He would have done similarly in due time. Thankfully he will not be alone."

"Wouldn't have been able to help as much as I did if not for you," Albert said.

"None of us assisted you in befriending Prince Makani." Sariel added.

Albert shook his head. "I just followed Kargon's lead. He's always supporting the Hero. Figured I could do the same."

Kargon scoffed, "I don't remember instructing you. Just make sure to keep up with him. So, he doesn't feel alone at the top."

The boy contemplated the words and nodded.

"You take care of yourselves, okay?" Louise instructed. She hugged Avant and whispered, "I packed some extra snacks for you." He nuzzled against her before being placed in the carriage.

"Thank you for giving us a place to stay while we were here," Aisha said.

Louise tightly grabbed the Hero's hands and smiled. "You're family now. Come back any time."

Aisha stepped into the carriage followed by Vofric. Kargon thanked the Greycastles and joined his party. Sariel readily took the wheel and started the engine by cranking the lever on their right. One last cheer erupted from the crowd as the party drove out of the gate.

"Thank you, heroes!" King Nasim and his family bellowed as a powerful gust of wind pushed the cart forward.

Vofric hummed softly while Avant sniffed the bags in search of food. Aisha sighed, leaning on Kargon and wiping her tears. Their time in Dawncaster was far different than what the young adventurers expected. But they would remember it fondly. Kargon took a long breath, his heart pounding with anticipation at the sight from the front of the carriage. There was a long road ahead.

CHAPTER TWENTY-THREE

Routine

Within a couple weeks the party encountered their first snowfall; a sign of the coming new year. Worldwide beliefs stated that the heavens provided a white sheet to clear away the marks of the past ten months. Which was an intriguing idea but didn't diminish how annoying it was to deal with. For privacy the party used routes that few people knew about and thus they were packed with snow. Navigation would have been harder if not for the map provided by the Dicoris family.

A carriage's thin wooden wheels were especially slow in inclement weather. While everyone else considered normal ways to traverse the perilous roads, Sariel handcrafted a solution. They examined the tires and firmly grasped one. Vines emerged from the central structure and wound around each spoke while firmly digging into them. Simultaneously, the wooden pieces grew thick and wide. The final step involved crawling under the wagon to thicken its base to protect from corrosion.

"The engine will fail if we do not lower our speed to compensate for extra weight," Vofric said.

Sariel smirked. "Correct."

They had begun teaching Vofric how to handle the mechanical carriage as the machinery drew his interest. In theory he could operate the carriage like a beginner. In practice, however, the carriage became an extension of the dwarf. Vofric piloted the vehicle as if he'd done it all his life regardless of weather or road conditions.

Nights were often spent off the road to camp. Sometimes, Sariel opted to continue the journey in the middle of the night as they required half as much sleep. Darkvision worked well enough for navigating and if it failed they needed only to wait for sunrise. When no safe camping locations could be found Sariel would drive with light from Vofric's hammer. Unfortunately, it made them obvious targets for anything hiding in the night.

After such an encounter Vofric stated, "It is rather odd that you cannot make a pillar of flame to deter assailants."

"I've tried but my flames refuse to leave me. Even my astral hands can only pass a fire on contact," Kargon said.

"Why not keep stamping the ground in front of us then?" Aisha asked.

"Either you get the nice warm wagon or I attempt to use my astral hands. But I have to ignite for that and I doubt we want to set the carriage on fire."

All of them wore light clothing without the need for their warm outerwear. Through constant practice Kargon learned to radiate heat without igniting. It tempered the wagon and gave respite from the increasingly cold weather.

"We'll keep the warm wagon. It helps us conserve energy so fighting and hunting isn't as rough," Aisha explained. Kargon didn't need convincing since producing heat had become second nature after his tribulations.

"Even when we do, Avant handles the tough part."

The owlbear tilted his head at his master and chirped softly. After repeated responses, Kargon had come to understand the motion as acknowledgment. Though it was odd to see it come from a different colored beast. During the cub's seasonal molting, his feathers went from dark auburn to white with gray specks. Only his snowy undercoat remained unchanged.

People often scoffed at the idea of domesticated owlbears. They were considered too aggressive and prone to bestial rampages. Those exact qualities made Avant the perfect adventurer. His persistent focus was the reason he led hunts. Vofric and Aisha stayed with the carriage while Sariel and Kargon accompanied the owlbear. In order to avoid giving themselves away, the monk stopped emanating warmth and everyone equipped a coat.

With his beak in the snow, Avant blended in perfectly with soft layers covering his fur. Working together, he and Sariel could track things with pinpoint hearing. Silent and specific movements were all they used to communicate. Once Avant caught the scent of something he moved quickly, pushing through the snow without a care. When they got close he was much more deliberate. Slow steps carved a path for his master to follow without disturbing anything.

A group of deer grazed on leaves and plants amongst tightly packed trees. If not for Avant's sudden stop Kargon wouldn't have noticed. Cold air formed a cloud of vapor as he let out a steady breath while waiting for the next signal. Avant leapt into the crowd and roared, hoping to scatter the prey. Unfortunately, some were ready to attack the small beast they outnumbered.

That was Kargon's signal to move.

Using the trees for leverage, he quickly closed the gap with the closest prey. Antlers were far too threatening for the docile nature deers displayed. Head down, it charged at Kargon. Avant behind his master and ready to fight. If Kargon dodged, the deer could skewer or trample the cub. Snow crunched with each furious step. Several more and it would be within reach.

There was no reason to wait. Kargon opened his palm and slammed it to the ground, igniting it mid-motion. Instantly, an astral palm appeared over the deer and pressed it to the dirt.

A messy pattern appeared around the blazing fighter's palm where snow had rapidly melted. The beast fought back but Kargon continued to hold it down, hoping not to needlessly kill it. If the final signal didn't happen soon, there was no other choice.

An arrow whistled through the sky before hitting something that yelped. Sariel had successfully hunted something nearby. Carefully, Kargon released the deer and it dashed away.

Avant chirped for his master's attention and led the way to their ally. Sariel examined a deer carcass for safe consumption. Once confirmed, the group could return to camp. Being the owlbear's backup wasn't the reason Kargon joined the hunts. Rather, Avant and Sariel requested the monk come along to transport their quarry.

"As a physical combatant, you must train your muscles," Sariel had explained.

Originally Kargon complained about the comment but the elf was right. Rage and instinctual movements were unreliable. Numerous hunts helped the brawler pack on muscle. But he still moved slowly on the way to camp while the others sought out firewood. Aisha suggested using the monk as a fire but the idea of smelling like an inviting meal was detrimental. They already attracted predators while camping, there was no reason to make it worse.

Bandits were the least of the party's concerns. Shambling undead of all kinds wandered the land. Humanoids and animals alike hunted living beings—making the untraveled road more perilous. The adventurers always stopped to deal with them lest someone unprepared succumb to the monsters.

Fortunately, any adversary they encountered had to contend with the Hero. Lightning bent at impossible arcs to collide with targets. Regardless of the speed of their dodges, they couldn't escape. Even with her back turned, Aisha could fire a bolt through an enemy before they reached her.

For battles on the road, Sariel built a grid of foot high rails across the wagon roof. With precise movements Aisha locked herself in place to retaliate even while the carriage sped through the forest.

"Are you sure you can't warm me up while I'm out there?" Aisha asked as she returned to the wagon after an attack. She tossed her snow covered coat into the corner with the rest.

"For the last time, no. I'd have to go up with you and that'd make me a hindrance. Not to mention the rest of the carriage would get cold," Kargon protested.

Aisha pouted and sat down. "Avant, help me since your father refuses."

The owlbear trilled and cuddled with her. A low grumble emanated from Kargon as he kept his focus on the trail behind them in case there were any remaining enemies. Vofric chuckled while stepping into the cart from his perch out front.

"Intriguing that you don't contest being called Avant's father," he said.

"I know what I am," the monk replied absentmindedly.

"Kargon, we have escaped. Shut the door, please. I would like a brief moment to drive smoothly," Sariel complained.

"Right."

Once he was situated, Kargon unfurled the map. Marks all over represented their past campsites. While he didn't have Sariel's natural sense for navigation, Kargon was quickly learning the lay of the vast land. Aisha tried to learn it as well but outside city gates she was seemingly incapable. The roads stretched for hundreds of miles in every direction. Some towns and forests sprinkled the continent in inexplicable ways. Only one thing was abundantly clear; Gromsev, Elmud's home, was still far from reach.

CHAPTER TWENTY-FOUR

Brief Respite

Fog laid across the dark forest like a thick mass and clouded stars from view. No amount of darkvision provided a clear perspective. Vofric's light hammer had its light suffocated by the surroundings. Even the length of the carriage proved too much to see across. Something about the situation sent a chill down Aisha's spine. Without hesitating, he rested a hand on hers with Avant underneath. It was all any of them could do to comfort Aisha in an unfamiliar situation.

"Are there any landmarks near our destination?" Sariel's disembodied voice asked.

"It's a small town," Kargon replied. "There should be a gate. Maybe some lights."

"Vofric, watch our flanks. The road is difficult to view."

Light footsteps on the roof echoed in every direction. That compounded with every unseen thing Aisha sensed made her shiver furiously. Every part of her hoped it would reveal itself for battle. At least then she wouldn't feel out of control.

"Sariel, make a sharp right. We almost passed Foxhill," Vofric commanded.

They gripped the lever to their right while simultaneously tapping the pedals in front of them. A forceful shift in momentum caused the carriage to skid sideways before facing the correct direction. Dim lights in the distance invited the adventurers to approach.

Vofric grumbled as he climbed down from the roof. "Normally such a maneuver does not upset my stomach."

"Probably because you can usually see what's around us," Aisha said, peering into the fog.

Spherical lamps atop stone pillars straddled a metal gate that sat open. Loose pebbles rattled furiously when entering Foxhill. Decrepit wood hung in shambles overhead and dull lights flickered along the street. It was odd to think of Foxhill as a town. A single long street with buildings on either side was less than Wolden had to offer. At the end was the town hall, equally as worn down as everything else. Service Towns were common but Kargon imagined they would be better maintained to entice adventurers.

There was no one in sight and the only interior lights came from a building near the center of town. Signage hanging on the front had symbols representing an inn and tavern. A man stepped out and greeted the party as the carriage slowed.

"Welcome to Foxhill! Are you folks looking for a place to refresh from a long journey? Foxhill Inn is the place for you!" he said. "I'm Troy, the proprietor of this fine establishment."

Aisha poked her head out of the wagon and examined the man. There was nothing out of the ordinary at a glance. Patchwork clothes laid loosely across his easygoing form. Wearing a sunhat at night was odd but eccentricities were commonplace in Tetria.

"Hello. Is there somewhere to store our carriage?" she asked.

With a nod, the man led them to the side of his inn. White lines on the ground and an already stowed carriage made it obvious where Sariel should stop.

"This area is under our watch. Feel free to leave anything you need here until you head out," Troy said.

Disregarding the suggestion, Vofric made sure everyone carried their necessities. It was an innocuous word but the party knew it meant to grab their armor and weapons.

While double checking their gear, Sariel's ears twitched. "Keep your wits about you," they whispered while going into the inn.

The interior was better kept than everything else in town. Bright lights hung from simple metal structures over wooden tables and chairs. A door led to the kitchen and stairs on the opposite side of the room led upstairs.

"Two rooms," Aisha said as she slid into a seat.

"With your pet that'll bump the price up to ten silver," Troy replied while pouring water for each guest and placing a bowl on the floor for Avant.

Aisha nodded to Vofric and he passed a gold coin to the innkeeper.

"Oh ho! A proper gold coin! Let me put this away and get you a meal," Troy said excitedly.

The moment he turned his back, Aisha looked around with her magic eye. The water was safe and there didn't seem to be anything else in the tavern. She cautiously sipped her water as Troy hastily returned with stew and placed them on the table; smiling widely at the impressive meal.

"I've got plenty ready since everyone's still out," he said.

No one thought Troy would be the first to acknowledge the lack of residents in Foxhill.

"Where are they?" Kargon asked.

"Barone, our mayor, went out earlier and hasn't returned," Troy replied with a nonchalant wave of his hand. "She can't remember directions very well and likely got lost in the forest. Some other adventurers offered to search for her and our townsfolk joined them. I stayed back to greet anyone who arrived. I'm really sorry if our little town isn't what you were expecting."

"Please don't apologize. We appreciate your hospitality," Aisha said.

Something triggered her instincts and sent her knee into the bottom of the table. Quick reactions stopped her from cracking the simple wooden furniture. No one turned to Sariel as they could all hear soft taps under the floorboards.

"Rats," Troy said readily. "Been an issue but I have trouble evicting those little vermin."

"Understandable." Sariel nodded then shot a glance at Aisha.

She took a purposeful sip of her stew and hummed in delight. "I'd offer our help but we've been traveling all day. May we rest before assisting in your search?"

Troy nodded and placed two keys on the table. "Don't worry, miss. I'm sure we'll find her by morning. Please enjoy your stay. Your rooms are at the end of the hall upstairs. If you need anything, just shout my name. Thin walls can be useful."

Leaving a woman wandering a forest at night went against everything Kargon believed an adventurer should do. Fog was still present and made it nearly impossible to navigate on foot. But he knew better than anyone that Aisha wouldn't do something like this without reason. Even Vofric was nonchalantly eating his meal instead of demanding they aid the lost woman. Something was amiss with the party but neither Nevesi could put a finger on it.

Once Troy collected the bowls, everyone went upstairs. Kargon's memory of the meal was hazy but he felt full. It wasn't a concern compared to whatever his allies needed to talk about. The moment a door was unlocked, the party pushed inside and Aisha locked the door. Everyone hurried to the far corner of the room to huddle.

"Why are we denying him help?" Aisha whispered immediately.

"Something is wrong," Sariel replied with the same hushed tone.

"I agree. We'd normally help find the mayor," Kargon said.

Vofric shook his head. "No, Kargon. Sariel is saying something in this town is amiss."

"What?" Aisha asked with an impressively quiet fury.

"I do not know but what kind of adventurer allows civilians to assist in a search?"

Kargon huffed. "Vofric! Albert helped us in Dawncaster."

"Because I vouched for him," Vofric protested.

"Maybe someone vouched for the civilians," Aisha said.

Sariel rolled her eyes. "All of them?"

Aisha clicked her tongue and sighed while meeting Kargon's gaze. A similar groan passed his lips as realization dawned. Something so obvious shouldn't have slipped either of their minds. The stew couldn't be drugged since, unfortunately, the party knew what that felt like. But something was clearly affecting their minds, clouding their judgment without overpowering it.

"Troy is likely involved," Aisha said. "Things seemingly bend to his whims."

"The stew came out too fast," Kargon muttered.

Sariel grunted. "The carriage lot did not exist until I asked about it. Though I do not sense anything happening there through my ward."

"Equip your armor and make ready to depart," Vofric said. "We should not remain here any longer."

"Agreed," Aisha said.

They carried their armor during every break yet Kargon was thankful Vofric had insisted. Though he and Sariel didn't need to add anything to what they already wore, Aisha and Vofric needed to equip their platemail. An ear to the door allowed Sariel to listen for movement nearby. Meanwhile, Kargon put on his goggles and stood watch by the window. With the useless lamps outside it was difficult to discern anything in the fog. The curtain didn't help but parting it risked them being seen.

Focusing was difficult with rats continuing to scurry throughout the building. With every passing moment the sounds grew more fervent. Tiny claws scratched against stone floors with maddening clarity. It was impossible to discern distance based on the frequency of the sounds. Especially odd was that hundreds of unseen rats were capable of completely masking their chatters.

The stress of the situation allowed Avant to pace around the room without supervision. Surprisingly silent steps carried him towards the wardrobe where a small crack in the door was used by the owlbear to pull it open. Fine wood grain defined its walls except for a small broken piece at the back that led into a tiny passage. Even a newborn Avant wouldn't have fit inside.

The unnerving sound of him chomping something caught everyone's attention. With a fierce twist, he threw the morsel into the middle of the room. Five slender fingers wriggled furiously as their palm fought to turn over. A bone jutted out of the end of its severed wrist. With a powerful push it flipped over before slowly facing each adventurer; its nails scratching against stone. The claw dashed for the door but was stopped by a sword stabbing through the palm.

"That's what was bothering me. We've been surrounded since we got in the fog," Aisha said with relief. "Kargon, window. We need to go."

Within seconds of her best friend pulling open the window, Aisha leapt through. The fog was so thick it barely dispersed when she landed past the surface. Standing tall revealed only her torso. Sariel followed their leader with Vofric close behind. The clouds of vapor moved around his head as he let out a low grumble. Only his head peeked out from under the mist.

"Avant, the fog's a problem. You're with me," Kargon said.

If not for the monk's training, he would have been bowled over by the growing cub. Everyone had drawn their weapons by the time he landed nearby. Sariel guided them towards the carriage, keeping a sharp eye on their surroundings. Puffs of fog shifted as crawling claws underneath rushed at the adventurers. Before anyone could act, Avant jumped from his master's arms. Bones broke in the unseen cloud as the young beast crushed his foes. Some claws leapt from the ground but were stopped by Kargon, Aisha, and Vofric. He only used his light hammer in fear of hitting Avant. There wasn't a clear sign that there were fewer monsters but the sound dulled enough for Sariel to acknowledge it.

"We're clear!" they said and ran for the carriage.

In response, Avant roared to stun any remaining claws long enough for everyone to disengage. Sariel opened the wagon door then rushed to the driver's seat before belting out the power word. The party piled in with seconds to spare before the carriage peeled out of the alley. Squelches and screeches accompanied bumps on the road. Crawling claws couldn't move fast enough to outmaneuver Sariel.

The adventurer's carriage burst through the metal gates but everything was still impossible to see. Lights from the lamps vanished from view behind the party and blurred luminescence appeared ahead.. Following the presence brought them back to the gate of Foxhill.

"Peculiar," Sariel muttered.

They turned around and drove as straight as possible. Without the slightest deviation in their movement, they returned to the gate. Just in case, Sariel had Vofric take the wheel. Within seconds, they were within the walls again with loud tapping below the wagon.

Vofric grumbled. "We're trapped."

"This may be a spell cast by Troy," Sariel answered.

"He had no magic around him," Aisha said. With a gasp she attempted to detect magic again. "The town hall! There's a strong aura coming from there."

Kargon grunted, "Go! Maybe Troy wasn't lying about the mayor being in danger."

"That's... twisted. Vofric, go for it."

Crawling claws slowed their assault as the party approached the town hall. No fog clung to the building and by the time they reached the entrance, it was safe to get off the carriage. Rotting wood defied logic to stay upright as misaligned planks held the door in frame. It fell from a single knock. The only source of light in the building was Vofric's small hammer. What appeared from outside as a large multi-roomed structure was an illusion hiding a single room with a stone slab covered in engraved names.

Kargon was the first to notice that amongst the rows of names were Troy Oakenheel and Barone Xande. Bloody handprints marked the long forgotten individuals.

"Why would you do this?!" Troy screamed from outside.

The power of his voice forced away the remaining fog and revealed the decrepit town. Flattened claws littered the street. Those with life remained still at the innkeeper's side. The party exited the town hall to face what was obviously no longer humanoid. Large gashes revealed necrotic muscle across his body. Teeth clattered against each other through his cheeks. Without a hat it was possible to see the massive pieces missing from his skull and brain.

"You went to the forest! You could escape!" he yelled. "I did not act suspicious for you to come back here!"

"Act?" Aisha gasped as realization dawned. "The stew. You were supposed to drug it—"

"But I didn't! I forced the claws to move actively to scare you off. Why did you return?!"

"Foxhill is enchanted. We are unable to leave," Vofric insisted.

Troy's face dropped. "No... That would mean she's aware..."

Something entered town, grotesquely crawling across the stone pavement at high speed. Within seconds it was across Foxhill and behind Troy. A long breath accompanied a chorus of creaking bones as it stood upright. Crimson orbs hung in hollow sockets where eyes should be over jagged teeth drenched in viscera. Tattered rags draped over the creature held a damaged badge.

"Mayor Barone, you've returned," Troy said meekly.

"They no...t sleep, Troy," she panted hungrily. "I lock Fo...xhill. No one go."

"You can't keep doing this. They are innocent."

"Adventurers help. Need... food. Help with... food."

Troy yelled to the adventurers, "Run! Please!"

Barone moved unlike other undead and was on Kargon in seconds. Nails like jagged claws ripped through his armor and into his chest. During contact, the image of a black crystal flashed in his mind. Aisha threw the creature off and Kargon fell to his knees, choking on blood. Adrenaline wasn't enough to protect him from failing organs. Thankfully, Vofric began healing the moment Barone was thrown back.

Even in the air she was able to dodge a rain of arrows. Only one got close but unfortunately it passed through an opening in the ghoul's leg. While Barone focused on Sariel's volley, Avant rushed in—fur bristling in rage. With a wild charge, he knocked Barone to the ground. She maneuvered with ease on all fours; arms functioning as pivot points while kicks riddled the owlbear. One landed firmly on his side and threw him to the ground. An axe kick threatened his head but was blocked by Aisha's sword. With careful movements she threw the monster off balance and tried to cut through its torso. Barone placed all her weight on one hand and ducked under the blade before retaliating with a roundhouse. Disgusting claws on her toes cut Aisha's arm. The zombie tried to attack again but stopped short as a golden glow wreathed the Hero.

The wound wouldn't heal without contact but it was less painful. Vofric's eyes were trained on the creature as he muttered a prayer. No fear was evident on his face and Barone dashed up to him then stopped. Cackles echoed through the empty town as she stood over him. Foolish confidence never went far with the dwarf. Barone brought her claws down on his armor only to be burned by holy light on contact.

While the creature remained distracted, Sariel fired two barbed arrows; piercing the monster's feet and binding it to the stone floor. Trying to pull herself free left Barone unaware of the fast approaching owlbear. A mighty leap sent Avant hurtling at her torso from the right. In tandem, Aisha swung her blade from the left. Barone took the brunt of the owlbear's charge and used it to twist away from Aisha. It was to no avail as *Valefor* ripped one of the creature's arms clean from the socket.

The zombie released a guttural roar, spewing remnants of her meals on the warriors. With Vofric's help Kargon rejoined the fight and approached the monster from behind with ignited hands. A firm grip and shove jerked Barone's head back. An astral hand at her torso mimicked the motion and forced the monster prone.

"There's a crystal in her neck!" Kargon yelled.

"Shatter it!" Troy screamed.

Whenever Vofric empowered his war-hammer it was like light was fighting to burst out of the weapon. Its radiance was almost painful after being in the dark so long. Barone screamed in horror while lashing out at the monk who responded by burning brighter while awaiting Vofric's attack. There was no need to aim a weapon that eclipsed its target in size. The paladin grunted to signal the stone bludgeon's descent towards his ally's hands. Once it passed Kargon's eye line, he jumped back. One second later and he would've been minced like Barone. Bones, stone, and muscles turned into a fine paste that gripped at the war-hammer as it was pulled back.

Slowly, the haze around Foxhill lifted and stars illuminated the night sky. Every illusion vanished with only Troy left standing on the empty streets of his town.

"She hunted adventurers since we returned," he said shamefully. "I was a husk like her. Thank you for ending... this place."

"How long have you been doing this?" Aisha asked with the same hunch the rest of her party had.

"Weeks ago we awoke in a version of Foxhill that no longer exists," Troy explained. "Adventurers unaware that the town had fallen came seeking aid. Barone was hungry and I felt a compulsion to help her. As time passed my mind grew clearer and I could no longer stand for what she was doing."

Vofric inquired, "Why did you not release the curse sealing the town?"

"There wasn't one before. Barone was capable of it in life and seemingly reacquired the ability..."

Troy's legs wavered and the light in his eyes vanished. The sound of a body collapsing on stone masked his last thanks. Aisha silently lifted the man's body and placed it on what remained of Barone. As she stepped away, she whispered something to Sariel. Roots burst from the ground and laid across the corpses before Aisha looked at Vofric. The holy man nodded before saying a brief prayer. Even Avant remained silent, watching the late funeral. Finally, Aisha looked at her best friend. They knew not everyone followed Nevesi traditions but it was the safest choice at present.

Two flaming astral hands appeared over the roots. A slow, deliberate descent touched the flora and set them ablaze along with the last Foxhill villagers.

Once the fire died down, Aisha walked towards the carriage. "Elmud... their master's power reanimated people who've been dead."

Vofric grimaced. "To be forced into the role of a monster against one's will is a nightmarish curse."

"Yet we must defeat them. Lest the deceased be remembered for the actions of a husk." Sariel added.

They climbed into the carriage with a collective sigh. Though the day's journey weighed on them, no one shut their eyes. Sleep was unwelcome after the night's events.

CHAPTER TWENTY-FIVE

Inferior/Superior

It took another month before the Hero's party arrived at the base of Mount Ikrali. A small town, Lokral, provided a place to rest and gather supplies before attempting to climb the mountain to find Gromsev. As badly as the group wanted to press forward, it wasn't possible during the early parts of winter.

"How long do you think we should wait?" Aisha asked while cupping her hands under a mug of hot chocolate.

"Travel will be safest in five months," Vofric answered, already dreading the response. "At the earliest; two months."

There wasn't much debate beyond that since it was impossible to see the mountain path. Exploring the nearby forest and assisting townsfolk made the say much easier. Many tried to give the party goods for free but Aisha refused to take any unless she could pay. It was almost peaceful if not for the ever-present weight of what Elmud and their master were doing. The moment a path appeared on the mountain, the party would continue their quest.

Snow began to melt and cool rain fell from the sky. The party knew spring was coming when Avant began to molt; his chocolatey brown fur returning. Sariel returned the carriage to its original form albeit with channels to divert water. They were off before anyone could protest.

Wet stones reflecting bright light made the path easy to find but difficult to look at. Light rain was manageable but on the off chance of a downpour, the party had to stop. It was too late to turn back but Vofric would be damned to risk everyone's lives in hopes of traveling a few miles.

It took a week of slow maneuvering to reach the mountain village of Gromsev; a rest area for anyone crossing the mountain.. Sturdy wooden structures bridged gaps off wide roads snaking back and forth along the ridge. Silhouettes of flying humanoids hovered in the sky, going about their business. There was no reason to attack the village's dragominn unless they acted first.

Large holes carved into the mountain were modified into enclosures. One by the village entrance had stables for horses and stalls for carriages. Sariel slowed down to speak with the large dragominn operating the garage.

With a skeptical eye he examined the modified vehicle before addressing the draconic elf. "You must rent a stable and a carriage stall," he grumbled.

"We do not possess a horse," Sariel replied.

"I'm aware. You must pay for both."

The half open door to the garage revealed only a single used stable and slot out of several empty ones.

"It's fine, Sariel," Aisha said and stepped down. "May we leave our bags?"

The dragominn was hesitant at the sight of a fully armored adventurer. But it was expected for bestial humanoids to be on high alert. Within seconds, the operator was composed again.

"Five gold pieces," he replied.

"Five?!" Kargon asked loudly, stumbling off the carriage. "That's unheard of even with a horse. I'd understand two but—"

Aisha fished five coins from her pack and handed them over. A studious expression appeared on the dragominn's face as he examined the coins carefully and waved Sariel in. More arguments were on the tip of Kargon's tongue but Aisha dragged him away by the arm he did something stupid.

"Remember where we are," she whispered as they walked behind the vehicle. "This is Elmud's home. They may not accept us simply due to our races."

Vofric exited and shook his head. "That is incorrect. I have visited this village in the past. They are likely wary after news of Dawncaster spread."

"It is also possible they recognize Aisha." Sariel added.

Kargon sighed. "So, the weather and the people will be cold here. Wonderful."

Avant chirped in agreement as the upper half of Mount Ikrali was perpetually covered in snow. Everyone dawned overcoats to stop Kargon's heat and avoid unnecessary attention. It was the last thing they needed while looking into Elmud's past. The garage operator checked on the party, noticed they were done retrieving their items, and waved them out of the stall. After the last of them stepped out, he pulled the doors shut then muttered something. A near imperceptible wall grew from the top of the fence and completely surrounded the carriage.

"If you must retrieve anything, let me know. I am always here," the dragominn said and walked away. His attitude was unwelcoming but he took his job seriously.

Upon exiting the garage, everyone's attention turned towards the paths connecting the village. Large amounts of space covered by bridges made the village feel bigger than it was. Absentminded explorers could easily find themselves plummeting to a lower level or further. Sariel and Aisha couldn't easily leap from around without risk of breaking something. Vofric, on the other hand, needed to jump between planks due to spaces being too large for his size. In order for Avant to get around he needed to remain in Kargon's grasp. The monk's experience clambering around Dawncaster was useful moving around Gromsev.

The first step to uncovering Elmud's secret was complete yet they found themselves stagnant once again. Villagers intermittently descended from the sky only to avoid the outsiders and continue about their day. Signs were written in a script only Sariel understood. All nearby enclosures ended up being private domiciles. Gromsev didn't see outsiders nor care to welcome them.

"This does not make sense," Vofric said. "Gromsev must be encountered to pass Mount Ikrali. The lack of an inn or tavern is illogical."

"Was there one when you visited last time?" Kargon asked.

"I did not stay long enough to warrant seeking one out."

They stood on one of many bridges scattered along the snowy cliffs. While Aisha looked out towards the horizon, Sariel squinted at the carvings in the mountain. Kargon followed suit and noticed a larger enclosure in a deep gouge of the mountain with a stone door. A plaque was bolted to one wall with symbols he couldn't read.

"Sariel, is that what I think it is?"

They smirked. "Outsiders are not welcome to stay, only imbibe."

Only dragominn occupied the tavern and glanced towards the new entrants. Thankfully, the villagers didn't seem to care and continued discussing recent events. Namely, the changes Tetria went through as a result of the Dawncaster attack. Rumors of a failed undead attack on Gromsev caught the party's attention.

"When did that happen?" Aisha asked loudly to the small group at a nearby table.

They looked her over and their faces sank.

"We had nothing to do with it," one replied defensively. "It's just something we saw." They led their group away before more questions could be asked.

A waiter approached the adventurer's table with their costly mugs of mead. She nodded to Aisha and said, "You're the Champion of Dawncaster. We all know why."

"I won't apologize for killing someone who sent an army of monsters to attack a city of innocents," Aisha grumbled and took a swig of her drink.

"No one's demandin' it. But they ain't gonna welcome you either. You killed one of our own."

Sariel furrowed her brow. "Are we to assume you hold the same beliefs as the fanatic?"

"No, of course not!" the waiter replied immediately. "It's just... You're the first adventurers who've come here since the news spread. Are we wrong to fear your wrath? Or to think you see us all as monsters?"

"I fail to see why you would be equated to monsters," Vofric pried.

"Well— It's—"

An older dragominn woman approached the table and softly patted the waiter's back. "That's enough dear. I will speak with them."

Defeated, the younger dragominn nodded. Chairs scratched against the ground as more patrons left. It wasn't due to the party but a sign of respect for the village elder. Her request informed the others that privacy was needed which left only the party and a guard inside.

"I apologize for our young one's outburst. One of my lessons was misunderstood," the elder said and sat down.

"Did the same lesson cause Elmud's mindset?" Kargon asked.

The elder nodded sadly.

"Can you tell us more, Elder...?" Aisha said.

"Zhusthum," she answered, then took a long breath. "Gromsev residents are descendants of dragons. Acceptance of our race happened within the last century. I raised many of our youth to use their abilities to help others. To prove dragominn meant no harm. Instead, many secluded themselves in our village."

Aisha shook her head and sighed. "You put a lot of weight on an entire generation's shoulders. It's no wonder Elmud turned out the way they did."

"You are correct," Elder Zhusthum replied sadly while rising to her feet.

The party followed her out of the tavern as the original occupants flooded back in. Slow footsteps led the group upwards. Many of the areas they passed had previously been searched to no avail.

"During their childhood, Elmud began to resent being a dragominn. They believed we were inferior due to humanoid laws that controlled our abilities," Elder Zhusthum said.

"There is no sense behind that thought. It's completely illogical," Sariel replied.

The elder agreed. "There is rarely hope in finding logic behind a child's thoughts."

Homes that weren't built into the mountainside were secured to wooden pathways. One of which sat near the top of the village on long rods that set it hundreds of feet away from the mountain. A thin rope bridge allowed for one person to cross at a time which the party crossed slowly while Elder Zhusthum flew over the gap. Shaky planks that made up the house floor seemed to be placed with no regard for security.

"Elmud rarely placed their feet on Gromsev once they grew wings. It did not take long for them to understand we are more powerful than other humanoids," the elder said. "My teachings of keeping their power under control were seen as heresy and they wanted to prove me wrong. Though I never learned how. Thirty years ago they suddenly left for Dawncaster. I assumed they had calmed down in their middle age but upon seeing images I realized they never did."

"How would you discern their personality from an image?" Vofric asked while looking around the hut.

Elder Zhusthum paused. "I miscommunicated. Elmud had not aged since leaving Gromsev. They had lived nearly sixty years but looked half their age."

"Meaning they probably aren't dead," Aisha said while leafing through loose notes on a shelf of the empty home. "A spell must be helping Elmud keep their youth."

Kargon agreed. "With how they disappeared; Elmud is probably still out there."

"If so, another attack is possible," the elder said sorrowfully. "This is all I can provide you to help discern Elmud's motives. Please stop them however you can."

"We will do whatever is possible. Do not tell your youth to hide their capabilities. Simply educate them on how their actions dictate the opinion others hold," Sariel suggested.

Elder Zhusthum shut her eyes tightly but accepted. "I will do so as long as I remain and teach the next elder to do the same. However, little can be done to garner their support for you as long as Elmud's motives are unknown."

Kargon scoured every nook and cranny for any out of place notes based on damaged clues. For the hut to be smaller than the Dawncaster bunker was ridiculous even if it was on stilts. Elmud clearly only came to the room to sleep and make plans since there was no place to prepare meals.

"Is there somewhere else they went regularly?" Kargon asked. "What happened when Elmud got hungry?"

"There are eatery caves for Gromsev residents who do not have the means to cook at home," Elder Zhusthum answered.

"Lead the way," Aisha said and nodded to her friend. "Good call."

Sariel stopped them and added, "If there are multiple caves we will need to discern which Elmud used."

"Don't overthink it," Vofric said with a hum. "It is likely whichever cave is furthest from here."

It was located at the lowest level of Gromsev. While a dragominn could descend quickly, the party had to slowly trek back down to find the alcove hidden by misshapen rocks. Stools, tables, and cooking pits were carved from the stone that surrounded the room. There were four well-worn stations but they were ignored during the investigation. A small bookshelf near the entrance grabbed everyone's attention. Recipe books both official and homemade were left unattended. Aisha scanned the contents and was drawn to a notebook with handwriting matching the notes in Dawncaster.

Recipes were quickly skimmed over and unrelated notes were too scarce to bother with. That was until the Hero reached the last page and traced her fingers across the final passage.

"These are fresh compared to the others," Aisha explained.

"Elmud returned to leave notes?" Kargon asked,

Sariel scoffed. "The bastard is taunting us. They demand our attention."

"Have they left a location?" Vofric inquired.

Aisha slowly leafed through the notebook again. "There are a lot of recipes with strong effects. It's probably enough power for Elmud to stand with their master."

"The demon king..." Kargon muttered unintentionally when trying to utter his name. "What sort of meal gives enough power to match him?"

"One made of their ancestors."

Elder Zhusthum let out a shaky breath. "The fool is hunting a dragon."

CHAPTER TWENTY-SIX

To the Summit

According to Elder Zhusthum there was only one dragon in the Ikrali region. Legends spoke of a cave at the summit but no one had seen it for centuries. Gromsev residents avoided flying nearby out of concern for their safety. Records proved that dragons had as innumerable personalities as any other race but that didn't lessen the fear people felt in the face of mystical beings. Based on the fact that this one hadn't ever attacked a nearby town, one could only hope it was amiable.

That was assuming Elmud hadn't succeeded in killing it and getting more powerful. It was unlikely they stayed behind. If they failed, it meant a pissed off dragon waiting for the party. Kargon wasn't sure they could defeat such a powerful foe.

There was no way to scale the upper half of the mountain with their carriage. It wasn't so perilous that climbing tools were needed but the path was narrow and unpredictable. Much like midwinter, snow stacked a few inches high with spring showers freezing it near solid. It couldn't hinder Kargon and he could carve a path forward. Camping gear, food, and the sensation of warmth was too inviting for animals not to approach the party. Some were easily scared by the adolescent owlbear while others had to be fought back.

Normally, Sariel would know when threats were coming but their mind was elsewhere. Thankfully, the mountain path had little in way of cover —allowing the others to see incoming danger.

Corpses of long dead kobolds crossed the terrain by digging their boney claws into the ground and wall. Having fought enough undead, the warriors knew they could take some hits. Death was the only way to be turned into a Husk. It put Kargon's mind at ease due to nothing keeping his body away from the monsters. Without hesitation, he grabbed the snouts of the scaled canines and ignited them. If that wasn't enough to kill one, he followed up with a fist through their torso. It was more work than throwing them off the mountain but if they survived the fall, innocents would be attacked.

Precarious footing forced Avant to learn how to fight while remaining grounded. Tackling his opponents knocked them to the floor where he tore them apart with his talons. Meanwhile, Aisha relied on her lightning to avoid unnecessary risks. Fierce shocks cracked bones and left nothing but dust in their wake. The fastest fighter turned out to be Vofric with his blessed light hammer. A single throw tore through multiple monsters before it came flying back.

All the while, Sariel remained absent-minded and silent. A monster could have snuck up on the elf whose eyes were trained on the skyline without a care in the world. Or rather, their cares were unrelated to the matter at hand. Sariel awkwardly apologized after the battle and started walking before anyone had a chance to acknowledge it.

"Are they okay?" Vofric asked.

Kargon shook his head. "No idea."

"I think it's related to their lost memories. Something might be triggering them," Aisha said. "Keep an eye out but let them follow their instincts."

Avant took the instruction in stride, keeping pace with their elvish companion while the others followed close behind. Whenever Sariel muttered something, the young owlbear responded with a series of chirps and growls. In turn, Sariel spoke more. Kargon couldn't help but feel a little jealous at their fluent conversation. Though that faded when anything important happened and Avant relied on his master.

The owlbear barked for Kargon to examine the path ahead. Jagged rocks and broken stone melded into slate into a smooth, cohesive road that spiraled upward to the summit. Sariel paused at the first step off the rubble let out a slow breath; tears welling in their draconic eye.

"Lead the way," Aisha said softly and patted Sariel's back.

"I am unsure why but I require time to collect myself. You may go ahead," they suggested.

Avant let out a soft bark and turned to Kargon.

He nodded and said, "We'll wait."

"Take your time, friend." Vofric added.

Shakily, Sariel wiped their face in confusion. They'd expressed emotions before but having only their mutated half do so was jarring. Everyone stood in silence as the elf muttered quietly. A memory flashed in Kargon's mind and demanded explanation. There may never be a proper time to ask about it and though he'd be going against his word, Sariel would surely understand given the circumstances.

"Did your memories start coming back when we heard the demon king's name?" Kargon asked.

"Why do you ask that?" Aisha inquired.

"Kargon is always observing us." Sariel explained, "My memories did not return but his name triggered a sensation like my scales were tearing through me. I do not know how it relates to my amnesia."

"Why not tell us?"

Sariel sighed. "I am still unsure what it meant. The undue stress is better kept to myself."

"Sharing one's concerns with friends eases stress," Vofric said. "Do so when ready."

Sariel looked at each of their friends slowly and nodded before silently continuing towards Mount Ikrali's summit. Light shined on the precipice that stood over all of Tetria. The southwest was covered in forests that hid Neves. Unsettling waters rippled violently to the south. Particles of moonlight encompassed the land—originating from the western Dawncaster.

"I can't believe Kharim protected all this," Aisha said, turning to the unknown east. "From this high it's impossible to even see who I'm protecting. Not to mention how much Tetria's evolved since Kharim's time. Am I really supposed to protect more than the first Hero?"

It was obvious to everyone that their leader was overwhelmed. Unfortunately, this was unlike Balur where her doubts were rooted in lies from the elves. Logical concerns were harder to alleviate. But some part of the Hero always fought back against encroaching fears. A part that Kargon was thankful for and glad the others were growing familiar with.

"Fighting for others does not guarantee recognition," Vofric said. "I cannot remember how many people I have defended in my time adventuring. All I know is to hold my ground. Every enemy vanquished saves lives."

Sariel grunted. "Assuming Tetria has evolved, you must accept that all its inhabitants have as well. Thus, Kharim would not be enough to protect it now."

Aisha slowly outstretched her arm, her palm facing an unknown city in the distance. Blocking it from view was difficult and she slowly waved to obscure different parts but never the entirety. "It'll take a lot of effort to even protect one place," she said sadly. "And the chances I fail are astronomically high."

Kargon mimicked Aisha, making a point to block another portion of the city from her view. "You keep saying 'I' need to protect the world. Consider that you have a party fighting with you that you handpicked."

"Avant was your choice." Aisha smirked.

Kargon rolled his eyes. "I asked permission."

Avant grunted affirmatively, flopping onto his stomach and blocking a random portion of the city with outstretched paws. A large eastern portion was blocked by Vofric's worn right hand. Sariel hesitated, staring at their hands before slowly reaching out with the draconic claw.

They sighed. "My bow would reach farther than this."

"My hammer would not cover even this much space." Vofric chuckled. "Though, with us working together, Tetria will be protected. Am I correct, Hero?"

Aisha smiled and nodded. "You may have a point." With a step back, she finally examined the flattened peak they occupied. "Where to next?"

Instinctively, everyone looked towards Sariel whose arm remained outstretched. As if a layer of dust was stripped by the sunlight, their forest green scales transformed into a shining metallic emerald. Both eyes turned luminescent citrine as Sariel let out a groan of pain. They roared and swiped a claw over the land, shifting the ground to reveal a hidden entrance.

It dropped into a cavern which snaked all the way through Mount Ikrali. Sariel was the first one down and rushed into the dark. The opening disappeared under rigid vines that locked into place; hidden within the rocky outer layer.

Sariel led with confidence and caution since whoever, or whatever, claimed the cave as home would be a threat. Elder Zhusthum's warnings remained at the forefront of the party's minds. There was little doubt they had entered the lair of a dragon. Glowing stones embedded in the walls provided dim light that bounced off melted gold fused to the ground. There were no stories about dragons parting with their horde so it was likely this one had been robbed. The path widened to reveal a distinct lack of treasure as it grew scarce.

"How is this structure standing if it gets wider as we descend?" Kargon asked as he stared at the distant ceiling. "It should have collapsed."

"We've seen plenty of bolstering spells. Now shut up! Our voices might alert someone," Aisha whispered.

Kargon forgot a possible encounter—a dragon's Husk waiting for a fresh meal. He shut his eyes to quiet his fears and nearly tripped, only stopped by Vofric's out-stretched arm.

Four paths stood in front of them led into random tunnels. No treasure remained to follow but large gashes in the wall made clear where gems were once embedded. Kobolds rested nearby and stared at the group. Aisha held up her hands in a sign of mercy and the creatures returned to their business, seemingly accustomed to the presence of adventurers.

"We could split up," Kargon said. "Once each of us—"

"No," Sariel interjected. "This way."

There was no hesitation in their words or actions. That was one of the reasons Kargon felt more assured about an even tempered cave denizen. Elmud would have eradicated the kobolds and a violent dragon's underlings wouldn't have let adventurers pass peacefully. Without a single hindrance, the Hero's party arrived at a large chamber with few gems remaining in the walls.

Scratches near them showed hesitation in removing them. Gold coins laid in a pile between the party and a huge creature with its back turned. Aisha rested her hand on *Valefor's* hilt but it felt unnecessary as the beast showed no aggression.

Everyone wished for a calm dragon but it was hard to accept what they saw. Myriad scales trailed over every inch of its massive body and tail—wrapped snugly around its side. Claws were stowed under its torso and wings folded on its back.

"There is little left I can offer in payment." A deep voice spoke directly into the minds of the adventurers as the dragon's long neck curved outward, carrying its head into view. Forest green scales complimented jewel-like orange eyes.

"What new knowledge have you acquired?" it asked while scanning over the party. The dragon's gaze froze each of them like a child being scolded by their parents—though significantly more frightening.

Sariel stepped forward with their bow drawn, unable to hide their fear against the daunting opponent. Shaky legs barely kept them upright while summoning the courage to speak. "Did you… do this to me?"

The massive dragon stared soberly at the elf and let out something like a sharp exhale. Without a second thought, the creature morphed. Kargon had heard of dragons taking a humanoid form but seeing it first hand was unfathomable. There was more logic behind Albert's transformation than how the dragon restructured itself into a high elf. Sariel's bow clattered to the floor and they let out a soft whimper as the dragon slowly approached. One hand softly rested on the mutant elf's shoulder and another on their cheek. Something resonated between them, causing Sariel's scales to glow emerald again.

"No, Sariel," the dragon said with tears streaking his face. "No father would hurt his child so."

CHAPTER TWENTY-SEVEN

Dragon Born

Centuries ago, Vethyeans spoke of an emerald dragon seen over the skies of Tetria. Edthecridaldyrth, eclipsed many of his kind in size and had to transform to walk amongst humanoids. No one had proof of the ability and it could only be found in his hidden cave. Fortunately for him, the climb to Mount Ikrali's peak was impossible.

Remnants of failed expeditions were buried under layers of snow. Within the sheets of powder hid rigid vines that stopped anyone from getting halfway up the mountain. The trek couldn't be completed in a single stretch but taking time to rest left expeditionists open to danger. Gear would be shattered or eaten by the land itself—especially those made of precious metals.

Though none reached Mount Ikrali's summit, everyone returned alive. Climbers would fall from great heights and land safely in soft snow. When hunger struck and reserves ran dry, food would appear before them. Edthecridaldyrth was unwelcoming but not murderous. All he wanted was privacy to safely raise his child.

Sariel spent their time digging intricate tunnels under Mount Ikrali to protect their horde. Paths wound underground to traps and dead ends, all manned by kobolds sworn to the dragons. Every once in a while Sariel's tunnels would break through to the outside world. It was crucial they inform Edthecridaldyrth so he could seal the path.

However, rebelliousness is a phase all races go through. Openings that led to the surface became less accidental and haphazardly covered with less secure magic. Light eked through the cracks and shone into Sariel's room. The open sky and fresh air called to the young dragon who'd never flown higher than a few feet off the ground in a looping cavern. Even the kobolds had more opportunities to leave the cave and some chose to never return.

"I wish only to see the mountain range, Ed," Sariel complained. "Allow me to hunt at least."

"It is dangerous," Edthecridaldyrth said as he looked over his recently acquired treasure.

Sariel groaned. "You retrieve treasure and explore Tetria near daily. I simply wish to join you on occasion."

"I understand. It is too dangerous for a child."

"I have lived eighty years! I am not a child!" Sariel roared.

Edthecridaldyrth sighed and looked at his child. "We are dragons. I do not care what others consider a seventy six year old to be. You are a child!"

"What age were you when you could explore the world? Did your mother not allow you to learn through experience?"

"I will not repeat her mistakes." The elder dragon threw down the remaining treasures and left in a huff.

There wouldn't be any further discussion no matter how much Sariel pushed. Tension after arguments made the cave unbearable and Edthecridaldyrth often left to regain composure. The young dragon remained by their horde and stared at the intricate goods from far away lands. Armor worn by knights who served distant royalty laid in a massive pile with intricate jewelry filling the openings. Sariel dreamed of seeing crafters work their talents first hand or whatever else the world had to offer. Waiting for permission would result in never getting a chance to explore.

Sariel returned to their room and stared at the cracked stone walls. Based on the direction of light the sun was setting. No cave denizens came near this room so it was the dragon's only chance to get some fresh air. They placed a claw at the base of the opening and magically tore the roots apart, revealing a sizable hole in the mountainside.

Cool air tickled the muscle beneath Sariel's under-developed scales. The scent of flowers carried from fields at the base of Mount Ikrali. It didn't taste like anything but was more pleasant than the dust and stone they were accustomed to. Slow steps carried them to the edge which provided a clear view of the land below. Cities in the distance were blocked from view by dense forests which housed small villages. It would be days before Edthecridaldyrth's return—plenty of time for the young dragon to explore.

Sariel lifted off, sealed the window, then descended into the forest. All the time spent hovering proved useful within the foliage. Unfortunately, trees often got in the way but were of little consequence. While Sariel was small compared to Edthecridaldyrth, she was massive next to anything else. Trees crumbled from a light impact and crashed in a cacophony. Woodland creatures scurried to safety in fear of the predator above.

Sariel's first stop was a small town nearby with a stone wall surrounding it. A sign hung over its gate marked it as Foxhill. Incapable of transformation, Sariel stepped over the entrance to get into town. There was no way to maneuver without hitting a building so they remained rigid while walking down the single wide street. Sariel's neck craned at awkward angles to look into stores with a massive eye that eclipsed the windows while staring at goods and occupants. Different styles of clothing and armor made it clear that few hailed from Foxhill.

Villagers screamed in horror at the massive beast while others drew weapons. Four different adventurers wielded different kinds of swords Sariel had never seen. Questions flooded their mind but none could be asked before someone lunged and cut the dragon's snout.

Sariel staggered back and yelped, believing the small town wasn't pleased with her lack of decorum. Disappointed, Sariel flew away as scales peeled from their muzzle. This time they went northeast past Mount Ikrali towards a larger city. It had to be more open-minded towards foreign visitors.

Innumerable obelisks stretched high into the sky across a city on unknown terrain. Yellow and brown minerals collected together into a malleable form that blanketed the land; similar to snow but hotter. Unfortunately, Sariel couldn't stay near the ground for long.

Stones launched from trebuchets scattered around the city. They were too fast for an inexperienced Sariel to maneuver around. Vitriolic commands sounded from small humanoids preparing for battle. As the dragon flew higher, they saw hidden warriors launching projectiles of all kinds.

It dawned on Sariel that people feared a dragon's form. It was no wonder Edthecridaldyrth perfected his transformation before stepping into foreign lands. But logic didn't soften the blow. Sariel returned to Mount Ikrali and absentmindedly picked at the stone behemoth they called home. What appeared as small scratches would be the foundation of future paths. Each gouge would be a safe haven for travelers or part of a village. Massive sorrowful tears splashed away snow and debris as Sariel buried their dreams of exploration. Head hung low, they returned to their small window, opened it, and crept inside.

It didn't take long for Edthecridaldyrth to find out what happened. Not due to the massive changes on the mountain but because his child never mentioned the outside world. Sorting treasure and talking to the kobolds was all Sariel did. Any details Edthecridaldyrth tried to share were brushed off. Sariel openly admitted to seeing the world and rejecting it. The truth wounded them more than they cared to admit.

Like any caring father, Edthecridaldyrth tried his hardest to help Sariel. Rather than treasure, he retrieved books and new foods to expand Sariel's mind. The furthest he went was an offer to hunt together.

"I cannot hunt if I cannot transform. Am I correct, Ed?" Sariel asked.

"Yes. We can find a solution," their father replied.

Sariel sighed. "You would have already if you believed me capable. I was only twenty years of age when you began teaching me magic and continued until you were satisfied with my abilities. Something informs you of my skills... or lack thereof."

"My child was bound to be talented at our magic. I expect you will outgrow myself in the coming years."

"But I will remain unable to transform, correct?" Sariel asked.

Edthecridaldyrth looked hurt. "I do not know why but yes. I wished to create a world more accepting of our kind before allowing you to travel. Some places will be open to you—"

"However, I will not be able to walk amongst the citizens." Sariel interjected. "I do not wish to lord over the denizens of the world. There is no reason to travel if I cannot interact with the people of those lands."

"I understand," the elder dragon sighed. "Allow me some time to look for a solution. I only ask that you do not recluse yourself from me. Please."

***

Edthecridaldyrth failed to reset his traps after Sariel changed the face of Mount Ikrali and within months people succeeded in scaling it. The cave mouth sat open at the summit since no one should have ever reached it. Cold air permeating through the tunnels required adventurers to remain cloaked and obscured. It didn't take long for them to cross paths with kobolds guarding a path that went towards the treasure chamber. To the monsters' surprise, they weren't attacked. Instead, the adventurers asked for an audience with the dragon residing in the cave.

Meetings with humanoids were common for Edthecridaldyrth; though he'd never faced them in his abode. However, it was an opportune chance to allow Sariel interaction with beings they wished to meet. If it went poorly, it would be a poignant lesson in how to kindly handle threats to life. Though the concern seemed unwarranted as none of the adventurers brandished weapons.

One of the three humanoids stepped forward and removed his hood. Fur covered ears poked up off his snow covered face that grinned with awe at the dragons. Sariel had only seen felminn in one of the many encyclopedias their father gathered. The adventurer kneeled in front of the giants.

"Hello, honorable ones. My name is Veil. We come from the eastern city of Shusyoun," he said. "Months ago we saw an emerald deity mark a path along Mount Ikrali and saw it as a sign of where to continue our search."

The man's direct form of speech pleased Edthecridaldyrth—usually displeased by the meandering nature of humanoids. "What is it you seek?" the dragon asked. "Our treasure is considered ineffective by your kind."

"Our journey is to gather knowledge. We wish to bring peace among the races on Tetria using magic and science," Veil explained. "Many creatures judge others without interacting with them. We wish to change their opinions. A deeper understanding of one another will diminish their fear."

"Some months ago," Sariel muttered. "I presume you saw what happened when I approached the... desert in the east."

Veil nodded slowly. "Khergrin's reaction to you was uncalled for."

"Our kind are feared. If what you say is true; you seek to assuage the concerns of many," Edthecridaldyrth said.

"Exactly," Veil exclaimed. "If you would be willing to travel with us, you could help spread the word about your kind."

Sariel frowned—another opportunity for their father to travel around the world. The young dragon would be left alone to die in the cave until something changed about the world.

"I have traveled the world for many years. It is no longer of interest," the elder dragon said. "I must refuse your request."

"Based on what we saw, your child wants to learn about the world. Can they join us?" Veil replied.

Sariel blurted out, "I cannot transform. Though I would like to join you, it is not possible."

The figures behind Veil murmured before one handed the felminn a corked vial. He smiled softly and held the shimmering amber liquid forward.

"You are in luck, my lord. We created this potion to assist us in settlements dominated by a single race," Veil explained and popped the cork.

With a deep breath, he drank the concoction. His visible extremities became dull gray as fur turned to scales and he grew taller. Soft paws transformed into scaled claws and the felminn was gone, replaced by a dragominn. Only his eyes remained the same silver orbs that looked at the dragons in admiration. Neither dragon could hide their surprise.

"This form lasts until I drink another potion," Veil explained. "However, we will likely need to modify it to work on you."

"Can you do so and return here with the new concoction?" Edthecridaldyrth asked.

Veil shook his head. "It's possible but I don't recommend it. Shusyoun takes months to reach on foot. We can collect data here and take it with us but finding the correct measurements takes many attempts. I foresee us having to travel back and forth for years, maybe decades, before finding a successful concoction."

Edthecridaldyrth hesitated to say anything. A few decades was nothing to a dragon with their multi-century lifespans. Waiting for the potion would pass in an instant. But that knowledge came from experience—which Sariel had little of. They couldn't hide the craving for adventure and it would be wrong of a father to stand in their child's way.

The elder dragon nodded to Sariel. "The decision is yours to make, young one."

"I will go," Sariel replied immediately. "Traveling will not take long with me by your side."

The hooded figures murmured while Veil smiled widely at his new traveling companion. More research would slow his ultimate goal but the assistance of a legendary creature was nothing to scoff at.

"We are ready whenever you are, my lord. Do dragons need to pack?" Veil joked.

"Of course not," Edthecridaldyrth said then smiled at his child. "I will not stop your search for knowledge. But, please return to me every so often. To put my mind at ease."

"I will come back to you, Ed. Do not worry," Sariel said.

The elder dragon couldn't help but feel sorrow as his child exited the cave. Radiant emerald scales reflected sunlight but didn't compare to the smile on Sariel's face. With a wing planted on the ground, they provided a platform for the smaller beings to mount. Once the dragon was familiar with the weight, they flew away without turning back.

The adventurers used magic to keep steady as they approached the heavens. Veil's voice carried to Sariel's ear, guiding them towards a laboratory. Clouds provided ample cover and the sun blinded anyone who might look towards the group. Within hours, they arrived near the lab. Trees and remnants of collapsed civilization kept them from view at ground level.

Unfortunately, Sariel's size was not conducive to stealthy movement. An old tower crumbled when they took an unfortunate turn and nearly landed on the riders. Some debris hit the base of the dragon's neck and sent a chill down their spine. Luckily, the passengers were unhurt. They arrived at a group of buildings hidden within an alcove surrounded by tightly packed trees and covered by a magical dome. Other researchers greeted the adventurers as they dismounted.

"This is the next step in improving the potion," Veil said.

"Has it been… briefed?" someone asked.

Veil's lips curled into an unnatural smile that triggered Sariel's instincts. Every fiber screamed to flee but their body didn't move. Sulfur and lavender mixed into a pungent odor that overwhelmed the senses and blurred Sariel's sharp sight. Willpower was the only thing keeping them upright and it was quickly fading. When Sariel finally focused on Veil, they saw a familiar sight.

The dragominn's body morphed but not even a drop of the concoction was used. Long white hair hung over a gray humanoid with only a single distinct feature—two silver orbs staring at its collapsing prey.

CHAPTER TWENTY-EIGHT

Time Marches On

Centuries worth of memories weighed on Sariel as the past flooded into their mind. The adventurers sadly watched pained expressions flash across their friend's face. It was hard to catch a breath with everything they divulged. Torture Veil committed over two hundred years was recalled in seconds. It was like the wounds burst open but there was nothing to heal.

Involuntarily, Sariel reached for their father's hand. Vulnerability was especially difficult to express when they prided themself on silence and stoicism. Edthecridaldyrth's perfect transformation made clear just how roughly Sariel was treated and how poorly the mutation was tested. The emerald claw dug into the elderly elf's palm but the pain was incomparable to the sorrow in his gaze. Shame was evident on the face of a father who sent his child into danger.

"I researched many beings during my travels before joining you all. Based on those findings and my memories, Veil is a changeling," Sariel said.

Kargon looked at his friend and awkwardly asked. "Is there anything you remember that might explain why you were taken?"

It was insensitive and Edthecridaldyrth made his displeasure known but Kargon didn't waver. Sariel was too scrutinizing to take his words at face value.

"The memories are not cohesive. I see brief flashes that could have occurred at any time," Sariel explained, trying to stay calm. "I do not recognize all the languages spoken. However, at some point, someone with silver eyes mentioned the demon king; likely Veil or a descendant."

Their measured response eased Edthecridaldyrth and he said, "I am having trouble understanding his motives. Why would a demon wish for the world's inhabitants to find common ground?"

Sariel huffed. "Ed, it was a lie. They did not seek acceptance for monsters. We were sought out for experimentation. We—I was easily fooled due to my isolation."

The elderly elf furiously shook his head. "Blame lies with me for sending you alone."

"But why experiment on you? What connection does a dragon have to the demon king?" Kargon asked quietly.

"Power," Aisha muttered. "Dragons are powerful and Veil stumbled on one that couldn't transform. What if the demon king can't either? The experiments could have been to find a solution."

"Suffice to say, the demon king's subordinates have worked towards his return for centuries." Vofric sighed.

Aisha let out a frustrated sigh. Eight years of training already felt like too few to face a being known as "the demon king." If his underlings had been preparing for centuries, it'd be even harder to find victory.

"268 years I have searched. After only five, I broke our promise and sought you out," Edthecridaldyrth said soberly. "Shusyoun was a distraction. I learned of a group spreading misinformation and ravaging settlements. But I refused to give up. A dragon cannot succumb so easily."

"Few individuals remained who knew my true form and could aid in my search. Their guild delegated specific members to work with me."

Sariel stared at the damaged walls and empty coffers littering the room. "Why did you part with so much of your treasure?"

"By providing income, the adventurers could focus on the search. Some had families of their own and I wished to ease any hardships my request created," Edthecridaldyrth explained. "Our rapport has grown to the point that Barbatos aids me even while my coffers sit empty."

Vofric furrowed his brow and hesitantly inquired, "I understand you trust others based on their actions. Even so, how can you ally with a group of demons? Did you not suspect they had ulterior motives?"

"I did not," the dragon replied. "Barbatos is filled with individuals from many races. Their name originates from a belief that a demon can only be defeated by another."

"So it's a group of adventurers that help people while fighting demons," Aisha said.

Without thinking, Kargon said, "I wonder if they're preparing to fight Aeraza."

Utterance of the name silenced the room and he clasped his hands over his mouth before cautiously whispering again. Silence caused the name to echo through the halls.

"Do you always say... Aeraza?" Aisha whispered?

"Normally, I don't need to worry about anyone hearing me," Kargon replied. "Using his name makes everything seem more manageable."

He didn't go into detail how scared he was. Not of the demon king but for Aisha's life. It had always been in danger but knowing the threat made it worse. For eight years the Hero had a daunting task in front of her. Kargon believed that whatever came at her couldn't be too powerful. But learning the challenge's identity—learning of the demon king changed his outlook.

"Why is everyone silent?" Edthecridaldyrth asked quizzically. "Aeraza's name holds no power."

"But it should only be able to be spoken in a specific magic circle." Aisha replied.

"You speak of the silencing seal. It was cast during Aeraza's downfall. Any who were born after that time are bound to it but those of us who lived during the spellcast are not. Our existence creates an anomaly in the seal, allowing others nearby to utter his name."

Sariel grunted. "Why would the creators of the seal leave a glaring issue in a spell that affects the whole realm?".

"Did you not teach them the intricacies of magic?" Vofric asked.

"They were a child when last we spoke," Edthecridaldyrth said defensively. "The age of teaching them magic outside their own had not arrived."

Vofric grumbled and nodded. "Apologies. I must remember you are from a different time." He turned his attention to Sariel and explained, "All spells have a weakness, whether they are like Kargon's reliance on physical contact or the limit of my and Avant's supportive magic. The more powerful a spell, the more glaring its weakness. Whoever cast the seal made a choice to allow living beings to continue speaking of Aeraza."

"There are only a few races that live long enough to have the anomaly come to light." Aisha added.

"Exactly. But such refined definitions allow for a stronger spell to hold."

Sariel nodded. "Do you know who cast the spell, Ed?"

The elder dragon shook his head. "I avoided the outside world during Aeraza's uprising. What happened afterwards is unknown to me."

"What if I asked for your assistance?" Sariel asked.

Edthecridaldyrth silently studied each adventurer, less harshly than when they arrived. There was little recognition from the transformed dragon when looking at Kargon, Vofric, or Avant. But he paused on Aisha and glanced at *Valefor*, resting on her hip.

"I see," Edthecridaldyrth said. "You stumbled upon this cave on your journey to fight Aeraza."

"Yes, we have reason to assume his underling is hunting a dragon," Aisha replied.

"There are others in the vicinity of Mount Ikrali. Though what I consider nearby is likely several weeks away. Even so, I request that you continue your search as another of my kind is still in danger."

Sariel asked, "Is it possible for you to carry us during our search. It will be significantly faster with your help."

"Our kind are territorial on most occasions. Worse, many are monstrous and violent. When I hunted and hoarded; it was from the extinct civilizations of Tetria. Others would rather be the cause of extinction."

"I have finally returned to you and again you refuse to join me." Sariel huffed.

"In this case, you are correct," Edthecridaldyrth smiled softly. "This is a journey you have chosen. My child was not one to seek me out for solutions."

"Are you truly willing to let Sariel go? You just reunited." Vofric said sadly. "How can you trust us?"

Edthecridaldyrth nodded slowly, his smile unwavering. "When it came time to trust again, I was discerning and allowed my allies to prove themselves." He gestured toward the party and said, "You brought Sariel home. In the short time I've spent with you—I see how you care for them. Likewise, I see that they trust you. That is all I need to know my decision is correct."

Sariel grumbled but didn't contradict their father. Trust was obvious ever since the battle in Balur. Mysterious habits and silent demeanor didn't change that.

"Where is the closest dragon located?" Aisha asked.

"One hundred years ago the city of Khergrin was destroyed during a monster raid. Survivors rebuilt around the remaining spires," Edthecridaldyrth explained. "Spirefell is little more than a collection of villages but they are the most likely target of the Desert Ruler."

While everyone was listening attentively, Kargon's eyes were drawn to Vofric. Normally, the dwarf calmly listened to the most horrible news. But hearing about Khergrin made his eye twitch and a tight grip dug into his knee. The longer Kargon stared, the higher chance his friend would catch on.

To refocus on the conversation, he asked, "Is the dragon's temperament anything like yours?"

Edthecridaldyrth inhaled slowly. "It matters not. If I were hunted, I would retaliate with all my strength. Any individual hunting my kind is likely aware and confident in their own strength. The collateral damage during such battles is astronomical. Khergrin's curse of destruction may befall Spirefell."

"We will prevent it," Vofric said. "The villagers must be protected by any means necessary."

Sariel nodded. "Then we must hurry. The opportunity to evacuate the villagers before an attack may yet be possible."

They got up to leave and hesitated, realizing the cave was nothing like they remembered. Everything below the treasure chamber was sealed off, shrinking the home significantly. It was a self-imposed punishment for losing a child. The dragons shared a silent glance before the elder led everyone out of the cave. Edthecridaldyrth's presence was enough to open the hidden entrance.

He placed a hand on each adventurer's head as they walked by. "Ancient prayers hold little power now. Nevertheless—" Edthecridaldyrth's eyes shined. "—Eyes of the dragon watch over you."

He didn't wait for the party to start their descent. The cave was sealed moments after they stepped outside. It was all Edthecridaldyrth could do not to join them and, in turn, diminish their hard work. Doing so would not only bring shame to him but his child. One who already brought a dragon's strength to the Hero's party.

CHAPTER TWENTY-NINE

Race to the Bottom

The flood of memories provided Sariel with full awareness of Mount Ikrali's many inhabitants. Previously hidden routes were theirs to travel and completely avoided wild beasts. Kargon presumed all the detours would slow the descent but they arrived at Gromsev in three days, none the worse for wear. They would have rolled right into the village if not for Vofric's wariness. No one else in the party had experience returning to a settlement after a quest. According to the dwarf, there were certain expectations to be aware of.

"Keep your answers vague. Do not tell them anything they do not need to know. We needn't spread information relating to any dragons," he explained.

"You say that like anyone other than Elder Zhusthum will care about what we've been doing," Kargon replied.

"With good reason." Vofric pointed towards a group of villagers waiting with the elder at Gromsev's gate.

All shared similar looks of disbelief at the unscathed adventurers. Whatever story they were told was clearly more harrowing than what they thought the party could handle. There wasn't a way to avoid the encounter as Elder Zhusthum rushed to the party with a studious look on her face.

"You are unhurt. Was one of our ancestors atop Mount Ikrali?" she asked.

"We achieved clarity atop the mountain," Aisha said.

It was barely an answer but the elder was clearly satisfied as she turned to the villagers and announced, "Behold the Hero has been guided by our ancestors."

How she reached that conclusion was beyond Kargon. But it fooled the villagers. Murmurs of awe and amazement passed through the small crowd. They had seen few outsiders, let alone ones who returned from the summit. Questions compounded from individuals trying to be heard over one another. However, no one in the party felt like they'd accomplished more than helping a friend visit home.

"Right..." Aisha replied. "Elder Zhusthum, we won't be staying. There's plenty of daylight left and the rain's died down so we can get pretty far down Mount Ikrali today."

"Of course, Hero. Is there any way we can assist with your departure?"

The adventurers looked at each other and debated quietly. Camping supplies were plentiful and they preferred hunting. Not to mention their distrust of cuisine from unfamiliar places. But it would be unbecoming to deny villagers eager to help.

"Is there a courier here? Or someone who can reach Neves?" Kargon asked.

"The garage gives any mail to traveling couriers when they pass through Gromsev," a villager said.

Aisha silently thanked her friend for remembering Foxhill. Then she addressed the villagers. "Thank you for the hospitality but we should be going."

"Understood," Elder Zhusthum replied. "I will guide you."

For all the praise the elder gave her people, none stayed to see off the adventurers. Disappointment was evident on her face but she remained dutiful in leading the party back to the garage. The owner was as unenthused as ever to see them approach.

"I was told you hold mail for traveling couriers," Kargon said.

The operator grunted affirmatively and held out his hand. Two rolled scrolls passed between them. One was a message for Dawncaster regarding Foxhill. Aisha was more intrigued by the other, marked for Zigon and Velana. The garage owner double checked them while the adventurers piled into their carriage. Listless and tired, Sariel entered the wagon with Kargon, Aisha and Avant. In turn, Vofric took the driver's seat and rolled out of the garage.

The road that brought them to Gromsev led to another path which crossed the mountain range. Driving took Vofric's mind off their destination, but it clearly weighed on him. Kargon wanted to comfort him but felt queasy as the high speed carriage bounced on the rocky terrain. Retreating into the wagon, he sat next to Aisha and prepared for questions.

Sariel tilted their head toward the half-elf and grunted. "Who are Velana and Zigon?"

"Kargon's parents," Aisha answered while petting Avant. "Why'd you contact them?"

"It is possible he misses them," Vofric said.

"No," Kargon replied. "Well, yes. But that's not why. It's been bothering me how the Dicoris's and Victor mentioned that I'm immune to fire. I thought it was just something weird about me. But after seeing Sariel and Edthec—" He hesitated, realizing he couldn't pronounce the dragon's name. "Sariel and her father together I realized how similar their magic is. It made me remember that my parents weren't surprised by my immunity to fire. They have to know why."

Aisha hummed. "I don't know how neither of us thought of that. Any ideas what the cause might be?"

"Yeah..." Kargon ran a hand through his hair. "It's that thing I'd complain about when we were younger."

"You can't be serious."

"It makes sense!"

"Kargon, you're half elf, half human. It's obvious," Aisha huffed.

"Humans aren't immune to fire!" he argued.

"To be fair, few creatures are. None of which could necessarily breed with an elf," Sariel said.

Vofric chimed in with, "It is possible that Kargon comes from such a monster. He is rather unique."

"No way, Zigon is very... average? But even more so. His most unique feature is the red hair which, obviously, Kargon has," Aisha said.

"Pops is incredibly normal now," Kargon said. "I'm different from when we left Neves. He may have been different in the past."

"Why don't you believe you are half-human?" Sariel asked.

"Because of how obvious other half-elves' features are. Aisha has Tiefling horns. Captain Julian's crewmates had fangs, wings, or tails. I have fire immunity. Fire immunity seems to be all I have other than my hair. So Pops has to be hiding what he really is."

Vofric chuckled. "As silly as it sounds, I believe Kargon is correct. All we can do is wait for an answer. Though it will take a long time for a courier to find us by following our trail."

"I hadn't thought of that…" Kargon admitted.

Aisha chuckled. "You're an idiot."

"We will receive the information when it is most pertinent," Sariel said with their eyes shut.

Avant chirped in a manner that told Kargon to be patient. He ruffled the owlbear's head as the beast got comfortable between the Nevesi duo. Without bothering to ask, Aisha rested her head on Kargon's shoulder and shut her eyes. He had enough experience to use her as a pillow without stabbing his eye out on her horns. Rhythmic bumps in the road were so powerful they pounded inside Kargon's chest. By some miracle, he was still able to doze off.

Rain showers didn't last long as spring reached the halfway point. Gravel squished into the mud as wooden wheels smoothed the terrain. There was no denying Vofric's masterful operation of the carriage. He knew exactly how to move to minimize the rough environment's effects. Speed barely fluctuated as they steadily traversed the mountain. If not for a peculiar feeling of ascension, no one would have awoken from their slumber.

"Vofric, are we still trying to reach Spirefell?" Sariel grumbled.

"This portion of the path rises and then falls. We will have no more flat roads until we leave the mountain," Vofric explained.

Aisha groaned as she awoke. "How much longer until we reach the bottom?"

"I have only traversed here on foot. With the carriage I assume we will reach the bottom after nightfall."

That was still hours away which Vofric would have surely pointed out if he wasn't interrupted by the sound of another artificed carriage climbing the mountain. There wasn't a chance to point out the peculiarity before a swarm of vehicles presented themselves as the party ascended. The road flattened into a large platform like the central square of a town with dozens of modified carriages lining either side of the road.

"What's going on?" Kargon asked.

Aisha shrugged. "Vofric, pull off to the side."

He parked near the vehicles on the right side and everyone got out to seek another path. Crossing the area seemed impossible with two carriages blocking the only obvious road forward. Their engines roared as the drivers poured in mana to increase the output. A woman stood between both vehicles and screamed for them to get ready before signaling the start of a race. The drivers tore out of the starting position and off the edge of the platform, vanishing from view instantly. Only their engines could be heard descending the mountain.

"Nice ride you've got there. Custom made, I take it," a person said, kneeling close to the party's carriage and examining the tires.

"Yes. Handmade, in fact." Sariel replied.

The enthusiast approached the engine and said, "It's a solid piece of work. Ever thought of seeing how it'd do against other modified carts?"

Sariel scoffed. "It is meant for travel."

"So, you're not good enough to race with it."

"Excuse me?" Sariel grunted. "Who are you to judge our carriage? I built this with my own hands. It can handle anything."

The racer laughed while walking to a nearby vehicle. "The name's Taze Fehlam. And I didn't say the carriage was an issue. It's probably your driving. Didn't even pick up speed when the road was clear."

"We don't have the luxury of playing around with no responsibilities." Sariel said.

"I've got plenty of responsibilities," Taze said and slapped the side of the white carriage next to them. Etched on the side were the words "Fehlam Delivery Services." "I just know how to take a break. Ease my mind with a distraction."

"Apologies, young one." Vofric interjected. "We are simply trying to reach Khergrin. Is there a path we can take that will not obstruct you and your compatriots?"

"I think you mean Spirefell," Taze scoffed. "Cuz, you know, the spires fell."

Aisha interjected. "Sorry about that, we're not familiar with the area."

"Right, whatever." Taze replied nonchalantly. "Go past these carts on the right and there's a road down. You'll reach the bottom in a few hours."

"Thank you," Vofric said.

Taze glared at the dwarf. "My mistake, really. No reason to challenge a Starcaller disciple."

Regret and shame mixed into one attack and struck Vofric squarely in the chest. "I'm sorry. Do you know me?" he asked.

"I know your kind. Worthless cowards. No reason to bother challenging a party that keeps one of you around," Taze spat.

"What are you talking about?" Kargon asked.

"He must not have told you. A party of disciples came to Khergrin a century ago. Left us to fend for ourselves during an orc raid. The spires crumbled and by the time the orcs were finally killed only a fraction of the citizens were left. A dwarf was the only Starcaller disciple that returned—spouting nonsense about taking out the orc leader. My ancestors were some of the last survivors who built Spirefell on top of crimson sand." Taze nodded at Vofric. "No one in that village would expect anything but a cowards attitude from a Starcaller disciple. I should've known better with that sigil around your neck."

Kargon couldn't help but see Vofric's defeated attitude as admittance. With a thousand yard stare, Sariel shook their head in mourning for the lost lives. Avant opted to comfort the dwarf with a light nudge.

Aisha sighed and said, "If we race you it's a distraction from our duty. But if we deny you, we're cowards. It seems there's no winning for us."

Taze perked up and replied, "It would prove me wrong about Starcaller disciples. I'd definitely make sure Spirefell knew about it. Not to mention, it might ease that tension your friend is feeling."

"The way you challenge people is infuriating," Kargon said.

"I'm aware. So, what do you say?" The racer was clearly addressing Vofric.

With a grunt, he forced himself to calm down and consider the options. After brief contemplation, he said, "We must reach Spirefell as quickly as possible."

"It'll still take weeks to get there but the race track gets down the mountain in a few minutes compared to the hours long road down the side."

"How?"

Taze smiled coyly. "Only a handful of turns and we shoot down the mountain at max speed."

"That cannot be safe," Vofric replied with wide-eyed curiosity. An opportunity to go all-out with the carriage excited him. Aisha patted his back and looked him in the eye. They both knew what needed to happen but only one of them could accept. The dwarf stepped forward and put out his hand. "We accept."

Taze smiled and shook hands fervently. The starting line was cleared before both carts took their places. Even while inside the wagon, Kargon could feel electricity in the air. Drumming heartbeats drowned out the excited cheers of the onlookers. Powerful fingers gripped the steering wheel as Vofric slowly inhaled. Something was still eating away at him but he forced it down with focus.

A man sauntered between the vehicles and nodded to each driver. Taze energetically declared their readiness while Vofric replied with a gruff, one word response. Both engines started as the drivers steadily poured in mana and shook the ground with revs. The crowd shouted as the man from the starting line pointed to the side.

"Three!"

Another gesture to the other side of the crowd.

"Two!"

Both arms to the air lifted everyone's spirits.

"One!"

The Hero's party was filled with regret the moment they peeled out. Not checking the drop beforehand hid the sharp angle of descent. Both carts barreled down the mountain at unprecedented speed. Kargon couldn't make out a single thing in the landscape even with his goggles. Avant could barely stand and used the walls to keep steady. Speed was Aisha's forte but that was on-foot. This was beyond anything she'd experienced in battle. Only Sariel's eyes could see anything and based on their reactions, it wasn't good.

What Taze shared with them had implications they didn't understand. A large section of the mountain was flattened by something long forgotten. Now a completely smooth road with few turns led to the bottom. One improper maneuver would send the carriage careening off the mountain and all passengers to the afterlife.

"We needn't win," Vofric said. "Reaching the bottom of Mount Ikrali is our main goal."

"But, you want to win right?" Kargon asked.

"Not by risking your lives," Vofric stated and slowed down. With Taze already in the lead, all it did was widen the gap.

Kargon crawled to the front of the wagon and rested his hand on Vofric's shoulder. "What happened in Khergrin?"

"We chose the incorrect option," Vofric grunted. "It wasn't like Dawncaster where Elmud needed to be stopped in order to halt the attack. The orcs should have been killed before we targeted their leader. Instead, the city was forced to fend for itself and we were outnumbered in the orc camp. By the time the orc chief fell, only I remained."

"But that wouldn't stop the other orcs," Aisha said sadly.

Vofric nodded. "I was young and foolish. Monsters traits were unknown to me yet I acted like it was obvious. We sought glory like my grandmother without truly understanding her lessons. I cannot blame Spirefell for seeing Starcaller disciples as cowards."

"But by not trying in this race, aren't you just doing the same thing?" Kargon asked. "I'm not saying we'll win but putting in the effort matters. Show Taze— Show yourself that you're different than before. Don't worry about us. You know we're sturdy."

Vofric stared blankly into the distance, unknown miles away, where hundreds of spires stood long ago. Few remained intact with small buildings around them adding color to the desert. Aisha swallowed hard, approached Vofric, and slapped him hard on the back.

"Decisions are bound to go poorly sometimes. What matters is how you deal with the consequences. Didn't you teach Albert that?" she asked. "Heroes aren't perfect. What matters is owning up to your mistakes and being better. Is the better version of you one that coasts through the Hero's quest?"

A golden light burned in Vofric's eyes and calmed his nerves. The memories would never go away. Pain caused by failure would persist. But this was a step towards fixing it.

"Brace," he commanded.

"Aisha, keep a hand on the lever and release mana into it," Sariel said.

With a simple nod, she placed her hand on the metal rod at Vofric's side. Golden light fused with purple lightning as they wreathed around the lever. It flowed into a conduit under the seat connected to the engine. New life roared into the machine and the world turned into a blur. Within seconds, they could see Taze—grinning widely as the real race began.

"Might wanna slow down on the turns!" they screamed over the engines. "Otherwise, you'll blow right through them and crash!"

Vofric remained silent and slowed just enough to safely take the upcoming turn. Taze, on the other hand, didn't heed their own advice. They cranked the lever and initiated brakes before turning outward. Another crank and acceleration pulled them into the turn sideways. Horse-drawn carriages couldn't hope to mimic the maneuver. Most of the party thought it wasn't possible for them either.

Turns were becoming more frequent and Taze continued to drift through them. Vofric sped up, gradually matching the timing of the experienced racer. With each curve, the surroundings became blurrier but neither slowed down. Rough terrain was always an inch away from the tires. One wrong move would send them off course. But they continued fighting for the lead. The familiar tension of a brawl tickled the spines of every passenger in Vofric's vehicle. Even Sariel couldn't hide the spike of adrenaline that brought a grin to their face.

"Slow down for real this time! Or your cart's done for!" Taze commanded as they finally lowered their speed.

A sharp turn fast approached but Vofric's speed remained steady. "All of you, to the right of the wagon. On my command, jump to the left side."

The others didn't bother arguing or asking why. Not that there was a chance as the dwarf took a left turn that made the right set of tires lift off the ground. It was overkill for the slightly curved road and unwise for the next sharp turn. Staying upright was incredibly difficult as the cart precariously balanced on two wheels.

"NOW!" Vofric commanded.

As the party's feet landed on the opposite side of the carriage, the dwarf turned hard. It felt like the world momentarily slowed down but their speed never dropped as they ripped through the sharp turn. Simple curves and straight roads were all that remained ahead. Without a miracle there was no way for Taze to catch up to Vofric and Aisha's combined efforts.

Vofric let out a long breath as he slowed the carriage to a stop at the bottom of the mountain. A large crowd cheered for the victor even though they didn't recognize him. Looking back at the track, Kargon couldn't comprehend how far they'd traveled in a matter of minutes. It was possible teleportation felt similar but there was no way it was as exciting.

Taze skidded to a stop nearby and jumped off their vehicle. It felt like an attack was coming until their excited smile became more clear. "That was amazing! How did you turn like that? You were on two wheels!"

"My party trusted me and lent their aid," Vofric said.

Taze nodded. "For them to trust you with something like that, you must've done plenty of wild stuff already." They put out a hand and continued, "I'm sorry for antagonizing you earlier. I can't say some Spirefell folks won't react similarly but you've proven me wrong. I'll spread the word and try to get them to ease up. What's your name?"

"Vofric Starc," the dwarf said while shaking our new acquaintance's hand.

"A gift for the Starcaller's disciple," Taze said and passed a coin to Vofric. "It ain't much but crack that and toss it, you'll send out a flare. One of a kind and I'll come to you. Maybe I'll see you in Spirefell."

"We appreciate your help," Aisha said. "And the challenge. We didn't know Vofric was capable of that."

Kargon chuckled. "Don't think he was either."

"It's an indispensable skill," Sariel said.

Maybe the compliments were too much but all Vofric could do was choke out a quiet, "Thank you."

The crowd pushed for the party to stay but a single race was enough distraction. They were ahead of schedule by at least a day. It wouldn't be wise to squander it. Who knew how many weeks ahead Elmud was. Letting them press forward any longer was unwise.

CHAPTER THIRTY

Blazed Trail

Two uneventful weeks of travel wasn't what anyone expected after leaving Mount Ikrali. After half a year of adventuring they'd grown accustomed to encounters being relatively frequent. A couple days of peace was welcome. One whole week was a nice surprise. Now the party was anxious and looking for any clue they were making progress. Kargon was starting to miss the claws from Foxhill and that was a concerning feeling.

Sariel sat atop the wagon and tested their improved vision. Memories of training their ancestral abilities helped improve them. The worn map from Dawncaster had no clues about how to reach Spirefell and the party wasn't sure of their location. Triangulating the spot was their best option but the dense forest stopped Sariel from doing so. From atop the mountain, the village looked so clear and the desert manageable. Unfortunately, everyone failed to see all the hindrances on the way.

"Your father really would've made this simpler," Kargon said from his perch at the back of the carriage.

"I swear everyone wants this to be harder than it needs to be," Aisha complained.

"Ed believed us capable," Sariel replied. "I do agree that a little assistance was warranted in this case. Vofric, have you not visited this region before?"

Vofric grunted from his seat. "Minor changes in landscape would not be reported."

"Not unless it indicated something big was happening." Kargon added.

Normally when the group talked Avant chirped up or let his thoughts be heard. Aisha said he took after Kargon in that way. The growing owlbear—as tall as Vofric on all fours—was even more expressive now. When he noticed something from inside the carriage, he shot up and shook the back. Slowly turning, Avant stared out the front of the wagon and approached the driver's seat. The carriage barely slowed when the beast leapt off and ran towards the forest. Sariel immediately leapt into the trees to follow. For once, the carriage wasn't left behind as the forest had a wide, unmapped road that Avant stuck to.

He tracked for several minutes without stopping—far longer than usual. Whatever got his attention wasn't average prey. Neither was the road they used. Large shattered trees laid messily along the path. Crushed foliage and animals littered the dirt, seeped in blood and viscera to the point of painting it crimson. Avant returned to the carriage out of discomfort but remained at the front. With a hand resting on him, Kargon vocalized movements to guide Vofric.

After a couple hours they were deep in the forest with no roads or landmarks. Tetria was rumored to have undiscovered land but none that was untouched by humanoids altogether. Not even orcs or goblins had taken refuge in the forest even though it was perfect for a long term settlement.

Shifting stones drew the party to hidden remnants of a stone watchtower. Something had hit the building and shattered its supports. People who said watchtowers could withstand the harshest conditions referred to only what they could perceive. Few considered the effects a dragon could have on a structure. Aisha was the first to notice chipped red scales flickering within the rubble. Stones likely tore them off during the collision.

Everyone exited the carriage to investigate— stepping onto squelching dirt that caused viscous ichor to rise to the surface. Torn apart goblin pieces were infused with the ground. Pointed ears and crushed teeth peeked through the grass. Broken weapons were scattered within the tower with melted pieces stuck to the floor. Charred wooden beams snapped as they crumbled to ash.

"They couldn't put up a fight," Aisha said.

"That's assuming the dragon even looked at them. It's like it passed through here and they happened to die," Kargon responded.

Sariel shook their head sadly. "It was aware of their presence and chose to ignore them. Whoever this Desert Ruler is, they believe themselves mightier and more prestigious than any other being."

"Elmud has lost their mind to challenge such a creature," Vofric said.

Avant growled affirmatively while ransacking the remaining food reserves of the goblins.

"We're equally foolish," Aisha replied. "I mean, either we have to fight Elmud after they beat a dragon or we have to face a dragon to protect Spirefell. Maybe having some unearned confidence would be good here."

Sariel grunted in agreement. "We must convince ourselves of victory. It is the only way to succeed."

A new path presented itself behind a fallen wall of stone. The carriage could barely squeeze through and the party thought their luck turned around. They disregarded that notion the second they found the first giant bloody footprint. Charred corpses of overconfident beasts blended into the environment. A smoky layer of ash settled over the forest in search of a loose spark.

Surroundings became more distorted with every bit of progress. Trees bent at odd angles where the dragon had rushed through. Stray fireballs killed any flora on contact while wild tail swipes created massive dead ends. As the beast barreled through the forest, it crushed every animal and splattered them across the floor. Avant shuddered at the sight and curled into his master's arm. It was a mystery why a domestic beast like himself felt a kinship with the forest's denizens and pain from their deaths.

"Loss is felt because we share a spirit. Relations are not necessary for sympathy," Vofric said soberly.

With a soft trill, Avant moved between Kargon and the dwarf, hoping to comfort them. The moment was short-lived as the temperature spiked around them. It was obvious to everyone as past the devastated foliage, they saw a sea of sand. With Vofric at the wheel, Sariel could modify their carriage without stopping. Tires widened to handle sand and a thin sheet of bark draped over the wagon openings to block out minuscule particles.

Sunlight assaulted the senses and bounced off the smooth land ahead. Vofric's natural squint provided the perfect measure against it. The nearer they got to the desert, the more sure Kargon became that something was off—deserts shouldn't be reflective. Light could be brighter with the lack of cover but not blinding.

As they reached the edge of the forest, Kargon's suspicions were confirmed. What he assumed was a mirage turned out to be a layer of glass spread across a portion of the sand. Rolling hills and stones were all over the desert yet this entrance was completely flat.

"It's melted," Kargon muttered.

Aisha gasped. "No way. You can't mean—"

"I can't even reach those temperatures."

"The dragon," Sariel grumbled. "We can reach heights impossible for humanoids."

Vofric shook his head. "It really is like facing a deity. To change a landscape with a single attack is no simple feat."

Avant let out a shaky breath and slumped onto his stomach.

Though Kargon understood the intention, it wasn't the same as his exact words. "What's up, little guy?" the half-elf asked.

Sariel replied. "He says, 'so much for convincing ourselves of victory.'"

CHAPTER THIRTY-ONE

Spires in the Sand

Thick films of sweat lined everyone's brows except Kargon's. Lessening the heat around them was beyond him. All he felt was a presence and based on how prominent it was, he could understand why it bothered the others. Not to mention low water reserves and food. Hunting wasn't possible without a means to hide and everyone was too focused on the dragon to consider an alternate solution. Either they finished the quest and left the desert or reached an oasis.

"That's big debris! We have to be close to Spirefell!" Kargon pointed to a half-buried stone—the only unique thing he'd seen for a while.

"We've passed that before," Aisha groaned. "Though I don't know how since we haven't turned at all."

Tremors shook the ground as the stone lifted from the sand and pulled other rocks towards it to take a humanoid shape. Pieces rubbed together and allowed the talos to mimic a roar. Swinging its arm detached the furthest stone and sent it hurtling at the carriage.

Vofric masterfully weaved around it and accelerated. "We cannot waste time here!"

"Keep us steady!" Sariel barked, firing blunt projectiles to knock more flying stones off course. The lumbering creature couldn't keep up with the speeding carriage and dropped back to the sand, separating into a pile of innocuous rubble. Unfortunately, it wasn't the only one.

The ground rumbled as more talos rose up. Swift movements got the party through but it was impossible to avoid the monsters entirely. A rain of boulders chased after the carriage and shattered multiple planks. Only half the vehicle remained when the party got away—awkwardly balanced on the back axle. Sariel worked quickly on makeshift repairs, knowing the carriage wouldn't last.

In the distance were four small villages surrounding a collection of damaged obelisks. Even broken they stood nearly as tall as Dicoris Castle. Any joy the party might have felt was crushed by the looming shadow overhead. Desert Ruler was a red dragon only slightly smaller than Edthecridaldyrth. Plumes of fire instantly melted clumps of sand. Citizens were attacked by crimson kobolds supporting their master. There wasn't an opportunity to look for Elmud or their allies.

"There's no undead! Sariel, do Kobolds regenerate?" Aisha asked.

"No! Kill the fodder and we can attack the dragon collectively," Sariel replied.

"Vofric, get as close to the spire as possible. You and Avant go north. Sariel, you go west. Kargon, east. I'll go south and try to keep the dragon there."

Scattered acknowledgments sounded as the carriage rattled forward. Shards of glass erupted into the sky and blades rained down. A high pitched whine emitted from glands in the dragon's mouth as gas poured out. Fire violently burst out into a massive orb that soared toward the party's cart.

"Split up!" Aisha yelled as she leapt off.

There was no way to dodge the attack with the vehicle intact. No one could spare a second for goodbyes. Everyone jumped off the carriage moments before it exploded, propelling them towards their destinations. Sariel quickly disappeared to the west while Aisha began an onslaught on the nearest kobold. The center of Spirefell caused the rest to hesitate. Each obelisk drew sand towards it with a massive sinkhole appearing in between. Vofric slapped Kargon's back and pointed to the outer parts of the southern section of the village. By hugging the walls it was possible to get to their assigned locations.

***

Sariel didn't bother taking the high ground to catch sight of her prey. Bright scales were easy to catch in the middle of panicked masses. Arrows harmlessly brushed past citizens before piercing their targets. It was obvious the lizard-like creatures would be stronger than undead but Sariel had still underestimated them.

Modifications were needed if their arrows were going to trivialize the monsters' defenses.

Spirefell guards saw the elven ranger in battle and rushed to their aid. Two swords replaced Sariel's bow as they got in melee range of the monsters. A group of kobolds beset upon the temporary allies. The draconic elf blocked one with their blades, forcing it back but not breaking through its armor. But assessment was simpler at close range. While defending with one blade, Sariel modified the other then swapped stances.

With each transformation their attacks grew more finessed. Serpent-like strikes weaved through wild kobold flailing. Thorns sprouted across one of Sariel's blades, creating a serrated edge. A furious swipe tore through a kobold's hide and stunned the creature too much to protect itself from the next strike. Sariel's second blade grew deadlier seconds before decapitating their opponent.

Blood sprayed across the floor as the corpse dropped like weights. The sight of a deceased kobold invigorated the Spirefell combatants and caused them to fight with ferocity matching the raiders. Sariel stepped back into the crowd and properly studied their weapons. Replicating it as an arrowhead created heavy projectiles that needed to be aimed high to land properly.

Drawing the bow was unruly when using a barbed arrow. Nevertheless, Sariel remained firm, light reflecting in their focused eyes. The arrow boomed as it loosed from the bow and flew skyward. Seconds later, it plummeted downward; drumming in the wind. The sound pulled a couple kobolds' attention but they couldn't dodge before the arrow pierced one through the head. Momentum carried the projectile through its body and into the leg of another beast before jamming into the sand. Using the snare, a villager lopped the trapped monster's head off.

"Again!" a guard commanded.

Sariel was multiple steps ahead as a rain of arrows fell upon their enemies.

***

Vofric and Avant arrived at an area with multiple buildings under attack. The kobolds were chaotic yet had a loose formation. As treasure collectors, they had unique tactics for hunts—many that worked well in combat.

With a deep breath, Vofric drew his war-hammer and swore to break Khergrin's curse. "Avant, aid any building under attack. Use a mana fueled roar if you need backup."

The owlbear growled then charged down the street into a building where a group of citizens cowered behind a single guard. A broken sword was all she had to face the kobold attacking them. A single misstep would cost multiple lives. Someone screamed at the sight of an owlbear and pulled everyone's attention. Luckily, that included the kobold.

With a roar, Avant lunged at his prey with a shield of feathers. The kobold mistook him for an ally, leaving itself wide open. Avant's beak pierced into the monster's hide then tore away, leaving a massive gash on its side. When it dropped its weapon from shock, the guard grabbed it and used the opportunity to slice through the monster's torso. Even as it died at Avant's feet, the civilians stayed wary of the blood soaked beast. He shook his head and nodded to the door, hoping they'd understand as he left.

Thankfully, Vofric showed where the adventurers' allegiances lied. A few kobolds had heard Avant's roar and approached the building. The paladin didn't need to worry about their scales. With a prayer, he bolstered his war-hammer and slammed it into the nearest enemy. A tilt in midair allowed the dwarf to smear the monster on the sand. It left his back wide open and Avant rushed in to defend. Their combined efforts took out many kobolds but they kept coming. Spirefell guards and villagers stood by and watched in awe.

"Are you really a disciple of the Starcaller?" someone yelled.

"The... very same... that failed you," Vofric admitted while fighting.

Another scoffed. "Isn't there some better way to stop the kobolds? Shouldn't you focus on the dragon?"

"It is of... no concern... until you... are all safe."

Avant growled while tearing apart another kobold—distinct sarcasm in his voice.

"Let us speak on this later," Vofric demanded. "If you do not wish for my assistance, raise your arms. Fight!"

He emitted a golden light that wreathed selective weapons— empowering them while conserving mana. Thankfully, no one was hateful enough to standby and punish the adventurers. Guards rushed at unoccupied kobolds while others secured buildings; ensuring no monsters got away.

***

It was unsurprising how readily villagers and guards accepted Aisha's help. Some recognized the Hero from stories while others felt her powerful aura. Unsheathing *Valefor* drew the eye of every nearby entity. Kobolds that were mid-rampage took pause and made a slapdash plan to attack together. Little did they know a numbers advantage meant nothing in the face of Aisha's magic.

Every swing of her sword cut the life of multiple kobolds short. Surviving was only possible if they were outside *Valefor's* range. Foolishly, they rushed in for a chance against the Champion of Dawncaster. Having learned from the last onslaught, Aisha summoned lighting to her right hand in the form of a second blade. Its immaterial shape easily covered any opening *Valefor* couldn't reach. Physical manifestations of mana were unhindered by monstrous scales and sent violent jolts of electricity directly to blood. Not even a minute passed before more than half the kobold raiders were killed.

One stood back and watched the slaughter closely. It didn't bother with civilians while studying the swordswoman's majestic combat. Sharp silver eyes tracked every movement until the last kobold fell.

Aisha didn't underestimate the bystanding kobold as it rushed forward. Even then, she wasn't expecting its deft dodging. Both sword and lightning blade couldn't connect with the kobold yet it never tried to attack. Aisha swung again and the monster jumped over her blade. Before lightning could connect in midair, the kobold pulled itself away with its tail.

Two arrows flew past Aisha and nearly connected with the monster but it leapt back; stretching nonchalantly.

Sariel rushed to Aisha's side with their bow drawn. "The western sector is secure. Is this kobold really troubling you?"

Aisha grumbled. "Something's weird about it."

The kobold's silver eyes glinted in the sun. "My lord, it appears you have decided to trust others again. Is that a wise choice?"

Short breaths were all Sariel managed as the kobold transformed. Grey skin hugged a humanoid form with nondescript features except for two silver orbs staring maliciously at the mutant elf.

"Veil!" Sariel roared and loosed an arrow.

He sprouted wings that carried him away from the attack. Upon landing, the wings vanished as quickly as they appeared. More projectiles targeted him but he easily side stepped; only flying when necessary. "Are you sure you should attack me, my lord?" he taunted. "Isn't our friend here worth your time? He is a ruler after all."

A thick cloud of sand kicked up as heavy wings flapped overhead. The pungent odor of blood and fire grew thick in the air. Horrified screams drowned out whatever else Vail said as he vanished into the fleeing crowd. It pained Sariel but they stood with Aisha as the Desert Ruler descended upon the village.

***

It didn't take long for Kargon to dispatch the kobolds in East Spirefell. Their resistance to fire did little to protect against his raw strength. Crushing scales was never something he anticipated being capable of. But protecting civilians while alone against a dozen kobolds required strong focus. He assumed that was what caused his flames to solidify beyond even his astral hands' density. It made little sense but there was no time to question it. The solidified flames were unmatched in power, exploding on impact and eviscerating monsters.

Civilians and guards alike were in awe of a firebrand and he couldn't deny it boosted his confidence. So much so that Kargon didn't fear the dragon descending nearby. Vofric and Avant ran past on their way south and Spirefell citizens cheered as Kargon joined.

He wasn't two steps into South Spirefell when a creature dropped from the sky in front of him. Crimson scales across the dragominn's body shivered in excitement. Tar-like scars traced its visage as if one well placed strike would sunder it. Kargon's instincts failed in assessing the individual's strength—likely because he'd beaten them before.

"Let your party handle the beast. Got a score to settle," Elmud said.

Before Kargon could respond, they grabbed him by the collar and flew back to the eastern sector. One swing of Elmud's arm sent the half-elf across the sand covered street with unexpected force. Upon finding his footing, Kargon ignited. He couldn't close the gap with a lunge but powerful strides worked well enough. Elmud didn't bother moving and took the full brunt of a straight punch. Fire resistance shouldn't be enough to handle the explosive force of Kargon's new magic. Instead, they stood unscathed with Kargon's fist against their face.

"Again. Been a year. Have to show more for it," they said in an unamused tone.

Kargon sent a quick jab accompanied by an astral hand—both ineffective. Something was wrong with his magic. The sturdy flames weren't reappearing no matter how much he tried. With an obvious wind up, he sent a burning punch towards his opponent.

Elmud grabbed Kargon's fist mid-swing. "Disappointing," they muttered.

"Disappointed in me? Or yourself for losing to me?" Kargon scoffed.

The dragominn silently tightened their grip. It was impossible to describe the feeling of bone against bone. They popped, fractured, then tore through skin as every part of Kargon's hand shattered, blood pouring from the wounds. It didn't register that the scream he heard was his own.

Elmud's serious facade gave way to a familiar cockshire attitude as they used their free hand to pull down the monk's goggles. Once his face was unobscured Elmud pulled Kargon's arm from its socket. Bones cracked from the rebound before Kargon was flung skyward with the dragominn flying close behind. Every use of their claws showed the difference in races as Kargon's skin flayed. It took everything to mount a defense but each attempt was stopped by a clawed strike. Sand burned against his exposed muscles that only stayed inside by sheer luck.

A tight grip kept Kargon in midair before he was furiously spun and released—his limp body careened towards a South Spirefell wall. Before the collision, Elmud flew directly over his victim and kicked him straight to the ground. Sand was softer than the thick walls of a building but it was hard to say the landing was any better. Stones and glass cut Kargon as he skidded to a stop. Elmud crashed down next to their ruined plaything and propped him up.

"You've done nothing for a whole year! To think you beat me before," they scoffed and scratched Kargon's chest. "Some hero you turned out to be, Kargon."

Another attack ripped through him. "Overconfidence is your undoing."

More rapid strikes tore into the monk—a bloody pulp waiting to fall. "You're a fool for believing you could help the Hero."

Through bloodied vision Kargon could barely make out Elmud's next attack. It was a mocking stance similar to his haymaker. And Kargon could do nothing to stop it.

"Enough." said a soft voice that somehow reached every person in Spirefell. A figure emerged from the center of the spires clad in intricate onyx armor. Two cobalt horns curled out of his forehead, hanging over jet black hair. Cerulean skin amplified black eyes with cobalt irises. An elegant tail with a barbed tip provided balance as the man ascended unseen steps. On his back was a steel greatsword that put Rusty's to shame.

Every eye in Spirefell turned towards the tiefling—including those of the Desert Ruler. Even in Kargon's haze, he knew who approached.

"Aeraza."

"Do not speak his name!" Elmud barked. They dug claws into Kargon's face, lifted him up, and threw him towards the Hero's party.

Though the demon king walked slowly, his gait carried him further than it appeared. Desert Ruler was the first to leave its stupor, readying a flame for its new prey. But there was no battle. An imperceivable swipe from the demon king's greatsword cleanly split the dragon's head from its body. The Hero's party remained frozen as the gigantic monster crashed to the ground—defeated by their nemesis.

Aeraza stared at Aisha. "Kharim's successor." He let out a soft hum then turned to Elmud. "We go."

The dragominn grumbled then took to the sky, carefully picking up the demon king and a silver-eyed villager. To take the dragon head with them, the changeling transformed his arm into a massive claw. Desert Ruler's body remained untouched as the demons flew away.

Sariel almost fired an arrow but Vofric stopped them before pointing to Kargon with a panicked look. Avant ran to his master and stared, unaware what to do. Tears freely flowed from Aisha as she rushed to her childhood friend's side. Kargon could no longer hear what was being said. He couldn't even sense pain. There was simply nothing.

CHAPTER THIRTY-TWO

Splitting the Party

"Kargon? Kargon!" Aisha wept over her friend's body as his blood pooled under them. Avant approached slowly and pressed his body against Aisha's side for comfort. No amount of support could stop her shaking. Trembling hands reached for Kargon's face but feared making contact.

Sariel stood behind Aisha, looking at Kargon with a dour stare. All the dragon's skills were made for combat and yet they were powerless against a daunting foe. They were useless when it really mattered and now could only listen to Kargon's fading breath.

"He has little time. Vofric, can you do something?" they asked.

"I have little mana left..." he said, slowly meeting Aisha's tearful gaze. "It is enough to close his wounds."

The paladin knelt next to Kargon with clasped hands, a soft prayer on his lips as golden light wreathed them. Nothing could be allowed to break Vofric's focus lest he hasten the monk's journey from the mortal realm. Slowly, the dwarf separated his hands and hovered them over Kargon. Bones reshaped and fused with their shattered remnants while deep cuts sewed themselves shut. That was already pushing Vofric to his limits but he kept going. Ribbons of loose skin rapidly stitched together but left small openings. Scars and bruises remained prominent all over Kargon's body.

Civilians slowly exited their hiding places all over Spirefell and traveled to the south. Whispers carried through the gathering crowd about everything that happened. Most, however, joined the Hero's party and prayed for the monk's wellbeing.

Vofric panted as he exhaustively looked over his patient. Thankfully, the prayer was mostly successful before his mana fully depleted. With a soft word of thanks, Aisha placed a hand on Kargon's cheek.

"Come on. Wake up," she pleaded. "Why isn't he waking up?"

Vofric shook his head. "He has many wounds. Some beyond the physical."

"Are we expected to wait in the street?" Sariel asked.

"I'm not leaving him in the middle of the street!" Aisha argued.

A villager approached cautiously and said, "He may rest in one of our cots." Noticing Aisha's wary glare, she continued, "My name is Ciora. I'm a nurse at the local infirmary. We can bandage the remaining wounds and let him rest."

Aisha and Sariel shared a look and lifted Kargon by his shoulders. No matter how slow they moved, there was no avoiding blood loss. A pained groan would be welcome just to ease the party's nerves but the unconscious half-elf remained silent.

Entering the infirmary was promising as stone walls caused the temperature to cool. Kargon was carefully placed on a soft cot and Aisha brushed his wild hair off his sweat-drenched forehead. The others grabbed seats nearby as Ciora bandaged any visible wounds. It was nerve wracking while Aisha scrutinized every movement but the nurse remained steadfast.

As she worked, a halfling approached the solemn adventurers. "My name is Orin; chief of Spirefell. Thank you for protecting us. I cannot convey my sorrow for your comrade's fate."

"Be careful with your words. He has not passed," Sariel said venomously.

Orin held up his hands fearfully. "I misspoke. I regret the pain he is in." He turned to Vofric and said, "You are different from previous Starcaller disciples we have encountered."

The dwarf shook his head. "I am the very same one who failed you in the past."

"I see. I commend the change in your actions."

An absentminded grunt passed Vofric's lips. Success in protecting

North Spirefell had lost its luster as he studied the faces of the Nevesi duo. Aisha blankly stared at Kargon, not bothering to wipe her tears. Sariel's hand rested on Avant while they stared out the window, contemplating their next course of action.

The village gave the adventurers privacy and focused on the dragon's corpse. Repeated strikes with simple tools broke scales, revealing meat that would feed the village for months. Other parts were torn apart to be repurposed. A mixture of emotions weighed on Sariel as the Desert Ruler was butchered. Disappointment at the dragon for its violence and humanoids for readily tearing it apart. And understanding that anyone would defend themselves when attacked without warning.

"How long will it take?" Aisha asked suddenly.

Nothing had changed about Kargon's situation. But there was no training to watch over a dying comrade. Whatever Aisha felt was beyond comparison for the rest of the party.

"I do not know," Vofric said.

"Guess."

"I cannot."

The response hit Aisha like a punch to the chest. A monstrous grip tightened around her heart at the thought Kargon may never wake up. She unconsciously placed a hand on his arm, focusing on the heat he unconsciously permeated. He had to be alive. Kargon was too resilient to fall now. There were more people to meet and things to do. There was no way Aisha could tackle them without her idiot. The Hero needed him to succeed on her quest.

"What was at the center of the spires?" Sariel said, staring at the obelisks through the window.

Orin had remained nearby, assisting Ciora with her needs. "I cannot explain it here. You will need to join me at the village meeting hall."

"We should not leave Kargon alone. Vofric, you and I shall go."

He didn't need an explanation. While Aisha's eyes landed on whoever was speaking, her attention never actually left Kargon. His arm in her grip was the only thing stopping her shaking. A teary eyed Avant approached her and leaned against her legs.

"Rest if you must, Aisha. We will return shortly," Vofric said, then turned to Orin. "Lead the way."

Aisha barely acknowledged her friends leaving.

***

Hours passed before the others returned. The Hero hadn't moved a muscle; her eyes transfixed on Kargon. Lightning crept along her fingers as she lifted a hand over the man. The effects of an electric shock to the chest were unknown. It might defibrillate Kargon. Or maybe his fire immunity made him especially susceptible to lightning. Aisha was too frazzled to think about it. Footsteps were approaching and she made her move.

As the door to the infirmary opened, Aisha leapt out of her seat. Sariel and Vofric weren't quick enough to stop her and Avant only woke up because they screamed. Electricity crackled around the Hero's palm as she slammed it against Kargon's chest. His body jolted upwards then immolated.

Aisha staggered back in fear as everyone rushed to stop the blaze. Bandages burned off while wounds cauterized. Even in tatters, his armor withstood the intense flames. Ciora grabbed buckets of water while Vofric and Sariel moved things away. Only the cot was set ablaze.

"How do we stop him?" Sariel yelled.

"Is there anyone in the village attuned to fire?" Vofric asked.

Ciora replied while pouring water on Kargon. "No. The climate doesn't agree with them."

"Aisha? Aisha?!" Sariel screamed.

The commotion drew a crowd that drowned out any conversation. Avant charged at the Hero, tackling her to the floor and forcing her to focus. Slowly, she looked away from Kargon as the panic and screaming reminded her of a similar occurrence—a vague memory from before his monastic training. "We need his master. The monk in Mount Iana."

"That's at the most southern point of Tetria! We need a faster solution!" Vofric argued.

From within the crowd someone yelled, "I can get you there!" Taze pushed through the door of the infirmary and explained, "If you can carry him, I can send you to Mount Iana. It's the least I could do for you helping Spirefell."

"I can carry him," Sariel insisted. They had only a little mana left and created a stretcher. It would surely burn but could be magically repaired. the last of their mana went to building a stretcher.

Taze nodded and commanded Ciora. "Get the mirror from your office. The big one next to the closet."

"I will help!" Vofric said and ran out of the room. He and Ciora returned with a mirror taller than Sariel that stood on simple wooden legs.

"Vofric, the coin." Taze demanded. Holding it in both hands, they snapped it in half. Silver powder puffed out and the coin shimmered. Throwing it at the mirror morphed its surface into liquid metal with no reflection. "It's made from controlled Traveler's Dust. Only five people can go through. I doubt I'm replacing any of you."

Aisha rose to her feet and grabbed one end of Kargon's stretcher. "We'll handle it."

One step into the liquid metal instantly transported them in front of a lake atop a flattened portion of a mountain. Behind them stood the entrance to a seven story temple that curved around the land to create a wall. Both ends met at an arched gate that led to stairs descending the mountain.

Frantically searching for someone to help, Aisha ran towards the temple. She was stopped by the door swinging open as a feathered humanoid with the head of an owl stepped through. A tuft of feathers on the front of his round face gave him a perpetual look of aggravation. Sandy feathers encircled large gray eyes that stared intently at the adventurers. The owlminn balanced atop clawed talons, blocking the path with two freckled wings.

"What are you doing?!" he squawked.

"Avant, your disciple is on fire!" Vofric yelled.

The bird-like humanoid took pause as did the young owlbear standing below the stretcher.

"Vofric?" Master Avant asked quizzically before turning this attention to the burning half-elf. One flap of the master's wings brought him near and he exclaimed, "Kargon!"

The owlminn lifted his left arm—slender and clawed—over Kargon, rows of beaded bracelets rolling down to his bicep. Directly across from the master appeared a white shade of his visage. Plunging their arms into the fire, they slammed against the half-elf's chest. The impact sent a surge through his body and a force akin to wind stopped the flames instantly. Without hesitation, Master Avant gripped his disciple's bracelet and tore it off. The cracked chains rustled in his feathers as he studied the individuals who appeared at his monastery.

"I demand an explanation."

***

Air in the Sanctuary of Spiritual Combustion must have had magical properties. Passing through the monastery entrance calmed the party. Students of many ages and races explored the halls between their studies. Some looked to be getting specialized training from mentors. All of them took notice of the Hero and her party meeting with the headmaster in the tea room. Disciples young and old wanted to eavesdrop but knew better than to interrupt.

Master Avant listened intently while sipping tea from a fine cup resting on his palm. "For the demon king to not only show his face but let you live is astounding. Did you say his greatsword was black?" he asked.

Aisha answered. "Yes. But about Karg—"

"An onyx blade able to kill a dragon. *Brachynox*; sealed for centuries and lost to time. Found by one who can utilize it to its fullest potential."

"What is *Brachynox*? The chief of Spirefell mentioned it was a powerful sword." Sariel said.

"An Artifact of Arcana. You have encountered one in Dawncaster. The stave wielded by the prince," Master Avant explained. "I know not what the demon king seeks but his goal will be easily reached with that blade."

Aisha hummed. "We can look into it while waiting for Kargon to recover."

Master Avant grunted. "No. The boy must be trained once he awakens. Otherwise, he will become a hindrance further along your journey."

"We can do our research while we wait!"

"Are you saying you will leave innocents to defend themselves while twiddling your thumbs in my halls?"

"No! I mean, I also need to train and the facilities here—"

"Cannot handle your strength," Master Avant interjected again. "Are you aware of what you need to do? During the battle you shared with me, not once did I hear about you using *Valefor* for its intended purpose."

Years of ignoring the obvious hit Aisha like a brick. Eyes widened as realization dawned. "It's a conduit! I'd forgotten. I couldn't do it before. Maybe—" She reached for the hilt of her blade but Vofric forcefully grabbed her wrist.

"Not here. The effect of your magic on such a powerful conduit is unknown," he said. "It could be catastrophic until you master it."

Sariel nodded. "Doing so during our travels is the best option."

"You two sound surprisingly okay with leaving Kargon behind," Aisha spat. "He's my friend! And he's not waking up and it's my fault! We can't just leave him here!"

Sariel cleared their throat to stay calm. "Kargon is our friend as well. He is resilient and will find his way back to us."

"The sanctuary must have means to contact us when Kargon is ready. Or they could contact Taze to bring him to us," Vofric said. "Much like you trust Kargon, I trust Avant to take care of him."

Avant, the owlbear, growled at his namesake and demanded proof before he left his master. The bird-like beings stared at each other in brief silence.

"We could not be more different, little one," Master Avant said while slowly resting a hand on the young beast's head. "However, I do care for Kargon. He will be under my direct care and tutelage. It will depend on him how quickly he can rejoin you." He turned to Aisha. "Is that agreeable?"

Before answering, the Hero looked at her companions. It was selfish to think only she cared for Kargon. But the world—the demon king—would not wait for him to recover. The journey needed to continue and everyone needed to improve. Waiting around was the worst possible choice.

"Can we see him before we go?" Aisha asked.

"Of course," Master Avant replied.

The group traveled to the infirmary where other disciples watched over Kargon. They departed as the adventurers approached and surrounded their ally. For the first time, he looked calm in his unconscious state.

"Can I have a moment alone?" Aisha asked.

"Of course," Master Avant replied and took the others to wait by the door.

She sat on the edge of the bed and ran her fingers through Kargon's hair, unable to feel magical heat radiating off it. All their life he'd been a light sleeper—always waking up when Aisha stared too intently. It was possible to count on one how many times she got to enjoy his calm demeanor. Tears welled in Aisha's eyes but she held back. Slowly, as to not disturb him, Aisha leaned in close and kissed Kargon's forehead.

"It'll be weird not having you by my side," she said, rising to her feet.

The group walked with Master Avant back to the lake in the courtyard. Few leads existed but someone had to know more about the Artifacts of Arcana. The best bet was Shusyoun, the city of scholars, easternmost city of Tetria, and a place that sent chills down Sariel's spine.

Master Avant could send the party to the east exit at the bottom of Mount Iana. It would take months to reach Shusyoun on foot but there were no other options. A spell caused stones inside the lake to glow and turned the water into bubbling silver tar.

"I will take care of Kargon," the master said.

Vofric and Sariel thanked him while Avant nuzzled against the owlminn.

Aisha simply nodded, stepped into the lake and commanded, "With me."

CHAPTER THIRTY-THREE

The Hero's Conduit

Within days everyone had figured out ways to train during the trek to Shusyoun. Vofric empowered the base power of his magic by reciting the Starcaller's "teachings." The journey was less mind numbing as he shared Yuna's adventures. Even with hazy details, it provided insight into the hardship Kharim and his allies faced. Each story strengthened the dwarf's connection with his grandmother. Understanding helped him find forgotten spells, like the ability to wash away fatigue with a wave of his hand. Multiple nights of camping could be easily skipped thanks to holy blessing.

Hunting was all Avant needed to grow stronger. Rage was unnecessary during battle with small morsels but he still empowered himself to an unstoppable form. Aggressive roars scared away prey so the owlbear could get the chase he sought. Nothing could stop his rampaging charge through the forest. As his rage infused blessings grew, the energy around him morphed. Mana-filled feathers turned into a metallic shell bolstered further by his already tough hide. As long as Avant raged, nothing could escape unscathed.

Sariel was luckiest in that crafting and dismantling tools empowered their combat techniques. When camping, reshaped trees magically bound together to form a platform above the forest floor. Two tents were built on top with a rope ladder hanging down. At first, the treehouses took hours to construct as bending trees proved difficult. But with each newly crafted tool, Sariel's abilities improved until the forest danced to their whims. Camp was often ready within minutes of finding a safe area.

Aisha had no such luxury and needed to carve out time to practice her magic in solitude. Lightning was too wild to safely strengthen around others. Electric control had a limited distance and there was no telling where it would go if it traveled far enough. Aisha wouldn't allow the others to get hurt from her irresponsibility. The solution was creating a large distance from them every time she intended to train.

Time used to find a solitary area was perfect for thinking about her fallen friend. An aching weight laid in her chest every time Kargon came to mind. If the thoughts arose during training it would be a problem—worse yet if they appeared in a fight. Thus, she acknowledged the feeling during treks then pushed them away while training. Nothing could be on Aisha's mind when she tried to use *Valefor* as a conduit. If she succumbed to memories of Kargon, it was a squandered night of training.

As she arrived at an acceptable clearing the thoughts dissipated. A firm grip on *Valefor* pulled it from the sheath while walking to the center of the area. With a forceful stab, she planted the blade in the ground then held her hands over the hilt. Crackling purple electricity bounced between her fingers longer than she normally held it. The element was best used quickly and allowing it to weave around her for minutes was unfamiliar. Every bit of focus sped up the frequency of flashes and jolts but none leapt far from her palms. The bolt would launch at unprecedented speed once released and needed to be strong enough to affect *Valefor*.

Aisha had tried pouring mana into Kharim's conduit when she first acquired it. That was how everyone learned to wield magic—to connect to the energy that flowed through the world. But her refined mana didn't empower *Valefor*. When Aisha tried the same thing recently, each attempt was met with failure. In frustration she'd launched a bolt of lightning at the sword and the magic wreathed around it. That caused her to start searching for the minimum required power needed to fuse her magic with the blade.

An orb of electricity lowered slowly from Aisha's hands to *Valefor's* leatherbound hilt. Sweat dripped from her brow as mana poured into the destructive force. No spell in her arsenal could compare to the creation. Even if it didn't help with her swordsmanship, it would be a boon in the battle against the demon king. Deep in the recesses of Aisha's mind, an inkling that this could possibly damage the weapon reared its head—enough of a distraction for the half-elf to lose control.

The time it took for the lightning to make contact with *Valefor* could not be described as a second. For anyone other than Aisha to perceive it would be a miracle. What anyone could sense was the massive shockwave from the legendary sword. There was no sound as it took on the force and deflected electricity outward, followed seconds later by a ground-shaking boom. Surrounding flora was decimated by the blast and expanded the alcove in size.

"Dammit!" Aisha yelled, wild bolts flying from her hands at *Valefor*. Each dissipated on contact and she sat with a huff. Intertwined fingers rested under her nose while she grumbled at the sword.

A figure appeared in the clearing and took note of the damage. Aisha was aware of the presence but knew it posed no threat.

"That was quite an attack," Vofric said groggily while stowing his war-hammer and walking to Aisha's side. "Are you still having trouble using your weapon?"

The crash had to have awoken the party as Sariel appeared in a tree at the edge of the clearing. Avant lumbered to the base of it and slumped onto his stomach.

"Kharim's weapon," Aisha said.

Vofric furrowed a brow. "What do you mean?"

"It rejects me every time I try to wield it as a conduit."

"Flinging magic wildly at a conduit does not constitute 'wielding' it." Vofric rested a hand on his friend's shoulder.

Aisha stared daggers at the stout man but said nothing.

"Do you know what I utilize as a conduit?" Vofric continued.

"Your hammer. I get it. You know how to do this and I should've asked for help."

"You are partially correct. Asking for help would have been wise but you have made peculiar decisions since the events of Spirefell. None of which I blame you for," Vofric explained. Pulling the front of his haphazardly equipped chestplate, he fished out his pendant—a golden four pointed star.

Aisha furrowed her brow. "That's not the Starcaller sigil."

"It does not represent a Starcaller's connection to Yuna but her grandson's. A conduit she passed down to me," Vofric explained. "I produce holy magic through it then pass it to my war-hammer." Without unsheathing his weapon, he caused it to glow. "Even if you cannot use it as a conduit, that doesn't mean it can't be infused with lightning. Simply guide your magic into your weapon."

"It's not mine," Aisha huffed.

"My second argument; *Valefor* is known as the Hero's sword. Not Kharim's. Ask anyone who has crossed our path and they would state that it is your weapon. Do you know why?" Vofric asked rhetorically, reminding Aisha of her mother. "*Valefor* chose you. You are trying to overpower it when you should be working alongside it. You must choose *Valefor*."

The idea that Kharim's will was rejecting Aisha felt similar to the unwarranted expectations others had in the Hero. Scrutinizing glances accompanied the smallest failures even when she was new to her role. The acceptance of her flaws from allies was a shield that provided room to master her abilities.

"I guess *Valefor* has some expectations that I have to meet," Aisha muttered and rose to her feet. A quick pat dusted the dirt off her armor as she slowly approached the sword. Its unaging leather invited her worn palms like it had countless times before. There wasn't a single speck of dirt on the blade as it released from the ground. Waving it slowly through the air reminded her how comfortable the weapon felt in her grip. A meek jolt of lightning danced along her open hand's fingertips. Softly, she traced them against the flat of the blade.

The sound of crackling lightning was accompanied by a faint metallic hum. *Valefor's* silver light became surrounded by an unending torrent of purple electricity that drew mana from Aisha without any exertion. It wasn't perfect; she still couldn't use *Valefor* as a conduit on its own. But it was the first real progress she'd made. As long as she had enough time to connect lightning to the weapon, there would be no problem.

"How does it feel to swing?" Vofric asked after stepping to a safe distance.

A forceful swing created an electric line that followed the attack's arc. Each follow-up created an aftereffect. Without thinking, Aisha collided with one and it painfully surged through her. Her immunity to lightning had often protected her but this was more powerful than previous backfires.

An idea popped into Aisha's head and she muttered something about Kargon rubbing off on her. Not bothering to consider the consequences, she swung her blade then quickly jabbed her free hand at the trail of electricity. After the shock and pain wore off, she produced more lightning in her free hand. The crackling magic was softer than *Valefor's* but greater than other spells Aisha created before. Not only had her magic empowered the weapon, it had amplified her in turn.

The space in front of her became clouded in a flurry of strikes. Metal clashed with lightning and shot out sparks that quickly disappeared. For almost a minute, she attacked relentlessly at speeds the rest of the party could barely perceive. But they knew something was wrong as frustration was evident on their leader's face.

"What's wrong?" Vofric asked.

"I'm too slow," Aisha grunted without stopping her swings.

"Your physical capabilities cannot produce the results you desire," Sariel snorted.

With a sudden stop and pivot, Aisha stared at the figure in the trees. "Excuse me?"

"I spoke improperly. Allow me to elaborate." The dragon jumped from their perch and landed softly before walking to the Hero. "You wish to attack as fast as lightning travels, correct? Your body cannot produce such speeds naturally. However, I believe it can be guided to that speed."

Sariel held out their draconic claw, summoning their bow instantly. They shot an arrow across the clearing. It appeared mundane until the projectile turned in the air and flew sideways until piercing the ground on an unexpected course. "Regardless of contact, I feel a connection with my creations," they explained. "Your lightning has a presence in your mind you haven't considered. Focus on the lightning on your blade; not the physical representation but the connection you feel."

Aisha was aware of the sensation but she'd never paid much attention to it. It was a faint presence like frayed rope asking to be grabbed. Launching a bolt of lightning from her free hand, she felt the frayed rope again—more prominently than before. Moving her hand felt like it brushed against it and forced the bolt to twist in the air. Sariel immediately backed up to Vofric's side.

The presence within *Valefor* was much fainter and felt like a tangled mess of rope. One momentary presence demanded Aisha's attention as she slowly waved her sword. It was near the blade's balance point and screamed out every so often. It took precise timing to pull when it was strongest.

The first time was sheer luck and had Aisha not released *Valefor*, her arm would rip out of its socket. Speed and force of the redirected attack put immeasurable strain on her yet she was too excited not to try again. Hurriedly she picked up the sword and traced lightning on it. This time she swung more seriously; as if attacking an invisible foe. Every attempt to grab at the sensation was a failure but it grew clearer with each swing. The tangled mess became faint and frayed ends bound into a sturdy point that called to the Hero.

Aisha pushed her awareness towards the sensation. In the middle of one of her naturally fast attacks, she shifted its trajectory. Her body roared in pain but she refused to let up. The lightning guided attack was immeasurably quick. Aisha groaned in pain but raised her sword. Once again, she was successful but without care there could be permanent damage.

"You both… made this simpler…" she panted while massaging her shoulder. "But it'll… take a while… to master."

Avant let out a drawl of a growl in response. Aisha looked to Sariel who wore a knowing smirk. "Practice."

Aisha was in too much pain to laugh but tried anyway. There was no stopping her so Vofric handed over a small bag of potions.

"I cannot convince you to rest now that you've made strides forward. However, the idea of remaining awake is unpleasant to me." Vofric chuckled groggily. "Use these as you see necessary. But make time to rest before we depart."

After a quick word of gratitude, the others gave Aisha the privacy she wished for. They were right about her excitement. She practiced once more before thinking about drinking a potion. It was an awful decision that resulted in her dropping to the ground in pain. Slowly, she dragged herself over and retrieved a drink, allowing it to take effect while she laid on her back. All the while, she held *Valefor* over her. Rest might be necessary but there was no way she would release the weapon again. No way she'd stop the flood of mana. Though it was making her delirious; giving her visions of an amethyst light muddying *Valefor's* silver glow.

CHAPTER THIRTY-FOUR

Heart to Heart

The party's ratty map was practically useless in the eastern part of Tetria. It dawned on them that half the continent wasn't properly recorded. Much of it remained undeveloped as wild animals roamed with no fear of the humanoids. Monsters of all kinds dominated the land and only served to hinder the party. Keeping track of their location was best done by following any river. It also aided in finding campsites and quarries to hunt. It wasn't as easy without Kargon but Avant and Sariel handled themselves well while Aisha and Vofric resorted to fishing.

A makeshift fishing rod was lightly gripped in Aisha's hand as she sat atop a boulder by the water. Experiencing the time it took to catch a single morsel made her appreciate Kargon's patience. Every passing day made it harder to ignore memories of him. Something about them made Aisha's heart flutter.

"Have you ever been in love, Vofric?" she asked suddenly.

He sat on another stone with his own rod and slowly turned his head at the question. "Excuse me?"

"It's just a question," Aisha replied listlessly.

Vofric reeled in a small morsel while contemplating. "A few times. Some have passed away and others went their separate ways."

"So, everyone does…" Aisha's line tugged in the water but pulling it out revealed nothing. With a sigh, she cast the line again.

"Separating ways does not mean love diminishes. I doubt yours has for Kargon."

"You mean as a friend, right?"

"I mean platonically and romantically." Vofric grunted.

Aisha blushed, trying to keep a straight face while staring at the river. "How would you know?"

Vofric crossed his arms with the rod held close. A deep sigh accompanied the recollection of past lovers. Memories of roaming the streets of myriad cities, hand in hand seeking views made worthwhile by the presence of a close companion. Gifts given with knowledge of a person's heart. A kiss shared at innocuous times remembered for the words shared around it.

"Hearts want companionship," he said softly. "My life feels fulfilled with friends but I cannot deny romance is enticing. A special person can turn plain days into unforgettable memories. They share your sadness in a way that lessens the pain.""

"It feels like Kargon's surrounded by lights," Aisha muttered. "In my mind, I mean. Every memory of him is shining. I had a mentor I saw that way for a while. She was the only one who treated me as more than just 'the Hero.' But once she left the shine vanished. For Kargon it's always been there."

A school of fish swam swiftly past the duo without disturbing the water. The shift in colors drew Aisha's attention and she nabbed the hook on one creature before flinging it towards her. Precise movements unhooked the dying creature before she binded fresh bait onto the hook and tossed the line back into the river.

Vofric chuckled softly. "Do you think that's why you asked Kargon to join you on your journey?"

Aisha shook her head. "No. Honestly, I never thought anything of it. He just always treated me like the kid he grew up with. We had a large group of friends in our childhood. They distanced themselves when I drew *Valefor*. Other people who were never close to me acted overly familiar. Like they deserved something from me and anyone else simply for knowing me. Not Kargon. He's the same idiot who's been there. Always."

"Was there a time in your life when Kargon was not there?" Sariel asked loudly as they returned with Avant with a bundle of fruit. The dragon sat near the campfire and began sifting through while Avant joined Aisha by the water and immediately ate the small morsel she'd caught. Everyone accepted that the first catch went to the owlbear.

"Not really. Our parents were old friends so we grew up together," Aisha answered. "There were the five years he studied under Master Avant. Even that didn't change Kargon much."

"He had a temper, no?" Vofric asked. "It seems to have returned."

Aisha nodded. "The anger helps him fight but it goes away the second things die down. Even as a kid he never took it out on anyone. Velana and Zigon were still worried something might happen."

Sariel scoffed. "It takes a strong personality to remain unchanged even after major events. Let us hope Elmud's attack does not overpower it."

"It won't," Aisha said confidently while pulling another fish from the water and slamming it against the boulder. It was much larger than the first and was placed opposite Avant so he knew not to touch it. One more catch would be enough for all of them.

"How long have you felt this way?" Vofric asked.

"My whole life. I just... didn't acknowledge it," Aisha replied.

"Will you tell him when we see him again?"

Aisha sighed. "I don't know. I'm worried he won't feel the same way."

"Foolish," Sariel grumbled.

"I have to agree. It is rather obvious how Kargon feels about you." Vofric added.

"What do you mean?" Aisha asked.

Vofric hummed and looked at Sariel. "I caught on during our time in Dawncaster. Was it the same for you?"

Sariel shook her head and said, "Balur."

Avant lazily chirped while eating his snack.

"He also says it was obvious in Balur," Sariel translated.

"The young often outpace their elders." Vofric laughed.

"That justification fails considering my age," Sariel scoffed.

Aisha huffed. "But, how do you know?"

"The way he looks at you is not mere admiration. There is wonder and awe with every glance." Vofric hummed. "Though I do not believe Kargon is wise enough to recognize his own feelings. As you said, you have been friends your whole life."

Sariel grunted. "He likely thinks all people view their closest companions the way he sees you. I care for you all deeply but I cannot match his adoration of you."

"Agreed." Vofric nodded. "Thus I ask again; will you tell him?"

Aisha watched her line bob in the water between a group of large fish avoiding the hook. It would be easy to shock the surface of the water to catch them all but it would unequivocally damage the ecosystem. There was no choice but to do the job properly.

"No," she answered. "We have a duty to complete. I have to train and focus on the job at hand. The fate of our world is more important than romance."

"Once our journey is complete, you will have ample opportunity," Sariel said.

"That is assuming we succeed."

"Considering that our quest is treacherous, you may not be able to tell him your feelings," said Vofric. "Are you willing to give up the chance entirely?"

Aisha turned to the dwarf and nodded. "If I must."

The brief distraction encouraged a sea beast to challenge the Hero's grip on the fishing rod. Without looking back, she forcefully pulled the creature from the water. It fought with vigor but was no longer protected by the river. A bolt of lightning from the Aisha's free hand fried the creature in mid-air before she brought it to land.

"There are more pressing matters at hand."

CHAPTER THIRTY-FIVE

Skybound

Everyone was growing antsy with the lack of progress towards Shusyoun. Each passing day was another that the demon king grew closer to his goal. It was no assumption—Aisha didn't entertain unprovable notions. Rather, the whole party had noticed more strength in their undead enemies. The frequency of attacks since leaving Mount Iana had ramped up once again but the monsters had changed. They took on a myriad of forms and their power was never what could be expected. Thankfully, the rate at which undead could grow stronger was nothing compared to the adventurers. While the first powerful undead had left them bewildered, it fell without causing any harm.

By now, Sariel didn't so much as leave their perch atop the trees during a fight. Initial hesitation regarding Shusyoun turned to frustration with its elusiveness. It had been so easy to find in their youth. Granted Veil guided the dragon away from it before locking them away for centuries. However, there were no records of it vanishing or being destroyed. This was different than Foxhill since Shusyoun was a mirror to Dawncaster.

Tetria was comparatively smaller than most other continents but was one of the most unexplored. Rumors of travelers getting lost in the eastern half of the land were starting to make a lot more sense. The forest felt endless, similar to the one separating Mount Ikrali and Spirefell, with no landmarks in sight. Weeks had passed since leaving

Kargon and no one knew how much longer it would take to find Shusyoun. No one wanted to even consider they might be going in circles.

At first, Sariel considered triangulating their location using distant vistas was the best option. Years of observation grew into a great skill of recognizing notable clues. Memories of far off views from sky high were burned into their memory. Tall trees that looked over the canopy provided a similar feeling. But Sariel hoped to go higher, so much so that they considered replacing their cowl with a magical alternative. They quickly brushed off the idea. Since waking up in the middle of some unknown field fifty years ago, the cloak had remained with them and replacing it felt inappropriate.

Instead, Sariel studied the ecosystem to track major changes on the party's route. If memory served, Shusyoun's surroundings were dominated by monsters rather than animals. The construction of the city centuries ago garnered undue attention but the defenses overpowered any creatures foolish enough to attack. During such studies, they relied on Vofric to aid from below. With both sets of eyes, the party was less likely to be caught unaware.

"Wooden structures... wooden... structures," Vofric muttered to himself while looking past the underbrush. What he lacked in distant vision he made up for with a discerning eye. "You do not expect them to be as advanced as yours, Sariel, correct?"

"It's unlikely but not impossible. Some monsters have the intelligence required to craft functional edifices."

Aisha raised her eyebrow at the suggestion. "Tetria has only a few monsters with that level of reasoning."

"That we know of," Sariel said from on high. "Goblins may appear unintelligent but even they are capable of building. What they lack in power they make up for with tools. But Veil's experiments had some successes. If they were released into the wild... There is the possibility of highly intelligent beasts who can empower their natural strength."

"Why's Veil on your mind?"

Sariel stopped suddenly and settled onto the branch under their feet. Traumatic nightmares haunted them but rarely did they think about it during waking hours. For memories to flash in their mind something needed to trigger them. Aisha, Vofric, and Avant stopped under the tree as Sariel focused on their surroundings.

A chill ran down their spine, making them acutely aware of the cowl. Memories of clattering scales on muscles were fresh as the day the dragon was captured. The scent of fear emanated from fleeing creatures in the forest. Soft whimpers and rabid growls cascaded in Sariel's mind. "Ravenous…" they muttered and dashed away.

Everyone else could barely keep up while navigating the difficult terrain. Avant's sharp eyes assisted in tracking the swift dragon and his large form was much easier to follow. Against small foliage he was something of an unstoppable force. Sariel's tracking might have been hindered if they didn't know the familiar's vocalizing. Though it was hard to mistake him for any other owlbear with his patchy hide of half brown, half white fur and feathers.

After ten minutes of constant dashing, Sariel stopped with their bow ready. The others caught up soon after and fanned out around the tree. Exhaustion was no issue with the Vofric's magic increasing their endurance The animals took no notice of the armed adventurers or even the almost fully grown owlbear baring his beak. What chased after them was far more horrific. The sight stunned everyone, barring Sariel—sure that Veil had discarded his victims.

Squirming veins bulged off the muscular deformity lumbering towards the fleeing animals. Whatever laid beneath the skin fought to tear through the surface. For a bipedal humanoid, it was incredibly animalistic. A rabbit's muscle structure connected to cat-like legs and jagged claws protruded from gorilla knuckles. Only the creature's head—a hobgoblin—remained relatively unchanged except for the strained blood vessels on the brink of exploding. So many mutations shouldn't be possible for a single creature.

Behind it were bodies of other slaughtered mutants of differing shapes and sizes. All were horrifically mangled when killed by the ravenous hobgoblin. It carried itself with uncharacteristic madness, likely resulting from Veil's experiments. Sariel thanked their draconic lineage for protection from a similar fate.

"Adventurer meat. Tough." The hobgoblin's voice warbled like bubbling acid. Even while addressing the party, it didn't take its eyes off the bear within its grasp. The animal flailed ferociously to no avail. Hefty swings dragged its entire body into the air before slamming it into the dirt. Bones crunched under the pressure and blood seeped out like water from a wrung towel.

While tearing into the morsel, the hobgoblin stared at the adventurers—clearly expecting a reaction. Much to its chagrin, they were unphased. Seeing a dragon beheaded followed by Kargon's evisceration had hardened them.

"Show mercy," Sariel demanded without explanation.

Aisha nodded, then looked at Avant. "Charge."

With a mighty roar, he charged and clawed at the hobgoblin's arm. Talons tore through muscle and freed the bear carcass. There was no saving it but at least the hobgoblin gained nothing from it. It angrily swiped at Avant but missed due to two arrows piercing its open wound. Searing pain coursed through its arm as poison burned within.

"Little one. Mine!" The hobgoblin roared and kicked off Avant to propel towards Vofric. Sturdiness provided an unfortunately secure foothold.

With a preemptive swing, the paladin caught his assailant against the heft of his war-hammer. It pushed the monster aside but did little else as it used the momentum to lunge towards Aisha. With each movement more arrows poisoned the hobgoblin.

Such a lumbering oaf was too slow to impact the lightning fast swordswoman. She sidestepped and brought her blade down on the wounded arm—changing direction midway through the monster's shoulder and aiming at its neck. The hobgoblin forced the weapon off kilter and sacrificed a chunk of muscle. Less than five attacks was all it took for the monster to recognize it was bested.

As Sariel expected, the hobgoblin was ready to retreat. But no one was ready for all its bulging muscles to explode, creating a veil that hid its transformation to the smaller form of an average goblin. It dashed away in flash with unseen mutations. Aisha gave chase, but the unfamiliar forest proved difficult to navigate. Fortunately, Sariel completely avoided the spray of blood and was close on their target's heels.

It moved irregularly, flowing between the trees like water. Mid-dash, Sariel shot two arrows far into the distance hoping to slow the monster. Though the projectiles didn't land on the target, they blocked its path unexpectedly. When slowed, it was possible to glimpse small draconic wings protruding from its back. Pity trickled into the dragon's mind knowing the pain such a mutation likely caused. It was their duty to kill the wild hobgoblin. To show mercy.

Continually shooting arrows only slowed Sariel down. Focusing on the chase helped but the monster used small shortcuts in the forest to vanish momentarily. Something in the distance reflecting the sun made it all the harder to track the fleeing hobgoblin. Sariel didn't dare look away—their heightened senses could still track the creature but a single distraction would allow it to escape.

It was aggravating to be bested by such a weakling. A hunter should never fall behind in their favored terrain and this was Sariel's. Visions of a time long past teased their focus but the dragon refused. Pain surged through them unlike any they'd experienced even after hours of hunting. It was as if hundreds of small blades were tearing through their back.

No. They were ripping out. Each time Sariel's cape flapped it tingled against their spine. A possibility occurred to them. It invited failure but that was already likely without taking a chance. While still dashing forward, they descended to the lower part of the trees where large trunks made maneuvering more difficult.

Instead of jumping off the branch and climbing higher Sariel aimed straight ahead. There was nothing to latch onto and they began to plummet. The ground wouldn't hurt them but there was no speed to be gained. But the dragon hadn't crashed in the forest centuries ago because of a mad dash but her size. Sariel was on course to slam into a tree if something didn't happen soon. But they'd learned from friends the benefits of a leap of faith.

Seconds before the collision Sariel was pulled to the side by a strong force before it turned and surged forward around the tree. Not even a glance was needed for them to recognize the familiar feeling. Their hooded cloak transformed into beautiful jade wings that poked out from beneath Sariel's cropped tunic. Each flap pushed them forward faster than jumping ever could. Sharp eyes working in tandem with Sariel's significantly smaller size blessed the dragon with unprecedented navigational abilities. The hobgoblin looked slower, a few dozen feet under its predator. Sariel glanced forward while considering their next action and caught sight of something in the distance.

Before understanding what it was, they began hurtling to the ground. The wings had transformed back into a cloak that rustled in the wind without slowing the descent. Sariel landed with a loud thud, momentarily dazed. The hobgoblin was wise to take advantage of it but it decided to turn back was unknown. It hovered over Sariel with a wild look of hunger. Slick claws protruded from bony limbs on a crash course with the dragon's head. They couldn't help but let out a scoff—their single mishap attracting the monster with ease.

A single long blade protruded from Sariel's palm and pierced through the hobgoblin's head. The skewered monster crumpled to the forest floor while Sariel rose to their feet, brushing off the blood. Aisha and the others were loudly calling out, directing Sariel back. Every few steps they summoned the wings but could only hover seconds before dropping back down. Using a magic item was completely foreign but made of Sariel's own draconic scales shouldn't be difficult to understand.

"What was that?" Aisha asked with a huff.

Sariel landed next to the party, satisfied with the extra second of air time. "My cape is… was my wing. I wondered why Veil had dressed me when I was abandoned. It was a sick joke," Sariel explained. "I will turn them into a boon."

Aisha shook her head. "Not that! I mean, I'm glad you understand it and would like to learn more. But what was that chase? You went mad. You said to show mercy."

"Ah, yes." Sariel said, as if forgetting their own demand. "Initially I wanted to follow it to wherever it came from. Then something came over me. I was reminded of what Veil did. Who he hurt. All the survivors carried rage that nothing could satiate. They even attacked each other when given the opportunity. I couldn't let it go free." They turned around and walked with purpose while the others followed with questions.

"It seems the encounter was integral in reacquiring your wings," Vofric said.

"Likely," Sariel replied.

Aisha inquired. "Are they the same as your old ones?"

"No, I have access to temporary flight. I must practice in order to master them."

Avant growled softly. Sariel slowed to ruffle his head. "Veil will harm no one else. Not if I have any say."

Aisha and Vofric shared a soft smile and continued to follow.

Neither could deny the peculiarity of Sariel remaining on land.

"Not that I don't like the confidence in directions but where are we going?" Aisha asked.

"A glimpse of something during the chase caught my attention," Sariel answered. "It is clear to me where we are."

CHAPTER THIRTY-SIX

Ancestral Blessing

Tightly packed trees encircled a crystalline dome hidden deep in the forest. Nothing resembling the shape was on the party's map. The only reason Sariel caught a glimpse was because of the shattered upper half that reflected light from certain angles. A collection of buildings inside made up Veil's laboratory.

Dried blood splattered across every surface from a long forgotten battle. Structures crumbled with shattered tools and scattered records littered about. Intact notes were gripped by decomposing corpses. No one in the party felt sympathy for the dead adorned in crimson soaked lab coats. The most peculiar finding was that some of the damage seemed relatively fresh.

"My best estimate is that something happened nearly two decades ago," Vofric said, crouched next to a skeleton with his thumb pressed against a rust smear. "Based on the angles of the fallen corpses, I assume the attacker came from within the central structure."

Most buildings in the clearing were small living quarters which surrounded the main lab. The party didn't bother searching for a door to get inside since most walls were severely broken. Tables filled with scientific tools and magical catalysts were devastated. Reports were torn to shreds without regard for what could be learned from them. As per usual, Aisha immediately looked for something out of place that could provide clues.

Sariel tried to help but couldn't hide their shaken nerves. Without a word, they approached Avant and kept a hand on the beast's back to ease her tension. The owlbear stayed while the duo carefully roamed through the building. None of it was recognizable; mainly because prisoners had been kept in one of two rooms. The "infirmary" was used to drug and operate on them. Potions caused horrid mutations which were followed by ruthless experimentation.

Unconsciously, Sariel gripped the ends of their cloak and wrapped it tightly around themself. Even while shaken, they guided Avant to the room that was most familiar. At the side of the main entrance hall was a hatch hidden under rubble. After moving the stones, Sariel unhooked the latch and revealed a ladder. The owlbear's large body cracked the wooden frame as he plummeted to the room below before Sariel followed. A weepy coo echoed from the beast as he slowly understood their surroundings. Long deceased beings were magically chained to impenetrable cages. Blood, guts, and every internal piece of the creatures had rotted into the stone floor. Each step squelched as the duo silently examined the dungeon.

Vofric aimed to protect everyone by figuring out what caused the extinction of Veil's compatriots. On the off chance they were alive, maybe a weakness could be deduced. Decrepit corpses in the laboratory were clearly the first who were attacked. Their blood was sprayed violently throughout the structure. Bones charred black from unknown elements seemed ready to crumble but touching them revealed how sturdy they were. Something about it was familiar but Vofric couldn't place it. That was until he turned back towards Aisha.

The records room was damaged beyond reason. Lifeless ivory skeletons laid amongst tattered papers and irreparable stone slabs. Aisha dug through piles of broken bookshelves in hopes of finding something. In the clutches of a single soot covered skeleton was a leatherbound book. One check of the surroundings made her feel safe enough to retrieve it.

"Aisha, no!" Vofric yelled but it was too late.

The book was in the Hero's grasp as she stepped back. Simultaneously, the black skeletons throughout the facility rose from the ground. Tar bubbled in their chest cavities like a makeshift heart. Some retrieved weapons while others began to conjure spells. One was hindered momentarily by an arrow from Sariel as they returned from the dungeon with Avant in tow.

They rushed to Aisha's side and Sariel asked, "What did you do?" At least a dozen skeletons had resurrected around the lab and moved to encircle the party.

"I just grabbed a book!" Aisha replied. "It was dumb. I realize I should've considered undead!"

The book might be a problem but it was the only chance of learning what happened here. She stowed it in her armor and unsheathed *Valefor*, unafraid of the undead with everyone's growth. That was until her blade made contact with a bone and felt like it hit reinforced metal.

"Aim for the heart!" Vofric commanded.

An arrow whistled through the air on a crash course with one of the farther skeletons. Its bones morphed into tendrils that deftly knocked away the projectile. Avant tackled the legs out from beneath a nearby monster and moved to bite its heart out. Bones once again transformed and bludgeoned the owlbear with enough force to throw him back several feet.

Aisha quickly electrified her blade and rushed towards an opponent. By now she could handle thirty swings before feeling any strain—more than enough for these monsters. An imperceptible attack launched at the skeleton's heart and tendrils had no opportunity to react. *Valefor* pierced through the black tar but slowed from high resistance. It was enough hindrance for a tendril to hit Aisha's back. Ignoring the pain, she pushed her blade through the organ. It fizzled before the skeleton crumpled to the floor. Aisha hadn't caught her breath before the bones rattled once again. Tar bubbled in the fallen monster's chest cavity and it was soon back on its feet.

Aisha swore under her breath. "I need time to think. Focus on breaking the bones. Don't worry about the hearts!"

While Sariel and Avant could only hinder the skeletons, Vofric was a different case. Golden light rippled off his war-hammer as it shattered bones with ease without considering the heart. It couldn't recover from holy magic's might. Such powerful strikes couldn't be ignored and more monsters lumbered towards the dwarf.

A tendril wrapped around the war-hammer's shaft at the end of a swing, disarming Vofric moments after he decimated another skeleton. Five more fell over each other as their wild tendrils tried to reach the glowing paladin.

He capitalized on his small stature and dove through the tall monster's legs. Strikes pounded heavily against his platemail but a controlled roll landed Vofric next to his war-hammer. The skeletons made an inviting target as they fought against each other to get untangled. But Vofric was worried about his allies, unable to make progress in the fight.

Slowly, he drew the light hammer from his waist then studied it — giving the skeletons time to recuperate. Runes were engraved along the shaft with magical stones inlaid along the bottom of the head. Yuna's stories mentioned it was used to temporarily empower others. It was about time Vofric used it for its intended purpose.

The golden light of Vofric's necklace never dissipated but it was nothing like the molten orange glow radiating from his light hammer. Quickly shifting his other grip placed it near the head of his war-hammer. He hummed, raising his left arm and glowing light hammer to the sky before bringing it down forcefully against the anvil of a war-hammer. A wave of light pulsed through the lab that forced the interwoven skeletons apart.

One attacked the glowing paladin in a panic but was blocked by his light hammer. Mere contact caused the reanimated bones to disintegrate. When the monster pulled back it was met with the force of the molten orange war-hammer. Using weight and momentum, Vofric lifted off the ground before returning with a fierce swing that crushed a black skeleton and eviscerated its heart.

Undead creatures were not known for their personalities but these ones seemed confident due to their overwhelming numbers. Even the sight of a strong ally's demise did not deter them. But they hadn't noticed the glowing bodies of Aisha, Sariel, and Avant—holy magic infused into their strikes. Sariel's creations were empowered, able to drill through bones and pierce hearts. A golden Avant ripped apart the magic that bound the skeletons together. They clattered to the floor and couldn't reconnect before he stomped out their hearts.

In the time the others took out a couple monsters, Aisha wiped out the rest. With nothing hindering her, it was only a matter of how fast she could attack. One skeleton seemingly burst from *Valefor* being near its chest. It hadn't fallen before the half-elf engaged two more; their movements too slow to combat the lightning fast Hero. Any remaining monsters were dispatched in short order.

"Vofric, what was that?" Aisha asked excitedly as the glow faded.

Sariel snorted. "Quite a powerful trick to keep hidden."

"I apologize. I had forgotten the stories regarding its ability until I saw the black skeletons rise," Vofric explained. "I did not expect the properties of the hammer to transform so significantly when used as a conduit. Now I feel foolish for using it as a projectile for so many years. Though, this kind of blessing is only useful against obvious forces of evil. Zombies, skeletons, and demons are the most common foes I have felled."

"It'll definitely help against the demon king," Aisha said.

"Agreed but what of his army? I highly doubt he will not raise another before our journey is complete."

"We'll cut them down."

Vofric shook his head. "I believe you're missing my point. There are only four of us. Five if we include Kargon. Wasting your energy against the demon king's forces puts you at a disadvantage during an important battle."

"We are lacking in numbers." Sariel nodded.

"That is one option. The other is that I refine the shockwave in such a way that it single handedly wipes out droves of enemies."

"There's time to train," Aisha said confidently.

Vofric sighed. "The demon king's hordes will be endless. My attack, and its range, are finite."

Aisha grew frustrated, realizing she hadn't considered anything beyond her final opponent. Elmud and Veil were obvious obstacles but the idea of more enemies slipped her mind. Of course the demon king had fodder to do his bidding. That was why Kharim needed innumerable allies. It was the reason he led armies to fight alongside his party. A pleasant hum escaped Vofric as the Hero berated herself and she turned to him with raised brow.

"Did you think of something?"

"I believe so," Vofric answered. "I must forgo improving the shockwave that occurs when my hammers meet."

Aisha squinted and said, "You'll focus on making the blessing stronger?. But you just complained about our numbers." She slowly contemplated her words and continued, "You want to make your spell more widespread... You have some idea where we can find an army."

"A hunch, yes. Thanks to Sariel, in fact."

Sariel quizzically turned to the dwarf. "If I have had any role in a scheme, I am unaware."

"Not directly. Edthecridaldyrth mentioned a group that has worked with him for centuries; Barbatos. I had also heard of them during my previous adventures," Vofric said. "They have many numbers and focus on hunting the forces of evil. Based on the changes happening in the Tetria, I am hoping we can rely on them."

Aisha hummed. The logic was sound and with a pre-existing group at their side the party wouldn't need to find more people. "But that involves reaching out to them."

"And rumor has it they have a station in Shusyoun," Vofric said with a smile. "Granted, it is a gamble and if you wish me to refocus my effort, I will—"

"It's a good plan."

Sariel scoffed. "There are risks but they are outweighed by the potential reward."

Avant seemed uninterested with the conversation and nudged Aisha's leg. His eyes were focused on the half-elf's hip where a forgotten journal rested.

With a gasp she fished it out. "Shusyoun is still a ways away. We'll look for Barbatos when the time comes. For now let's figure out what happened here."

"That is if such information is within that tome," Sariel said.

Aisha took a knee while reading the journal to facilitate Vofric reading over her shoulder and Sariel stood over them. Owlbears lacked the ability to understand written language but Avant stayed close and listened intently as the Hero read aloud.

According to the notes, Veil's experiments focused on mutations and the effect they had on hosts. Some individuals were weakened to provide a myriad of abilities to others. The most recent experiments started forty years ago and were cut short.

Only common monsters could be found during that time which facilitated a higher survival rate—but the reasoning was lost. Rather than spread themselves thin on multiple creations, everything was put towards a single monstrosity. Bestial tendencies and rampages designated it as nothing more than rage incarnate. Few details of what creatures were fused remained. Magical traits from humanoids were used so the party assumed it was a monster with some relation to their kind. The necessity of such a creature seemed pointless until the mention of an Artifact of Arcana. The being was meant to retrieve it from a cave hidden beneath the lab.

"I was unaware there was a hidden cavern here," Sariel muttered.

"It is unlikely they would let the information slip to their prisoners," Vofric said. "It is unfortunate but they were skilled researchers."

"Indeed." Sariel grunted. "What was hidden within?"

There were few details regarding the magical item; only that it had been wielded by the abomination to seek revenge. Bloody notes detailed how researchers and prisoners alike were killed before the monstrosity returned to the cave. Unfortunately, nothing explained why the researchers had returned as skeletons.

"I can't believe there's Artifact in this place," Aisha said absentmindedly. "If the demon king is planning to collect them, he'll return here at some point."

"It is in our best interest to leave before he does so," Vofric stated.

"I suggest we retrieve the Artifact prior to our departure." Sariel added. The others turned to the elf with questioning eyes. "There is little to elaborate. The demon king will be hindered and we will be empowered. That is assuming this Artifact and creature still remain."

Aisha placed the book on the floor and sat back. If an Artifact really was around, the demon king would come for it. Overpowering its guardian would be child's play for him. "We don't know where to start."

A growl from Avant was the only reply before he approached a ravaged wall. Only rubble remained where structural components once stood. Deliberate swipes cleared the area and revealed a loose hatch. The entrance of a dark tunnel stood behind the gateway.

CHAPTER THIRTY-SEVEN

Attunement

Without Kargon it fell to Aisha to care for Avant. He'd been antsy, dismissive, and absentminded since entering the lab. It got significantly worse upon entering the cave. Being perpetually paranoid ruffled his hide, disturbing nearby surroundings. No amount of instruction reached Avant as he broke the usual formation and stayed many steps ahead of his pack. Maybe it was an instinct of growing owlbears to lead but his obvious distress made everyone uneasy.

Had he been able to explain what bothered him, the others wouldn't blame his irate demeanor. In the dark corners of the dungeon he saw the bones of his kind. Cuts on the cage bars matched the shape of his claws. Fear that his own future would be marred by uncontrolled rage and violence shook Avant to his core.

The language of owlbears could not be translated to express such complex thoughts. No matter how much he growled and roared, Sariel would never understand. The only option was to find whatever monster wielded the Artifact and prove it was nothing like Avant. Logic dictated it would have died long ago but he still let out an inquisitive growl towards Sariel.

"It may have mutations prolonging its life," they replied. "Dragons are not the only beings with long lives. I recall seeing unicorns, gryphons, and other humanoids being sapped of life."

Vofric grunted. "Let us not forget the demon king's penchant for unlife."

"I would prefer not to kill someone or something forced into a state of madness," Aisha grumbled.

"Doing so at this time is showing mercy." Sariel insisted dryly.

Avant knew he didn't carry the same sadness as the dragon but the conversation was still uncomfortable. Thankfully he was far enough from the party to ignore it and think of how odd the cave was. From his understanding, there should be paths and monsters distracting anyone from thinking of their final reward. But there was nothing deterring the party from continuing along the singular tunnel.

Avant paused, turned to Aisha, and chirped inquisitively. The Hero hesitated and pondered—shocked that she clearly understood the owlbear's question.

"Um, Vofric, can you come listen to Avant?" Aisha asked.

"Should you not ask Sariel such a request?" he replied.

"Normally, yes. But I need to check something."

The hesitation confused Avant. Normally Aisha threw out a response with her best guess at his question but now he needed to repeat himself. When he chirped again Vofric raised an eyebrow and hummed.

"The dungeon is quite peculiar."

Aisha pointed at the dwarf and exclaimed. "You did understand him!"

"You say that as if you do as well," Sariel stated.

"I do!"

"It may be an effect of this mysterious place," Vofric said.

Sariel grumbled. "I agree. There were many encounters whenever we delved previously. Nothing has been like this odd path."

Everyone made a point to search for things off the obvious road. The closest thing to an opening were large claw marks along the walls resembling Edthecridaldyrth's cave. Otherwise there was only evidence of what once existed here. Destroyed mounts marked spots where torches hung. Shattered remnants of wooden supports littered the ground, leading to long decomposed corpses. It was difficult to identify anything about them. Something had forcefully ripped the bones apart and scattered them across the floor.

Tattered leather and metal were scattered everywhere from distant years. It was like walking through a timeline of armor through the years. Older ones had to be layered more to match up to the defensive capabilities of pieces like Aisha's. There was little worth salvaging from the half century old scraps, yet Avant stopped to examine each piece.

What he looked for wasn't useful armor but the cuts that marked them. Even the smallest ones eclipsed his claws in size and sent a chill through Avant. Whether the enemy was his kind didn't matter; any similar creature would be bad enough.

For once, Avant regretted his master's tendency to speak out loud. Kargon openly talked about how foolish others were to fear an owlbear without taking the time to train one. It was a kindness only Avant knew—from a man who could understand him with the smallest of movements. Kargon was able to calm the owlbear's nerves with no trouble. But he wasn't here now.

The possibility of losing himself to rage overwhelmed Avant. A wild roar is all he managed before dashing away from the party.

"Avant, wait!" Aisha yelled after him and gave chase with the others.

Rotting guts, muscle, and viscera messily splattered every surface of the tunnel, but skeletons remained relatively unharmed. They were the most recent victims and Aisha desperately wanted to examine them. But the idea of leaving Avant alone sat poorly with everyone.

The end of the tunnel opened into a room no larger than the barracks on the surface. Bones of bugbears and goblins littered the floor with monster parts scattered among them. At the far wall stood an armor stand with nothing on it. Assumedly, what was once displayed there was equipped by the large spectral beast that sat in the center of the room.

Avant let out a sad growl as he recognized the form of an owlbear— some relief felt by its obvious abnormalities. Smoke endlessly poured off the ethereal black creature which was significantly larger than adolescent Avant. The only part of the specter not lacking form was the stone chestplate molded to the monster's torso. As the party caught up and entered the room, the ghost's eyes opened—blue orbs of light staring at the intruders. The spectral owlbear bristled and in turn, each adventurer prepared their weapons.

"You abuse another of my kind?!" the specter bellowed then

charged. Much to the group's surprise, there was a distinct voice within the bestial roar.

Avant leapt in the way and roared back, demanding the specter stop.

"Why protect?" it replied. "Or do they command you?"

The young owlbear barked back defending his allies. None were his master.

"You are forced into servitude," the specter growled.

Once again Avant argued that his master was unlike what the ghost assumed. Much like him, the party were undeserving of the specter's wrath.

Aisha stepped forward slowly, raising empty hands to show she meant no harm. The others followed her lead and stood by Avant — willing to take the risk for his sake.

"We would never do something that harmed Avant. He is an adventurer like the rest of us. It is his choice to battle. Not for us, but with us," Aisha said.

"He shows not normal abilities," the ghost replied.

With a pet on Avant's head, Aisha replied. "Countless battles have made him grow exponentially. Though I admit we're not entirely sure what he is capable of."

"I believe he has shown bardic and barbaric capabilities." Vofric hummed. "They manifest in rather unique forms as well."

"It seems he recently became capable of communicating via growls," Sariel said then turned their attention to the ghost. "Are you truly so foolish as to assume an obvious mutant would abuse another of our kind." They made a point to have their left side prominently facing the specter.

It took the closest approximation of a deep breath manageable. "Apologies. I not seen peace from your kind since birth," it said. "My kind not have names except when companions give. Calling young one 'Avant' proved your motives. You wrong about new ability. I cursed to speak. Powerful enough to affect others near me."

"What other mutations did they force on you?" Sariel asked. It seemed like a common experience from their days as a prisoner.

The specter wavered and let out a grizzly sigh. "The mages... killed many warriors. Used tricks on travelers. Absorbed abilities and forced on me. Not know how many. Not know all abilities. Only know rage and unlife."

"They empowered you to retrieve that Artifact, didn't they?" Aisha asked. After receiving a nod in response, she continued. "We hatched Avant. Sure, he trains but that doesn't explain why he has unique abilities."

"Evolution," Sariel said. "The mages wished to push evolution. It was likely a goal chased through centuries. Little did they know natural evolution would provide similar results in due time."

The specter trilled. It was a kind sound like Avant's when caring for his friends.

"Brings peace that my kind grew strong with no torture," it said.

Sariel grunted. "I must agree."

"We still need the Artifact. The demon king will probably come for it. Especially with Veil at his side," Aisha stated.

The specter shuddered at the mention of Veil, knowing he would be a difficult opponent. They never crossed paths but what was done in his name struck fear into the undead being. It stared at Avant and stepped back to the center of the room. "I protect Artifact. Only give to strong opponent. I challenge Avant."

There was an awkward silence from the rest of the party. This fight could take time and they were sitting beneath a lair connected to the strongest being they'd ever seen. But hesitation and debating had caused enough problems already.

"Avant, prove your strength to your ancestor," Vofric said.

Inspired, the owlbear advanced as his party stood aside. Both beasts took a fighting stance but neither moved to attack. There was no electricity between the combatants. While no one expected animosity, it was peculiar that Avant seemed disinterested in battle.

In truth, he was distracted by memories of his master's fall. As much as the monk liked battle, he never did so without good reason. Failure came from poor assessment of himself and an opponent. But when Kargon fought seriously it was for a cause.

Avant growled inquisitively, questioning why he and the specter should battle. The Artifact was a threat to the specter as long as it remained here. If anything, they could travel together to protect the magic item. As a group, it would be possible for the specter to seek revenge.

"Kargon once said Avant should only fight when there's something to defend. He'll be proud to know the little guy learned from him," Aisha said. "The only defensible thing to do here is remove the Artifact from this place."

The specter once again dropped its stance. "Agreed. But the armor no go with me. Am bound here. When leave, cave collapse." With slow steps it approached Avant. "Can give armor. Accept and flee. Lab not survive."

Avant stared at his ancestor then turned to his party. His master wasn't amongst them but the monk's essence permeated from his best friend who gave a thumbs up. Even during situations with unknown variables, Kargon was always willing to do what was needed. There was no doubt in Avant that his master would be proud with this decision and barked affirmatively.

"It will be unfortunate to no longer understand the young one," Vofric said.

"Word not needed. Only trust," the specter said as it placed a ghostly paw on Avant's head.

There was a surprising warmth in the familiar gesture. Then the stone plate shattered explosively—lulling Avant into a false sense of security with its lack of sound and force. Beneath the stone was an intricate metal plate with an embedded gemstone that burst forward and collided with Avant. He let out a mighty roar, launching the nearby stones away and letting go of the fear that weighed on him.

There was only momentary satisfaction as the cave shook violently. The specter's form pulled apart in an instant with no explanation of the Artifact. Avant's growl was accompanied by a blue energy that surrounded everyone. While it was no longer magically explained, everyone understood the command.

The group sprinted out of the tunnel as a powerful black hole appeared in place of the specter. With Avant's magic, the party could fight against it. Unfortunately, skeletons and rocks flew at them as sharpened projectiles. Everyone was too focused on defensive maneuvers to realize what another bark from the owlbear had done. Aisha and Sariel knocked down anything nearby while Vofric charged through with his war-hammer.

By the time they arrived at the cavern entrance, the tunnel had crumbled in on itself. Even then, magic pulled them back as the black hole was more powerful than they imagined. The fact that Avant's magic could challenge such a surge was astonishing. Everyone rushed for the opening in the trees as dirt and stone were violently torn out of the ground. Massive clumps floated in space momentarily before vanishing into the expanding black hole.

Sariel had the easiest time traversing by flying over. Lightning wreathed around Aisha's legs to assist in dashing through the small platforms. It was growing harder for Vofric to get across the damaged land but a mighty force sent him airborne and onto Avant's back. The paladin hadn't realized the owlbear would grow so much in less than a year. A stone saddle appeared on Avant's back with structures that kept Vofric in place. Their combined magic augments made it possible to maneuver across the quickly dwindling platforms.

Unfortunately, there was one last obstacle for the party to reach safety—a wave of massive glass shards rocketing towards them. Everyone prepared to protect themselves but hesitated at a clear command from the owlbear. His intent wasn't to stop his allies but another attempt at the spell no one saw in the cave. Gravity twisted around him and forced all the nearby blades to the ground. Shards continued to drag towards the massive pit behind the party but there was nothing blocking the path forward anymore—minus their shock at Avant's new power.

"Go!" Aisha commanded, pulling the others from their stupefaction.

Only a few empowered steps carried them out of the opening as the circle of trees crumbled and black hole imploded. Sariel was the first to turn and look at the remnants. The expression on their face was one the others hadn't seen before. Dazzling eyes and a wide smile basked in the destruction of the source of their nightmares. The anger would not fade but it could exist alongside joy. After all, only a massive crater was left of Veil's laboratory.

CHAPTER THIRTY-EIGHT

City on the Edge

Openly carrying an Artifact was a dangerous prospect considering the demon king would likely seek it out. Thankfully, the destroyed lab provided an unforeseen boon in a clear line of sight to a well constructed watchtower in the distance. Sariel flew up to get a better assessment and saw the massive city of Shusyoun surrounding it. After months of searching, the only thing slowing progress was blankets of snow.

It took almost a week before the whole city came into view. Where Dawncaster was a large circle, Shusyoun spread out against the coast. Instead of a standard city wall, a waist high stone perimeter with gates interspersed surrounded the settlement. Entering from any location would be no issue but the party had to find the fastest route to people who could help uncover the demon king's true motives. The best option was marching up to the main city gates and requesting assistance from a guard. With the number of gates around the city, there was no line for inspection to enter Shusyoun. Half a dozen soldiers clad in steel armor with covered helmets stood spread out near stone arches leading into the city.

"Where are you coming from?" a guard asked as the party approached.

"We trekked from Mount Iana," Aisha replied.

The guard whistled. "I hope you mapped that route. Go on in."

Aisha hesitated and asked, "Won't you inquire about our

business?"

"Most folks don't want to share their business. Anything untoward we should be wary of?"

"No, not at all. We wanted to know where we can speak with the Shusyoun scholars."

"They're around," another guard huffed and waved his hand dismissively. "Look for anyone with a triangle shaped pin. The pattern's also embroidered on the back of their robes."

"I take it they aren't your favorite people," Aisha said.

Getting more information from someone was always Kargon's wheelhouse. Connecting with others on a personal level helped. While the Hero may come off as unreachable, a normal swordswoman could easily relate to a town guard.

The guard scoffed. "No. They're fine folk. But if someone comes searching for them I can see how unreliable they are. Probably stumbled through the forest with no clue what you were doing."

"Excuse me?"

"Let me guess: You found some scroll or something. Was missing information, I bet. Couldn't find anything else on your own?" The guard's words grew louder, drawing the attention of his comrades. "Recent adventurers exploring Tetria have been too stupid to offer mapping the unknown. You can't do anything without our scholars and waste their time while they've got enough on their plates. Do you see what's been happening on our continent? Is your quest more important than the Husks? Or the-"

"Damian! Enough!" The first guard barked then turned to the party. "You all go about your business. Like he said, triangular symbol on the robes and pins."

Aisha was taken aback and seconds from saying something. Thankfully, Vofric waved her along with Avant leading their small group. He growled at the guards while passing by but they were unphased. What bothered them were the sharp hateful eyes of a dragon who threatened them without a word. Some soldiers reactively glared at Damian for spouting off.

The streets of Shusyoun were paved of stone and brick. Buildings of all shapes and sizes lined the roads with wooden structures atop flat roofs. Cloth screens overhead provided cover from the light snow. People roamed the streets without a care—seemingly unaware of the dangers around them. Many greeted the party with a smile before continuing the day. Guards amongst them looked on with disdain. They carried the same disgruntled attitude as the ones at the gate.

"The rooftops appear to be openly accessible," Sariel said and pointed at roaming citizens. "Our chances of finding scholars at a street level will rise."

Aisha agreed and quietly followed her allies; still frazzled by the earlier encounter. No one needed to recognize her but it was peculiar that Shusyoun guards knew about the Husks yet not other details. They should know her role in hindering it and protecting Dawncaster. It should be obvious she was working to protect Tetria and not blindly exploring the continent. Regardless, she pushed it aside and forged on.

The rooftops were primarily used for relaxation by civilians with guards keeping an eye out. Only a few areas were off limits like the large watchtower and a handful of highrises. Mistakenly visiting too many in the search for scholars would likely draw further ire from the guards.

Avant took careful steps on rooftop pathways. They seemed sturdy but a creature of his size was rare even amongst the familiars roaming the city. It proved to be a blessing as his shadow projecting to ground level drew the attention of onlookers. Majesty wasn't what any of his ally's would use to describe Avant. Shusyoun citizens would call that a travesty as they took in the sight of a beautiful snow white fur and feathers. Some saw it as a blessing and moved on while others sought to learn more.

"Sariel, do you see that kid running?" Aisha asked.

They grunted affirmatively.

"Follow her."

Sariel dashed away without summoning their wings to avoid undue attention.

"What is your reasoning for following the child?" Vofric asked as the rest of the party jogged after their swift friend.

Aisha explained, "She just saw something amazing and wants to learn about it. I'm guessing her elders taught her to ask scholars questions about things she doesn't understand. It was similar in my village."

It wasn't long before Sariel found what they were searching for but realized the others fell far behind. Small wooden structures surrounded the dragon so they rocketed skyward like an emerald flare. The sun reflected off Sariel's scales and drew more attention than intended. More whispers spread through the city about a tiny dragon that vanished from sight. Sariel remained hidden until the others arrived.

Together, they watched over the child as she spoke to a woman in a gray robe. She was around Vofric's height which made it difficult to find any pin that might be adorned. Embroidered on the back of her cloak, however, was a large blue triangle with silver engravings. The party considered jumping down to her but seeing a group of armed warriors dropping from the sky might send her into a panic. Instead they found the nearest descent and made their way to the scholar.

Clearly the snowy owlbear caught her attention and she pointed it out to the child. The scholar assured that it was a tamed familiar. There was nothing to fear or to be in awe of. Some adventurers simply had unique tastes. It was a satisfactory explanation for the child so she ran off as the party approached.

"Your familiar has garnered quite a bit of attention," the scholar chuckled.

"Apologies. We seek to learn from the scholars and Avant's presence made finding you easier," Aisha said, petting the owlbear.

"Of course. We expected your arrival, Champion of Dawncaster."

Without another word she walked away, not so much as glancing back to check that the party was following. The cloak made it look like she glided through the busy streets. Buildings got more spread out, interspersed with intricate paths that led to a tower surrounded by more robed individuals. Above the front arch were intricately carved letters that read "Bridging Athenaeum."

Abstract metal structures extended out from the sides representing hands grasping distant knowledge. Stone pillars along inner walls functioned as doorways that could be accessed by anyone. Beings capable of flight jumped from one story to another without hesitation. Guards stood at each doorway and checked the identification of all who passed. None of these mattered to the party entering through the main gate. Others took notice but turned away quickly to not disturb the Hero. once the group passed. Even the receptionist paid no mind as the adventurers walked by without any pause.

Such nonchalance was still unnerving after the experiences in Balur. Aisha's off hand hovered near *Valefor* as the party was led to an inner room. There was a single wooden door, no windows, and a large stone table with metal seats surrounding it. High backs accommodated the tall brimless hats worn by the scholars awaiting the party. Discerning glares studied each adventurer as they lined up in practiced positions. The furthest right was the dwarven paladin with a wounded elf to the left. The Hero stood on the elf's other side with the owlbear. An awkward space was left between them that Avant shimmied into after realizing his mistake. The guide stood aside silently.

"Welcome, Hero. We are the high minds of the Bridging Athenaeum. We have awaited your arrival," a woman said calmly. "What has delayed you?"

"Apologies, high mind. We sought information in Gromsev which then led us to Spirefell," Aisha replied. "I am sure you are aware that the demon king has made his presence known. He has allies, one of which gravely injured our comrade and we searched for aid in his recovery. The land between Mount Iana and Shusyoun is expansive and difficult to navigate."

"Are you saying you were present when the demon king retrieved *Brachynox*?" another high mind asked.

"Yes, we—"

"Did you do nothing to stop him?!" a different man yelled.

Aisha took a deep breath, holding back her frustration. "We were ill-prepared to face him."

"Ill-prepared," the first high mind huffed. "What other information do you bring?"

Aisha already had a hunch of what the reaction would be but answered anyway. "The demon king wields *Brachynox* and was able to single-handedly defeat a dragon. We suspect he will seek other Artifacts of Arcana. Please tell us about the remaining ones."

A high mind scoffed. "You come with a request yet have nothing to offer."

"We have retrieved an Artifact," Aisha said and gestured for Avant to step forward. "The stone chestplate worn by our familiar."

The high minds muttered amongst themselves before one replied, "That is simply a piece of magic armor. It is as much an Artifact as that war-hammer. How were you unable to deduce such a simple fact?"

No one knew about Artifacts except people who uncovered them or records relating to them. Outside Tetria the knowledge of them was even more limited. Any expectation that someone not specialized in the field could identify one was foolish. There was no way the high minds didn't know it and yet they looked down on Aisha for a simple mistake.

"You are dubbed the Hero yet fail to identify magic items," the high mind scoffed.

Another grumbled, "And she allowed many to perish during the Dawncaster attack. Can we truly trust her capabilities?"

"It is the limit of an amateur adventurer."

It stung but Aisha remained silent. The high minds didn't seem like they'd stop rambling from her reaction. Their voices cascaded over each other as they voiced their complaints.

"You have yet to uncover the demon king's plans or motives yet seek guidance."

"If you saw the demon king, why not fight back?"

"Why did you let him flee with no challenge?"

"You should have let your ally fall for the greater good."

Aisha's hand shot up before she could stop it—silencing everyone. After a few seconds, she dryly said, "Anyone who takes up arms against daunting odds is a hero regardless of capabilities. We will study public records and conduct research on our own." She took a step back and almost turned but hesitated. "146 people fell in Dawncaster. It is better to admit you lack information than needlessly waste time berating those who seek your aid."

Somewhere during the high minds complaints Aisha saw the obvious fear in their eyes; reacting like children caught in a lie. Spewing false claims was the only path they saw when they couldn't provide useful information. Saving face was all that mattered even if it meant insulting the Hero. And all that could be forgiven.

But the high minds weren't near the demon king. They didn't comprehend the silent overpowering aura he emitted. Cutting down a dragon may have been something they learned about but seeing it down with such efficiency was wholly different. Above all, Aisha couldn't forgive anyone who suggested sacrificing an ally—especially not Kargon.

The rest of the party wore similar faces of disgust as they turned from the scholars. They weren't the only option to move forward. Access to information was never something the party had luck with. There was no reason to expect it now.

"Vofric, we'll look into available records about the Artifacts. Start the legwork on any hint of Barbatos in the area," Aisha instructed as she pushed open the exit.

"Allow me to be of assistance," said the scholar who brought the party to the meeting.

"With all due respect, we don't want your help."

"I understand that the Bridging Athenaeum can be unwelcoming. Our leadership is... hard to get along with. That is why volunteers like myself are necessary," the woman said. "From the bottom of my heart, I apologize for their behavior. My name is Freckle. Allow me to guide you to the public records of the Artifacts of Arcana. They are not kept on premises."

Aisha stared at the halfling woman with discerning eyes. Having a guide around town would be helpful. Not to mention the time wasted from dealing with the high minds. It could even unlock avenues the party hadn't considered. But they had to keep a distance and be ready to cut their losses the moment something unfavorable happened.

"Lead the way," Aisha said with a nod.

Freckle weaved through busy streets in a manner similar to Vofric navigating Dawncaster. Every so often the party lost track of their guide but after some searching she would pop up nearby. The robe was a hindrance while the halfling woman dashed through the streets. She roughly bunched up the bottom of the cloak while the group arrived near a busy bridge. It crossed over a river that flowed towards the East Ocean.

"There is a shortcut below; by the river," Freckle said. "I understand if you would rather avoid less sanitary areas of the city but I wanted to put the offer on the table."

Aisha turned to her allies but was sure of the response; two shrugs and a flustered head shake with a coo. Upon confirmation, the guide continued.

Discreet stairs descended to an incomplete lower part of the city. At a glance only a single long passage stretched through the area near the river. Freckle's time in Shusyoun had taught her to look at unassuming corners. Under this specific overpass—near a wall with an awkward indent—was a passage deeper into the city. The party was immediately on alert but their guide was unphased.

As they walked, it became clear that this was no ordinary passage. Markings on the wall glowed softly from Freckle's touch and shifted nearby stones. After a few minutes of travel she stopped and removed her robe. Underneath was leather armor covered by long dirty blonde hair that spiked all the way down her back.

Aisha drew her sword while Sariel checked behind them for an escape route. With a flourish, Vofric unhooked his light hammer and nodded to Avant. None of it phased Freckle. With obvious movements, she tapped at small stones on a brick to her right that opened a closet with a fur-lined trench coat inside.

"It's good that you're on edge. Wouldn't do if you just accepted an invitation carelessly," she said while donning the jacket. "Gotta say, some of our other recruits aren't the biggest fans of dark and mysterious hallways. The lack of panic is a good sign. Makes me glad you're the one who's supposed to face Aeraza."

Even though they were surprised at the name, no one let it be shown. No route remained from the way they entered. A bow might have rested in Sariel's hand but there was no arrow. Within the stone closet was an innocuous brick that Freckle pushed. The wall in front of the group opened to reveal a bustling establishment.

"Allow me to introduce myself once more. My name is Freckle Kiraan," the halfling said with a coy smile. "Welcome to Barbatos."

CHAPTER THIRTY-NINE

Brink of Existence

The lack of windows didn't make the Barbatos hideout any less vibrant. Carvings in walls magically showed what was happening in different parts of Tetria. Plants grew out of cracks and stretched out of well-maintained containers. Rooms were occupied by groups of diverse humanoids as they planned excursions. None hid their apparent awe at the sight of the Hero and her party. Some bowed while others simply waved; balancing reverence and equality in a way Aisha wasn't accustomed to. She had to admit, it was nice.

"I assumed you'd be hidden in the big forest between Mount Iana and Shusyoun," Aisha said while absentmindedly looking around.

"It's called the Agrestic. One of our bases is there on the off chance you stumbled across it," Freckle replied while leading the group to a room deeper inside the base. "There's a bunch spread across Tetria so we were bound to cross paths."

"How many of you are there?" Vofric asked.

"We're more than one thousand strong."

Vofric hummed. "It must have taken quite some time to gather that many allies."

"Almost five hundred years."

Aisha hummed softly. "Barbatos has been around almost as long as the demon king's been gone."

"It's no coincidence," Freckle said and opened a door with her name scratched into it. The office was messy with papers stacked high on the desk. Cabinets and drawers were left slightly ajar from past interactions. A detailed yet worn out map hung on the back wall with pins and symbols interspersed across Tetria. The most well-kept object in the room was a hovering disk intertwined by rope with a glowing stone in its center. From the wooden filing cabinet, Freckle retrieved a dusty gray journal and handed it to Aisha.

"Kharim might have retired as an adventurer after his journey but that doesn't mean he stopped protecting Tetria. Allies consulted him while mapping the continent." Freckle explained. "The findings were difficult for many to grasp. Even so, they shared the discoveries with descendants who expanded their knowledge and faced threats. They became a slowly expanding group that faced stronger than average monsters. As time passed, and the name of Barbatos spread, we began taking jobs from individuals who had no one else to turn to. Whether because of the cost or due to secrets that needed to be kept. Never anything villainous. Though I won't pretend we haven't gotten our hands dirty in five centuries." Freckle sighed, remembering something unpleasant. "We realized if growing threats didn't awaken *Valefor*—whatever did would be catastrophic. Whoever drew the sword would need more than a few allies. That is why Barbatos remains. We are here, in every sense, to work with you."

Though Aisha and Vofric were processing the statement, Sariel latched onto an earlier phrase. Not from Freckle but her father. The halfling hadn't mentioned it but everything she said matched Edthecridaldyrth's words.

"You are named after a demon in order to face a demon," Sariel said. "Edthecridaldyrth informed us of the meaning."

Freckle raised an eyebrow at the mention of the dragon. "He's an old friend. Barbatos' relationship with him started as a benefactor providing a quest. Over time, however, he has aided us with knowledge while we continue to search for his child. How do you know him?"

"I am said child," Sariel replied, a smile pulling at the edge of their lips.

"Oh, that's wonderful! He can hopefully breathe easy now."

The genuine relief in Freckle's voice pleased the draconic elf. It was obvious the guild, regardless how mysterious, cared for those who trusted them. At least that was the case for this halfling of unknown rank.

"What is your role?" Sariel asked.

"I'm one of several captains," Freckle answered. "We don't have fancy badges but we're the only ones with access to Farspeech Coins."

"I take it that's how you share information that's been gathered without having to physically travel," Aisha finally said.

Freckle nodded. "It bypasses the need to interact with guards or scholars who may hinder us. Or if someone gets lost in the Agrestic."

"It's still a mystery," Aisha muttered while staring at the map.

"No one has created a complete map but it has been studied rigorously. Villages are scattered throughout but they are often under siege by powerful monsters. I can't imagine what the Husks are like there."

Aisha cursed to herself that they hadn't crossed any of these mysterious settlements. Any bit of humanoid contact would have likely cut the trek to Shusyoun short. It wasn't lost on her that all her luck had run dry since Kargon fell.

"Where's the information about the Artifacts?" Aisha asked, trying to stay on task.

Freckle responded by pulling a small key out of a pocket on the inside of her jacket. It opened a drawer at her desk with a folio regarding discovered Artifacts of Arcana. There was no record of Avant's armor but with how many magical items were being discovered every year it was possibly on par with the Artifacts. Aisha hoped it was the case so that the high minds were wrong.

"Do you know why they are referred to as Artifacts of Arcana?" Freckle asked. "Magic items follow a well-known classification system. Those that break the bounds are known as arcana class. Tetria was an unremarkable piece of land until multiple Artifacts were discovered here. It's what caused the Age of Exploration and why people still enter the Agrestic even though the chance of death is so high."

Red ink marked *Brachynox* as taken by the demon king. The page for *Lightbringer* was marked with blue ink. Instead of a name it simply read "allied." Many questions swam through Aisha's head but she pushed them, slowly reading through the other pages.

"Unbinding Chains, *Judgment*, Pyro... manic?" Her heart skipped a beat on the last page. "Ring of Dominion. There's not much history about that one."

Skimming the files told of brief instances when every other Artifact had been utilized. The Unbinding Chains erratically changed the user's beliefs and caused them to target their opposition. Similarly the tome *Judgment* was capable of eradicating anyone the wielder deemed an enemy. *Pyromanic* was eyewear forged by fire giants to control their kind. Even a cursory glance made it apparent they all had devastating consequences.

"It's especially destructive when the chains and tome are used in tandem," Freckle said. "The wielder could theoretically wipe out all the Hero's allies without losing themselves."

"*Brachynox's* ability is simply to amplify the wielder?" Sariel asked while studying the single document repeatedly. "That seems rather underwhelming."

"All its wielders went undefeated before the weapon was sealed. None could explain why it was so powerful but its true potential is hidden." Freckle sighed and kneaded the bridge of her nose. "And even still, none of those compare to the Ring of Dominion. It creates a sphere of influence around the wearer—a god-field. Everything within is under their control, even magical ether."

Something so powerful should have been written about in history books. But all Artifacts of Arcana were scarcely mentioned in public records. How they were handled after the Age of Exploration was almost unknown. Barbatos was ahead of the curve but lacked full awareness.

"Why were only some destroyed?" Vofric asked, waving sheets with crossed out drawings.

"According to our records, some were too strong to break. Thus they were sealed away. Unfortunately, my predecessors followed that wise decision by wiping out any memory of where the Artifacts were kept." Freckle nodded to the sheet about the ring. "I've traveled a lot in my life and that is the strongest magic item in existence—which is both a fact and an understatement."

Aisha rifled through the pages and huffed. "I understand the ring, tome, and swords. But what about the goggles? How come it survived? I've never heard of fire giants making something indestructible."

"They lost it."

"They lost it?"

"Yes, so well in fact that it's seemingly vanished." Freckle clarified. "Even if it hadn't, its power is so niche that we don't need to—"

The sound of running overhead cut Freckle short. Guards were making their rounds with more fervor than usual but the group ignored it.

Sariel grunted. "Considering the power of each lost Artifact, the demon king will likely seek the Ring of Dominion. I assume you have come to the same conclusion. Have you made any progress seeking it out?"

"None so far." Freckle replied, twitching at the chatter overhead. "We have many members searching the continent. Obviously, that's assuming it remains on Tetria."

"Let us hope that is an impediment for the demon king, as well." Vofric suggested. "It is possible he could—"

A loud crash overhead shook the hideout and couldn't be ignored. Heavy boots rapidly sprinted through streets; accompanied by fearful screams and panicked chatter. Another crash and Aisha immediately recognized the sound of thunder. A Barbatos member rushed to Freckle's office and shoved the door open.

"Boss, head for the main gate!" he yelled before running off.

The party followed Freckle out of the office. Other members were scrambling for exits but Aisha's eyes were trained on their guide. There was no doubt she knew the quickest route outside—an innocuous closet with a ladder leading to a ceiling. Freckle clambered up while rapidly reciting an incantation that allowed passage onto the roof of an apothecary near the main gate. All attention was on something far in the distance that could only be seen through telescopic monoculars. Freckle unhooked one from her hip and climbed onto some crates strategically placed at one side of the roof. A flick of the wrist extended it with a satisfying series of clicks before she put it to her eye.

"Oh my gods."

The utterance held more shock than someone of Freckle's caliber often felt. Tetria was divided down the middle by two mountains; Delras Range to the north and Mount Iana to the south. A chunk of land was torn between them and for the first time, it was possible to see the western half of the continent from Shusyoun.

Black bolts of lightning rained from the sky where the mountains were separated. Each flash created parts of a building; hundred foot tall barricades; towering spires; stories upon stories of stone. The central spire stood significantly higher than any other, a protected keep within. It was an unrecognizable structure that left every citizen across the land dumbfounded.

The final lightning strike was not atop the castle but spread across the whole of Tetria. It was a storm targeting the island continent. One streak crashed into the land between the Agrestic and Shusyoun's main gate. From within appeared a giant cyclops who angrily lumbered towards the city. Black leathery skin stretched across its facade instead of the natural muddy tones. Crimson light shone in its single eye as it glared at the gate. Its goal was clear; honor the king's arrival.

Worrying about other cities and villages had to wait until Shusyoun was safe. Regardless of how unsavory its government had been, the Hero was bound to protect it.

"Freckle, get everyone away from that thing," Aisha commanded. "Sariel, Vofric, Avant; with me."

The Barbatos captain wasn't used to following orders but with everyone already moving, she had little choice. No use challenging the pecking order when the Hero was involved.

Vofric climbed onto Avant's stone saddle to easily traverse the rooftops before leaping over the main gate and landing heavily in front of the massive brute. The moment Sariel reached the gate they sprouted wings and flew over the monster. Poisonous arrows rained over it before the draconic elf landed behind their target. Seconds later, Aisha landed next to the cyclops, delivered two swift lightning empowered strikes to its heels, then jumped back.

Attacks of such caliber were of little note for the monster. It didn't stop due to pain but because of how boring it would be to crush a city with no opposition. A tenderized meal before work was well worth the effort. With a hefty swing, the cyclops swung its arm—the size of a tree trunk—in a circle around it. It missed all its targets but one dodged in a punishable way. Sariel flew upwards and their wings suddenly vanished. Momentum from the cyclops' swing carried its other arm towards the mid-air target. Avant ran through the cyclops legs and propelled Vofric off to block the attack.

"Do not underestimate me," Sariel spat as they summoned their wings—powering through the burning sensation. The pride of a dragon wouldn't let them succumb so easily.

The cyclops' massive size and strength left it with abysmal speed and redirection skills. Its open palm smash was easily dodged by Sariel flying through the fingers. While the hand plummeted, they created an arrow. Normal ones were like needles to the cyclops and it had some resilience against poison. But the arrow of a ballista would be devastating.

Aisha caught on when the projectile began to eclipse Sariel in size. The cyclops was about to pull back and she yelled, "Avant, bring the arm down! Sariel, get some distance then fire! Vofric, brace then hammer the nail!"

If not for the sound of battle, everyone would hear three sets of teeth and a beak tightly grit. Cyclops did not train in order to be strong. Thus its natural abilities were not enough to draw its hand back as a powerful invisible force pulled it to the ground. The roar of an owlbear was enough to send humanoids into a panic. Avant could make even a giant shrink in fear. Dirt and clay shifted on the pavement as the monstrous hand displaced them. One day, people would pause to admire the massive imprint left after this battle.

There was no more pain as Sariel pushed their limits to fly higher. Dragons did not waver in the face of opposition. The loosed ballista arrow did not whistle as it drilled downward—air broke apart near its four blades. Blood erupted from the back of the cyclop's hand as the projectile pushed crimson ichor out of the wound. Stone against heavy wood made a distinct sound only the party was familiar with after so much time with their artificed carriage. That was the sign for Avant to release his downward force.

Fluctuations in gravity could knock over the most trained fighters but experience and evolution made the shift negligible for Vofric. While the cyclops wildly watched every attacker, it only heard one thing; a deep throated prayer. Drawing his war-hammer was never a swift action and Vofric learned long ago it was better to take his time to make a statement. It mattered not that his grandmother was a peaceful god. The fear of such beings was ever present in the hearts of mortals. Golden light erupted as he hefted it onto his shoulder and leapt upward.

"Glory to the Starcaller."

It was a whisper drowned out by the slam of stone against the arrow shaft. Magic surged from one weapon to the other as the projectile dug further into the ground. The cyclops screamed in horror, flailing wildly to grab the arrow and get free. The adventurers knew what panic and fear did to people. It made inevitability all the clearer. When the cyclops finally got a grip on the bolt stuck in its hand, realization dawned. There was a fourth adventurer that had yet to act.

Lightning crackled from *Valefor* as Aisha deliberately advanced towards her target. Each step forced more mana out of her, wreathing electricity around her body. Field testing new techniques was never preferred. But to negate the demon king's powerful message, the Hero had to send her own. Shusyoun's panic had subsided as the adventurers held back a massive threat with ease. That wasn't enough. Word needed to spread. Spectacles had their place and this was it. The memory of the demon king beheading a dragon with a single swipe haunted Aisha's nightmares. It pushed her to become a warrior that would put her past self to shame.

Onlookers only saw her take a single step. Trained eyes watched her lunge forward and jump. Even her allies only perceived further movement but couldn't track it. For all intents and purposes, with that one step, Aisha vanished from sight.

Unseen steps carried her over the cyclops' trapped arm at imperceptible speed. Silver light traced a line through the air following *Valefor's* point. It crossed the monster's neck and lingered for a moment as Aisha reappeared past the beast. She dropped to the ground as the silver line erupted into a bolt of purple lightning that violently tore through the cyclops. Precise force decapitated the monster and Aisha's boot hit pavement at the same time the cyclops' head launched backwards. It landed heavily across the open field near guards planning to flank the creature from another gate.

Stunned silence was quickly overtaken by bombastic cheers. Guards held back citizens trying to meet their heroes. Freckle easily bypassed the blockade by leaping off a bannister near the gate.

"That was incredible," she said with an even keel.

"Freckle, we were discussing a plan of what to do about the

Artifacts." Aisha replied. "We clearly can't only focus on them."

Vofric interjected, "Villages will require aid in defending themselves."

"Turn all of Barbatos's efforts towards helping areas struck by black lightning—especially in the Agrestic. Following that, seek out the Artifacts." Aisha instructed. "Be prepared for my call. When the time comes, we will face him. If you are willing to aid us, that is."

Freckle smirked. "It's the very reason we were created. I won't try to command you on your journey so do what you feel is right. My time on the sidelines ended once you found us. If you find yourself by the Bursbo Shallows look for the village of Deriich. There are contacts in the area. Now go! Oh, and welcome to Barbatos."

Aisha smiled and looked at the city. Celebratory airs and jovial cheers reminded her of home. It was understandable that Shusyoun would want to honor the party. But this was just an equalizer for the party—proof they had grown since Spirefell. Nothing like that would happen again if they had any say.

CHAPTER FORTY

Settlements Under Siege

After a year of adventuring, no time passed faster than the two weeks spent hunting down empowered demons. Knowledge of the Agrestic allowed the party to find hidden settlements and protect them. Roaming packs of blackened monsters ferociously attacked the party at every opportunity. Their features were dyed like the void and all displayed unique abilities unseen in their species. Exhaustion weighed heavily on the group as they only got to rest every few days.

There was no shame in accepting offers from the settlements they saved. A proper meal and good night's rest went a long way but stopping for too long meant others were in danger. But limits were present for even the strongest warriors. The Agrestic wasn't magically hindering their senses yet was harder to traverse than the island leading to Balur. Villages in the forest were naturally hidden and easily destroyed by the demonic monsters. Worse yet were the intermittent black lightning strikes that brought more threats. During any break the party got, Vofric prayed for help to arrive elsewhere.

"That's the seventh squadron we've cleared today," Aisha groaned while wiping black goo off her horns. "I'm so tired."

Anything more than zero was too many. Some recent encounters were unrelated to the black lightning. Rather, the presence of the demon king's castle strengthened Husks throughout the land. Their newfound power was too much for some adventurers—transforming them in turn. Defeating them left a sour taste in the party's mouth as they couldn't take time to honor the dead.

The only blessing was that the new monsters were unlike the soot skeleton's from Veil's lab. Powerful holy magic was unnecessary in defeating the creatures. Aisha assumed it had to do with Prince Makani's moonlight blessing—its particles perpetually carrying in the wind.

Thinking that way bothered the Hero since she preferred absolutes. Similar ideas wasted everyone's mental energy unnecessarily. Even after months apart, Aisha wasn't used to not having someone to handle voicing the concerns. Kargon did it all his life and could move on without issue. The others easily deduced what was on Aisha's mind from her longing eyes staring blankly into the distance.

"I can only suggest we contact Avant about Kargon's condition so many times before I assume you do not wish to see him," Vofric said. "Though maybe your feelings have changed since our last conversation."

Aisha immediately argued. "That's not it! I want to! It's just-"

"You are concerned about whether he will match our current strength," Sariel interjected dryly. "Training can only provide a finite amount of growth. Our own training has been bolstered by frequent bouts with the demon king's minions."

Avant bumped the Hero's leg and cooed quietly—similarly feeling Kargon's absence. The possibility that he couldn't continue the journey with them felt unfair. But Aisha knew it was a possibility since parting ways. Dawncaster's records stated as much with how many allies parted with Kharim. Sometimes the power needed to continue on a quest was too much. Better to live a long life aiming for a different goal than battle the demon king's army.

"I'll still make sure to go back to him when everything's done," she said confidently. "Plus, I'm not convinced that he can't match up to us. I mean, it's Kargon. Elmud got lucky..." Her voice trailed off before finishing the thought.

Sariel looked down at their stout ally who was doing poorly to hide his annoyance. It happened whenever Aisha avoided the topic of what happened to Kargon. Normally Vofric would bite his tongue but repeated avoidance was grating.

He hummed gruffly. "Pray tell; why have we not contacted Kargon or Avant?" Aisha hesitated but the dwarf needed no answer for the truth. "It is a given that warriors are wounded during battle. Kargon would willingly take one thousand cuts for his allies regardless of the consequences." With each word the paladin's footsteps grew heavier. "Fear that he will fail to rise from a fall is not love; it is disrespect. Concern for his well-being is fine but the prevailing belief should be that nothing will overpower his will."

"Nothing should outshine your faith in Kargon." Sariel added. "Mutual trust proves that you believe we will push through any adversity. As foolish as he is, I believe Kargon will too. Your relationship with him eclipses ours by many decades and yet something stops you from placing the same faith in him."

As badly as she wanted to, Aisha couldn't argue with her friends' words. Kargon had shown his capabilities long before adventuring. Every unfortunate examination as a soldier was met with reactive training. Failed missions were studied repeatedly in hopes of diminishing losses. Unfortunately, Elmud reacted similarly to their defeat and trained to humiliate the firebrand. But habits dictated Kargon would overcome this hurdle.

"I can't bring myself to believe training will match up to real combat," Aisha said weakly.

Vofric huffed. "Aisha, your growth is not simply from combat. Much like we assisted you in unlocking your potential, so shall Avant for Kargon. On that point, even if growth was only from combat I would still trust that bird. He will drill everything our foolish friend needs to know into his very bones. I would readily bet my life on it."

Aisha was taken aback by the statement by the life-threatening absolute. Stories about Kargon's harsh master didn't carry the same image that Vofric had. Then again, he was the only one able to cease the flames that engulfed the unconscious monk. There was obviously more to the owlminn than what he showed.

"You're right." Aisha admitted. "The next opportunity we get, we'll send for an update. That is if a postage station is still standing."

"It was acceptable collateral to protect lives," Sariel replied immediately. During a recent battle they tore one down to kill a group of fanged imps.

"You're not wrong," Aisha said.

Since leaving Shusyoun, the party had unfortunately caused the destruction of many buildings. Nothing that was completely irreparable but resources were scarce with monstrous threats all over the Agrestic. It hindered the general functions of some settlements but was a necessary sacrifice to avoid lost lives. After some battles, citizens blamed the party for not being fast enough regardless of how many people were saved. Not preventing every single death was inexcusable—ignoring the fact it was also impossible. Thankfully, some places were able to fend off their attackers without delay. Sometimes it was due to the residents while others were assisted by strong adventurers. Barbatos had received Aisha's orders and were moving to fight the black lightning spawn.

"Something's wrong," Sariel said abruptly, their ears twitching at the sound of a distant crackle. "Ahead of us. One mile."

It wasn't hard to identify what they were referring to. Winding paths and thick trees covered the next village. Wooden partitions surrounding it blended into the forest and further skewed the party's vision. What was unmistakable were wild flames within the walls—a common sight ever since the black lightning storm.

"Screams. We must go!" Sariel commanded and broke into a sprint.

Avant immediately belted out a spell to speed everyone up then signaled Vofric to get on. If the danger grew, Aisha would speed herself up more but wasting mana before battle was ill-advised. Coming up short in a foreign situation would be devastating.

Flames easily eclipsed the seven foot high walls and drowned out the sound of demonic screeches. Wooden structures shook from an unknown force terrorizing the village. A crowd of monsters had to be in the village based on their cascading breathing. Yet, citizens and guards stood idle at the edges of the village as they watched the carnage.

The Hero's party pushed through to the makeshift arena. To their surprise, buildings remained unscathed with charred monstrous corpses nearby. Embers only radiated from a moving pyre which danced across the settlement with such frequency and strength that it was almost flying. Within the flames was a black silhouette with two glowing blue eyes furiously striking any monster within the village walls. No creature in the demonic horde was capable of withstanding the blazing attacks.

"If it ain't Aisha and her cadre," a familiar voice said nonchalantly as it approached.

"Taze? What's going on?" Aisha asked.

The delivery driver grinned widely. "Special delivery."

A furious brute pivoted away from the inferno and took notice of the chatting adventurers. Demons were dwindling without leaving any mark on the settlement. But all were aware of the Hero and leaving a wound on her would make the monsters' losses worthwhile. Standing two heads taller than the half-elf cemented the brute's confidence before it dashed towards the party. Running on four muscular limbs provided ample speed on par with Avant's unempowered abilities.

Aisha stepped forward, ready to draw her blade. But she hesitated at what appeared behind the demon—an arm triple the size of the flaming humanoid. Their position across the village was no hindrance. The fiery hand easily wrapped around the hulking creature and forcefully pulled it back. Simultaneously, the ethereal limb phased through the monster and left burns all over its body. A powerful explosion tore apart the brute's torso before burning its heart to smithereens. Its final scream was too short-lived to echo around the silent village.

Ashes drifted up from burnt Husks and demons riddling the street. The massive pyre slowly dissipated as the warrior within pulled down their goggles. Daggers stared at the monster that foolishly rushed at the Hero. A breath held far longer than necessary finally escaped the brawler's lips.

"You're not worth her time."

CHAPTER FORTY-ONE

Origins

Kargon awoke with a choked out breath and chill through his body as cold air passed over him. Groggy eyes examined a clay aligned window allowing sunlight into a brick room. No bars or screen stopped nature from entering and leaving as it pleased. Residents were expected to deal with any issues that arose from the small opening. The memory of such an expectation informed Kargon of where he was since the Sanctuary of Spiritual Combustion wouldn't change rules that worked.

He had trouble rolling over with all his bandages. Forcefully, he reached his right hand over his torso to tear off the tightest bindings—following that by removing the rest. It was the first time he'd been left with scars after battle. The most prominent was one cutting from the left side of his forehead, across the bridge of his nose, to his right cheek. There was a persistent pressure across his body that Kargon focused on ignoring. Part of him felt weak for having been scarred so heavily while another was proud of the marks of a warrior.

"Kargon, there are robes on the table," Master Avant said loudly from the other side of the closed door.

Being focused on his scars, the half-elf didn't register he was nude. "Ah, thanks," he replied.

The small room only had space for a bed, end table and medium sized desk with two chairs. Kargon took one look at the cream colored robes and sighed. They were loose fitting and never felt secure regardless of who wore them. A cloth belt wrapped tightly around the waist made it marginally comfortable. With both chairs pulled from the table, Kargon opened the door to invite Master Avant inside. A tray with a tea kettle, cups, and biscuits were balanced in one hand. A white and orange robe was draped over the owlminn. Over a decade since their last interaction, the bird still sent a chill down Kargon's spine.

"How long have I been out?" he asked, as the master placed the tray down and took a seat.

Kargon moved deliberately as he lifted the kettle and slowly filled both cups. The warmth helped ease the tension in his fingers. He sat down and munched on a biscuit while patiently awaiting a response. A long breath hung in the air as the master appreciated the drink.

"One month," he finally replied. A long explanation informed the younger man of what led him here.

"I need to thank Vofric for saving me from the brink." Kargon sighed. "I'm guessing none of my stuff survived."

Master Avant shook his head while retrieving a pouch from his hip. Two talons reached inside and revealed a familiar pair of goggles. It wouldn't have surprised Kargon if his master held onto them. Instead, the elder passed the eyewear over with no coercion. Upon closer examination, the goggles were completely unscathed.

"May I ask where you received those?" Master Avant asked.

"Pops gave them to me."

"I see. Do you know what an Artifact of Arcana is?"

Kargon nodded. "The prince of Dawncaster had one."

"Yes. The demon king retrieved one in Spirefell as well," the master sighed. "Rumors dictate that diverse groups crafted said tools; one of which was created by a conglomerate of fire giants and dwarves."

Kargon couldn't help but snicker. "I don't see how seeing through fire matches a staff that harnesses moonlight."

"Seeing through fire is a well-known ability of the goggles but it is secondary. A necessary component to assist with the unseen effects of the primary function." The aged mentor took a long breath and leaned back. It might have been prudent to refresh himself on the research he conducted to inform Kargon—weeks had passed since he found it. Master Avant would never admit how excited he was to see his disciple in good health. A strict attitude is what Kargon was most receptive to.

"Fire giants are unable to refine their mana," Master Avant explained. "Little focus is needed for them to produce fire but it is wild. Uncontrolled. *Pyromanic...* the goggles enable the wearer to refine and empower their magic. Records indicate that it put fire giant magic on par with high elves."

Kargon's eyes went wide at the mention of matching a high elf. The Balurians were blessed and yet he was able to break through a fiery barrier summoned by their chief. But he didn't dare mention that to his mentor.

"Pyro... manic?" Kargon muttered. "Pyro is understandable but why 'manic?' I know fire giants are inclined to rage but the goggles have little to do with it."

"I do not have the answers as to another race's thought process when naming their creations."

"That makes sense..."

The goggles hung from Kargon's hand as he lifted them to eye level for examination. There was no concern in using them even if all their capabilities eluded the monk. Zigon wouldn't have given Kargon something that could harm him. He set the accessory down when he saw Master Avant patiently waiting with an empty cup. After a quick refill, Kargon retrieved the goggles.

"I'm confused about something," he said. "If fire giants and dwarves made the goggles, shouldn't they be... bigger? Maybe smaller? And how come I can use them?"

It was almost a rhetorical question as an idea of the answer nagged at the half-elf. But it didn't make sense no matter how he considered it. Obviously, Zigon wasn't an elf but he wasn't significantly short or gigantic, standing only a few inches taller than Kargon who himself was barely six feet. Sure, he had a beard but it wasn't comparable to the magnificence of a dwarf's facial hair. The only traits Kargon knew about fire giants were their magic and their rage. While Kargon couldn't deny his swift anger in a fight, that felt like something that happened to everyone. Meanwhile, Zigon hadn't so much as raised his voice during his son's life.

With every thought, the confusion grew more evident on Kargon's face and it was harder for Master Avant to remain silent. He retrieved a scroll from his pocket, placed it on the table, and pushed it forward. With a nod, Kargon knew to unfurl it.

"Take your time. I will wait," the master said as he sipped his tea.

After everything that happened, Kargon had all but forgotten the letter to his parents. Quick fingers undid the knot binding the scroll before he opened it fully. Reading the first line took Kargon back to his last stay at the monastery—when he was called back home.

My Little Firecracker,

Your father and I were expecting a letter sooner regarding your origins. We should have discussed it before you left but hesitated. Zigon holds much fear in regards to his past but it is outweighed by his concern for your well being.

You are correct in assuming your fire immunity comes from him. Few races have such an ability and I'm sure you've deduced that he is a fire giant. He is the cause for your elemental affinity as well as your explosive temper. It was a concern for us as you grew and we turned to Master Avant for aid. He can explain anything else you may need to know.

I know you are likely wondering why your father is so small for his race. I would say it is unimportant at this time but you never did like that answer. Years before you were born, he chose to sacrifice all his abilities and power to be with me. We can talk about it more after you return from your journey.

We miss you and wish you luck on your adventures. Take care of Aisha.

Love,
Mom and Pops

Kargon read over the letter a few times, becoming more aware of the messy hair in his periphery. Gently, he pulled off a few strands and examined them—the physical trait he shared with Zigon.

"Pops is a fire giant. I'm a fire giant," he said. "Or half of one. Guess that's good enough for *Pyromanic*."

"It is not simply 'good enough' but better due to your elven descent," Master Avant explained. "It allows you to refine your magic naturally. The goggles improve it further. That is why your flames have begun to take a near solid property."

"You're the one who taught me to refine my flames in the first place. I take it you knew what I was the first time I came here."

Master Avant chuckled. "You say that like you had any say in coming here. We both know that isn't the case. Your rage manifested wildly. Simply being near your mother manifested flames. Neves was in danger the moment you had an outburst."

"Right." Kargon sighed. "They drilled into me that you did them a big favor."

"I offered to mentor you since no one else could handle your fits of rage. It brings me joy to see the lessons were not forgotten."

Kargon could never forget the harsh training he went through. It's why he had trouble accepting the calm tea-drinking master who sat in front of him. There was a time when Master Avant only showed anger—ruffled feathers giving him the visage of a monster. The smirk on Kargon's lips quickly faded as his thoughts turned towards Elmud, a slow breath escaping his lips as he stared out the window.

"It wasn't enough to win against—"

"The dragominn. I'm aware." Master Avant interjected. "Training alone is not enough to prepare one for a journey like the one you accepted."

"I couldn't deny Aisha. The other options wouldn't show her the respect she deserved."

"Does she deserve to kneel next to your decrepit body and weep?"

The words stung worse than the pangs of pain from Kargon's scars. Though he was unconscious, the memory of Aisha screaming over his body was burned into his body. Brief consciousness gripped him when she tried to shock him back to life. Nothing should ever make Aisha unhinged enough to try that.

"I need to join them again," Kargon said.

Master Avant wasn't the kind of bird to beat around the bush and firmly stated, "You need to train."

"Master, while I understand the thought, I don't think the other mentors here will do much good for me," Kargon said. "And, like you said, training on my own is pointless."

"Do not presume to know my plans. The other mentors are meant to train our students to find balance. That was never what you needed. You may no longer have fits of rage but I am the only one capable of training you."

The words made Kargon shudder but he tried not to let it show.

Master Avant stood up slowly and continued. "You must learn the proper utilization of your magic through a conduit. Combat techniques must be altered to overpower enemies you never expected to face." He stood over his student and said softly, "Since the day we met you have refused to wield a weapon. I will refine you into one that is unmatched. That is, if you agree."

"Why wouldn't I agree?" Kargon asked.

"Your allies and enemies are actively growing in strength. While you may accept my training, there is the possibility I won't allow you to leave. My expectations are higher than they used to be. And if I recall you were quite vocal about their level of impossibility." A brief smile passed Master Avant's beak before the firm demeanor returned. "If you agree, it is while knowing that I will push you further than any past student of this monastery. And you must pass all my tests satisfactorily for me to approve your departure." He turned and opened the door. "Take the night to think about your choices and come to my office tomorrow."

Before Master Avant could take a step, Kargon answered. "I'll do it. I get everything you're saying but it's just a long winded warning."

"Are you only saying you'll do it due to my 'long winded' phrasing?" Master Avant grumbled and turned to face his student.

"No! Of course not. You've always been long winded, anyway." Kargon protested. "It's just that Aisha... Everyone is waiting for me."

Even while stumbling over his words, Kargon's resolve was clear. Short of threatening to end his life, nothing would stop him. Even that may not be enough. It was the same assured look a young half-elf had worn when swearing to run off and help his family. The wild abandon of a fire giant burned in the easy-going man wrapped in loose fitting robes.

CHAPTER FORTY-TWO

Untamed Magic

What Master Avant referred to as his office was an open air training area halfway up the monastery. It was a perfect square stretching for a few hundred feet in every direction with a pond connected to a small mountainside waterfall. Grass and stone was planted deliberately in an attempt to ease the tension of any student's who ended up here—it never worked. Only the headmaster of the sanctuary taught here and his lessons were anything but serene.

Flames flickered and wisped away from Kargon's arms as he focused on the shattered chain in his hands. The conduit Commander Ivana provided was barely functional. Containing the blaze was harder than ever and left his robe singed with pieces fluttering away after each ignition. Empowered flames from Shusyoun burned deep red in Kargon's memory. It would be easy to brush them off as a dream if not for Master Avant confirming their existence.

He twirled Kargon's goggles around one finger while walking circles around the stationary student. Whatever piece of the master made him a calm and doting caretaker was silenced—leaving the strict mentor Kargon remembered.

"Reinforced flames are the strongest form fire can take. They can even withstand a fully powered fireball," Master Avant said. "*Pyromanic* allowed you to cheat out that quality of flame."

"So then... why am... I trying... without it." Kargon strained to speak while keeping his focus.

"Cheating it out proves that your body is capable of producing reinforced flames. In fact, some part of you is accustomed to them and aware of how to properly wield them."

Kargon grumbled, loud enough for Master Avant to hear. Both were aware that the younger man had a taste of the flame. On his first attempt, several days ago, they wreathed his fingers before loosening into their natural wild form. But Kargon was wearing his goggles at the time which his master swiftly took away.

With every attempt, something nagged at Kargon. Master Avant was fully aware of it and simply waited for his student to say something. Though neither man expected how the realization presented itself.

A raging fire encompassed Kargon's arms; burning cloth licking at his skin. The distinct sound of a whip lightly cracking in the flames called to him. Growing rage made the blaze expand and the monk did everything he could to keep his emotions in check. Every second he struggled made the cracks louder and their source more obvious. The conduit was breaking, each shattered chain making the flames more vivid.

Clear as the day he fell, crimson flames wrapped around Kargon's fingers. In an instant his arms were alight with the intense blaze— then they were gone. Silver shards melted on his palm with a fine red powder being all that remained of the ruby.

Master Avant hummed lightly. "That was unexpected."

"The conduit wasn't... meant for reinforced flames... Was it?" Kargon asked while lapping up as much air as possible.

"No, it was not. I was expecting you to realize that much sooner."

"Dammit, master..."

"Yet I am delighted by the outcome you stubbornly worked towards." Master Avant insisted as he stepped in front of Kargon. "To produce that fire from such low quality equipment is quite a feat. Try this."

With a swift wave, the remnants of the silver bracelet were brushed away before something else was placed in Kargon's open hand. Over one hundred black wooden beads and a matching ruby were strung together by enchanted rope. It wrapped around Kargon's right wrist twice with enough give to rattle as it shifted along his forearm. A smile appeared on his face upon realizing it matched

Master Avant.

Slow, steady breathing accompanied focus on shaping fire. The overexertion was entirely unnecessary as crimson flames burst out of Kargon's palms. Without intending to, he ignited his feet and melted the shoes he'd insisted on borrowing. Outwardly, there was a wild fire leaping off him but underneath was a thin layer of reinforced flames.

Kargon's eyes lit up and he stared at an empty spot in the sky a few feet away. A flick of the wrist summoned a burning astral hand similarly engulfed in fire. As long as it remained a fist, there was no discerning it from a fireball. But the longer he stared at the projection, the more frustrated he got.

"I can't move it independently."

"It is good you noticed," Master Avant said.

Kargon huffed angrily, embarrassed at how obvious it was to his master. Some part of the disciple wanted to show that his old training wasn't a waste. But everything he did felt like proof he hadn't grown.

"I should be able to by now! I've been summoning them for almost a year and all I can do is make them imitate me. There's more to astral magic than that!"

The flames dissipated as he wiped frustrated tears from his eyes. For some reason, he felt like a child in front of Master Avant.

"You are incapable of astral projection, Kargon." Master Avant stated candidly. "However, that has always been the case."

For some reason that straightforward attitude actually calmed Kargon down.

"Gee, thanks." It was a fully sarcastic and unnecessary response. The master wasn't so nonchalant that he'd leave half an explanation unsaid.

"People who have only seen astral magic assume it is all the same," Master Avant explained. "In truth there are two distinct categories: the first, and more explored, is astral projection. That camp encompasses my abilities like creating several ethereal limbs and even cloning myself to a degree."

Master Avant liked demonstrating his skills during an explanation. It was both to help his students understand as well as keep himself sharp.

"The other camp, which is often lost within the first, is astral extension. That, my boy, is where your abilities lie. Your creations not only mimic your actions but cannot move independently."

"Seems like the lesser camp," Kargon groaned.

"While there are weaknesses that are not present in projection, there are also strengths. For example, you can modulate the consistency of your creations. They can be sturdier than your physical body or as immaterial as mana itself."

"That doesn't sound too bad."

Master Avant smirked, having saved the best for last. Practice allowed him to sell having almost forgotten the information. "Ah, also it is not bound to your size. I can't imagine all the possibilities that entails."

Kargon's mouth was agape as he stared at his palms. Fresh flames wreathed his arms and while they were aloft, he summoned an astral hand. It had never occurred to him that they were ever so slightly larger than his. What was more intriguing was a faint line connecting the creation to his own palm that crackled when he focused. The wire expanded outward and revealed an entire flaming arm that slightly encompassed his own. In shock, Kargon pulled his arm back while dousing the flame. The force created a small explosion around his fist and lit the grass ablaze. Even while shocked he made sure to put it out.

Before Master Avant had a chance to complain about the damage to his office, Kargon reignited. This time the astral hand wreathed around his own—the reinforced flame he'd felt earlier. It was probably what Master Avant meant when comparing astral extension to mana. While Kargon was aware of its presence, it was physically nearly nonexistent. With a forceful step forward he punched the air and launched the blazing astral fist outward. It solidified slowly as it traveled. Much too slow for real combat—for now.

Another punch sent forward the second hand then Kargon kicked the air. A previously unsummoned foot appeared and burned wildly. Each aggressive movement was wholly different from before. This was the attack that was intended for Elmud that day. One empowered by Kargon's entire being. One that carried his rage. His fury. His disappointment from being held back. His sorrow from falling at the feet of his friends. His self hatred for making Aisha cry.

Kargon roared cathartically as he propelled his fist forward. Mana poured into the astral imitation faster than he intended and its form changed. In place of the normal projection was one triple its size. Calmly, he held his hand out to familiarize with the feeling of transformation. That was what got him to create the reinforced flames in the first place. Master Avant made clear what a single display of power meant. Replication was possible. More power was possible. Drilling a giant fist of fire into Elmud's cocky face was possible.

CHAPTER FORTY-THREE

Combat Proficiency

Kargon foolishly assumed he was ready to depart after summoning reinforced flames within a week of training. In truth, the size and consistency of his flaming appendages couldn't be reliably controlled. Fire was easy to manipulate but his astral magic had yet to be tamed. When Master Avant asked for a detailed report of last year's adventures, Kargon thought it would prove that he could improve while traveling.

Master Avant gave an unimpressed sigh. "With your strength, you can easily scale buildings in a single bound. Not only that, you are incapable of maintaining ignition while focusing on physical effort. As a combatant reliant on his own body, that is a significant problem."

"I could master it while fighting Husks on my way to the others," Kargon argued.

"Are you sure you will master it on the way?"

"No, but—"

"What will you do if your flames injure your friends?"

Kargon let out a sad sigh. "I hadn't thought of that."

"Thankfully, I know the perfect training method," Master Avant said with an unnerving smile.

Part of Kargon hoped the smile came from pride in the question. But another, more intelligent part, knew it was something more sinister. But that confused the disciple even more. Controlling the flames was difficult but the training sessions hadn't been that bad. In fact, Master

Avant had been pretty easygoing; all things considered.

The first goal was to stop Kargon's flames from dying out when he exerted himself. Every morning, he meditated in the master's office for an hour while maintaining his ignition. Following that, he went to a larger training ground. The center was an empty field used for group activities with a looping track around it. Students were taught balanced combat techniques by other mentors; all of which watched Master Avant's disciple during breaks. Fire around his legs left charred footprints with every dash and leap. With every day of training Kargon got faster and jumped farther. It was almost possible to bound across the field in two steps. Unfortunately, blazes disappeared when he got too focused on surpassing limits. Frustrated slow steps allowed him to reignite before attempting to exert himself again. Ashes and burn marks stopped getting cleaned and created a way to measure Kargon's progress.

Having trouble here was within Kargon's expectations but made his shortcomings in combat training more frustrating. Flaming punches doused themselves if he swung with all his might. When focused on staying alight the attack would be significantly weaker. Worst of all was the method of training—the reason for Master Avant's wicked smile.

Wind whipped in the air as Master Avant walked into his office while twirling a bo staff. There wasn't a single word shared between him and his disciple before the owlminn dashed forward. Every student knew if the headmaster wielded his weapon, someone was learning a harsh lesson.

For months, that was for Kargon to block without losing his fire. The caged inferno around his arms provided the perfect shield against the swift strikes but tightening his block made flames waver. Furthermore, his vision was obscured due to lacking *Pyromanic*. It was the perfect advantage for Master Avant to get around Kargon's defense. Magically refined wood felt like a heavy metal rod against his legs before he was thrown to the ground. Landing heavily on his stomach, he was held down by the crushing weight of his master's weapon. It happened enough times that Kargon stopped panicking after getting knocked prone. Gritting his teeth, the disciple conjured a large astral hand to push himself aside. He only moved a couple feet but there was enough momentum to sweep out Master Avant's legs.

The owlminn quickly recovered using his wings.

"Acceptable," he said. "Though I fail to understand why you allow yourself to get hit by even my most obvious attacks."

"I can't see some of the ones I could dodge because of my fire," Kargon groaned.

"And the rest?"

"I have to face them head on," the firebrand replied and took a seat in the grass.

"Commendable—" Master Avant shook his head. "—but foolish."

"When I'm in a fight I have trouble turning my focus away from my opponent. The most I can do is use my body to protect my friends."

"I failed to consider how your rage would affect you." Master Avant landed heavily in front of his student and slammed the staff on the ground. "Such a style of combat is not unheard of. It functions best with a weapon but I will not waste time convincing you. Kargon, you must drill this lesson into your very soul." He stared intensely at his disciple and continued, "Hit and get hit."

Kargon chuckled. "That's not as long-winded as your usual lessons."

"You must never let up when attacking. If you are to be struck, do not take the full brunt of it. You must learn to redirect its momentum towards your enemy."

"That's more like it."

As nonchalant as Kargon was, he did think carefully about what his master was saying. Especially since it was the first time a lesson was based on his stubborn demand.

It was true that he relied on his own momentum to empower attacks. Redirection would allow him to amplify them further. Not to mention he could protect others without putting his life on the line. There was little pride in falling at his allies' feet after taking attacks that could be dodged without putting others in harm's way. But sometimes he'd need to take an attack head on. Reinforced flames did a lot to weaken blows but only covered his limbs. A proper defense relied on him fully igniting.

The pressure of a staff against Kargon's chest pulled him from his thoughts. He let it push him back then planted his left hand on the ground to flip while kicking his opponent away. A gruff response was the master's sign of approval. The owlminn rushed towards Kargon with the staff swinging in a wide arc. Kargon dodged underneath and advanced. With the movement from both attacks to amplify a single punch, he could overpower Master Avant. The disciple's fist wasn't ignited but the force launched his master hundreds of feet backwards. Swift movements stopped his momentum in mid-air.

"Much better," he said nonchalantly.

The attack wasn't enough to phase an experienced fighter. It lacked the explosive impact of Kargon's flames—an obvious note the disciple was aware of. As he was reigniting, Master Avant retaliated. Without any time to think, Kargon leapt over the staff and punched downwards. It missed by a wide margin and Master Avant smacked his weapon against Kargon's face before he could land. The attack pushed him to the ground but he didn't falter. Using the speed of the fall, he rolled back onto his feet and dashed towards his opponent.

Master Avant knew his own vice of being quick to judgment. Years of meeting different students and travelers proved his assessments correct. But surprises had come and gone—and he'd learned to invite them to the monastery.

Giving Kargon time to think would be a detriment. Instincts drove him to improve and Master Avant could guide them. He presented an obvious opening to Kargon's left. Stepping forward with a heavy foot placed him within reach of his target. Fury gathered behind his fist as it traveled towards Master Avant's face. He let it get within an inch of contact before summoning an astral hand to push himself out of the way.

Kargon pivoted angrily and stomped towards his master—burning footprints trailing behind. Rage filled his entire being.

"I see," Master Avant said calmly.

"What?" Kargon barked back. Even with all the anger in his eyes, he stopped moving at his master's words.

"You spoke so candidly I assumed your rage forced a simple level of focus. We both failed to consider its full effects."

"Speak plainly."

Master Avant sighed and ran a finger across his forehead, searching for the correct words. "Fire giants are driven wild by their emotions. They are quite literally blinded by them. In place of a level head, they wield great power."

A drumming beat pounded in Kargon's head and his left eye twitched wildly. Blood boiled from the sensation of the scar across his face. Yet all the anger flowing through him didn't force him forward. Higher reasoning prevailed in keeping him steady. Slowly, he was able to think about the emotions overwhelming him. They made no sense. Sure it was frustrating to get toyed with but Kargon felt no ill will towards his master. The longer he thought about it, the calmer he felt.

"The fire persists when I'm emotional," he said while staring at his arms and willing the flames to finally extinguish. "I end up focusing on my strength without thinking about it."

"Furthermore, your mother's clear head keeps you calm. It covers the biggest weakness of a fire giant," Master Avant explained.

"Relatively calm," the half-giant said and shrugged awkwardly. "You didn't teach me this before."

"No, I didn't. Your parents wanted you to learn balance. I am proud that you have learned it. But in a fight it hinders you. Contradictory to my teachings, you must succumb to your emotions in combat."

Kargon nodded absentmindedly and muttered, "It's different."

"I assure you my reasoning is as I stated."

"Not that. I mean the emotions. I've felt anger like this before. Not the times when I was a kid. But in Dawncaster. I was furious but it felt like joy. I could fight and move freely without a care in the world. But my focus was better. I didn't need to calm myself down."

"There's a rather obvious difference, isn't there?" Master Avant asked. "You may not see it now. It will come in due time."

Kargon silently nodded and raised his fists. There was already enough on his mind without piling on specific emotions. It would push his strength to a new level but he couldn't control the current one. A few lucky attacks against Master Avant meant nothing as long as he went easy. Kargon needed to focus on the task at hand—the opponent flying nearby.

The goal of his training was inherently contradictory. How was he supposed to focus without focusing? Then again, maybe the idea itself was wrong. Focus was necessary to solidify and amplify his astral magic. But flames came naturally—to the point that he unconsciously ignited. He recalled when Vofric told him to maintain focus for perpetual heat.

But that was unnecessary when burning wildly. Prior to shattering his first conduit, that wasn't how Kargon set himself ablaze. During training his frustrating failures were followed by immediate reignition. He wasn't even thinking about it. There was no fuse to the match and he didn't need to insist on creating one.

With a sharp breath, he reignited—the flames flashing into existence across his arms and legs. Rage and fury burned in his mind but he remained steady. Twinkles of joy, pain, sorrow, and every other emotion appeared and vanished under the sturdy surface of anger. It flooded his mind but maintaining control was paramount. Kargon had to bear the torrent of emotions colliding with his perpetual rage. This was new territory and it was his to rule.

CHAPTER FORTY-FOUR

A Reason to Fight

Almost half a year passed before Master Avant suggested taking a day-long break. There was something he wanted to discuss. They met in the observatory; a room that took up the entirety of the highest floor of the monastery. Multiple openings along the wall allowed a pleasant breeze to pass through the building. A large balcony stretched around it and looked across Mount Iana and some of Delras Range. Relaxing there was a pastime for all residents of the monastery.

It was difficult for any of them to ignore Master Avant's presence at a table that overlooked west Tetria. Two chairs sat on either side, one of which remained unoccupied. A covered teapot and two cups rested on the table. By now Kargon was used to the glances from his peers. Many had grown to respect the adventurer who held his own against the headmaster.

Kargon paused briefly as his eyes took in the view of a distant opening in the forest. Past thick foliage it was possible to make out the familiar buildings of Neves. After a minute, he sat down and poured tea—first for the master, then himself.

"Master, are you sure you want to give these to me?" he asked and handed over a filled cup. "You said you'd tell me when I could leave but with these I could make a run for it."

He wore an outfit similar to his old adventuring gear, though definitely better quality. Dyed feathers lined the crimson sash around his waist and the bindings on his arms magically wrapped around him without hindering the mala bead conduit.

"You are not one to run," Master Avant stated. "They were simply cheaper than commissioning replacement robes for the ones you continued to burn."

Kargon chuckled. "You say that like these won't."

"Neither did your previous garments. Though these will handle reinforced flame better."

Instead of grabbing his own cup, Kargon pulled away and ignited his hand before slowly patting his belt. It took the flame as expected but there was no scent of burning cloth. Flames danced along the crimson sash until he doused them. Similarly, his bindings were unscathed by the astral flames around them.

"This had to cost a fortune," Kargon muttered then shook his head. It was untoward to deny a gift from his master. "These are much tighter than the robes you had me training in."

"Indeed. They are better suited for an adventurer's quest. I used similar equipment long ago," Master Avant answered.

It was hard to imagine the burly master letting his feathers be pressed under tight wraps. The bird was so adamant about wearing loose fitting robes that all inhabitants of the Sanctuary of Spiritual Combustion were required to. Then again, they didn't come here to train as combatants and only learned a little self defense.

"What about the belt? It always seemed a little pointless." Kargon asked as he patted it. "And where'd you get all these feathers?"

"When you are ignited, your body appears as a black silhouette. Full ignition will cause the tassels to mask your movements." Master Avant explained. "As for the feathers. I have collected my molted ones since the creation of this sanctuary. It is a blessing imparted on my students when their studies come to an end."

Kargon gasped unintentionally and forgot decorum. "Master, I— Are you sure? I'll admit I've gotten stronger but I still can't fully ignite. The only reason we know it's possible is because of what happened when I was unconscious. There's no guarantee I can do it—."

"You can. I have never been more sure of a disciple's capabilities."

"What makes you so sure?"

Master Avant took a sip of his tea while collecting his thoughts.

Deafening silence of a contemplative mentor made Kargon nervous. He carefully drank his own tea while waiting. Eventually, cups were returned to the table and refilled by the younger man but no words were said. Almost ten minutes passed before Master Avant finally spoke.

"You have trained rigorously for the last half year. Consider that you were on the brink of death prior. That is why I believe you are already unleashing your magic to the best of your ability."

"Oh," Kargon replied sadly. "So what was that about me igniting completely?"

"You have a talent for misunderstanding me without listening to my full explanation." Master Avant said plainly. "Your ability to wield magic is at its upper limit. However, your magic itself has further potential. Pushing past this wall will allow you to master it with ease."

Kargon nodded slowly, still not entirely sure what his master meant. "I guess punching through the wall isn't possible... Is that why we're taking a break today?"

"Correct. I hoped this was not the case but you are dealing with an unfortunate affliction. A few of my past students have dealt with it and overcome it via deep introspection. Unfortunately, it involves a lot of sitting and talking."

"Master, you love sitting and talking. Especially if there's tea involved." Kargon replied.

"True," the master hummed. "But certain students are easier to deal with when communicating through violence."

Kargon couldn't help but laugh. Here was an enlightened monk talking like a fight crazed soldier. Though he wasn't wrong that recent training had been more fun than either monk anticipated. If not for Master Avant's insistence on training Kargon personally, the half-elf wouldn't be half as accomplished as he was now. Though, it felt odd to be thankful for multiple beatings.

"You sound too easy-going for this affliction to be that serious," Kargon finally said.

"The severity is not life threatening but can affect if you will be able to face the oncoming challenges," Master Avant explained. "Pardon the terminology but you are magically constipated."

"You make it sound so serious yet it has such a stupid name."

"It is simply the best descriptor. Something is hindering your magical growth—likely mental. Possibly emotional considering your heritage."

Kargon nearly made a retort but thought better of it. Normally he wouldn't mind sharing his feelings but hesitated when considering that it may not be enough to break through this wall. It was completely possible that this was his limit and Master Avant was wrong.

Little did Kargon know that centuries of astute study had given the master experience in reading a person's soul. It often took the form of someone's most prominent magic—in Kargon's case, a flame. Suffice to say, any reaction it had was beyond his notice and the master wouldn't mention it unless absolutely necessary. Though, if this all went according to plan, the wooden seat beneath Kargon would be incinerated. Master Avant rose to his feet and walked towards one of the balcony doors to get a better view of the land.

He asked, "You are unable to detect magic, correct? Unless it is highly concentrated according to what you've told me."

"Yeah. The only times I've been able to sense it were when Makani cast his Moonlight Beam and whenever Aisha creates a lightning explosion." Kargon replied, following his master. He remained silent about Balur.

Master Avant hummed affirmatively and took a sip of tea. "Kargon, why do you adventure? What do you seek?"

"Aisha asked me to." Kargon replied. "Oh, you probably mean what my personal motivations are, right?"

"That is correct."

"I want to protect people. It was why I became a soldier. That's why I originally left this place."

"It is commendable to wish to protect every life. But, in truth, no one holds all lives to be equal. Individuals hold others to different levels of importance. Don't you think so?" Master Avant asked.

Wind tickled Kargon's skin as he leaned against the stone parapet. With training he'd grown more precise in feeling temperature without any focus. He noted how warm it felt while considering an answer.

"There is no shame in it." Master Avant encouraged.

"It's not that," his student said softly. "I think protect is the wrong word for my party. I want to fight by their side."

Master Avant noticed a forceful crackle from the depth of Kargon's soul. Staring into the distance, the old bird radiated a softness few were familiar with. "Tell me about your friends."

The words rattled in Kargon's head as watched a large bird fly overhead. Few others passing by held a candle to the magnificence of the first.

"Did you know Sariel is a dragon?" Kargon said it more as a statement than a question. "Not figuratively or spiritually. They are literally a dragon. It's not some secret they hide. People just assume Sariel's an elf who got wounded. Can you imagine what it's like to hear that your actual being is a curse? I can't. And I can't even sympathize with Sariel because they won't open up." There was a hint of frustration in his voice. "But it's okay. Without realizing it, people are eased by the presence of a dragon. I don't think Sariel's aware of it either."

Master Avant noticed sparks within Kargon's soul as his mind wandered. Without prompting he moved on.

"When we met Vofric, he was a priest. He'll deny it but when you guide people the way he does, it's an understandable assumption," the half-elf said candidly. "I think he's making up for not speaking up in Khergrin. Maybe he did back then and no one listened." Kargon's gaze shifted towards distant routes along the mountain where minuscule humanoids trekked. "He tells us about his grandmother a lot. How amazing she was and the people she inspired. There's no doubt in my mind that Vofric's remembered similarly by all the people he's helped. I feel similarly since Avant wouldn't be in our lives without him."

Master Avant scoffed, remembering the young owlbear who fiercely defended the unconscious half-elf. It was clear that the man who raised Avant was far different from the undisciplined boy from a decade ago.

Kargon chuckled softly and ran a hand through his hair. "Sorry about naming him after you. You're just… really similar. He likes berries a lot. And I bet if he could cook like you we'd be eating fish every night. I wrongly assumed he'd stay back and support us in battle but he ended up like me." Absentmindedly, he traced a finger along his sash. "I kinda get how my parents felt when I was blowing a fuse over everything. Thankfully, Avant is much calmer than me. The only time his rage comes up is when a fight's brewing. I wasn't that way until recently."

It was astonishing to Master Avant how peacefully his disciple spoke. To the master, his disciple was still the child that spent his first day at the sanctuary looking for fights. The fire in his soul burned steadily but the master was hesitant to ask Kargon to ignite.

"What about Aisha?" he asked.

"She's my best friend," Kargon replied nonchalantly.

Master Avant raised an eyebrow. "Is that it?"

"Yeah? What else is there?"

It took more control than expected not to shout at the foolish young man. After nearly a century of students coming and going, Master Avant finally found his stupidest disciple. Part of him was furious that Kargon ended up being his favorite. How he had gotten so far without a modicum of wisdom was beyond the owlminn. A long sigh was all he could manage while pressing both index fingers against the sides of his temple.

"Kargon..." Master Avant started then immediately paused to think over his words carefully. "In one word, tell me what you remember of your first experience at my monastery."

"Discipline?" Kargon answered.

"May I tell you what I remember of your time here?"

The silence made Kargon more confused while angering his master further. Maybe that was for the better since aggression was all the half-giant responded to.

"Aisha!" the master squawked loudly. "You spoke of her during every possible interaction! There was never anything prompting you to do so! I have never read a word of her endeavors yet know more than the Hero's adoring fans! And all you can say is she's your best friend?"

Kargon listened with mouth agape. Partially because of the yelling. Mostly because his master's bristled feathers reminded the student of his pet. When the anger subsided, Master Avant's furious eyes silently burrowed into his disciple. The younger man turned away and focused on a far off alcove he'd repeatedly stared at. Under shaky leaves and sturdy trees he could almost make out the opening where Aisha and he received their first carriage a year ago. All to avoid a party in her honor.

"Aisha hates being complimented when she hasn't done 'anything of note.'," Kargon said softly. "I once told her she was a hypocrite since she compliments me and I don't do anything. She took me hostage for three hours and ranted about all my accomplishments. This was before she asked me to join her or anything. I think that was part of the reason I kept up on my training. It impressed her. It made me happy to know she thought of me even while dealing with the Hero's responsibilities."

It was hard talking about his best friend while not knowing where she was for the first time. "I think I'm finally understanding how she felt being alone," Kargon said. "People stopped treating her like a person when she drew *Valefor*. They saw deification as a compliment and forced her on a pedestal in solitude. But she's never been anyone but the girl I grew up with. Maybe that's why I had an easier time sticking around." Kargon laughed as a soft blush covered his cheeks. "You should have seen her in Dawncaster. The way she cut down two assassins while drawing the eye of every person in the room."

Master Avant chuckled lightly. "I doubt they saw her as you do."

"Because they only see the Hero! I see Aisha. She didn't need to be anything else to convince me to join her," Kargon admitted softly. "But that's not special. Everyone's close to their best friend."

The raging inferno in place of his soul demanded Master Avant's attention but breaking through Kargon's mental wall was a delicate endeavor. "You are correct that people with such a relationship are close," Master Avant started. "Would you describe your parent's relationship similarly?"

"Kinda?" Kargon said then shook his head. "I mean yes but also they're not just best friends."

"How do you mean?"

"Based on Mom's letter alone; Pops sacrificed something big to be with her. I've seen both of them give up things for the other. They fight each other and together. I learned what a best friend is from them."

The master worded his next words carefully. "They are far from simply friends to one another, no? Answer me honestly. What is Aisha to you?"

Kargon started strong then faltered. "She's my…"

His attention drifted from Neves to Wolden then Sespik. Water fluctuated near the Balur Sea and vast miles separated it from Dawncaster. More trails raced by until he was staring at the peak of Mount Ikrali. Finally, Kargon's eyes rested on a clump of spires in the desert. A deep sigh pulled his attention back to home. Every memory he had, regardless of how he felt about it, involved Aisha.

"She's my everything."

The roaring inferno that was sealed within Kargon engulfed him physically. Crimson embers wreathed tightly around him under the wild blaze. With a sharp gasp, he stepped away from the bannister and blindly threw embers before quickly pulling them back. All he could see was a cascading firestorm as a torrent of emotions flooded his mind. Finally, Master Avant's cryptic words about his emotions made sense.

"Master. My goggles," Kargon requested with his hand extended.

A smirk that was impossible for him to see appeared on Master Avant's face who'd carried the goggles daily since hinting at their necessity. Handing them over fused them into the silhouette, revealing only two cobalt circles that eventually rested on Kargon's face.

A sharp inhale extinguished the inferno and revealed his shining smile. With a little willpower he immediately reignited completely, no longer overwhelmed by his emotions. Kargon tilted his head towards the direction of Master Avant's office.

"I think there's time for a spar."

CHAPTER FORTY-FIVE

Battle Ready

"It's not a standard package, ya know?" Taze Fehlam said.

They sat with Kargon and Master Avant in the observatory. The functionality of the room had changed since the black lightning strikes a few days ago. Intermittent bolts struck daily and monks manned the balconies to assess where to send aid. They could only get so far. Thankfully, the light particles of hope continued to inspire people to fight.

"I do not disagree," Master Avant replied. "However, you can navigate the Agrestic better than others. Finding the Hero will be easier than asking her to return here."

Taze sighed. "We can't be sure she's in there. What if they reached Shusyoun?"

"They'd go right back in. No choice with where the castle is." Kargon said confidently while studying the massive forest.

"Looking for your friends is going to be rough. And we'll cross a lot of Husks."

"I'll handle it," Kargon insisted.

Taze looked over at the scarred warrior who radiated a calm ferocity even while sipping tea. The delivery driver had seen their fair share of jaded adventurers but this was different. Whatever happened over the past months changed Kargon physically but the confident light remained in his eyes. Even Master Avant seemed more amiable after spending so much time with his disciple.

"I can't believe I'm accepting this," Taze said with a soft laugh. "Okay, we teleport to the base of Mount Iana. We aim for any places that are under attack. I assume your friends will be doing something similar so we'll cross paths eventually. Though they're probably pretty far north."

"That may not be the case," Master Avant interjected. "Assuming they reached Shusyoun before the storm, they would have re-entered the Agrestic from the southeast. Even without monsters to face, it would take months to get north."

"How big is the Agrestic exactly?" Kargon asked, unable to process what he was looking at.

"It takes up over half of Tetria and remains the least explored region of the continent."

Taze chimed in with, "I've been trying to get someone to vouch for my discoveries but a delivery person doesn't hold much weight for folks."

"Hopefully we can do something about that once everything calms down," Kargon sighed then turned to Master Avant. "I can't go until you say so."

The old bird sat silently while staring at an empty cup on the table between the trio. His student immediately grabbed the teapot and steam wafted off the liquid pouring out. It should have been room temperature by now but Kargon's heated palm at the bottom of the kettle instantly warmed it up.

The disciple had high quality magic and great control but he'd never defeated Master Avant in battle. But both knew it was never the goal. It would be selfish of Master Avant to keep the Hero's ally simply for the thrill of sparring. Part of him was convinced it was for Kargon's safety but another knew it disrespected Kargon's autonomy.

"I have little to offer in the way of supplies. Though that may be for the best as you seek your friends," Master Avant said contemplatively. "Taze, are there any preparations needed for your vehicle?"

"Not a one. I'm good to go when Kargon is," the speedster replied.

Master Avant rose to his feet and gestured for the others to follow. "Kargon, I acknowledge the vast difference in who you are now versus the man who landed in the infirmary months ago." His feathers bristled from a surge of cold air as they descended steps of the monastery. "Expectations are set when first measuring one's capabilities. The rate at which you evolved makes me thankful I never judged you. As you know, very few students are my direct disciples. Even fewer have the honor of saying that I could not properly gage their ability. I am proud to say you are one of them."

The group approached Taze's carriage outside the sanctuary gate. Weights and locks kept it bound to an intricate stone carved out of the ground nearby. It was made specifically for the delivery driver since they were the only one who delivered to the Sanctuary of Spiritual Combustion.

"Go with my blessing, Kargon," Master Avant said and patted his disciple's arm. He fished a coin out of his robes and passed it to Taze. "I will cover the expense of conducting this delivery."

Taze knowingly stepped away under the guise of looking over the vehicle. After silently thanking them, Kargon stared at his master. Long-winded diatribes and honoring traditions were well known habits of his—often causing annual send offs to run long. Yet Master Avant was willing to bid farewell to his personal disciple with only words.

"I haven't proven myself yet," Kargon blurted out. "You normally make every student prove themself."

"True. However, that test is often a battle against myself which we have repeatedly conducted for the past several months." Master Avant answered quickly.

The speed of his words made Kargon sure that something was wrong. While the master stood with confidence, he couldn't hide his concern as he turned around moments before a bolt of black lightning struck one of the monastery spires. Cacophonous thunder shook the ground and part of the roof collapsed. There was no depth or reflection within the void that streaked through the sky before shifting around the shape of demons. Students screamed within the halls as a pack of monsters rampaged. Some mentors rushed inside via the opening while others dashed through the front gate. Another lightning bolt struck the observatory and summoned a brute. Spittle and mucus erupted from its maw during its lumbering attacks.

"Taze, take Kargon!" Master Avant commanded while marching to the monastery.

Kargon didn't turn even as Taze attempted to pull the monk away. Their vast difference in strength was apparent.

"We need to go!" Taze pleaded.

"I'm going to fight," Kargon said.

"Master Avant and the others will handle it."

Kargon turned to look at Taze with a fierce gaze. The driver expected to be berated but was met with a calm explanation. "The mentors can handle the small fry but Master Avant is about to fight that behemoth alone."

Students were filling the courtyard as their mentors fought the small horde of demons. Dozens of astral projections provided cover for the fighters. The observatory's destruction slowed as shimmering reflections of Master Avant goaded the brute away from innocents. Even so, he was out of practice and the demon would be advantageous in a drawn out battle.

"I've got this," Kargon said aloud and strapped on his goggles. The words were meant for no one else. With a powerful leap, he landed near the students who immediately parted as Kargon launched skyward again. This time powered by an explosion, he left a burning footprint and crashed straight through a wall to the observatory. He skidded to a stop between the behemoth and students struggling to escape.

The brute raised its arm and prepared to squash Kargon. Fire engulfed him the instant he got solid footing. As the monstrous hand plummeted towards him, Kargon punched upward with an astral fist twice the size of his own. It not only stopped the demon's attack but pushed it back. It stared in astonishment at the half-elf before turning to the owlminn descending nearby.

"Why did you return?" Master Avant asked.

"I can't face the others if I don't protect my home." Kargon grunted. "With me."

While Master Avant appreciated the gesture, he doubted the monks' clashing styles worked in tandem. It was clear the moment Kargon dashed forward with two massive astral arms. The attack was too obvious not to retaliate and the brute interlocked its fingers with the hardened flaming projections. It screamed in pain, trying to pull back. Kargon obliged by pushing forward.

In that instant, Master Avant realized his student's plan. Shimmering clones rippled off his form and darted at the monster to aid in pushing it over the edge of the balcony. But Kargon didn't let go like the master expected and plummeted with the demon off the observatory. A loud crash pulled Master Avant to the sight of a prone brute laying in his office with a fiery warrior rising to his feet nearby.

Kargon hadn't seen the effect of his flames for far longer than he realized. The crash landing was accompanied by a burst of fire that completely engulfed the monster. Bruises and burns spread across it like a wildfire. Silver apparitions continued their onslaught as Master Avant arrived in the arena. The brute lashed out and immediately destroyed two clones. A grunt of pain sounded from the master—feeling a portion of the pain his projections would have. At least that's what Kargon assumed since Master Avant never explained the secrets of his magic.

"I'll take care of this one, master. Watch over me," Kargon commanded.

Any words that might have been said were held back. Silver apparitions disappeared and Master Avant glided away, praying his curiosity wasn't at the cost of his disciple's life. The demonic brute was clearly insulted as it rose to its feet. Growling, it turned to the puny flaming monk. Without considering what the man could be thinking, the demon advanced. Kargon raised both fists and let out a slow breath. Unmoving blue orbs focused on the charging demon.

A left jab was all the monk sent out. It was nowhere near its target. However the massive fist that emerged from it engulfed half of the brute's body. Purposefully leaving the hand ephemeral allowed it to pass through the creature while causing both an impact and leaving sizable burns. Unfortunately, it allowed the monster to continue its charge.

Kargon pulled back his left arm and followed with a right jab—causing another astral fist to make contact. Rapid punches flew from his stationary position with astral extensions accompanying each. A constant state of rage boiled in Kargon's mind but he remained under control. Steady flames riddling the brute caused patches of fire to crop up all over its body. By the time it could reach Kargon, the monster had no strength and fell to its knees.

The disciple slowly curled his flaming right hand into a fist and pulled back his arm smoothly. A motion practiced thousands of times before his horrific failure. One Elmud mimicked to taunt the weakened adventurer. But now it felt firmer. Burned brighter. Deep crimson flames hidden under a wild blaze turned into a near magmatic state across the empowered fist underneath. Even on its knees, the monster was much too high to reach from the ground. A wide grin cracked on Kargon's face as he launched his fist forward, feet planted firmly. The magmatic form grew exponentially as it plunged into the monster's chest. Roasted guts and viscera erupted through its back. Torn apart bones were all that remained in the large cavity of the lifeless corpse as it crashed to the floor.

"Sorry about your office," Kargon said sheepishly.

Master Avant scoffed again. It was all he could do not to admit he was at a loss for words. Once again, his disciple had eclipsed all expectations.

CHAPTER FORTY-SIX

The Way Forward

The Hero's party remained silent at their table as Kargon finished the recollection of his time alone. Only soft coos came from Avant as he rested against his master's leg. As soon as the adventurers reconvened, Taze left on another delivery. Villagers gave them space at the local eatery where Aisha already filled in their missing ally on what they'd been up to. Granted she opted to leave out private matters. That didn't stop Kargon from sharing every detail of his training.

"We stopped over in Shusyoun for a bit to help with a dead cyclops they were having issues moving. Otherwise we've been weaving through the Agrestic to deal with Husks and the lightning strikes," he explained. "I've been going all out so we could catch up to you. Luckily, you found me!"

Sariel grunted. "It was difficult to miss your inferno."

"It wasn't bright enough if you couldn't see it from the sky," Kargon said with a smirk, matching his draconic friend.

"Do you not consider it odd that your father had an Artifact? Or that he readily gave it to you?"

"That'd be like me asking if you thought it was odd that your father spent centuries searching for you. And I don't know what to think about Pops having these things,. Kargon flicked the goggles around his neck. "What matters is that he willingly gave me something so powerful so I wouldn't hold anyone back."

Sariel snorted. "Understandable."

"You did quite a few impressive things, Kargon," said Vofric while contemplatively brushing his beard. "And we must discuss your possession of an Artifact. But, first, I would like to inquire about something." It took all of his focus to keep a smirk subdued. "What you said in order to unlock your full ignition. Am I correct—"

Aisha kicked the barrel Vofric sat on, causing it to spin a little. He turned back to the table and gave a wide grin to the blushing Hero. No one else had latched onto the words Kargon said more than Aisha. Their meaning could be anything. He was too stupid to realize his feelings. Vofric confirmed it. Sariel agreed. Surely, Avant did too. There was no reason to ask for clarification. Out of habit, Aisha ran a thumb and finger against her horns to focus.

"What's on your mind?" Kargon asked reactively.

The Nevesi woman firmly planted her hand on the table and slowly met her best friend's gaze. It always struck her how clear Kargon's hazel eyes were.

"What did you mean when you referred to Aisha as 'everything?'" Sariel asked directly.

Whatever emotions they felt were well hidden behind a placid expression. It still drew Aisha's blustered ire, staring with mouth agape. While acting like they didn't care, Sariel and Vofric were equally motivated to support their young friends. They stared intently at Kargon who turned his attention to the owlbear nuzzling his hand.

It wasn't shame or embarrassment that turned the half-elf away. Rather he wasn't sure of the answer himself. In the moment, he'd said what felt right. Any other time he spent thinking about the conversation never led anywhere.

A soft trill grabbed Kargon's focus. His hands had gone still and his pet required attention. The monk laughed softly and obliged. Even without looking up, he was acutely aware of Aisha staring at him.

It dawned on her that she was unprepared to face her old companion—things had changed between them. Even without Kargon's statement, she'd begun to see him differently. By ignoring the long past conversation near the river, she'd fooled herself into thinking it was avoidable. Seeing the firebrand in the village completely shattered that idea. Watching him battle quickened Aisha's heartbeat more than she'd ever admit. The moment he appeared, she felt safe. And he all but admitted they felt similarly about each other.

Aisha let out a shaky breath. "Kargon."

It sounded no different than any other time his name was uttered. Except he recognized the faintest shake in her voice. One that had disappeared by the time they became soldiers. It's appearance signaled she was scared of something unknown. Something she couldn't think her way out of alone. Kargon pulled his hands away from Avant and stared across the table at his dearest ally.

"What did you mean?" she asked.

Aisha's lips were quivering like they never had before. Or maybe they did. Kargon had never focused on them much but couldn't help looking now. That was all it took for his realization to click into place. Months of agonizing about what he'd said—solved within moments of drawing Aisha's attention. A smile unintentionally stretched across his face.

"What?" Aisha asked intently.

"It's like Pops and Mom," Kargon answered with a soft laugh. "How I feel about you, I mean. You're the most important person in my life." He ran a hand through his hair as his cheeks flushed intensely. "I hope you get what I mean. That's the best way I can word it right now."

Wide eyes and a sharp inhale accompanied a wave of red encompassing Aisha's face. Her ears rang as unsaid words repeated in her head. It was impossible not to crack a smile at her best friend's awkward admittance. Part of her was infuriated at the reaction since it was unbecoming of the Hero. But she never agreed with that idea of her mentors. She couldn't help the response elicited by the person across from her. Much like he couldn't keep her mouth shut around her.

"Aisha, should we step out?" Vofric asked quietly.

"I think it would be prudent." Sariel answered.

Avant walked under the table, within reach of the dumbstruck woman, and lightly tackled her seat. Without effort, she steadied and looked at the owlbear before turning to the others.

"If you don't mind. I know this concerns our whole party but—"

"You needn't explain," Vofric said and led the others to a table away from the Nevesi duo. In truth, they could still be heard but the space was appreciated.

Aisha and Kargon briefly looked at their allies getting settled before turning back to each other. Suddenly it felt like no one else was in the entire eatery except the old friends. Both were continuing to redden as they studied the other.

Finally, Aisha stammered out. "What do we do about this?"

"Oh." Kargon frowned. "I guess it would be awkward. Right. I can leave if you want me to. I'd rather stick around and help with the quest though. After it's done we can go our separate ways."

"No! That's not what I mean! I mean what do we do about this!" Aisha said defensively while waving a hand between them.

"What do you mean?" Kargon asked.

Raw emotions still overwhelmed the Hero and she fell silent. It would be hard for Kargon not to understand Aisha after all these years. But it would be better to guide her to the answer. At least so he was sure about the signals he was receiving.

"Do you remember when we first met?" Kargon asked innocently.

"No," she replied. "Why?"

"Well, I do. I've always understood your intent but that doesn't mean it's easy. I can't be sure what you mean if you don't tell me sometimes. You asked me what we're going to do but I don't get why my answer is an issue. Explain."

Aisha sighed and nodded. "We have to finish the journey. I assume it's also your focus based on the training you put in. With the demon king's castle and everything going on, we can't turn our attention to this."

Kargon raised an eyebrow. "This?"

"I'm..."

The word came out before Aisha could stop herself. Years of being stringent with her voice easily unraveled near her best friend. Habits were hard to break and their question-response style of planning was proving a hurdle. The reason was obvious to her and fighting it would just be a hindrance moving forward.

"I feel the same way about you that you feel about me," Aisha said. "And I figure if we feel the same about each other then our relationship would change. I mean, that's how Mom always described it."

Kargon laughed softly. "Master Avant must be rubbing off on us if we're being so long-winded about three words. But I think you're wrong about something. We're not our parents." He slowly waved a hand between them. "Whatever this is; we can figure it out slowly. I'm happy to just be by your side like I've always been."

"You don't want anything from me?" Aisha asked.

"Do you?"

Aisha caught herself again but didn't hesitate. "Your attention and care. Maybe a few words that go past being friendly. If that makes sense. Kinda how Zigon talks to Velana," she admitted.

It shouldn't have been possible for Kargon to blush more yet that didn't change the fact he did. Calling his parents lovebirds was an understatement even decades into their relationship. Part of him desperately wanted to inform Aisha of that fact. Or maybe she knew and didn't care. But Kargon definitely couldn't bring himself to speak that way. At least, not in the open.

"When we're alone. I can promise that much," Kargon said with a nod.

"What about when we're with the others?" Aisha asked.

The man smiled. He'd never been courted but was sure this wasn't the norm. "I'll treat you like I always have. The person I care for most in the world."

This time the words carried more than a simple admittance. Respect, trust, and admiration were only some of the meanings both of them discerned. Even Kargon was aware there was more to be interpreted than he was capable of.

"I promise to do the same." Aisha awkwardly repeated herself. "Is… there anything you want from me?"

"Say the words when you're ready," Kargon answered immediately.

Aisha nodded fervently. "I just hope the others won't push too hard."

"Can you tell Vofric, Sariel?" Kargon said and turned to the table his friends occupied.

The dragon coughed, turned to look at Kargon and smirked knowingly. Eavesdropping was too easy not to do but Sariel didn't expect the monk to openly acknowledge it. After some whispers, Sariel, Vofric, and Avant returned to the Nevesi duo.

"Don't wait too long, please," Vofric said as if he'd never left the conversation.

"Just agree to the request," Sariel insisted.

Avant rolled his eyes and cooed.

"Busybody, indeed." Sariel said.

"It's fine," Aisha replied with a snicker. "We're done here anyway. Right?"

Kargon nodded as both half-elves rose from their seats. However, Aisha did not step around the table.

"Will you join my party again?" she asked with her hand extended to Kargon.

"You're asking again? After all this?" he replied.

"Is that a no?"

"Of course not." Kargon chuckled and gripped Aisha's hand softly. "I'll follow you anywhere."

CHAPTER FORTY-SEVEN

Motivation

Black lightning strikes—known as Void Storms—took weeks to become a biweekly occurrence. Less attacks were a blessing but made experienced adventurers suspicious. Some assumed storms targeted specific locations while others thought they were tests. Regardless of which camp people fell in; all agreed they were only a precursor.

With fewer encounters, the Hero's party was able to start mapping out the Agrestic. They made little headway towards the demon king's castle while assisting every possible settlement. Some villages couldn't be saved, leaving the party to clean up Husks wandering the remains. Worse yet was how often they found themselves outnumbered. Bolstering their numbers was paramount but Aisha refused to invite individuals they crossed.

"I can't trust someone who looks halfway to death after fighting a small group of demons. They'd fall when facing stronger threats," she explained. "I don't want that on anyone's conscience."

"Their abilities will be best against demonic fodder but not their leaders," Sariel said.

"Harsh way to word it but yes."

"Aisha, adventurers go on quests knowing the danger they will face. We must provide the opportunity for them to prove themselves," Vofric insisted.

Kargon hummed. "You both have a point but aren't considering everything. Vofric, they need to prove themselves with these fights.

They shouldn't be holding back like we used to. We need allies who can stand with who we are now."

"What he said," Aisha chimed in.

"Aisha, you're also forgetting that they might be weak or tired from helping folks just like we have." Kargon stopped abruptly and looked around to make sure no one was listening in. "Not to mention, we don't know if anyone we've met is part of Barbatos. From everything you've told me, they can be relied on. Let them hinder the demon king's overarching goals and we can take him out directly."

"You're right," Aisha conceded. Normally she'd have argued more but it was hard to deny the obvious. "Sariel, how close are we to the next village? Maybe we can start gathering forces for the trek to the castle."

The dragon has sketched a vast map across multiple pages of their notebook. Some things were already incorrect based on settlements falling or expanding. According to the information they'd gathered from other villages in the Agrestic, another would be up ahead. With summoned wings, Sariel took to the sky. They could easily hover for minutes but only needed seconds when surveying the land.

Upon landing, they said, "There are sounds of battle coming from the village. We should arrive momentarily."

Without a command the party knew to rush in. Aisha always took the lead with lightning fast speed with Sariel keeping up while flying. A few steps behind were Avant—ridden by Vofric—and Kargon. When they arrived at the village of Maccfeld, it was clear they were unneeded.

Civilians stood in awe as they watched a sole adventurer battle the demons. Metal clashed against bone as the swordsman deftly blocked a monster on the verge of attacking a bystander. With a smooth tilt of the blade, he parried the creature and cut through it. Demonic corpses littered the ground around him as he sheathed his sword onto his back to the sound of cheers and applause.

The party watched in silence as he was offered food and a place to rest. Graciously accepting the meal while smoothly mentioning his need to depart proved it was commonplace. Villagers gave him reverence for a few minutes before leaving to deal with the corpses. It was peculiar for the Hero's party to see such an event from the outside. Especially after having experienced it dozens of times themselves.

"A good candidate?" Vofric asked. The wariness in his voice didn't go unnoticed. It wasn't from fear of displeasing Aisha but something nagging him. There was no reason to hide it from the others.

"I want to talk to him alone. But I need you to stay close without it looking weird," Aisha replied.

Kargon nodded his head towards the outdoor seating of the tavern where the swordsman was relaxing. "Let's get lunch."

The group split up with Aisha still standing near the village entrance. Something about how she was approaching the encounter bothered Kargon. It was like she was preparing to fight, her left hand hovering inches above *Valefor*. Even as the party sat down and ordered, Kargon kept an eye on his partner.

Unlike the others, Aisha knew exactly what made her hesitate. Magic was clearly identifiable through her prosthetic eye which glowed a dim purple when used in such a way. Mana that looked like black ink cascaded off the mysterious swordsman. Only one other being had ever presented mana similarly. But Aisha felt less fear this time. Striding forward, she pulled out a chair, and sat down confidently. It was the most intense way someone could approach a table, causing the man to look at her curiously.

"What brings you here?" Aisha asked directly.

"I have no idea what you mean. I am simply exploring the Agrestic and happened upon villagers who needed assistance," the man replied. "Thankfully, my abilities were enough to protect them properly.

"That's a lot of words to say you don't understand my question. Try shortening your answers if you want to be believable."

The man narrowed his eyes and took a slow bite of his sandwich. Chewing food wasn't meant to look so threatening. Slowly, he craned his head back and swallowed the morsel. When he looked back down, the white of his eyes had turned black and his irises a haunting cobalt.

"Magic detection. Commendable. I expect no less of Kharim's successor," the man said.

"My name is Aisha Ilphekiir," the Hero said intently.

"I am Aer."

Aisha raised an eyebrow. "Aer... I see. Your name can be said and shortening it avoids detection."

Aer chuckled before taking another bite of his meal. With each passing second, the Hero was able to discern his true form beneath the human facade. A hazy aura turned his jagged horns into wild black hair. The end of his jacket was actually a slender tail. Most disconcerting was his sword—*Brachynox* in an unrecognizable form.

"You have grown more confident since our last encounter," Aer said while wiping his fingers on a rough leaf. "Unexpected but that is of no concern."

"Why. Are. You. Here?" Aisha asked deliberately.

"Much more confident." Aer studied the woman in front of him. "Those who inhabit the world must be unified. Do you agree?"

Aisha replied trepidatiously, "Yes."

"Do you know what is needed to unify wild, manic, and unreliable groups? Power. Something you, me, and my subordinates have. Something needed to uncover the mysteries of this land inhabited by weaklings who do not seek strength. Rather they wait for a powerful being to do everything for them and provide a pittance as a reward." He lifted the last remaining piece of bread and tossed it in his mouth with thinly veiled disgust.

"They give what they have." Aisha growled.

"Resources taken from those more deserving. Cowards are an unnecessary plague on your redeemable land. I am here to erase them." He lightly laid a fist on the table and pointed the index finger at his tablemate. "Your kind — adventurers — have caused a slight hindrance in my plans. Thankfully, Kharim's actions taught me many things about Tetria. Sufficient measures will be taken to impart... knowledge on the people of this land. Following that, I will educate all of Vethyea."

A chill ran down Aisha's spine while she made eye contact with her adversary. There was no emotion visible from the king who stood above all others. It didn't matter if this wasn't his land. To him, it was only a matter of time before his rule.

"Strength should be used to protect those who can't defend themselves," Aisha said. Continuing the conversation was difficult but she refused to let it show. "Noncombatants have skills in other fields. They provide for the world in their own way."

Aer replied immediately. "I agree. We will keep them as pets."

"Doesn't that go against your purpose of erasing them?"

The demon king hesitated and glared at his opponent—unable to stop a smile from tugging at her lips. And yet she refused to let it overpower the fierce stare on her face.

With a sigh and a crack of the neck, he continued, "You are correct. I shall opt to simply end their lives. Thank you for convincing me, Hero."

Aisha hesitated even though she expected the reactive response to backfire. It was foolish to succumb to her emotions against such a foe. Regaining her composure, she rested her right hand on the table and left on the *Valefor's* hilt. Though her intent was clear, she didn't move to attack.

"What if you were stopped here? Before you can hurt anyone else?" Aisha asked.

Aer cracked a smile. "Do you believe yourself strong enough to defeat me?"

With a tilt of the head, Aisha pointed to her friends, seated several tables away. Plates stacked with delicacies spread across it and to a bowl in front of the owlbear. The group partook as if nothing was on their minds. In truth, all of them were aware of the man sitting across from their leader. Kargon's spot at the table was deliberate—directly behind Aisha and across the demon king.

"Sariel, he said his name's Aer?" Kargon whispered.

The draconic elf furrowed their brow and nodded slowly. Obviously, they heard the entire conversation but waited to inform the others.

"Vofric, is he speaking at a volume you can hear?" Sariel asked.

He only shook his head before tilting his head at Kargon. "Observation, I assume."

"My eyes are far sharper than yours yet I am unable to understand their words without hearing them," Sariel said to Kargon.

He gulped down some food and replied, "You've spent your life studying landscapes and information. The only skill I had as a kid was talking. I got good at reading people, even from a distance."

"Vofric also spoke to many people in his retirement. However, he is unable to deduce their intentions so easily."

"Haven't you noticed how he understands battlefields faster than any of us? Including you? Sure, as a priest he might've trusted people a bit much. But he conducted an investigation on his own and only clued people in when he thought it was necessary. I couldn't do that."

The dwarf nodded. "Your deductive abilities would have aided in knowing who to trust back then."

"Well, you've got it now and more." Kargon cleared his throat and nodded towards their leader.

"Back to the topic at hand. His name, it hides the real thing, right? I can say Aeraza safely." He made a point to whisper the demon king's name even quieter than he already was. Only Vofric seemed surprised that the name was uttered but quickly understood why.

"What shall we do?" Sariel asked.

It wasn't lost on Kargon that the dragon was open to guidance from him. Clearly, something had garnered enough respect to trust Kargon's words.

"Wait for Aisha's signal," he answered.

Each of them slowly raised their heads and turned to look at the demon masquerading as a man. Much to their surprise, he was looking back—slowly shifting eyes studying the adventurers.

"Your party consists of a wild beast, a weakened dragon, a failed paladin, and your lover." Aer said and turned towards Aisha, "I ask again; do you believe yourself strong enough to defeat me?"

"Yes," Aisha answered—as shocked by the words as the demon king. Unfortunately, her mask slipped and Aer capitalized on it.

He stood up slowly with his arms raised. "Consider this, Aisha Ilphekiir. Are you willing to sacrifice this peaceful hovel in order to challenge me?" No part of him cared who overheard the conversation. When Aisha didn't answer, he continued. "I assumed so. Allow me to take my leave and we will continue this conversation another day. Maybe one day we can come to an agreement."

With his final words, Aeraza turned and walked away. Aisha's hand still hovered over her blade unwilling to grip it. Slow steps carried the demon king to the edge of town and around the gate. Once he was out of sight, the adventurers rushed to the exit but he was nowhere to be seen.

CHAPTER FORTY-EIGHT

Guided Exploration

Aisha's adrenaline slowly lessened once the party left Maccfeld. Every unknown sound garnered an overreaction but the others remained calm to ease the Hero's mind. While the others were uneasy from the encounter, none of them had to directly interact with Aeraza. No one could fault Aisha for needing time to calm down.

As much as Aisha hated how she was reacting, there was pride in conversing with Aeraza. There was a time when it wasn't possible to even think of him by his name. Next time they faced each other, she wouldn't freeze—being able to fight was another concern entirely.

As Aisha was lost in thought she felt a presence near her right hand. With a smooth motion, Kargon slipped his left hand into hers and squeezed tightly before letting go. A wave of heat passed between them that comforted Aisha. They smiled softly at each other before refocusing on their surroundings. Both knew it would be a while until she felt better but the gesture was appreciated.

Every moment in the Agrestic made it feel bigger than anticipated. Trees broke apart as the group exited via the northwest and saw a sheer cliff covering the plains east of Delras Range. Vofric said a prayer that they hadn't found themselves near Aeraza's castle. Stones were partially buried in the ground from falling long ago. Boulders and uneven terrain made the land hard to examine even from Sariel's aerial view. The party almost returned to the Agrestic when Avant roared for their attention.

A trail of long brown needles camouflage in the dry grass. Mistakenly stepping on one sent a shock of pain through the owlbear's paw. Pulling back only brought the needle along and made him stumble into another. It would have been upsetting if not for the confused trill Avant kept making. Aisha chuckled at the sight and though that brightened the owlbear's mood, it didn't help his predicament. Kargon stepped up to assist with safely pulling each splinter out.

Following the trail led to a large hedgehog covered in specks of blood. It watched the group with an intense gaze, making sure they remained at a distance. Somehow it produced a similar aura to Avant even at half his size. The owlbear bristled to scare the hedgehog away but it responded in kind. Before either mistakenly attacked, Sariel held out a hand in front of Avant. The dragon slowly approached and took a knee in front of the bloody hedgehog.

"This is not your blood," Sariel said. "We mean you no harm. Please, guide us to your master so we may assist them."

The hedgehog studied the odd elf and their draconic mutations. After nearly a minute of silent introspection, it turned away. Slow and deliberate steps carried it towards its goal. Every few paces it would turn back to make sure the adventurers were still following without weapons drawn. In truth, Sariel could hear where the wounded master was but running in suddenly might cause the hedgehog to retaliate.

A familiar scent tickled Avant's nose as they neared a large stone seen from afar. The hidden side had a small indent carved out—big enough for a small humanoid. It seemed the woman inside would make it her grave based on the large gash across her body. Her consciousness was quickly fading from the massive amount of blood loss.

There was no hesitation as Aisha said, "Heal her."

Vofric stepped forward but was blocked by the angered hedgehog. Even Sariel couldn't calm it down with a sudden command.

"Spike, stop being... dramatic. Let him... heal me," the woman choked out. The commanding voice of Freckle was familiar even if she was on her last legs.

As soon as the hedgehog moved, Vofric rushed forward. Golden light burst from his palms and encompassed the tired warrior. He expected to use a vast amount of mana to seal the wound but far more was used before the Barbatos captain finally opened her eyes with renewed vigor. Vofric stepped out of the alcove as Spike rushed in to check on the patient. Freckle's rugged hand brushed his quills and calmed the flood of concern in the beast. With a huff, she rose to her feet and stepped out of the shadows.

Everyone was astounded by how much blood soaked into Freckle's armor from whatever attack threatened her life. Sariel, on the other hand, noticed the short woman's hair. It had shifted from blonde to a smoky black with a sharpness that matched her familiar's hide. Freckle was obviously not a pureblooded halfling but Sariel was unsure how to broach the subject.

"It's hedgehog," Freckle said as she studied the gaze of her saviors.

Sariel twitched as realization dawned. "You were mutated against your will."

"My parents, actually. At least I assume so since they were never around."

"Why would you hide this?" Sariel asked.

"I didn't hide anything. My abilities weren't needed in Shusyoun," Freckle said.

"And your friend here?" Aisha asked.

"He was on his own missions."

"Right," the Hero replied slowly. "Do you mind if I ask what you're doing out here? How'd you get so close to dying?"

Freckle paused and looked away as she debated how many details to share. It wasn't a case of keeping secrets but rather protecting her pride. Then again, it would be folly to hold onto such a vice when offered aid from the Hero. With a wave, Freckle brought everyone closer and whispered. "There's a dungeon not too far from here. Based on my findings there should be an Artifact inside."

It was a welcome surprise to stumble onto one of their goals while aiding someone. Even though Aisha was still recovering from her talk with Aeraza, she was able to keep a straight face. Calmly, she asked, "Do you need help getting it?"

Where she and the others expected enthusiastic acceptance was instead careful suspicion. Freckle's smile did not waver but remained silent as her eyes flitted between the adventurers. Spike slowly paced around the group waiting for his master's command. Aisha realized Artifacts needed to be monitored carefully—regardless of who had them. Barbatos's goals aligned with humanity but that didn't mean they trusted everyone with tools that could change the course of history. It was the wise way of tackling such dangerous items. Both women began to speak then stumbled. Aisha put out a hand and gestured for the other to start.

"I contacted other captains for assistance," Freckle said. "That was weeks ago and even with less Void Storms no one has come this way. Normally I'd say you're above doing a menial retrieval delve but the guild makes us equal. At least until it's time to fulfill your purpose."

"Battle against the demon king," Sariel muttered. "It is inevitable."

"Exactly. I'll happily take the help in getting an upper hand against his army. Plus, maybe we can handle that dragominn together if they come back."

The words sent a sensation through Kargon like the scars across his body had reopened. Wild heartbeats pounded violently against his chest and his breath quickened. Rattling beads on his arms invited flames to burst forth. Thankfully, he had enough control to contain them on a single arm. That was the best he could do to stop from completely razing the dry field. With a shaky hand, he pulled his goggles up and strapped them tightly to feel like his head wasn't splitting apart.

"What... which Artifact did you... find? Any clues?" Kargon asked as he slowly regained composure.

"*Judgment*, the smiting tome," Freckle answered, kindly not bringing attention to Kargon's panic.

"Master Avant mentioned half-elves made it. Most folks on Tetria could use it."

Freckle smirked then turned to Aisha. "With everything that happened, I was unable to inform your party."

"Are all Artifacts bound to the race that crafted them?" Vofric asked.

"Something like that. They're best used by the current generation of that race." Freckle debated continuing her explanation. It wasn't necessarily important but mentioning it could be helpful. "Why do you think the demon king went in search of *Brachynox*?"

Sariel grumbled. "Was it not the first in his quest to seek out all the

Artifacts?"

"Sure. We assume he wants all of them but there's a reason he went for the sword specifically."

Aisha sighed heavily with realization. "It's made for demons. During the Age of Exploration a myriad of races came through Tetria. They probably lost *Brachynox* and when it was found again, humanoids classified it as an Arcana class magic item. And since the era stretched almost fifty years, they lumped it in with the Artifacts of Arcana."

"Exactly. The Artifacts were always rumored to return to the hands of their creators." Freckle replied suspiciously quickly but turned her attention to Kargon before anyone said anything. "I mean, you've got *Pyromanic* so I assume you're part fire giant."

The half-giant nodded in response. Though he'd accepted his origin for the sake of training, parts of it still confused him. Not that his father was the size of an average humanoid. Not even all the secrets. Mainly that Kargon's parents bequeathed him a magical item with no explanation trusting that his journey would reveal its purpose.

"It's not important though. We should focus on finding *Judgment.*" He rubbed a thumb against his forehead scar. "Lead the way. Please."

With a nod Freckle guided the group, Spike and Avant by her side. Something about the peculiar halfling comforted and called to the owlbear. Though Sariel was ready for the quest, they were more focused on the mutant as well. Their differences spoke volumes as to how they viewed their accursed states of being. Vofric momentarily waited for the others but Aisha signaled him to leave. Once he was a few steps away, she grabbed Kargon's free hand and squeezed it.

There was no smile but a look of conviction in her eyes. Mention of a violent dragominn wasn't lost on her. But no one knew the pain Elmud wrought more than Kargon. Even though Aisha didn't smile, the firebrand grinned at her. It was his own form of resolution.

CHAPTER FORTY-NINE

Predecessors

"Calling this a dungeon is an understatement," Kargon said in awe, delving into the cave.

It only took a few minutes of trekking through tunnels to reach an underground cliff. Instead of another road, the party looked down at a decrepit city. Nature overtook buildings, crushing and encasing them at random. Roots from trees above ground stretched deep within the unknown settlement. Torches in the distance were barely visible with flickering embers. At the edge of the cliff were remnants of a charred rope staked to the ground by a thick quill.

"Spike and I spent weeks slowly scouring this place for *Judgment* only for that dragominn to show up and fight us off." Freckle groaned. "Do any of you have rope? I can make another stake."

Black quills stood on the back of her palm. With little effort she pulled one then transformed it into a conical spike the length of her forearm.

"Peculiar," Sariel said, then knelt on the ground to summon a braided vine. Technically the quill was unnecessary but Freckle planted it nonetheless. Few things had ever broken the dragon's creations and it intrigued them that the halfling's magic pierced through easily.

What the group assumed would be a short climb took almost a minute. The far off ceiling felt like a dreary gray sky. At street level, it was apparent how old the city was. Architecture that was only found in history books stretched above their heads. Nature easily broke through many structures, caving in ceilings. Signs of struggle littered the nearby area where Freckle had escaped.

"Less stuff is broken further in. It helped us sneak pretty far without getting caught," Freckle explained. "Then we got here and had to fight. There was no chance against that magmatic bastard."

The jab made Kargon let out a soft chuckle. Such a simple insult did a surprising amount to calm his thoughts about Elmud. They were a magmatic bastard. But that didn't lessen the threat they posed. It was clearly far above Freckle's ability to fight, meaning other Barbatos members would be similarly overwhelmed.

"I take it you've spent most of your time in Barbatos searching for things," he stated as the group moved forward. "When you're not commanding, I mean."

"I prefer the term delving. Or maybe exploring. My magic lends itself well to it," the spiky halfling replied.

With a nod she turned the group's focus towards nearby buildings. Thin quills were jabbed into the floor and let off a faint black smoke while vibrating.

"Grab one of those as you're going," Freckle instructed while stopping the vibrations. "If you see them in a building, I've explored it and found nothing on *Judgment*."

"You seem sure that Elmud is gone. The dragominn, I mean," Kargon said while placing a quill between the bindings on his arm.

"They flew off a few hours after I got out. That's why I was holed up in that rock."

Freckle turned to Vofric and thanked him. He shook his head in response before stepping away to focus on the search; a quill tucked into his armor. Aisha was further ahead with a quill in her bun and placing another in Avant's fur. The end of the street marked where they dispersed before vanishing into the city. A brief vibration went through the quills to confirm everyone's locations before Freckle continued the search with Sariel and Spike by her side.

The trio moved in silence, checking corners for any unseen threats. Empty buildings were searched easily with the sharp senses of a dragon. A simple tap of their hand against a structure produced myriad vines that crawled over every available space. Every sensation the wriggling tentacles felt was clear to Sariel.

Unfortunately, nothing of note was present. Tomes had been destroyed in a fiery blaze. Relics of a long forgotten city were broken from centuries of neglect. Sariel was careful when retracting the vines back into the ground.

"Kind of you to take so much care." Freckle dashed over an alley, throwing quills into the searched buildings.

From another building across the road, Sariel replied, "There is little left of this land's memory. It would be wrong to completely erase it."

"You sound like you're talking from experience."

Sariel hesitated and stared out the empty window towards the direction of the mutant halfling. "Our mutations are related."

"Seems likely, yes," Freckle replied nonchalantly.

"Do you have any idea the pain caused by the thing that did this?"

"I can't know. My mother died after childbirth. Father didn't fare much better with all the ailments plaguing him. I've been alone since I was a kid."

Spike barked as he scurried from his building to Freckle's. "Right, sorry. Spike's always been with me," she laughed.

Sariel finished searching their building and moved to the next. Without a word, Freckle tossed a quill from her spot through two windows and into the entryway. The precision and control dumbfounded the dragon. The halfling was young yet had experience beyond her years with a monstrous ability others couldn't stand.

"Does your ability not make you uncomfortable?" Sariel asked.

"It's itchy," Freckle joked, then sighed. "No. Not anymore at least. Gotten me out of my fair share of predicaments."

A soft contemplative hum unintentionally escaped the draconic elf. They had no idea why they asked such a question. The magic of a dragon was their birthright. It stemmed from their connection to the land. It was an ancient ability others could only dream of. For it to even bother Sariel felt ridiculous.

An errant glance pulled their draconic claw into view. Slowly, they looked at their non-scarred hand; the true mutation. It slowly reached over and ran across the scales on Sariel's face. "Apologies for the crude question but, does it not bother you how others view you? Do they not look down at you for your mutation?" they asked.

Freckle immediately replied, "Not the ones that matter." It was as if she'd practiced it—a mantra to remind her of her value. "Once I shut out the voices of my naysayers, I realized how few they were. Their shouts eventually got drowned out by the people who knew my worth. I only know the power of my quills because of those friends' enthusiasm."

"Your allies sound wonderful," Sariel said.

"You're one to talk."

Another involuntary hum was the last thing uttered by the dragon.

***

The adventurers reconvened within the hour with some books, personal items, and undamaged relics piled between them. Each took turns examining what they could understand but only Vofric read every book. Magical deciphering did little to explain what the books were about. The dwarf's upbringing and age allowed to not only understand old languages but to decipher their context.

"It seems Barbatos rebuilt this city and used for a hideout," Vofric said as he shut one of the intact books.

"Where exactly is it?" Aisha asked while looking over the dwarf's shoulder.

"You misunderstand, Aisha. This is the hideout. The entire city."

Freckle let out a whistle and looked up and down the street. "Barbatos could still use space like this. Wouldn't have to have our numbers so spread out."

"With large enough cities, your numbers would still appear thin," Vofric replied.

"That's not necessarily the case," Kargon interjected. "We call this place a city but that's more because of how it looks, not its size. Sure it's big, but not that much more than Neves."

"This wasn't only a hideout," Sariel said while examining one of the stone figures they found. "Families of myriad sizes called this land home before reconstruction. How much time has passed since the original city was buried?"

Vofric grunted as he flipped to the back of the book in his hands. Shaking his head, he handed it to Aisha and grabbed another. Swift skimming took him through three books before he slowed down. With a gasp, he glared at a tower on one side of the city. Much of the cavern had collapsed around it and made it difficult to reach. But the upper area remained unscathed with bare windows allowing entry.

"I don't know when this city was buried but I know why these tomes were written. It was to record the destruction of the Artifacts; nearly 200 years ago," the dwarf said while staring at the tower. "That was 150 years after the Age of Exploration ended. For two centuries, Barbatos safeguarded them before choosing destruction. Those that could not be were kept within their reach throughout Tetria. There is no information what hideouts or landmarks hold an Artifact or which might be there. Only that they would be guarded by powerful forces."

"Like the ever-flowing sands of Spirefell," Kargon said. "We couldn't so much as approach it before. But it didn't seem to stop the demon king."

Sariel scoffed. "He is powerful."

"An odd time to pay him a compliment," Freckle said.

"It is simply an observation and fact. He holds the strength to bypass a barrier intended to seal a tool that can shift the course of history."

Kargon hummed. "But not his allies. At least I don't think so since they mainly attacked the village. Meaning Aisha can probably get to the Artifacts with no issue."

"That confidence is what got you hurt," she said while looking towards the tower.

"Only because I didn't think before fighting Elmud last time. I know better now. And I know I'm right."

Aisha's eyes twinkled at her partner's determined words. It became clear to her something was wrong with the tower. Whatever caused walls to cave-in at its base should have brought the entire structure down. With a magical gleam in her eye, Aisha was able to view an aura permeating around the top of the obelisk—one that was slowly dissipating.

"I'll check it out," she said calmly as she strode towards the tower.

Everyone followed her wary approach to the base of the spire but only Aisha, Kargon, and Sariel climbed the rocks. The others stood watch at ground level, still expecting Husks. The stones were hardened and fused together from years of settling. Kargon had the easiest time ascending after decades of acrobatics. With his lead, the others were able to find footholds. Once they got near the top of the tower, he found a place to wait outside with Sariel. Aisha was the only one who stepped through the thinning aura into a once empty belltower.

Breaking in made clear what was causing the outpouring of magic. Floating at the center of the tiny room was a thick book with a chunk cut off. Frayed strings peeked out of the top of decrepit pages. A shredded golden ribbon was pressed between them and extended past the bottom. Gold engravings filled with dirt cut deeply into the dull gray hardcover marked with foreign letters. Aisha's focused glance couldn't decipher the ancient text but she knew it read *"Judgment."*

Delicate hands reached for the tome and effortlessly released it from its magical binding. The book hadn't only been a victim to time. Pages were sliced apart and burned with no rhyme or reason. Ink magically faded depending on how much damage a page received. Aisha absentmindedly flipped through the pages and stepped away from the center of the room. Tattered paper and cardstock littered the floor in a pattern that made it obvious they were used for kindling. Fire was such a common element yet Aisha only equated it to two people. She turned to look at Kargon outside who stared back and smiled.

The Nevesi duo often lost themselves in these brief interactions. Maybe they always had but now it was different. Even a simple glance lifted their hearts and soothed their minds. It was as though they were swaying together. That was new. Aisha blinked out of her reverie and reassessed the situation.

Stones they mistakenly thought had hardened began crumbling rapidly. The faltering wave of mana burst outward into a mist that encompassed the underground city. It was a mistake to assume the protection was only to block people from getting to the Artifact. A secondary spell that froze time had been set to stop its theft.

CHAPTER FIFTY

Escaping the Past

The immediate rain of stones didn't cause Aisha's air of calm to waver. Her entire party was rather unphased. The most direct path to the exit was obvious and keeping it clear was easy with Vofric's hammer and Avant's gravity magic. Any time loose dirt piled up, Freckle cut it apart with long blade-like quills. The adventurers who had climbed to the Artifact returned to the ground and caught up quickly.

"It is rather frustrating that we are prepared for this due to Veil's experiments," Sariel grumbled, swinging a wooden club to swat away errant stones.

"Pay it no mind and focus on reaching our destination," Vofric replied. "Lest we dawdle and succumb to an avoidable fate."

Everyone stopped as a high dirt wall blocked the road they followed. A building that stood minutes ago had succumbed to the rapid passage of time. It crumbled near instantly to the weight forced on it. Internal structures were breaking throughout the cavern in a thunderous applause of snapping beams. The party turned to a new path and continued at a quickened pace as Avant shifted gravity to push boulders with greater force. Some collided with others in the air, causing a rain of chipped rocks.

"Focus on keeping the path clear," Kargon said while punching away a large stone. "I'll deal with stuff coming at us."

Avant hooted affirmatively and used a more controlled force to carve a path. Within minutes they reached the rope leading to their exit. Unfortunately the rain of bedrock made it difficult to climb safely. Stones were piling up around the group. Manipulated gravity could only do so much before they were trapped in a spacious bunker. There was little time to decide what to do. All eyes turned to Aisha as she continually stared at the falling ceiling.

She turned to Avant and said, "Gravity shift our group towards the wall. Ignore the rocks."

With a powerful roar, he sent nearby debris flying and gave everyone enough time to get near the wall. Grumbles and confusion eked out of the owlbear as he worked out how to turn a force of nature. Kargon placed a hand lightly on the owlbear's back and Avant cooed softly. Falling rocks drummed around them but no longer distracted the beast. He forcefully slammed a paw into the wall and the group fell forward. Once everyone regained their footing, they ceiling was ahead of them.

"Kargon, Vofric. Clear the path!" Aisha commanded.

Fiery astral fists as large as the rocky storm easily swatted the projectiles away. Any that Kargon missed were quickly acquainted with the might of a war-hammer. Instead of falling away, they were shattered then sent directly into the wall. They made for comfortable footholds when vertigo momentarily overtook the group. However, running vertically was much faster than climbing. Less than a minute passed before they crossed over the edge and gravity reverted.

The tunnel had barely been affected by the quaking and everyone took a last look at the city. It had been completely destroyed, going through hundreds of years of damage in seconds. Vofric said a short prayer for the lost settlement before following Aisha to the exit with everyone else in tow.

The sun was crossing over the horizon, welcoming the adventurers into night. Though it was beautiful, no one focused on it or the tattered Artifact in Aisha's hands. None dared look away from the scarred dragominn casually leaning on a tree near the cave entrance. Wounds shining like obsidian trailed over gleaming crimson scales. A wicked smile of pearled teeth came across Elmud's face as they recognized the group. Aisha immediately drew her sword and put her right arm— book in hand— in front of Kargon. Simultaneously, Avant and Vofric flanked their fiery ally. With a silent motion, Sariel signaled for Freckle and Spike to stay back. Neither showed a semblance of fear and prepared for battle.

The dragominn exhaled sharply through their nostrils. "You really came out of the trap unscathed. Seems you've grown."

Though Elmud addressed everyone, their eyes were affixed on Kargon. It was plainly obvious they were studying the monk's scars. The one across his face was especially clear while his goggles hung limply around his neck. Multiple things had lined up for Kargon to be permanently disfigured and it made Elmud happier than expected.

Aisha stepped further in front of her friend and glared at the enemy. "I doubt you were able to destroy *Judgment* without the demon king's help."

"You'd like to believe so, wouldn't you? How could fire so easily destroy an Artifact." They said it with a knowing tone.

Freckle muttered, "Are you saying this isn't one?"

Elmud's smile disappeared and they slowly turned towards the small woman. In a hauntingly calm voice they said, "Be thankful the Hero saved you but do not speak when I address her." They faced Aisha and continued in a casual tone. "The rodent is wrong. Artifacts are really nothing special. Had some special materials and enchantments, sure. But they weren't so powerful they couldn't be destroyed."

Vofric bit his lip and turned away at the realization. Aisha only turned her eyes towards him and was met with a slight nod. No words were spoken but understanding was evident.

"It's not that Barbatos couldn't destroy the Artifacts. They chose not to," Aisha said with clear disdain in her voice. No one knew if it was oriented towards Elmud or the guild.

Elmud responded with a smirk. "No wonder Master Aeraza was impressed with you. Correct. The protectors of Tetria kept some hidden in case a threat arose. I'm sure you're aware they knew my master's promise."

"You mean his curse."

"Semantics do not change facts, Hero." Elmud insisted. "I did not require any assistance in broiling that flimsy book. None will be needed for any of the Artifacts. Though, I don't mind leaving one intact for our friend there."

Their eyes once again trained on Kargon. As if responding to the dragominn, *Pyromanic* reflected the setting sun. Of all the Artifacts, it looked the least sturdy. Kargon's firm grip wrapped around the goggles to protect them. Nothing would damage his family's heirloom under his watch.

Elmud scoffed. "Truly, we both have better things to worry about than an Artifact so useless it was lost by the fools who created it. After all, I must return to destroying the remaining items you surely seek."

Everyone's attention was focused on the dragominn but Aisha was more focused on an inkling of an idea. Even if all the Artifacts weren't exactly what she believed, they clearly held power worth seeking. The only proof she needed was the fact that Aeraza wielded one as his own weapon of choice.

"Why destroy the Artifacts when Veil could wield any of them to your benefit?" Sariel asked. If the venom in their voice could be used for battle, Elmud would drop dead on the spot.

A wicked smile stretched across the dragominn's face as they answered. "There is a certain joy in seeing the despair in our enemy's eyes as they lose all hope. We already hold *Brachynox* and are close to… nevermind. Simply put, Master Aeraza needs no other Artifacts to conquer this realm."

"The Ring of Dominion, right?" Aisha asked. "How close are you?"

Elmud grumbled and swore under their breath. "That mind may impress my master but keep pushing and he'll cut you down without a chance to join him."

"I don't need that chance. He'll be long dead before making the offer."

"And what of your allies? What if they are offered the chance? Will you be able to stop them? Or will you cut them down if they stray from your righteous path?"

Not a single person flinched at the ridiculous notion. Sariel continued looking for a chance to skewer the annoying dragominn while Avant and Vofric muttered spells. Giant quills rapidly grew as Freckle and Spike prepared to fire. Aisha remained unwavering in front of Kargon.

Elmud hated the lack of a vocal response. It was clear that their conversation partner was mentally indisposed. Something about Kargon's demeanor struck the dragominn as odd. Wide eyes were hyper focused on every minuscule movement. Trembling fingers twitched at the slightest shift in the atmosphere. His stance was solid, almost threatening. A faint flame was emanating from inside the monk's mouth. It was only possible to see due to his awkward toothy grin. As realization set, Elmud let out a hearty laugh. Reactively, for the briefest second, Kargon's fist tightened.

"I've spent enough time answering your trifling questions," the dragominn said while turning to Aisha. "Do not hinder your lover next time. Something tells me he's raring to go."

With that they sprouted massive wings and took to the sky with no intent to attack. At most they slowed the party's search by a few minutes but got clear information that Aeraza was being chased by the Hero. It wasn't as though the party thought he didn't know. It just cemented for everyone that few others could match Aisha or her allies' capabilities.

The group stowed their weapons and turned to Kargon who was as confused by Elmud's last words as them. What everyone else could see was the almost relaxed demeanor with which he stood. There was obvious tension inside him but it was unreflected outside. Only raw instincts and a joyous smile presented themselves. Once aware, Kargon knew the grin was different than any other he'd ever shown. Drumming heartbeats pounded in his chest like the cacophonous rain they just escaped. A high-pitched tone rang in his ears that drowned out everything but the sound of Elmud's voice until they left. Every sensation was extremely clear on his bare body as it prepared to attack.

They were all feelings he was familiar with. Remnants of fear that subsided with Master Avant's help. Anger with no tension since Kargon wasn't in battle. But the smile across his face made clear the most important emotion. When Kargon next faced Elmud, there would be joy in pummeling his nemesis.

CHAPTER FIFTY-ONE

Unexpected Company

Freckle and Spike were gone before the Hero's party made a plan. The realization that Aeraza and his peons outpaced Barbatos enraged the captain—along with the guild failing to record the reasons behind preserving Artifacts. But exhaustion and a life threatening battle were heavy burdens to shoulder. Rest was necessary before whatever next steps. If anything, other captains might be able to fill her in on what happened during her exploration. Thus the halfling and her familiar returned to the nearest village as the adventurers pushed onward.

There was little they could do to cross their enemies' lead on the Artifacts. All their information relied on the guild or their agents. Unfortunately, it seemed Barbatos was lacking intelligence or someone within the group was lying. Neither was good but the former was preferable and plausible. The lessening Void Storms would allow them to reconvene and properly share findings. According to Freckle, some of her agents might still be waiting in Deriich—one of many towns in Bursbo Shallows on the northwestern outskirts of the Agrestic.

With the location of the destroyed cave marked on their map, it was easy for Sariel to deduce the time needed to reach the town. Unfortunately, it would take a few days and they'd already spent many not going where they were suggested to. By the time the party arrived, the contacts may no longer be in Deriich. Even if it was the right place to go, it was based on Freckle's hunch bolstered by unreliable communication. The best option was to focus on getting to the town quickly.

"You cannot be suggesting that we ignore the plights of innocents that we pass," Vofric said cautiously.

"Of course not. But we can't have another Foxhill," Aisha explained.

"We can't accept anyone's hospitality. Breaks have to be dictated by our party." Kargon added. "And I think we need to ignore any hunches about the Artifacts. Just until we make contact with Barbatos."

"Exactly. The demon king's too ahead of us. We can't let ourselves be distracted."

Sariel grunted. "Worse yet is that we do not know the discrepancy in our knowledge."

A perpetual air of uneasiness weighed on the party as they traveled. Thankfully, it was one of few hindrances in their way. Being a month into summer meant there was no snow across the plain. Trees interspersed throughout the grassland bore fruit and allowed animals to roam near with no fear of Husk attacks. A lack of supplies proved no issue with the capacity to hunt. With Sariel's mastery over nature, there was no longer a need for carrying tents. The lighter load was an unexpected but appreciated result of the group's training.

Battles against strengthened Husks weren't difficult but casualties couldn't be avoided in villages the party arrived late to. Nevertheless, people always felt at ease the moment adventurers arrived. Word traveled quickly across Bursbo Shallows about the Hero's party defending small settlements. They provided what aid they could before sending the party on their way. Timing never allowed them to rest at a comfortable inn but they'd accepted it wouldn't happen again for a long time. Not that it mattered since one night of pseudo restful sleep wasn't enough to wash away all that weighed on them.

There was little ease for any adventurer currently traveling around Tetria. Greenhorns were met with insurmountable odds while experienced travelers had to contend with the weight of a horrifying future. Worse yet, all of them were second to the Hero and her companions. Though there were few complaints considering what she would be facing at the end of her journey. Whatever a normal warrior felt was significantly worse for the woman leading the frontline. Knowledge of what was happening was less helpful than anyone assumed. It only cast a shadow of fear based within the reality that

Aeraza would always be ahead of humanity. The day Aisha faced him, it would be from an unenviable starting point.

Kargon couldn't shake the flood of anxiety that washed over him whenever those thoughts arose. Voicing them was pointless since everyone was fully aware of them. It's not like it helped Aisha with the stress of planning for the fast approaching battle. She was trying to deduce every possible contingency to face her destined enemy.

Deriich was reminiscent of Neves with a guard tower at one side and town hall attached. People roamed the streets without care but none crossed the gate facing the party. Some walked nearby and looked towards the wooden observation tower outside before moving on. From afar no one could be seen inside but the party knew better than to trust the naked eye. Collectively they turned to Sariel for more information who was squinting at the hut atop stilts covered in shadow. In the corner was a hidden figure watching over the land.

A soft smile passed over the dragon's face and they said, "Let us continue forward. We shall not be attacked."

"How do you know?" Kargon asked even while following Sariel's lead.

"You will understand shortly."

As the group got closer, the covered figure slowly rose. The sun beat down on his back and hid his features but no one felt a threat coming from the being. He took slow steps towards the edge of the tower and stared at the party.

"Uncle Vof!" a familiar voice yelled happily. Albert's voice had dropped slightly during his year of constant training. Silver metal plating engraved with the Dicoris family crest covered his leather armor that tightly hugged his lean form. Telltale signs of youth were fading from the amateur adventurer. Stubble riddled his chin, giving him a faint shadow —it was a far cry from his uncle's beard.

Without hesitation, the boy leapt from the tower and landed with a thud in front of the party before crouching to hug Vofric. After the embrace, everyone received a firm handshake while Avant got a well deserved head ruffle.

"What are you doing here, Albert?" Aisha asked.

"It's a long story. Probably shouldn't spout off about it here. The guards will be back on duty soon so we can go talk," he replied.

"You're covering for them?" Kargon asked.

Albert paused for just a split second. Kargon instantly knew something was off but there was little reason to point it out.

The boy quickly nodded and said, "Something like that, yeah."

He waved at a group of approaching guards as they returned to their positions. Mere steps into Deriich made clear how few civilians remained in town. Many people had relocated after the appearance of Aeraza's castle. It was hundreds of miles away but could be seen from here. The vague spires that pierced the sky were daunting and its overwhelming aura put the most experienced adventurers on edge. Of course, townsfolk fled at the sight. Those who remained looked unphased by both the castle and the adventurers' presence.

"Some feel like this is normal and others gave up," Albert said when he noticed Kargon's wandering eyes.

"This isn't like anything they've seen before," he replied. "Not unless someone here is over five hundred years old."

Albert chuckled softly. "Yeah. It's weird that depressed people are having a more logical response to what's going on."

The group crossed the central inn and entered an alleyway. Weaving through the buildings wasn't difficult but it was odd that Albert was staying off the beaten path. They arrived at an establishment that was far less pleasing to the eye than the ones on the main road. Inside was an inviting tavern with few patrons and plenty of space. However, Albert passed by the front desk, nodded to the clerk, and stepped into the back room. Instead of a standard office there was a medium sized bedroom. A circular table sat at one side with a couple chairs; reminding Kargon of the monastery.

Albert quickly retrieved some more chairs and invited everyone to sit. "Okay, what do you want to know?" he asked.

Aisha stared at the younger man and contemplated the only question she had asked. What was Albert doing here? Obviously a lot had changed since they last met. Aside from a handful of scars, he had a discerning eye that studied the surroundings. Whatever he was searching for outside Deriich was rooted in the experiences that transpired over the last year.

"What's happened since we left Dawncaster?" she answered.

"That's... oh boy." Albert exasperated. "Remember how Makani said he'd be an adventurer to learn about the world? Well, he needed training. Mainly learning how to handle situations we'd face while on the road. So Victor trained both of us for half a year with some magic help from Queen Lyra. In order to avoid people revering the prince too much, his father teleported us to Shusyoun and we traveled to the northeast corner of the Agrestic. When the castle showed up, we helped villages across the forest and ended up here."

"So you're protecting Deriich?" Aisha asked.

Albert hesitated and looked around the room, obviously studying the party's faces. Everyone looked at Vofric as his god-son contemplated how to proceed. Unlike the aura outside, the dwarf's was calm and welcoming. Experienced eyes watched a child battle with feelings of trust and doubt. Something weighed on Albert that every adventurer—every person—needed to deal with at some point in their lives. Better for it to occur in the safety of a small tavern with friends than an unknown place.

"Kinda," Albert muttered as he lost his battle to doubt. "Makani can probably explain better. He's a lot smarter about this diplomatic stuff."

The room grew quiet with his response. It was only a few seconds but he couldn't handle what he perceived as scrutinizing eyes. "What are you doing here?" he blurted out.

Sariel seemed to perk up at the question. Only Kargon noticed the small twitches at the end of their ears.

"Looking for someone," Kargon said. "An ally we got separated from said we could find them here."

Albert smiled softly. "You guys make friends wherever you go. I hope we can do the same once after all this is over."

"Don't focus on an unsure future, Albert." someone said as the door to the room opened. Prince Makani stepped through and greeted everyone. "Aisha has grown far stronger than us. But she already carries much on her shoulders regarding the upcoming battle. Let us not increase its weight. The future may be enjoyed once we reach it."

The once reclusive prince had grown taller and more muscular with a sharpened jaw that was reminiscent of his father. Confidence and clear eyes resembled the queen. Strapped tightly to the prince's back was a staff magically bound in white cloth; *Lightbringer.*

"They let you leave the city with an Artifact?" Aisha asked.

"While locked in my family's vault, it provided a shield for Dawncaster. Removing it turned it into a weapon meant to be wielded. It wouldn't do to leave it behind based on the threats we face," Makani replied.

It was exactly as Elmud had said; the Artifacts of Arcana were left intact for defensive purposes even when they could end up in the wrong hands. Removing the weapon from Dawncaster made the city safer in the long run. Similar ideas came flooding into Aisha's head and she forced them back. A quick glance at Kargon made it clear to him to take over as the party's speaker.

"Albert implied you're doing something more than protecting Deriich. Is there some way we can help?" he asked.

"I'm unsure. We crossed paths with someone early into our journey. Constant contact has been kept and they told us to remain here to receive someone. That was over a month ago and they left no information regarding who we await," Makani explained.

Sariel shook their head and scoffed. "Freckle should have given you more information considering your lack of nuance."

Words muttered by the prince on his frustrated walk back had clued in the dragon. Freckle had instructed them to await important guests but the boys' different upbringings affected who they considered important. Only the calm dragon's striking tone brought back their senses and reminded them who both revered. People who didn't need almost a minute to realize what Sariel's words meant. Freckle had put the Hero's party on a crash course with old friends.

CHAPTER FIFTY-TWO

Astute Discoveries

After a year apart, it was no surprise that the young adventurers wanted to hear what the Hero' party had been up to. Staying on task fell to the experienced warriors. Thankfully, a few words of pertinent information got Albert and Makani on the same page. They listened intently as Aisha explained the party's encounter at Shusyoun. Each memory of the previous months sent chills down their spine. Makani's experience hearing dire news helped him keep a calm face but concern flared in his eyes. There was no reason for Albert to put on airs. Or rather, he couldn't. The horrific news of fallen villages and monstrous creatures left his mouth agape. While both boys were uneasy, they didn't waver and followed each piece of information with a nod or clarifying question. It was clear Freckle made the right call in trusting them. Experience would come with time but they were well along their way.

"Do you still have *Judgment?*" Makani asked.

Aisha retrieved the tattered book from her pocket and revealed it had crumbled to a quarter of its original size. Placing it on the table caused more ruined pages to turn to dust. Makani lightly rested a hand on it and sighed when the remnants disintegrated.

"Though the Artifacts are powerful, they are like any other magic item. The correct means can easily destroy them," he muttered.

"No wonder there's only a few left," Albert agreed.

"Is there any way we can contact Freckle?" Kargon asked. "She has to know something about what's really going on with the Artifacts by now."

Makani nodded and rose from the table, opening a bag leaning against the wall. From within came pieces of metal and rope along with a small conical piece of glass. As Makani sat down, Albert started to put the pieces together. Bent hollow tubes screwed together into a circle with small holes all over it. Thin ropes looped through each opening into a web. A metallic cup was placed in the middle followed by an intricate stone retrieved from Makani's pocket. Finally, he screwed the glass cone on top of the cup and encased the stone.

Albert placed the device in the center of the table while Makani composed himself. Wind whipped around the room and through the devices various openings, causing it to hover. A rhythmic tune emanated from the floating item. Only now did the Hero's party realize the device resembled the hovering object on Freckle's desk. The cobalt stone began to glow dimly but didn't refract off the glass cone above it. Amazement turned to impatience as nothing else happened for over a minute. The tired looks on Albert and Makani's faces made clear they were used to this.

Suddenly, the light grew brighter and bounced off the cone, turning into a wispy smoke that wreathed around the rope. A voice echoed on the wind.

"Captain Freckle, speaking," it said.

"Makani Dicoris and Albert Greycastle, reporting," Makani replied.

"I take it you finally met the contacts."

"It would've been helpful to know who to look for."

Freckle chuckled, "What's the fun in that?"

"Is this really the time for fun?" Aisha interjected.

"Of course, even a little bit eases the mind. Anyway, have any of you learned anything since we last met?"

Before anyone could explain, Makani blurted out, "Did you learn why the Artifacts weren't destroyed?"

"Patience, Makani." Freckle sighed. "I'm still unaware of the reason why the Artifacts weren't destroyed. Should have been possible in the last few centuries if not at the time of creation. But, I'm unsurprised that humanoids kept some intact out of fear. It was foolish but that's how we operate."

Kargon grunted, "Does that mean the other Artifacts aren't destroyed?"

"Unfortunately, no," Freckle answered. "It's almost systematic how the demon king and his troops are targeting the Artifacts. Reports have come in that sealed tombs around Tetria have been completely destroyed. Some had nothing left inside and others had new treasures. Everything was eviscerated and dozens of agents have died reaching the end of ancient dungeons."

A somber tension fell over the room as the group shared an uneasy silence. If not for the raw power the Hero's party possessed, Freckle would have died. Unplanned alliances and engagements would continue to fail. Even if one ended in success, it wasn't worth the sacrifices. The upcoming battle needed each and every member of Barbatos. Death was inevitable but an untimely one was avoidable.

Nearly a minute passed before Vofric broke the silence. "Have you any notion of where we can find the remaining Artifacts?"

"Artifact. Singular," Freckle replied. "I'm sure you can guess which based on Elmud's admittance. The Ring of Dominion may be able to be destroyed, I truly have no idea."

"Whether it can or not doesn't matter. We have to stop the demon king from getting it," Aisha said. "Please tell me you have some idea of where it is."

"In that regard we have... let's say good news and bad news. The good news is that we have information on where the ring may be located."

"Bad news is that there's multiple locations, isn't it?" Aisha replied immediately. "Whatever mistake Barbatos made with leaving Artifacts intact, they had to have known not to leave them in easy to find places. They probably took extra precautions with how strong the Ring of Dominion is."

Freckle let out a soft laugh. Information about the Hero could only explain so much. Details were always skewed based on people's beliefs. Drawing a sword could even be seen as a stroke of pure luck. But the mental and physical capabilities Aisha showed repeatedly impressed the Barbatos captain.

"That's right; Zeld's Shell and Natharia. In order to avoid any more unnecessary losses our members are gathering to tackle both possible locations. We're prioritizing Zeld's Shell, however. There is a small army of demons attacking it with a shapeshifter commanding them."

All of the Sariel's party members reacted by turning to the dragon. There was no panic or anger in their eyes at the mention of the shapeshifter. A calm aura permeated off the draconic elf as they asked the only necessary question.

"Silver eyed?"

Freckle let out a confused grunt. "Uh, yes. How did you know?"

"He ranks similarly to Elmud. It is understandable that they have equal responsibilities."

Something about the plan bothered Kargon. The names of both locations were familiar but he couldn't exactly place them. Squinted eyes looked into empty space trying to search for an answer. Aisha wore a similar expression as she scoured her memory for knowledge. Maybe it was the shared thought process or past experience that reminded both of where the information came from.

"The legendary turtle Zeld housed Natharia on his back. When he passed, the city was left abandoned and circling Tetria," Kargon said. "But the path is too erratic to follow."

"Not with enough time spent tracking it," Freckle replied. "Within the month it will be near the shores up north. But our agents watching the island reported demons already scouring Natharia."

Aisha groaned. "That's why Barbatos forces are gathering near Zeld's Shell. It's a vault made from his hide on the mainland. Even if there's no ring there, it might have information we need to retrieve the ring."

Assumptions were her least favorite path towards a plan but there were no other viable clues. All they could hope for was that Natharia didn't have the ring either. Maybe the demon king was still toying with innocent villages in the Agrestic and hadn't heard from his subordinates. Hoping for such a thing made Aisha's skin crawl. It was exactly why assumptions and uneducated guesses bothered her so much.

"Zeld's age eclipsed that of the Artifacts," Vofric said inquisitively. "Additionally, he only passed away two centuries ago. I was but a child but remember being devastated."

"What's that have to do with anything?" Kargon asked.

"It bothers me. You see, my statement isn't necessarily correct either. Based on what we know, some Artifacts actually eclipse Zeld's age. They were seemingly created at random."

"Not at random but not at the same time either," Freckle interrupted. "Some Artifacts were old and powerful magical tools that were reclassified due to their strength. Their power left a mark in many battles and resulted in a change to their legend."

Aisha was pulled from her reverie and stared at the floating disk in front of her. She'd almost forgotten Makani and Albert were there as the boys awkwardly watched the conversation unfolding. Next to the prince, leaning on the table, was *Lightbringer*. Its power was still beyond comprehension for anyone who didn't wield it.

"Which Artifacts were reclassified?" Aisha asked.

Freckle hesitated. It was the most flustered she'd sounded since the group met her.

"You're hiding something, Freckle," Aisha insisted. "The trust we have hinges on the fact that you know things about the Artifacts that we don't."

Freckle stammered. "I know, it's just—"

"Just nothing!" Aisha slammed her fist on the table. "I'm on a quest to defeat the demon king! The extra bullshit of the Artifacts is a problem. What is the point in hiding more information from me?"

She was seething with rage and no one faulted her, agreeing that it was unfair to be kept in the dark. Kargon softly placed a hand on his beloved's shoulder—not to calm her but in support. By now, the burden of the Hero's destiny only worsened as her goal neared.

"Freckle," the monk said. "I'm sure you have your reasons to hesitate but understand that the person who leads your agents into battle can't go in blindly. We want to work with you without doubts in our minds. I'm sure someone who deals in information can understand that."

There was a short pause before Freckle replied. "It's not confirmed but I've always believed a rumor passed down through generations of information brokers. During the Age of Exploration, a group of powerful adventurers found a portal to the demonic realms and retrieved a sword." She let out a staggered breath. "Only the tiefling in their group could use it. He got help from blacksmiths around the world in improving it. By the time he returned to Tetria and died, it was completely unrecognizable to the blade he uncovered. It was passed on to a commander of a tiefling army who deciphered its name; *Brachynox*." Freckle cleared her throat and continued. "Aisha, during your research in the Library Raebkayd did you learn about Kharim's nemesis? About his fighting style?"

Aisha's eyes went wide as she quickly turned to Kargon who threw his head back in frustration. Even Sariel couldn't hide the disgust of such an idea on their face. The tension was enough for Avant to shudder and seek comfort from his master. Only Vofric remained composed enough to speak.

"You're saying humanity uncovered the demon king's blade, improved it, refused to destroy it and now he wields it against them."

"It's just a rumor," Freckle protested meekly. Even she didn't believe her words.

Vofric shook his head. "No. Aisha said the demon king changed the weapon's form in Maccfeld much like the stories of Kharim's foe."

"At every turn he gets a leg up even though all he's done is sleep for five hundred years," Albert spat. "It can't ever just be easy, can it?"

"I learned long ago that those of us bound by destiny do not have the luxury to complain about difficulties on our path," Makani sighed. "I'm sure you agree, Aisha."

The Hero nodded. "Unfortunately."

While everyone else was reeling from the revelation, Kargon was focused on the sword hanging off Aisha's hip. There were few records about *Valefor* after it had been crafted—that didn't mean none at all. Kargon had dutifully memorized every tidbit he could about his best friend's sword. They seemed unimportant before but he'd never let a piece of information slip through his grasp. Not when it was related to Aisha at least.

"We'll be okay," he said calmly. "Kharim kept improving *Valefor* during his journey. And I know some of the swordmasters helped Aisha refine it. If that isn't an Arcana class item, my name isn't Kargon Meliamne." He stared intently at Aisha while everyone turned to him. "I don't know about destruction but with *Valefor* and your lightning I'm sure you can beat *Brachynox*. Regardless of who's wielding it."

"I have to," Aisha stated, smiling softly. "I've known my quest would be different from Kharim's since Mount Ikrali. This might be unexpected but it's par for the course." She turned back to the floating disk and spoke sternly. "Freckle, I know where Zeld's Shell is but I doubt you want us rushing in. Where's the base camp?"

CHAPTER FIFTY-THREE

Crashing Through the Gate

It took five days in a carriage to get near Zeld's Shell. It was one of the only known areas in the Agrestic, located near the center with roads east and west of it. Unfortunately, using such expeditious paths was impossible without approaching Aeraza's castle. Instead, they aimed to reach Jamoraz, a larger settlement in the forest turned base camp. With Sariel, Albert, and Avant using their senses in tandem, everyone was confident in finding the town.

On the fifth day, nearly fifteen miles from Zeld's Shell, did the party encounter the first signs of battle. Deceased humanoids and bloody demon corpses littered the ground. The unmarked area was one of many that symbolized a wall where civilians should not cross. Kargon would never admit it but was glad that Albert and Makani didn't falter at the corpses. Theirs wasn't a battle that could be survived if a sight like this hindered them.

Time passed not only in hours but sites of battle encountered. Settlements were evacuated as the onslaught of demons grew. Destroyed homes were surrounded by dead monsters and the adventurers who killed them. The forest was riddled with corpses of those who succumbed to wounds. Worse were the Husks of powerful warriors that needed to be defeated before the group could press forward.

By the time they arrived at base camp, they had crossed nearly two dozen battlefields. Jamoraz had been repurposed and fortified to fit troops and weapons within its walls. If all went according to plan, one day it could be returned to its original state. Though everyone involved knew that was wishful thinking.

Freckle awaited the group near the eastern watchtower. Seeing one of the captain's walking around the camp was astonishing to most Barbatos agents. Especially since many had never seen her beastly companion before. Add in her awe-inspiring guests and agents couldn't be blamed for faltering at the sight. But the adventurers' presence didn't bring levity or diminish the seriousness of the ramping situation. It did, however, give everyone hope and inspiration that Tetria could win this war. Such thoughts should have remained private. No sooner had whispers passed through camp that urgent news reached the gates.

"We're in danger!" someone screamed as she phased directly through the south gate.

There was no opportunity to check on her wellbeing as she continued in a panic. Gashes riddled her body and left a trail of blood in her wake.

"The demons, they're targeting us now!" she continued. "The gate opened and some went into the shell but there's hundreds targeting our scouts!"

Vofric ignored the chatter and pushed through the crowd to heal the woman. The aching sensation of large wounds sealing made her realize how wounded she was. Adrenaline vanished and pain washed over her as cuts shrank but refused to close.

"How many do you need?" Freckle asked, standing over Vofric.

"How many can we spare?" a Barbatos agent yelled. "Do we have more captains to go with them?"

"They're indisposed with plans for the next battle. Who can lead the cavalry alongside me?" Freckle shouted to the crowd.

Aisha frowned at the sight of the messenger as she slowly reached Vofric. The healing wasn't perfect but it was all that could be done. "If your troops die there won't be another battle," Aisha patted the woman's shoulder and met the gaze of her party members. Then, she turned to Freckle and said, "We're going. Anyone who wants can follow."

"What happened to not rushing in?" Freckle protested.

"I said you'd hate it if we rushed in—not that we wouldn't do it!"

There would be a smirk plastered on Aisha's face if it could overpower the anger swelling inside her. It was clear some members of Barbatos hoped the Hero would take charge. An agent approached the two women and placed a firm hand on their shoulders.

"There's plenty who will join," he said. Clad in familiar silver armor was Commander Rowen Telos of Dawncaster. Questions flooded the Hero's party but they ignored them. All that mattered was Rusty's readiness to lead and the calming effect it had on Barbatos. He patted Spike's head and grunted to Freckle, "Lead the way. We're right behind you."

Aisha was off without another word, following a thick trail of blood leading south. With Avant's empowering abilities the party would arrive in no time. The blessing even spread to the group of familiar faces behind them. Rusty, Freckle, and Spike led a group of fifty soldiers burning with fiery vigor. The Kingsguard commander had easily taken Makani and Albert under his command.

No matter how trained someone was they couldn't help but feel tense in battle. Stoicism often fell away in the face of a challenge but none of them showed fear—not unless the consequences were dire. No one could blame the agents of Barbatos near Zeld's Shell for succumbing to such an emotion. One seldom saw a mass of rampaging demons charging at them. Their attack was a celebration for breaking into the vault. Only a dozen Barbatos scouts were sent out to keep an eye on the demon's progress. Few remained in dire straits when the cavalry arrived.

A rapid chain of lightning arched off Aisha as she dashed into the fray. Even with the destructive bolts tearing through the monsters, many remained standing—this army was anything but "small." Their planning and strategy alone made clear this was nothing like Dawncaster.

That didn't matter to Kargon as he self-immolated and combusted multiple enemies. Powerful punches ripped through monsters and sent out large astral extensions that spread the blaze. Pressure from the strikes propelled Kargon around the battle at high speed. If no one knew better, they'd think he was flying.

But he was much closer to the ground than Sariel, who ignored the fight to search for Veil. Without a word they'd gained Aisha's approval for the plan. Both knew that the Ring of Dominion outweighed any thoughts of vengeance. The dragon's keen eyes were the first to see the shattered stone doors that blocked access to a cube built into the ground. Demonic corpses were piled around it from failing to break in. Survivors tried to attack the flying elf to no avail.

While their allies focused on pushing forward, Vofric and Avant looked to the surrounded Barbatos scouts. From weeks of fighting as a unit, Avant had learned tactics that were only possible with his unique magical abilities. At Vofric's command, he was pulled close by a pocketed gravitational field as the owlbear's hide bristled. With a mighty charge he opened a path through the monsters and a few allies kept up before the demons encircled them.

Being forced into close proximity didn't matter to Rusty as a single attack from his greatsword cut through half a dozen monsters. To create more space, Spike elongated his spikes and rolled through enemies. Any that avoided piercing by falling back were met with Freckle's saber quills. Near imperceptible slices allowed her to rend monsters in twain. Smoke poured out of the halfling's coat as she dashed from monster to monster. It was impossible to see the range of her strikes within the haze.

Unfortunately, for every fallen demon arose as a Husk. It had been happening since the Barbatos scouts retaliated. They could do nothing but cower behind Vofric and Avant. To their side was Makani with his staff unfurled in his right hand. Orbs of light burned through any monsters that stepped closer than he permitted. Few were able to bypass Albert's powerful punches. The gauntlets bound to his fists glowed with silver light that burned the demons on contact. However, monsters were quickly surrounding him and there was no way for him to take out multiple at once. Suddenly, a glowing beam of light shot out of *Lightbringer's* hooked end eradicated almost twenty monsters trying to reach Albert.

"Thanks, buddy!" he yelled before engaging the nearest living demon.

Makani simply nodded as he slowly produced more orbs of light that orbited him. Watching it gave Vofric an idea and he looked for Rusty or Freckle. Neither were in any place to command the soldiers at the edge of the battle. They were frozen with fear of the seemingly endless horde of monsters.

"Melee combatants, hold the line!" Vofric barked. "Spellcasters, utilize widespread attacks."

Even at his loudest, the dwarf's voice was kindly. Avant barked and sent a wave of blue energy far through the allied troops. The hesitant warriors felt a wave of serenity wash over them before immediately remembering why they came running to Zeld's Shell. A rainbow of light emanated from spellcasters deep within the army. Demons took notice and tried to stop it but were hindered by invigorated fighters wielding steel weapons.

"Widespread magic... is weak," one of the wounded scouts said.

Elements of all kinds rained around them and eviscerated packs of demons, breaking the encirclement and allowing the cavalry to properly join the battle. The silhouette of a kindly dwarf healing wounds seemed much larger all of a sudden. At his back were an armada of legendary heroes he trusted implicitly. For some reason he did not close the minor wounds on the scouts but they assumed it was to save mana in case anything went wrong.

"You are not incorrect. But combining overwhelming numbers with widespread spells makes the difference in damage unnoticeable," Vofric said with a smile after healing the last scout. "Fall back when an opening presents itself."

He turned away to hide frustration from not being able to completely heal the agents. Something about the demon's attacks caused issues with his magic. But centuries of failure made him a master of finding opportunities for victory.

"Rusty! Overwhelm them in crimson waves!" Vofric commanded.

The Dawncaster commander paused for a moment to see the blood pooled all across the battlefield. By waving his blade, the crimson liquid transformed into a torrent that cascaded over his enemies. Droves of monsters transformed into Husks and died instantly to the violent wave. Fresh demonic summons were destroyed before they had an opportunity to attack. With each bloody strike, the allied troops grew more fervent and thinned the demonic masses. The sounds of rage from the cavalry must have reached into Zeld's Shell as Veil finally stepped outside. A foolish assumption caused him to think only Barbatos troops were on the battlefield. He hoisted the ring up as a sign of victory and to bolster his subordinates. Triumphant roars passed through them and they matched the humanoids' might. Madness passed over every fighter as the changeling slowly lowered the ring.

Before it could travel far, an arrow pierced through the opening and pulled it from Veil's grasp. When the bolt hit a nearby wall, it sprouted roots that erupted outward. They bound into a tight sphere that locked the ring inside a small cage. The stunned changeling stared at the trap then turned to see Sariel drop to the ground nearby and dismiss their wings.

"How dare you?" he growled.

For the first time since they met, composure eluded him. Contrarily, Sariel felt calm in the sea of demonic beings. None had the chance to interfere as Kargon and Aisha reached the edge of the monstrous army. Their fearsome combination was overkill for small fry. Sariel might have chuckled if they weren't staring daggers into the monster facing them.

Without a word, the dragon transformed their bow into two scimitars. Wings instantly appeared on their back and they darted into range. One swing was easily dodged but the other caught Veil's arm. It was obvious that he allowed it to happen. Metal quickly replaced the skin across the indistinct form of the changeling. His unhindered hand became a morningstar that swung back at Sariel. They ducked under but couldn't dodge the following sickle strike that cut into their right shoulder.

"Your elven side is weak," Veil spat. "Release my ring!"

"Is it not meant for your master?" Sariel retorted.

The changeling grunted and swung his arms again which fused into a large blade. Had it landed, the attack would be devastating. But it was too slow for a deft Sariel. They flipped over it and cut two lines across Veil's chest. The blue ooze within was the same viscosity as blood. It didn't seem to bother the changeling as they quickly sealed the wound and attacked again; this time it was two flails. One arched wide and bound Sariel's wings while the other gripped one of their legs. A powerful swing lifted the dragon skyward before slamming them down. Bones cracked under the weight of gravity they'd long forgotten about. Reverting their wings to a cowl allowed Sariel to move freely. On a whim, they struck Veil's flail and watched carefully as he winced in pain before releasing his grip.

While Sariel's elven side was weaker, it moved more smoothly than the draconic counterparts. Their right leg was broken but remained steady with vines binding it together. Veil prepared another close range attack but the ranger reverted to their most accustomed weapon. The bow was more intricate than usual with rods to assist in balancing the arrow being created. Barbs and thorns riddled its shaft. Part of Sariel thought it would devastate Veil even if the shot missed. Another part doubted they had strength to land a shot with the magical arrow. But they'd learned well that a powerful threat could be as strong as any attack.

"We need not battle here," Veil seethed. "Simply release the ring and my troops won't destroy you."

"What troops are you talking about?" Aisha asked from behind Sariel.

Veil's tunneled focus dissipated as he stared angrily at the Hero. Then his attention turned to the fiery monk kneeling on top of a cyclops, angrily pummeling a hole into its head. An army of glowing adventurers followed an owlbear and dwarf. Fighters of all kinds finished the last of the Husks who once overpowered them. Sariel loosed their arrow and missed slightly—its poisonous barbs only slicing across Veil's arm. The wound didn't close for several seconds. It was unlikely anyone else noticed, maybe not even the changeling himself. But Sariel made a note of it.

"Mark my words; you will regret this!" the changeling barked as he sprouted bat wings and flew away.

The lack of movement from Aisha signaled for everyone to hold their ground. With slow, awkward steps Sariel and their party approached the caged ring. Vofric silently healed the dragon as they retrieved the Artifact. Surrounded by hundreds of demonic corpses and fallen allies, everyone waited with bated breath. Sariel extended a hand and placed the ring in the Hero's grasp. She did not foolishly raise it but held it to her chest before turning to the rest of her allies. There were no cheers.

CHAPTER FIFTY-FOUR

Partial Success

The fallen members of Barbatos were moved to the far side of Jamoraz where charred stones marked previous pyres. Names were noted down and valuables collected for next of kin before preparing each body for cremation. It was almost systematic how the guild went about sending off their comrades. They'd grown accustomed to losing people during large scale battles. No grandiose display would bring them back. But something would be done to make sure they were remembered once this tumultuous time passed.

Kargon, his group, and their trusted allies were invited to meet with the Barbatos captains. What was once a town hall had been repurposed for planning purposes. Freckle handled bridging the gap between the guild and the Hero's party. It was pointless for unknown people to try and build a rapport with Aisha at this time. She was stressed enough holding the Ring of Dominion for all to see.

"All that death for a measly ring," one of the captain's muttered, then looked away to briefly pray.

"I understand your sorrow, Micah. But you know this is no 'measly' ring," Freckle said. "According to all our information, it is one of four remaining Artifacts. And the strongest of any ever known."

Kargon softly ran a thumb along *Pyromanic's* frames. It was astonishing to him how vastly different his Artifact was to all others he'd encountered. Controlling the rage of a fire giant was no small feat but that didn't put the goggles in the same wheelhouse as *Brachynox* or

Lightbringer. The Ring of Dominion was especially different. That was apparent from the faces of awe surrounding the table.

"We can use it to end the demon king once and for all! We could even take over his army!" a captain said triumphantly.

Avant growled at the notion and stepped forward.

"It would be foolish to attune to it and the Hero has no such ambition," Vofric grunted, grabbing the owlbear by his scruff. "Attempting that level of domination would make Aisha no different than the demon king."

"Well maybe—" Another captain tried to speak but was stopped by a cold stare from Sariel.

"Do not utter nonsense without considering the ramifications."

The captain stared at Aisha's horns; scarred from years of training. An apology was barely audible from the shamed captain. Aisha brushed it off without hesitation. There were more pressing matters.

"It doesn't look right," she muttered. "Freckle, do you have the documents you showed us in Shusyoun?"

With an affirmative grunt, Freckle fished the papers out of her jacket's inner pocket. The fact they were still dry was surprising with how much monstrous blood coated her armor. Unfolding it quickly revealed what Aisha was talking about. On the paper was only an estimation of what the ring should look like. It wasn't so different that the group assumed they retrieved the wrong item. Rather, the ring in Aisha's hand looked like the image had been cut in half horizontally.

"For it to be such a precise cut... Barbatos really didn't want to destroy it," she grumbled.

"But they also didn't want it to get used easily," Kargon said. "Both halves need to be found so we can assume they had some forethought before leaving it."

Makani huffed. "If they were so concerned they could have split it further."

"Too much splitting and it might not be retrievable before things go from bad to worse." Albert pointed out.

"There was the option to seal it to a bloodline," Rusty chimed in with a slight nod to the prince.

"Many lineages end unexpectedly," Sariel replied. "There is also that chance that their descendants would not have been on our side of the fight."

Freckle sighed and shook her head. "That's such a depressing outlook on a theoretical possibility."

"Realistic assumptions often align with a downtrodden outlook," Vofric said.

Captains started spouting their ideas of how they would have sealed the rings. Some suggested never sealing it in the first place. Conflicts since the Age of Exploration would have ended shortly with its use. Others argued it should have been destroyed when the other Artifacts were. The room grew louder, vibrating from the overwhelming shouts. Kargon felt his heartbeat rising in the tense room. Veins were building out of Aisha's head and she quickly lost the battle to stay calm.

"ENOUGH!" she roared. "This isn't a time for hypotheticals! We are not using the Ring of Dominion! All we have is half of it. That means the demon king is going after the other half. If he finds it..."

There was a long pause as a stunned room stared at the enraged swordswoman. A long sigh left Aisha's lips as she deflated. It wasn't worth screaming at people in a time when they should work together. Devolving to baser instincts was unbecoming of the Hero.

"Look. We need to do something to stop him," Aisha said. "Otherwise Barbatos is finished. And after we're gone, Tetria is next and then Vethyea. So, forget what you'd do with the ring and think about where we go from here."

Quiet apologies spread through the room before people began planning. Kargon was in awe of how Aisha commanded the room. Every person's innate fear and distractions were overpowered by their respect and awe of her. Unfortunately, that made it harder for them to share their ideas in fear of saying something foolish. Sariel and Vofric had no such hang up but they were focused on helping the others reach logical conclusions. A smile crept across Kargon's face— realization that he was the only one prepared to speak around a stressed Aisha.

"Natharia is our best bet," he said, drawing people's attention. "If the Ring of Dominion is cut in half, that means there's only one other piece. We had two locations to search in and one of them is still out there."

Aisha considered the words and slowly crossed her arms. As the information became clearer she reached her right hand towards her horns. With her thumb and index finger running along them, she hummed softly. The contemplative figure triggered an immediate reaction from her partner.

"Do we know where the city is?" Kargon asked.

"If it'll reach north Vethyea in a few weeks, it's still at sea," Aisha answered before anyone else had the chance. "There's probably still demons there."

Kargon hummed. "Can we reach it before it gets to the mainland? Maybe stop the demons from finding anything?"

"We'd need a boat," Aisha said and her eyes lit up. "We know someone with a boat!"

"Right, Captain Julian. How can we reach her?" Kargon asked.

At the mention of a friend, Rusty perked up. All eyes that once bounced between the Nevesi duo turned to the Kingsguard commander. He retrieved an engraved stone similar to the one installed in Farspeech Coins. At the sight, Freckle retrieved the pieces of her device. She and Rusty wordlessly worked in tandem to reassemble it.

"Julian is likely aboard her ship. There could be prying eyes," a Barbatos captain said while watching their allies.

"Barbatos may have secrets but we don't work in the shadows. People need to know they can trust us when times are hard," Freckle replied.

"Not to mention, Julian's picky about her crewmates." Rusty added. "I trust her judgment."

Freckle's mana manifested as black smoke that wreathed around the communicator. Once again, the central stone glowed blue and its wispy light fused with the magic mist. Within seconds, connected with the recipient.

"Oi, Rusty, how in the world are you reaching me? The stones shouldn't be in range of each other."

"He's using a Farspeech Coin, Julian," Freckle answered.

A light scoff could be heard on the other side. "You're really lettin' him borrow one? Whatever. Why'd you contact me?"

Rusty replied. "We found the Ring of Dominion. Rather, part of it."

"Great, I'll head back—"

"No." Aisha interjected. "By 'part of it' he means exactly half."

There was a brief pause as the pirate muttered to herself. It was like a flood of familiar voices were bombarding her even when they didn't necessarily need to be together. "So the Champion of Dawncaster and her cadre ended up with us, too. That's more like it!" Julian exclaimed. "The other half of the ring... You assume it's on Natharia?"

"It's what makes sense. Can we use your boat?"

"Ain't no reason for me to turn back. My crew and I were already on our way to the drifting city," the captain said confidently.

Rusty's eyes went wide with panic. "No! Come get backup! Without Aisha and the others we couldn't have won the battle at Zeld's Shell."

"How handily did you win?" Julian asked.

None of the Barbatos captains reacted to the question but all of Julian's close allies felt something off about the woman. Not so much as a hint of sarcasm was in her voice. The silence was deafening and no one knew what to say.

"It was a hard fought battle," Rusty finally answered.

Julian hummed. "Lose anyone?"

"Many allies fell. However, we retrieved the Ring of Dominion."

"So, it was worth it."

"No object is worth lives lost. It was an unfortunate price we paid."

"That sounds like regret," Julian replied with a distorted voice. "I warned you, didn't I?"

Only the Hero's party recognized the voice and its manic nature. Sariel growled venomously, "Veil..."

"Will you not ask about the status of the captain and her crew? That's quite cruel," he taunted.

"We're not stupid enough to expect mercy from you," Aisha spat.

Concern and sorrow was palpable throughout the room as Barbatos agents realized they'd never see their ally again. None were more hurt than Rusty but he refused to detract from the conversation. As quietly as possible he stepped away from the table and exited the room.

Veil snickered. "I see Elmud was not exaggerating about your intelligence."

"Did you think doing this would get us to turn over the ring?"

Aisha asked.

"Half. You have half the Ring of Dominion and are nowhere near Natharia. Similarly, we have the other half and are nowhere near you."

"How did you reach the city so quickly?"

"There was no need," Veil replied. "I needed only to sink this ship as per my master's request. It's funny how worried you are about that. Don't you have questions about your dead comrades? How heartless. Even after all they did for you regarding Balur."

As soon as the name left his mouth, there was a yelp. Something rustled on the other side of the communicator before a much deeper voice spoke. The only person in the realm that every Tetrian knew. It was impossible to utter given the current group of people and lack of sigils.

"Demon king," Aisha uttered.

"My subordinate speaks as though my given order wasn't a test to prove his worth," Aeraza said with a slow and monotone voice. "Do not bother to seek Natharia, it no longer graces this realm. The eyesore was sunk when I retrieved half of the Ring of Dominion."

"You cut through Zeld..."

"What little was left of the beast," Aeraza stated plainly. "That is not my reason for contacting you, Aisha Ilphekiir. I would like an audience."

Kargon felt his emotions bubbling up and almost said something. A rough nudge from Avant kept the half-elf silent. Patient looks from Sariel and Vofric cooled the monk's temper. A steady mind was needed if Aisha asked for his input.

Without glancing at Kargon, Aisha asked. "Why would I meet with you? You know I won't just give up the ring."

"Consider it a stalling tactic," Aeraza answered. "Meet with me or I will begin the slaughter."

Aisha grumbled. "Just you and me. No rings."

"Bring your friends. Outpost Yazeum. I will wait for 48 hours."

It was more a demand than a request but Aisha knew she couldn't decline. But it was clear she had no inclination to. Before another word was spoken, the sound crackled and cut off. Aeraza and his underling were gone, taking the remnants of Captain Julian and her crew with them.

CHAPTER FIFTY-FIVE

Proposal

No one was capable of stopping Aisha from going to her meeting. Even some of her party didn't like the idea but challenging the Hero was a fruitless endeavor. Things like this often happened on quests and it didn't matter how wide-scale the ramifications could be. Stalling the meeting wasn't an option either. It would take almost a day of traveling west on the main road to reach Outpost Yazeum—halfway between Aeraza's castle and Jamoraz. A carriage had to be provided or the group wouldn't arrive in time and no one wanted to test Aeraza's threat. But the guild couldn't stand by idly. They looked to Aisha for instruction on what to do during the party's time away.

"Gather all the troops. And I mean all the troops," she said. "If you have contacts outside of Barbatos get them too. We were outnumbered even with fifty soldiers. It's only going to be worse when this fight starts."

Such commands made it clear there was a plan in mind. One that even her party was unaware of. Kargon had theories regarding what Aisha was thinking but brushed them aside. They seemed too foolhardy and risky for her to attempt. There was always the option to ask but part of him was scared of the answer.

The drive to the outpost was almost silent except for Avant's intermittent grunts. An uncomfortable harness was fashioned to his back, allowing him to pull the wagon with enhanced strength. A familiar perch atop the wagon housed Sariel as they sought out any threats. Surprisingly, none appeared—not even the Husks who had perpetually roamed the land for over a year. They'd clearly been there at some point based on the myriad of animal and humanoid corpses. There was no reason to check why the path was clear. It was likely Aeraza's way of assisting the party on their trek to the meeting.

Noon had passed when Kargon and his party arrived at Outpost Yazeum. Soft clouds drifted through the sky, providing a bit of intermittent shade. A warm breeze carried the scent of fresh pine and berries around the watchtower. Stairs spiraled hundreds of feet high in a double helix towards a balcony that surrounded a hut with doors on either side.

Leaning on the outside rail were two wicked creatures, grinning ear to ear. Veil waved casually at the group while Elmud simply stared at Kargon. Hunger for battle roared in both brawlers' eyes but neither moved to engage. Instead, the demons retreated into the hut while Aisha led her party upstairs.

The two monstrous subordinates had shed their taunting smiles by the time the adventurers entered the watchtower. They stood at attention behind Aeraza who sat at one side of a round table, no longer in his human disguise. None could deny the terror they felt from his true demonic form. Less so its actual shape and more from the memories of what the party saw in Spirefell. At his side rested a sheathed *Brachynox* in its original greatsword form. Imposing pressure made the demon king's welcoming smile all the more disconcerting.

Aisha sat across Aeraza with unwavering determination while her party found places to stand behind her. It had been a long time since they lined up in such a way. Kargon couldn't deny the joy in seeing his spot at the Hero's side hadn't been filled. But there was no expression of pleasure on his face. Tension in the room was heavy and almost had a physical presence. Kargon and Elmud looked ready to pounce at each other at a single command. Daggers flew from Sariel and Veil's glances as they studied each other. But everyone knew to stay calm while their leaders spoke.

"Welcome, Aisha," Aeraza said calmly; his baritone voice sending chills down the half-elf's spine. "I see you acquired a carriage to arrive in a timely manner. It is appreciated."

"I did. However, I wasn't expecting small talk. Why did you want to meet?" Aisha replied in a tone similar to her adversary.

"You are aware I seek to complete the Ring of Dominion. I am aware you will not simply hand over your half as I pose a threat to you. Thus I come to you with a proposal."

The moment Aeraza asked to meet, Aisha knew it would be regarding some sort of deal. It hadn't taken her even a minute to deduce what the demon king might request. He had years to take over Tetria while the Hero was being trained yet didn't move until recently. Based on the bit of Kharim's history regarding Aeraza, there was really only one thing he'd ask for. There was no reason to entertain that ridiculous notion.

"I won't join you," Aisha said.

Aeraza sighed. "Come now. Think carefully about my offer. I have even gone against my own beliefs to provide you with a gift."

He turned to Elmud who retrieved something from within his coat. As it passed between the demons, Aisha let out a disgusted grunt. Bisected elf ears were strung into a grotesque necklace on a metal chain slick with blood.

"We found records on the pirate's ship regarding Balurian elves. I will not deny the captain was honorable in turning those elves' attention onto herself. The Balurians were fooled and gave chase," Aeraza explained. "We met with them to report Julian Stormclaw's death. It seemed that their ideals were in line with my own."

Aisha swore under her breath. It seemed Aeraza had an abundance of Traveler's Dust to use as he pleased.

"Why did you slaughter the Balurians?" she asked, trying to stay composed. It took every part of her not to choke up. Partly because of the Balurian's that were slaughtered. Mainly due to everything Julian did without mentioning it to the adventurers. Aisha spent months thinking about why they weren't chased after by the elves. Neither the captain's involvement nor the Balurians zenocide had crossed her mind.

"They demanded assistance in ending your life to allow a Balurian to take your place," Aeraza scoffed. "All so they could turn around and face me in battle."

"Julian was able to escape them and then they asked you for assistance... you saw it as weakness," Aisha said.

Though his face didn't change, there was a twinkle in Aeraza's eye. "That mind alone is worth having on my side but your power is nothing to scoff at."

"But I sympathize with the weak. I believe they deserve aid. Protection."

"A symptom of the overpowering weakness present not only on this continent but your entire realm. Individuals like us—powerful warriors—are heavily outnumbered on Vethyea. Peace has made the residents here complacent."

Kargon winced at the words. Regardless of who he was now, there was a time that he relied heavily on others' strength. His capacity as a soldier was severely lacking. Even when facing Elmud in Dawncaster, Aisha had to make an arena for them to battle. Then again, that very same powerful leader guided her weaker allies to grow in strength. There wasn't a doubt in Kargon's mind that he would have stopped his monk training if not for Aisha's insistence.

"Peace is a good thing. It allows people to discover parts of themselves without relying on a world of violence. There is a life beyond killing others." Aisha stated confidently.

Aeraza snorted. "Is that the thought process you use to justify the existence of weaklings? They know nothing of battle except panicked reactions. They cannot comprehend the feeling of cutting down their adversaries. Of overcoming an opponent and growing in strength."

"Being capable of murder doesn't dictate strength. There are other ways for people to grow against adversaries without taking a life."

"One cannot rule over others without overpowering them," Aeraza insisted.

Surprisingly, Aisha smiled at the demon king's words. It wasn't lost on her friends that she'd been holding her own in this conversation. In fact, she was leading it in a way. That helped Kargon deduce what his best friend's plan likely was. And it took everything he had not to show his astonishment. There was no denying there was some logic in it but it was still a gamble. Though, risks were needed to face the demon king.

Aisha calmly said, "Gathering allies does not necessitate ruling over them."

"Groups such as those commit atrocities across your land," Aeraza argued.

"And they're dealt with by adventurers and soldiers who come together to protect the weak against people whose strength went to their heads."

Aeraza let out a long, tired breath. It was the most humanoid expression he'd displayed since they met. Glazed eyes stared at the ceiling as he collected his thoughts. The conversation was growing tiresome and so far he'd made no progress. For Aisha, it was a victory in its own right. But she and her party knew it could only last so long. Displeasing the demon king was ill-advised regardless of their strength.

"Let us consider a new agreement," he said. "You provide the other half of the Ring of Dominion and I rewrite the bodily chemistry of every being in Tetria. There will be no loss of life."

Aisha replied immediately, almost as if she expected the offer. "There's some problems with that suggestion."

"Such as?" the demon king grumbled.

"Tetria houses the most half-breeds of Vethyea. Evolution allows them to survive here. Rapid mutations would cause suffering and end their lives." Aisha met Aeraza's glare with her own. "You failed to mention what would happen after. Would you simply return to the demon realm? I doubt it seeing as you're sitting here in front of me. No, you'd likely use your newly mutated army as fodder on a quest to conquer Vethyea."

Veil stirred at the sight of the confident woman disrespecting his master. Each unwavering figure standing behind her only made him more aggravated. They appeared almost calm in the presence of the demon king. With a shift in weight, Veil grabbed the attention of every adventurer. None of them moved but their eyes were now trained on the changeling.

"Why are you humoring her, Master?! They need not leave here alive!" he barked.

"Do not speak out of turn, Veil," Aeraza said in a haunting voice.

"This is ridiculous! They are merely insects!"

"But he sees me as a warrior." Aisha's words were spoken with surety. Based on the fact that she and Aeraza hadn't broken eye contact during their disagreement, it was a solid assumption. It hadn't even wavered during Veil's outburst.

With a slow breath, Aeraza rose from his seat and turned to his subordinate. Not a word was spoken between the demons. Veil cowered at the placid expression on Aeraza's face. Seconds was all it took for him to return to a neutral, almost meek, stance. He hung his head as Aeraza continued to stare before slowly turning back and sitting down.

"You will not join me because you wish to protect weaklings. While Veil had a foolish outburst, he made a point," Aeraza admitted. "I could eradicate all the insects and leave you with no choice."

"You're right. I'll have no choice," Aisha replied as a smile slowly appeared on her lips. "But you never stated what that choice would be. You offered to let me join you but that was never the end goal, was it? It was to keep me around so we could battle."

"What makes you believe that?"

"The records about you and Kharim. You seemed to always grow just enough to be a challenge but never struck him with a killing blow. I'm sure it was a shock the day he overpowered you and didn't stop his blade."

Aeraza's eyes darkened. "He refused to show me the same courtesy I showed him."

"All to protect the weaklings of our world." Aisha added with a hum. "Now that we've cleared the air, how about I offer you a deal."

In truth, she expected a challenge. Instead, Aeraza gestured for Aisha to continue.

"Seven days from now. The canyon between here and your castle. Your army versus ours," Aisha said. "If you win, I will be your battle partner until the day I die."

"And if you win?" Aeraza asked.

"When I win you'll be dead. For good this time. I'm not like Kharim who gave you time to spout off some curse."

"My army will remain. Will you cut them all down?"

Aisha smirked. "Did you forget that I can see mana? Your pawns are connected to you. I've seen their mana and it always trails off. Right now you've got innumerable tendrils stretching off you." The purple glow of her eye grew to put a finer point on her statement. "When you go, so do they."

Aeraza sat in silence as he mulled over the offer. Clearly it wasn't something Elmud or Veil agreed to. Both had broken their neutral stances and were seconds from attacking. For all the years they spent with their master, they didn't understand him at all.

It bothered Aeraza that he felt a pang of jealousy for the friends Aisha had gathered. Whatever feelings they had about the deal could wait for later. Right now they looked steadfast and confident in their leader's choice. She didn't so much as turn back to check if her allies stood by her decision. Five sets of eyes carried the same conviction as they stared at Aeraza. He rose to his feet, donned his sword, then nodded.

"Make sure you possess your ring. In seven days, I will begin my conquest. You have chosen where I begin. Let us see if Tetria can withstand me."

With that he stepped outside, frustrated subordinates in tow. As before, Elmud sprouted wings before lifting his master and ally to the skies. A collective sigh of relief passed through the Hero's party. Aisha braced for questions from each of them, especially Kargon. All of them looked towards the monk as he silently contemplated what to ask.

"A stalling tactic, huh," he said.

"It was the best option with his ramping aggression," Aisha replied.

"You spoke well. Controlled the conversation as well as possible."

"I learned from the best."

CHAPTER FIFTY-SIX

Gathering

"What do you mean five days?!" Freckle asked incredulously. "You took one to get here. That means the attack starts in six days."

The Barbatos captain was running her hand along Spike's back to try and stay calm. Soft nuzzles were all he could provide to comfort his master. Unfortunately, composure was difficult after the Hero shared the plan to challenge a world destroying threat directly.

Aisha shook her head. "The demon king's attack is in six days. Ours will be in five."

"It isn't too much extra time but will provide a very necessary edge," Vofric said.

"Why do we not attack sooner if that is the case?" another captain asked.

"Is everyone you reached out to here?" Kargon asked.

A different captain held up their hand while sifting through papers with the other. "The remaining ones will arrive within a day. Considering the four day march to the canyon, we are attacking as early as possible."

Sariel let out a loud grunt that drew everyone's attention. "Have any of you considered that a four day trek will put our troops at a deficit in terms of energy? Mages who heal them will lose mana that will be necessary during battle."

It was a clear challenge to their party's leader. One that Aisha acknowledged but also admitted she hadn't considered too much.

Theoretically, it wouldn't have posed a problem for the numbers at the camp prior to the party's meeting with Aeraza. Upon returning, they were greeted by dozens more Tetrians willing to lay down their lives for their home. Hundreds more would be arriving before the trek and the repercussions of their exhaustion were obvious.

"It is possible for us to rest for a day upon arrival," Vofric said, then shook his head. "That many people would draw undue attention and leave them vulnerable."

Everyone in the town hall stood in silence while staring at each other. Sariel's anger made others give them a wide berth. It wasn't directed towards Aisha; rather, the fact that this was the most logical plan for the unfortunate situation they were in. Other captains from Tetria branches of the world government squeezed into the room but provided no other solutions. Wars fought during past centuries were nothing like dealing with Aeraza's army. No one wanted to admit how out of depth they felt.

"May I suggest an alternative option?" a voice said loudly. The crowd parted and a group of Barbatos agents led Master Avant towards the central planning table. His usual robes were replaced with a tightly fitted ensemble that matched Kargon's, save for the bright white color. The staff that had beat down the disciple for months was strapped to the owlminn's back.

"Who are you?" Freckle asked with a raised eyebrow.

Kargon readily answered. "This is Avant Qark. Master of the Sanctuary of Spiritual Combustion. He is my master and Vofric's past ally."

"So you're strong. What's that gotta do with the travel plans?" someone asked.

A soft coo passed through Master Avant's beak—sending a chill down Kargon's spine. The old bird's calm demeanor belied a strict warrior who despised when others jumped to conclusions. Dire consequences anyone who pushed the issue.

"What's your plan, Master Avant?" Aisha asked calmly.

With a smile, he nodded in greeting and answered. "The troops need not travel at all. My subordinates and I can reach the canyon ourselves—within two days to be precise."

"What good does that do?" Freckle asked. Stress from the situation made her sound more annoyed than intended.

"We can teleport the troops to the battlefield and strike far earlier than the demon king could expect. Our warriors will not have expended a single modicum of energy before the battle. In fact, all of you can focus on how to handle demons instead of worrying about travel plans. Spend time preparing your weapons and tools. Hone your skills."

Master Avant looked around the room as realization dawned on everyone's faces. In wide eyes and furrowed brows was the distinct sign of nervousness that the teacher was all too familiar with.

"Deal with your nerves as you see fit. Two days is plenty of time," he said.

Aisha couldn't hide the amazement at Master Avant's offer. "How would you do it?"

Master Avant retrieved a small pouch out from his hip and poured a silver powder onto his palm. "Traveler's Dust. I have collected it in many forms since opening my monastery. With the amount I possess we can teleport 10,000 travelers."

Uttering such a number silenced every person in the packed room. Not so much as a shuffle occurred in response. There weren't anywhere near that many troops but had they appeared, it would be nigh impossible to get them to the battlefield. Tools would have been sacrificed for carriages and carts. Shields and ballistas may have been dismantled in order to provide protection from the elements. Yet, in a matter of minutes, all those plans were dismissed. The wise owlminn was a guiding light for every warrior who heard his words and looked at him in awe.

"Be careful of errant attacks from the demons. Healing magics will be less effective," Vofric said. To him, Master Avant's journey was a foregone conclusion. "During the defense of Zeld's Shell my spells were weaker. I wasn't sure of the cause until we returned from our meeting with the demon king."

"His aura is poisonous, is it not?" Sariel asked.

Vofric nodded. "It hinders healing arts regardless of their nature."

"You need not worry about me, friend. I do not plan to engage in combat until the true battle has begun," Master Avant assured.

Avant cooed affirmatively while approaching his namesake. Roars and growls flooded out as he bumped his head against the master's palm. They both shared a similar smile that confirmed for Kargon that he'd made the right decision in naming his familiar.

"I promised to take care of Kargon. That extends to his people; including myself. And it does not end simply because he graduated from my monastery," Master Avant said and petted the grown beast.

"What... do we do with a whole day? Once everyone hears they don't need to prepare to travel, they'll check their equipment. But most of it is ready." Freckle said as her concerns turned towards the actual war. "A lot of them haven't been part of a fight like this."

Rusty sighed loudly and pressed two fingers against the bridge of his nose. Of the leaders in attendance, he was the most accustomed to large scale battles. So much so, that some of his new allies were previously defeated foes. But all of them could look past differences and memories in order to protect their homeland. This would be the first step in all of them coming to an accord after all was said and done.

"They'll panic and spiral. Any and every possibility of the battle will run through their heads," Rusty explained. "Many will default to the idea of dying on the battlefield. The simple idea of this type of attack will fill them with regrets of things that never were."

"What do you normally do?" Freckle asked.

"Well..." Rusty turned to Prince Makani and he replied, "Our guards celebrate their lives in preparation for the oncoming battle. It gets their minds off the unknown engagement ahead."

"I see no reason we can't do that now," Aisha said confidently.

Like a swivel, every head turned towards her. Only one seemed unsurprised by the declaration. It took over a year but the woman who ran from her departure celebration understood why others wished to engage in it. It was the one thing they did that respected Aisha as a normal person. Someone who felt fear and anxiety and nerves at the idea of a grand journey. The unknown weighed heavy on anyone's shoulders regardless of experience. But this time it wasn't just her who felt that consternation. Instead it was the thousands of troops gathering in Jamoraz. Sitting around for days waiting for a signal to fight would drive them insane. Mass panic would do nothing but weaken Tetria as a whole.

"All the food we stockpiled for travel can be used up. I'm sure there's plenty of ale to go around," Aisha continued. "There's no decorations but as long as everyone's distracted and happy, I don't think they'll care."

"Hours will be spent celebrating. It will require them to rest. There will be no time to spiral into a panicked state," Vofric added.

Sariel grunted. "Spending time frivolously may be the best course of action here. Master Avant, can you provide a clear signal to us before creating the portal?"

The master nodded and replied, "I will contact Kargon to send up a flare. I guarantee you will all see it."

"It will be best if we have an expected time of the portal opening," Freckle suggested. "We will spread it to everyone in the next day so they are ready regardless of if they see the signal or not."

"Noon," Kargon responded. "It's always noon with this kind of thing. Master and his people will have time to rest and prepare the landing zone. We'll also have plenty of light to work with."

A brief smile passed Master Avant before he nodded to the Barbatos captains. They looked at one another then to other leaders—all confirmed their agreement. Plans and ideas were quickly spreading around the room. Aisha had been swept up in it for far longer than the others. Days of rest were uncommon for her and she had no idea how to fill them. Even the words she said felt unknown.

Then, Freckle grabbed her attention. "Aisha, are you listening? Master Avant needs to leave soon. We have to announce the plan," she explained. "We've got a lot of troops. It's great for the battle but I'm not sure how we can get the message to as many as possible."

The Hero looked around the room and landed on Makani who was quietly deliberating something with Albert. As more eyes turned to them, they fell silent and looked up.

"Apologies, what is it?" the prince asked.

"Are you capable of amplifying my voice like your father does his own?" Aisha asked.

Makani nodded. "It's simple, yes. With some effort I can spread it past the town limits."

"Perfect. Master Avant, mind sharing the plan with everyone?"

"Of course."

"Good," Aisha stated and rose from her seat.

Others followed in kind while she led her party out of the room. There was a distinct shift in the air as the crowd parted for the Hero.

The sensation of recognition was familiar yet didn't displease Aisha like it had in the past. Onlookers knew the difference in what each of them faced. Tetrians were entering a fight they just heard about against an army of demons. But Aisha was ending a war she'd been destined to face.

The large group followed the adventurers out of the town hall and were met by an even bigger crowd of warriors. They meandered about and discussed what could be happening during the meeting. With each new leader that stepped onto the outside platform, more conversations ended.

The streets were packed with fighters of every race and creed. Faces marked with years of struggle looked to Barbatos for guidance. Aged warriors returned to the fray to provide a world for future generations. Doubt sat like a stone on the mind of every person joining the collective Tetrian army. Temporary structures built rapidly over the previous days nearly doubled the town's size. Waiting for every ally wasn't an option as more would arrive for hours.

Master Avant and Makani split from the leaders and stepped forward. The prince stood in front of the elder and put out his hands. Air fluctuated into a powerful stream and shot upwards when the caster upturned his palms. Rapidly expanding, the torrent of wind flowed through Jamoraz and as far out of its limits as possible. The chilling wind surprised townsfolk who were further away until the calming voice of Master Avant informed them. After a quick introduction he explained the plan to travel and teleport the troops. Bags of Traveler's Dust would be given to leaders which would in turn be sprinkled around the town walls to create a massive teleportation circle. The army listened intently, not daring to miss any important notes. Once the briefing was complete, Master Avant stepped away and gestured to Aisha to step forward.

The stunned expression on her face was humanizing for many. Any other day, that would have been a nice feeling for everyone involved. But instead doubt started to encroach on their minds. Unrelenting enemies never gave Aisha pause yet allied onlookers caused her to freeze. Even knowing they needed guidance, she couldn't speak. Kargon was ready to step forward but was stopped by Rusty as he approached Makani.

"Some of you know me as Captain Rowen Telos of the Dawncaster

Kingsguard. Others know me as Rusty of Barbatos. I am not as powerful as many of the people standing here." The heaviness in his voice amplified his words. "We have lost many comrades and friends due to the demon king's return. I'm sure you know we will lose more —some of us will fall."

"But that is no reason not to live!" Kargon said and smacked Rusty's back. "Let us celebrate the lives we've led. Prove they are worth fighting for with a day and night we'll never forget. Let's eat and drink like there's no tomorrow. Spend time with friends and comrades. Share stories of your experiences."

Rusty nodded and continued, "I will never forget the adventures of Captain Julian Stormclaw. I will not allow my own stories to be forgotten either."

"Today is not for battle. Prepare all you like but that will not change who you are in two days. Instead, come to trust the people standing next to you. Learn who they are and what it is they fight for. Come together in celebration to bolster each other. That is how we grow stronger for the coming battle," Kargon announced.

As the crowd remained silent, Freckle stepped forward. She laughed heartily and did her best not to trip over her words. "This man who speaks so boisterously is the Hero's most trusted ally. Trust in his words. Eat, drink, be merry. It may be your last chance." She took a deep breath and shouted even though Makani was still amplifying her voice. "Do so with no regrets!"

Quiet claps started in random pockets around the town and within seconds became a cacophonous applause that filled the streets. Cheers erupted from the surging crowd as they made for the food stores. Drinks were poured with abandon for anyone wishing to partake. The speed at which panic shifted to celebration was astonishing.

Many leaders of the Tetrian army shed their hardened facades to meet with their allies at an equal level. Unrelated groups came together to share stories of their adventures. Embellished victories had never been more welcome than from drunken celebrants. Clearly some had begun the party long before the announcement but no one cared to complain. The Hero's party and their allies were immediately beset upon to join the festivities. Only Kargon slipped away to see Master Avant off.

"Well said," the old bird complimented as he passed over a pouch of dust. "I have passed out the others and who better to carry this for the Hero than you."

"Thanks, master. Stay safe out there," Kargon replied.

Master Avant chirped, "I could say the same to you. I'll see you soon, my boy."

"Wait, how will you contact me? What's the signal? How will I know it's you?"

"You'll know," the master yelled as he took flight.

His subordinates separated from the crowd and joined the headmaster. Some had wings while others used magic to begin their pilgrimage. All carried themselves with unwavering confidence. Kargon laughed to himself, slightly annoyed at his master's coyness. There was nothing to do about it now. The signal would no doubt be clear. Likely something only the firebrand could understand. But that was something to worry about later. For now, he would get lost in the feast.

CHAPTER FIFTY-SEVEN

Alone Together

Jovial celebration could be heard for miles outside of Jamoraz. Every new ally was given a quick explanation of the situation upon arrival. It was their decision whether to partake in the festivities or rest. Any who opted to sit out changed their minds shortly after when wallowing proved unenjoyable. Camaraderie spread across the town was too enticing to ignore.

The sun was starting to set when Vofric finally got some time to breathe. Groups were challenging one another to friendly matches. Some took to barehanded brawling with healers on standby for any minor injuries. No one dared go too far even in a drunken haze. Others continued to gorge themselves which itself became a competition. Again, healers remained on standby for unforeseen issues. The only place they couldn't help were those who succumbed to emotions. Not everyone was joyous or rowdy as the night went on. Some split into small groups to talk and reminisce about less fearful times. They shared stories of allies lost and friends gained. Though they wore sadness outwardly, their burden was lightened.

Vofric walked through the crowd and studied everyone's calming rituals. The most surprising sight was Albert and Makani riling up a crowd to dance. An uncharacteristically wild smile was plastered on the stoic prince's face. Anyone who stumbled out of the circle towards the passing dwarf was quickly healed and sent back. With little effort Vofric tended to nearby drinkers and fighters alike. Normally he'd lecture them a little but felt it unnecessary at this time. Centuries of experience didn't stop his concerns and he nursed a mug of ale when the thoughts became overwhelming. Others might get completely lost in the merriment but Vofric wouldn't. His role went beyond the gathered forces of Tetria. He had to watch the Hero's back.

"Oi, Vofric. Come have a seat!" Rusty yelled from a table surrounded by other guards who were roaring with laughter at some unknown joke.

A simple wave was all it took for some of them to stand and make room for the paladin. Though rosy cheeks and a wide grin were apparent on the Dawncaster commander's face, something was bothering him. Vofric may not have Kargon's expertise in deciphering people's thoughts but he was familiar with inner turmoil. Though, anyone would have realized it after hearing Rusty's speech.

"You all don't know how great this man is!" exclaimed Rusty and pointed at Vofric with his mug. "He got civilians to fight during the Dawncaster attack! And protected each and every one of them!"

"I had assistance. Yet, some were lost during the battle," Vofric said calmly. "They laid down their lives for the city."

"An honorable choice! Some are bound to fall in battle. It can't be helped! I mean even Stormclaw…"

Rusty's voice cracked and he squinted at his empty mug. One of the soldiers poured the commander more ale and looked at Vofric knowingly. The dwarf realized the guards weren't simply making merry but caring for their leader. It was the only way to help him clear his mind before the battle. No one knew that better than Vofric. With an exaggerated motion, he took a large swig of ale then slammed the mug down.

He yelled, "You can't blame yourself for what happened!

"I should've seen it coming!" Rusty replied.

"How exactly? Were you aware of Captain Julian's location?"

Rusty hesitated. "Well, no. But, that's not the only time! I didn't realize Elmud was trying to attack the Dicoris's! They got so close to stealing *Lightbringer.*"

"That dragominn is a lunatic!" Vofric argued.

"I should have understood them!"

"Are you a lunatic? Because only one who's lost their mind could truly understand Elmud! I know of one person who can match that bastard," Vofric replied with a smirk.

Rusty couldn't help but chuckle at the obvious jab. His voice softened as he said, "You're right… About Stormclaw, too. None of us knew where she was. And trying to understand Veil is pointless."

Vofric nodded and asked for someone to fill his mug. A deep sigh escaped his lips at the memory of lost allies from his past travels. Khergrin's fall weighed on him to this day and yet he was comforting Rusty with false clarity.

"You protect anyone within your reach. I have seen it myself. Trust in that ability," the paladin said with a soft smile.

"And you watch everyone around you, realize what their shortcomings are, and immediately cover for them," Rusty replied immediately. "At Zeld's Shell you not only commanded our troops but reminded me not to hold back."

"Anyone is capable of doing so."

"That's literally not true, Vofric." Rusty placed his mug down and met his comrade's eyes. This seemed to be something he'd thought about a lot. Broaching this subject was the main reason he called out to the dwarf. By luck the conversation had steered in this direction. There was no way Rusty would miss this chance.

"During the battle, I want you to command the troops in our group." He took a deep breath and continued before Vofric could respond. "People the world over know who you are and would happily take your orders. You know what to do in dire situations. I can make plans but thinking straight in emergencies isn't my strong suit. With your mind… you're a better commander than me."

Vofric stared at the man hundreds of years his junior. Though Rusty wasn't wrong about his shortcomings, he exaggerated how bad they really were. Doubts had grown exponentially over years and couldn't be vanquished in a day. All the paladin could do was work within the constraints binding the commander.

"Experience has provided me with a skill for finding blind spots," Vofric said. "I will not replace you as commander but will lead alongside you. As you stated; you can create a plan. Make it airtight. Consider your subordinates' capabilities. It will be my task to find where it fails during battle. What do you say?"

He rose from his seat and extended his mug. With a blank stare,

Rusty considered the offer. Part of him regretted all the drinks as they made it hard to think straight. But no matter how drunk he was, Vofric could be trusted. There was no doubt that together they could empower the troops. Rusty pulled back his arm and slammed his mug against the dwarf's.

"You've got a deal, my friend!"

They shared one more drink before Vofric stepped away. Any excuse relating to healing others was met with more thanks than requests to stay. In truth, he needed to breathe after the offer he agreed to. Leading was not something he did intentionally. But denying his abilities meant succumbing to memories of failure. Rusty's request was surprising but not unwelcome. Vofric just needed to let it settle in his mind privately; which was easier said than done.

There were few places to rest so he opted to roam empty halls, not knowing where they led through the interconnected buildings. He'd simply retrace his steps when the time came. Minutes passed wandering the identical corridors until none of the surroundings were recognizable. Eventually, Vofric exited a stone door and found himself in an alley behind a local cafe. Few people noticed him enter as it was as crowded and rowdy as everywhere else. However, no one entertained going to the second floor. Shimmying through the crowd brought Vofric to the roped off staircase. and he ducked underneath before ascending.

The large room was empty with a few chairs and tables. Most of the curtains were drawn over shut windows. Moonlight shined through a single open door to the balcony where a shadow rested.

Vofric approached cautiously and said, "Apologies if I am interrupting your rest, I simply wished to sit peacefully."

On a wooden chair surrounded by dozens of empty mugs sat Sariel, calmly staring at the crowded streets. "No apology necessary, Vofric," they said, then returned to silence.

Vofric dragged a chair to the opposite side of the balcony and sat down. There was no doubt that Sariel didn't seek a conversation and he was happy to oblige. The deal with Rusty and its implications brought up memories of Vofric's failings. With a deep sigh, Vofric looked towards the stars to avoid seeing the warriors below. Lost comrades and loved ones stared back from distant stars.

How much time passed while staring skyward was unclear. The

only reason Vofric looked back down was because Sariel noticed someone inside the cafe. Their minor reaction faded upon recognizing the sound of a friend. It was the same reason Vofric wasn't driven away.

"Good job finding a place to get a break," Aisha said playfully upon noticing the others.

She pulled another chair to the balcony to join them in silence. None of them believed it would last for more than a few minutes. Primarily because of a fiery aura that approached from within the cafe. Avant stomped upstairs with Kargon close behind. A chirp from the owlbear drew the party's attention and he excitedly ran to them. Once Kargon noticed everyone, he grabbed a chair to join them.

"Group meditation is all well and good but I don't think a party is the time and place to do it," he said with a laugh.

"We were enjoying the view while recharging our energy," Vofric replied. "What brings you here?"

"I saw you from the street. A bunch of people have and are purposely giving you space. Some think they angered Sariel."

"Why is that?" Aisha asked, turning to her friend.

The dragon scoffed, "My limits were foolishly tested. Dragons and elves have unique constitutions that allow for certain feats. I am capable of the collective." They gestured to the mugs around them. "This is but a fraction. Over the course of this event I have drunk 348 mugs worth of ale."

"You kept track?" Kargon asked incredulously.

"Of course, it would not do to forget what I am capable of with this form." Sariel looked at their elven hand and clenched it. "I am not pleased with how I became a mutant but have come to terms with it. There are things I must acknowledge if I wish to continue on this path."

"It is quite an odd feat for a draconic elf to attempt," Vofric responded.

Aisha shrugged. "I think it suits Sariel."

"There are many things that likely suit me that I have yet to encounter," they said. "I wish to find them after our quest. It is only right that I follow the dream I expressed to Ed centuries ago. There are many things worth experiencing outside of battle."

The genuine expression of joy on their face made the others smile in kind. None felt the urge to bring attention to it. They wouldn't have said anything if not for Avant chirping. It caused an almost immediate response from Sariel.

"I am rather sure of my path," they chuckled. "I did not come here to consider other options. My intention when leaving the celebrations was to be alone with my thoughts and come to terms with it."

"Apologies for intruding," Vofric said and almost got up.

Sariel held up their palm and replied, "No need. You all... Being alone with you is a pleasure." They looked at everyone before focusing on the dwarf as he returned to his seat. "If I am honest, I would like to continue being in your company after everything. That is, if our paths permit it."

It was difficult for anyone not to look taken aback at the request of their most silent comrade. The strong will Sariel displayed never allowed for such a request to be uttered. Then again, they'd originally joined the party in order to reach Balur. Kargon always assumed Sariel stuck around to make their personal goals easier. In that moment he—and the others—realized it was because of something much simpler. The party's company brought Sariel joy that they'd wanted since childhood.

"I plan to follow my grandmother's footsteps," Vofric said. "I will share her stories with others and assist them in living a joyous life." He laughed softly. "Maybe I'll study artificing and race carriages. An exciting hobby but far less life threatening than our current endeavors. Sharp eyes and ears keeping watch are welcome to accompany me."

"An old artificer like you will also need spry adventurers as guards," Aisha said with a smirk. "There's no way I'll stop. Helping people and fighting monsters is what I'm good at and I like doing it. Our world isn't perfect so there'll be plenty to do even during 'peaceful' times."

Avant barked affirmatively which Sariel translated as, "Likewise."

"We'll all stick together but spend more time meandering around," Kargon said. "There isn't a better life to live."

As the conversation ended, everyone returned to silently staring off the balcony. Kargon focused on petting Avant so he had his fill before the next battle. Even so, the monk was aware that Vofric was staring at him. Silent agony nagged at the dwarf as he looked between Kargon and Aisha. Though everyone was happy with where the conversation ended, Vofric was uneasy. After repeated breaths and hesitation, he finally came to terms with what he wanted to say.

"While I understand your want to continue adventuring, should you not take time to explore the other parts of your life?" Vofric asked. Sariel hummed cautiously to the dwarf and he shook his head. "I am not teasing but asking a genuine question. Danger will always be part of our reality. That doesn't mean you should avoid other important aspects. I shouldn't be reminding you that you have feelings for one another."

Aisha reactively replied, "You aren't reminding us!"

"We just haven't had time to talk about the future!" Kargon explained in kind.

"You are the furthest along in preparation for battle," Sariel said. "Over a day remains until Master Avant's summons. Would it not be prudent to speak before then?"

Aisha turned to Kargon who stared back in silence. Both knew this topic would come up eventually but had been focused on other things. The celebration split them apart—making it hard to meet up. But months of slow days and quiet moments had gone by. Knowing looks and small signs of affection only meant so much when they avoided the meat of the conversation. In truth, both knew they were actively running from the verbal confrontation.

"I... Need to sleep on it," Kargon said. Only Aisha seemed unsurprised by her fiery friend's rush to leave. "Thank you for the break. Don't spend all your time up here and get back to the celebration. I'll be at our inn."

As the monk stepped away, the remaining occupants turned to Aisha. She waited to hear a door shut before rising to her feet.

While rubbing the few creases out of her clothes she said, "I think I'm gonna go for a walk. Mind keeping Avant with you?"

Sariel and Vofric shared a knowing look and agreed. They invited Avant back to the party and left once Aisha was surely away. No matter how much they wanted to, right now wasn't the time to follow their leader. Whatever happened next wasn't meant for the party, only the Hero and her right hand.

CHAPTER FIFTY-EIGHT

What Lies Ahead

Jamoraz inns weren't extravagant compared to others the Hero's party had occupied. The wooden ceiling was lower but it couldn't be denied that it was magnificent. A soft rug covering most of the floor made the room feel homey. Muted peach sheets covered the bed in place of silk.

It all felt familiar yet long forgotten to Kargon as he paced around the room, silently thinking about what Vofric and Sariel mentioned. The idea of a future with Aisha made him more nervous than expected. It was frustrating to feel overwhelmed when they'd been together all their lives.

But it was different now. Prior to his training, Kargon wasn't aware of the feelings he had. Now every memory was dripping with sweetness that he'd never identified. Innocent words spoken in the past were coated in unintended meaning. There was no way to tell if they were even correct.

The flood of thoughts distracted Kargon from hearing the light knock on the door. Clicks sounded as it was unlocked and Aisha stepped inside. She immediately locked the door behind her then looked at her friend. Both had trouble finding words that each needed to say. Neither would admit they were glad the other took this so seriously.

"I thought you were going to sleep on it," Aisha said softly.

"I can't. Lots on my mind," Kargon replied.

"So, the bed's not occupied."

It was said with relief. Aisha's shaky legs carried her to the mattress and she plopped down. With a smooth motion she twisted to lay her head on the pillow before staring at the mundane ceiling. Both half-elves were in a race to see who would bravely press the conversation.

Aisha won and asked, "Can we talk?"

Kargon nodded. "Yeah." He walked towards a nearby chair to grab it but hesitated. "Can we talk like before?"

"Yeah." Aisha's voice was soft and her face became warm.

The man slowly approached the bed and laid next to his childhood friend. Both tried to give the other space and left a clear divide between them as they stared upwards. Every passing moment allowed their screaming nerves to calm. Both eventually relaxed enough to loosen their muscles. Intentionally, Aisha reached her right hand towards Kargon and bumped his left. A practiced motion allowed him to slide a finger under her palm to lift it before taking her hand.

It was the only thing that had changed since their declaration all those months ago. They'd held hands plenty of times and it always surprised Kargon how soft Aisha's were. Callused and trained with dozens of scars yet they remained smooth. It was probably all in his head but he couldn't help but be enamored. Aisha's entire being made him react that way.

Kargon finally looked at her, appreciating every feature. Clothes thrown into a casual outfit laid softly across her form. The seemingly calm expression on Aisha's face was beautiful. If she didn't dare to look toward Kargon, that was okay. Her piercing eyes would see right through him.

Aisha was fully aware that she was being admired. A redness overtook her face but she didn't dare turn—fearing Kargon would look away. The roughness of his hands was different than before. Deep scars were scattered all over his body and could never be healed again. Yet he wore them with a smile that sent a shock through her heart. Fiery red hair was as ridiculous as all the Neves children always said. There was no denying it yet Aisha only remembered it as a feature of people she cared for. Seeing it whenever looking at Kargon made her feelings grow.

She turned her whole body slowly, cautiously, to face her counterpart. An internal battle raged as he kept a straight face while looking at her. The tightened grip of his hand would've hurt an untrained person. Instead it was met with powerful resistance from Aisha and a playful smirk.

"Everything's a competition with you, isn't it?" Kargon asked with a laugh.

"Only when it comes to you," Aisha answered and scooted closer.

"Don't let it happen when you're fighting the demon king. He's much stronger than Elmud."

"I know." Aisha frowned. "Kargon, I don't want to talk about the battle."

Kargon exhaled slowly. "I know. Sorry."

"Is it really so hard to talk about this? Is it just going to last as long as this quest?"

The pain in Aisha's voice made it clear she wasn't accusing her partner. Rather she was scared of losing him. Putting her in such a position made Kargon feel guilty. Especially since he felt the same way. They both knew it and yet hesitated to express anything further.

"I'm bad at recognizing things about myself," he said slowly. "Remember when we were kids and I said my only skill was understanding you? You were always so quiet back then." Aisha nodded but remained silent as Kargon continued. "Even during your years training you took time to lecture me about what I can do. Hells, I needed Master Avant to walk me through my own thoughts to realize how I felt about everyone—about you. For a while I thought it was a happy accident as part of my training. But the more I think about it I realize that Master knew I was unaware of my feelings."

"Don't be too hard on yourself. I needed Vofric to walk me through my feelings. Even Sariel had a better understanding than me," Aisha responded and shifted her gaze away from Kargon. "I was going to avoid telling you until after our quest was over. Then you went ahead and blurted out that I was your 'everything.' How can you say that and not feel embarrassed?"

Kargon noted that the Hero described her quest as a shared experience. But he couldn't think about it too much based on the other implication.

"You were going to make me wait and worry for over a year?!" he asked incredulously and sat up while still facing Aisha. "And what do you mean I should feel embarrassed? There's people who've only heard of you that love you. All they know is stories about the Hero. They see news about what you've done for Tetria. But they don't know your training or hardships or everything you put into being the Hero. I bet half of them wouldn't know what to feel after learning about your weird habits. Like how you can't focus without kneading your horns. Or how you shock yourself in the morning to wake up."

Aisha's eyes went wide upon realizing anyone had noticed a habit she tried to keep hidden. At that moment Kargon knew he was no longer in control of his mouth. Clenched fists were all that gave him a semblance of composure; what little he had.

"I don't feel embarrassed. I'd never feel embarrassed for knowing you. Or supporting you. Or feeling more strongly about you than anyone else!"

A smirk pulled at the corner of Aisha's mouth as she also rose to her knees. The look quickened Kargon's heartbeat but he didn't dare turn away. Her eyes were deep pools of purple that he happily drowned in. If not for Aisha's words drawing his focus, he would have lost his composure completely.

She asked, "Are you saying you like me more than you like other people or that no one else likes me as much as you do?"

Kargon's face went flush with color before he quickly covered it with his hands. A very deliberate turn and forceful plunge placed him back on the bed, facing towards the ceiling. Muffled groans pushed through his hands for a few seconds. He took a deep breath before shifting them; only enough to uncover his mouth.

"I'm saying I love you!" he exclaimed before forcing out an, "Idiot."

As confident as Aisha was in her question, she instantly regretted it. Years of pushing Kargon had proven him to meet tasks head-on. It should have been obvious that challenging his feelings would have a similar result. Somewhere in the mix of embarrassment and competitiveness, an idea bloomed. There was no need to hide her face in her hands. Instead, Aisha plunged forward and headbutted Kargon's chest. Reactively, he moved his arms but was too slow to block. He let out a grunt of pain as Aisha's horns got dangerously close to piercing through him. Then he felt her skating and moved his arms away so she had room to calm down.

"I—" Aisha stuttered.

"Feel the same way. I know," Kargon said contently.

She shook her head and let out a long breath. The sensation of warmth brushing against Kargon was unfamiliar. Even more so in a situation like this. The chill that ran down his spine was almost painful.

In the softest voice she'd ever used, Aisha whispered. "I love you too."

Kargon heard it clearly regardless of the commotion outside. Nothing short of a silencing spell would stop him from hearing the words. It put him in a brief daze, further enhanced as Aisha pushed his arm aside to properly lay her head on his chest. Both of them were acutely aware of each other's heartbeats. They'd felt similar sensations in battle but this was stronger. Aisha softly placed her left hand on her counterpart's chest, tracing her finger slowly against his muscular frame. For the first time Kargon wasn't looking up at his friend. In that brief moment, Aisha felt small. Like holding her too tightly could break her. In truth, anyone stupid enough to try would be the broken one. She'd been that way long before drawing *Valefor*.

"Do you remember when we met?" Kargon asked.

"Of course not," Aisha answered. "And you don't either! You're only a couple months older than me so don't give me that nonsense about you remembering."

Kargon laughed at the suggestion he'd made in the past. Then he focused on calming himself. What he said next needed to be confident. Wavering now felt akin to his loss against Elmud.

"I don't remember. We've been at each other's sides as long as either of us can remember. Even when it wasn't physically possible, we knew the other was by our side. My life is irrevocably intertwined with yours. There's no future I can imagine without you. If that means we adventure, I'll do it. If you decide to move back home, I'll be there."

Aisha interjected. "If I want to put Avant in a suit, will you help me?"

Kargon sighed then smiled. "I'll try to convince him. Everyday for the rest of my life if that makes you happy."

He could feel Aisha's lips curl into a smile before she pushed herself up to look at him. Her feet brushed lightly against his as she shimmied to get close. For some reason, Kargon could only think about how small a pillow was when two people tried to share one.

"Do you know what I'm thinking right now?" Aisha asked.

Kargon stared into her eyes and nodded in confusion. "That I'm talking a lot?"

"Correct, as per usual."

Kargon remained silent as Aisha slowly moved her hand to close his eyes. He didn't think it was possible to get any closer as she leaned in. Their breath became one as their lips pressed against each other. Neither really knew what they were doing but it felt right. Aisha's heart fluttered as something she'd waited for had finally come. Kargon was less eloquent with his thoughts. All he could remember was the word he'd always equated to the woman he loved. Soft.

CHAPTER FIFTY-NINE

Well-Laid Plans

Festivities ended long before the day of the planned teleportation. Everyone had sobered up and rested, allowing themselves to feel some nerves regarding the looming clash. Weapons were sharpened and armor modified for even the slightest edge against the enemy. Word had gotten around that the Tetrian allied forces numbered around five thousand. While it was larger than any army of this realm, it was vastly outnumbered by the demon king's forces.

Master Avant alerted Kargon of his arrival via a shimmering duplicate left hidden in Jamoraz. It followed the disciple as the troops readied themselves. The specter shared any information the master learned while his real form prepared the teleportation circle. Obvious details related to the ravine between where his group were hidden and the demon king's castle. The vast flatland was at least a mile long between the peaks and circled around the rock formation which held the demon king's castle. 20,000 demons that once spread throughout the ringed canyon all meandered on the eastern side. They paid no mind to the astral monks. Only three individuals watched Master Avant while they stood in front of the massive demonic castle.

No demons tried to stop the monks' spell. The demon king stood unmoving with his subordinates the entire time the teleportation circle was being created. When the information was relayed, Aisha was absolutely sure that Aeraza was inviting them to battle.

Allied troops were gathered as close to the five gates of the base camp as possible. Originally, Kargon, Freckle, and three commanders held the Traveler's Dust. Freckle handed hers off to another captain so all of the Hero's allies were by her side. Everyone sought her guidance as the Traveler's Dust was slowly spread around the town.

"Kargon, Sariel, Vofric, Avant. Can you guys come here?" Aisha asked her dispersed party members. "You've all been working towards this fight with me. Even if I face the demon king alone, I wouldn't have gotten here without you. I don't know if Kharim felt that way about his allies but I know the world didn't honor them well enough. King Nasim said it before but I want to articulate the best I can." Aisha took a deep breath and continued. "I may be called the Hero but I still don't think that's fair. 'Hero' isn't just a title given because of some prophecy—it's earned through actions." She huffed in frustration. Words flooded out but she couldn't reach the ones she wanted. True to form, she simply blurted them out. "What I'm trying to say is that you're all heroes. I'm only one of five in this party."

"It's not the Hero's party but the heroes' party." Kargon simplified.

Aisha excitedly pointed at the monk and exclaimed, "Exactly! This whole thing isn't just my quest. When the demon king falls, it'll be the end of our quest."

Kargon couldn't help but smile recalling the last time he heard Aisha say those words. Though he immediately blushed and pushed down the following emotions.

"Well said," Sariel complimented.

"Though it does not exempt you from rallying the troops," Vofric said while nodding to the giant teleportation circle.

As the last of the dust was dispersed elsewhere, a glowing silver light encompassed the town. Walking into it pulled people to Master Avant's location. There was no doubt he'd set it up a safe distance from the canyon so the army could be properly set before engaging in battle. Tetrians of all kinds pushed aside fear and doubt as they stepped into the silver light. Makani, Albert, Rusty, Freckle and Spike gathered together to assist Aisha in reaching the castle. Troops traveled through the portal first while the heroes' party waited aside. Footsteps became faster as safe arrivals on the other side were confirmed.

It wasn't long before only the heroes and their friends remained near Jamoraz. Aisha nodded to signal them forward. The secondary group teleported with confidence that drew the attention of nearby allies on the other side. Makani immediately prepared a spell that would send Aisha's voice in every direction. If he'd learned anything from his upbringing it was to show an enemy he wasn't scared. It didn't need to be the truth—a king simply needed to present a form that others could stand behind. But Makani's role was minor. The true face of the Tetrian forces stepped through with her party at her sides.

Seeing all the troops, looking back at her with expectant eyes, was daunting. Years of silence had made others think Aisha had more answers than she really did. No part of her liked being seen as mightier or more important than others. The duty thrust upon her shoulders had simply forced everyone into a position they believed necessary. But speaking as a girl from some small village wouldn't help right now. This may be the last time some of these people spent on Tetria. Their eyes looked towards her not only out of respect but fear of the massive forces down the large hill they stood on. Hateful eyes from the opposite cliff only made the situation worse.

Aisha needed to be the person everyone assumed she was but wasn't sure how. In front of her stood the secondary party with Makani's glow encompassing them. A short look to her left was met by Vofric's stoic glance and a fierce growl from Avant. To her right were a confident Sariel and calm Kargon. His eyes always saw the truth about Aisha. The person who needed to speak now was the one Kargon placed his faith in.

Shutting her eyes, Aisha faced forward, and let out a long breath. Luminescent purple light burst from her prosthetic so fiercely it could be seen before she opened her eyes. There was no way anyone could miss it. There was no fear in her as she stared at the trio of demons standing on the other cliff. Whatever aura of darkness radiated from Aeraza may scare others but meant nothing to the Hero.

"For over five centuries an obsessive demon has terrorized our realm!" she announced. "He chased after the first hero, Kharim, and demanded his attention. Many warriors were killed without a second thought and their struggles were forgotten. We will not allow that to happen again! Each of you has taken up arms against a daunting foe. Your actions will shape the future and create legends! We do not fight in hopes of driving back this threat but destroying it!"

Grips tightened on weapons and gazes became focused. An army of five thousand breathed in harmony as they took in the words of their leader. Electricity carried on the wind driven by Prince Makani. Killing intent permeated from the crowd with such intensity that demons took notice.

"We will carve a path through the shadows and cleave apart their very source! We will tear down their monument of darkness and bask in light!" Aisha yelled.

The crowd roared as they turned towards the enemy. Scattered sounds spread through the army as weapons were drawn and spells chanted.

"We do not fight for our cities!"

With the declaration, Aisha drew her sword and pointed it towards the sky.

"We do not fight for our factions!"

Electricity crackled as it grew in intensity.

"We fight for Tetria!"

Lightning streaked down from the sky and collided with *Valefor*. As the Hero swung it in front of her, she roared.

"With! Me!"

Thousands of soldiers charged forward with ferocity they thought impossible moments ago. Blades cut apart unprepared demons as they scrambled to retaliate. Raining projectiles pierced through monsters and hindered their movements. Violent blasts of magic eradicated sturdier beasts, leaving areas for Tetrian forces to push through. Makani and his group entered the fray and Aisha took her stance with intention to pierce through the crowd. Thinning the herd would be enough as long as she reached Aeraza with minimal wounds. Kargon tightened his goggles in preparation to aid her. Before either could take a step, a bestial roar halted them.

Gravity held them in place as Avant marched past them with a smile. Sturdy vines slowly emerged from the ground and bound into two large spheres—each encompassing a half-elf. Sariel's magic had advanced to the point that flora bloomed from the magical creations.

"What are you doing?" Aisha asked aggressively.

"Do not worry about carving a path," Sariel replied. "Allowing you to waste time on lower tier demons would be unbecoming of our allies."

Kargon groaned. "So, you're just going to keep us here?"

"Of course not," Vofric replied. "We spent quite some time concocting a way to send you towards your goal. It may not be perfect as I did not have the measurements of this canyon. However, it will put you close to your—our final target."

"I see," Aisha said and stared out at the lattice pattern of the orb. She sheathed her blade and nodded. "Let's do it."

Vofric placed the head of his war-hammer against the ground. The surprisingly large platform easily held Sariel. Normally, their wings didn't need focus to appear. This time, however, they burst out with large branches sprouting off them. They threaded tightly over other vines until the dragon's wingspan tripled. Only when they were fully produced did Sariel retrieve the orbs by magically binding to them.

"Avant, please lighten my load," Vofric requested.

The owlbear obliged and reduced gravity's sway to the point where Vofric felt like he could float away. Following that, both used magic to bolster Vofric's strength. A gruff exertion accompanied his wide stance as both hands gripped the war-hammer's shaft. Using all the strength he could muster, the dwarf swung over his shoulder. Even knowing the plan, Sariel was shocked by the speed of their launch. Flat wings allowed them to soar far over the demonic forces. Winged creatures occupying the space were kept at bay by ranged attacks from Tetrians.

"We will all plummet if I continue forward," Sariel said as they slowed. "This is all I can do to lessen your load."

With a controlled spin they hurled the orbs towards the cliff housing Aeraza. The orbs splintered seconds after leaving Sariel's grasp. Massive shards avoided Kargon and Aisha before raining down directly on Veil. He barely moved as the blades passed him. Only one left a minor cut on his cheek that he quickly healed before sprouting wings and leaping off the cliff. The soaring blademaster and monk weren't worth Veil's attention. With little interference they would plummet to the bottom of the ravine into a crowd of demons.

"Aisha, I've got an idea," Kargon yelled over the rushing wind.

"Just say it!" the Hero demanded.

"Plant your feet against mine!" With swaths of fire, the monk angled himself underneath Aisha. Once their feet were firmly in contact he instructed, "Use me as a launching platform! I'll give you a boost!"

Both crouched, though it took more effort for Kargon to do so against gravity. The adrenaline coursing through his veins was more soothing than the days of nervous anxiety that recently passed. As he focused on the remaining demons on the cliff, his gaze met Elmud's. Every insult and demeaning comment the dragominn made flashed in the monk's mind. With a smug grin, he extended a hand out and flicked his fingers back.

Electricity danced between the soles of Kargon and Aisha's feet. The idea hinged on the lightning wielder's ability to calculate a distance quickly. Pressure intensified between the half-elves as *Valefor* rested tightly in the Hero's grasp. She prepared to lunge, fully intending on striking her opponent first. A burst of fire and electricity exploded between the adventurers. One propelled forward like a beam of light directly on a crash course with the demon king. The other plummeted into a crowd of demons like a violent meteorite.

CHAPTER SIXTY

Dragonscale

Weapons clashed as Tetrians engaged their monstrous enemies. Magical and physical projectiles flew wildly through the air. Blood and viscera sprayed across the battlefield, tinting the rocks and soil in a mixture of red and purple. Demons' remains scattered across the land. But few monsters seemed to care for their fallen as they rushed into combat. Inexplicable traits appeared on many of the creatures. New demons were created from amalgamations of Tetrian life. The most obvious addition to many were wings that freed up their hands for attacks. Flying goblins dove down for quick strikes before retreating to the sky, only able to be killed during their descent. Unfortunately, some remained airborne and rained down their own long range attacks.

Sariel found themself deep within the enemy ranks after throwing the others. Winged monsters targeted the draconic elf who hovered in their midst. Straightforward flight paths carried them with single minded attacks at the ready. Some land bound creatures focused their long range strikes on the dragon. It was more of a gamble than a calculated attack but with their numbers, something had to hit.

Constant training had improved Sariel's aerial maneuvers. The obvious attacks from lowly demons were nothing but a trifle. Some were taken out from afar with a well placed arrow. Others needed to be handled up close. The bow transformed with ease into a sharpened sword that sliced the monsters' wings with ease. Overwhelming numbers were the only reason a few cuts appeared on Sariel's elven body but none were notable. Even so, death by a thousand cuts was an ever present possibility.

The flash of a well thought plan twinkled in the mutant dragon's eye but they held it back. Veil was fast approaching and he would likely hesitate if taken unaware. Such an opening needed to be timed perfectly.

Rather than taking a formidable form, Veil only sprouted wings to reach the battlefield. It was a peculiar choice but if anyone understood the benefits of a lean body it was Sariel. Instead, they focused on the incoming morphing weapons that Veil employed. Two longswords extended out of the changeling's arms and targeted Sariel's draconic side. Once they bounced off the scales, the weapons transformed into maces. The surety that they could wound a dragon had to have come from years of testing.

Veil's attack pushed Sariel upward, high above any other flying enemy. It took a concentrated effort to stop the momentum and get steady in midair. A twinge of pain passed through their arm as chips sprinkled off and plummeted like jagged blades towards unsuspecting creatures below. Unsurprisingly, the thick skin underneath was unharmed. Healing the scales was possible but the costs outweighed the benefits in a battle like this. More attacks would land and there wouldn't be time to seal those wounds. A better option was to focus on Veil's wild eyed aggression.

The maces were coming in fast but their weight was a hindrance. Sariel ducked under one and blocked the other with their blade. As the changeling pulled back, Sariel plunged their sword into his shoulder. Releasing the weapon, they swung an empty hand at Veil's side—summoning another sword mid-swing. Simultaneously, the changeling morphed his arm into a shield to block. When all the momentum stopped, he kicked the elf's stomach and sent both of them hurtling backwards.

With a crooked smile, Veil reverted his hand and pulled Sariel's sword out of his shoulder. Exaggerated examination of the blade was met with a comical, impressed look. Flourishes and twirls made it seem like it was crafted for Veil's hand. Having done nothing but research for centuries had opened his mind to what actions one should take in a war. Quick learning was an understatement when describing the processing power of the demon's advanced mind. It was possible to simultaneously study the battlefield and deduce a plan of action. Within seconds, he needed only to decide whether to engage with a direct strike or psychological attack. Then again, it was possible to do both.

Crawling skin sealed the shoulder wound while morphing Veil's hand into an unassuming hammer. Precise aim sent it down on the balance point of Sariel's crafted blade. It took more effort than expected but the wooden weapon broke nonetheless. An exaggerated sigh was all the changeling presented before looking back at his opponent. He rushed forward once again, increasing the hammer's size before slamming it against Sariel's scales. This time, they pushed back against the strike to keep from moving. Even more scales broke but the pain passed quickly thanks to a mixture of adrenaline and experience.

Another sword appeared in their arm while lunging at Veil. It was almost identical to the last time Sariel attacked. There was no reason to block what could be immediately healed. The welcome was appreciated as the weapon plunged into their enemy's arm. With intense force, Sariel ripped the blade out and left a large gash on Veil's bicep. Blood sprayed out wildly, raining blue droplets on demons below. The smile on Veil's face stunned onlookers. Dangling muscles stretched and twisted before binding together. Reverting to his prime state pulled back some of the blood that seeped down his arm. All throughout the procedure Veil stared smugly at Sariel.

But the slightest twinge of a smile on the dragon's face grabbed his attention. A portion of his arm—the size of the initial stab—remained unhealed. That shouldn't be possible. He went so far as to ignore Sariel and focus on healing but the cut remained. Presence of a foreign element in his body was obvious and it had a familiar feeling. Whatever it was forced more effort in healing.

"How?!" he spat.

Sariel simply stared back in silence, confirming their suspicions. Something the demons had done allowed them to hinder a godly healer. Vofric brought Kargon back from the brink of death and yet failed to aid people who were far less injured. While the loss of life was unfortunate, it made Sariel rethink their approach to fighting Veil. For all the research he'd done in his life, he'd failed to think of how to counteract the many natural poisons in this realm. Poison that could be replicated by someone who held dominion over nature. Sariel didn't speak a word of it.

"You truly think yourself better than me?!" the changeling growled. "Simply because you outnumbered me at Zeld's Shell; you assume yourself powerful. Had it not been for your allies I would have been victorious."

It was clear to Sariel that Veil was trying to get a rise out of them. Remaining steadfast was child's play in a situation like this. But pushing him further could provide an avenue for attack. The dragon smirked and scoffed. Their memories and adventure gave an understanding of how others might react to such a display. To push it further the dragon flew slightly higher to look down on the measly changeling.

Veil's silver eyes twitched as he rose further in the air. "That attitude of dragons has infuriated me far longer than you know. Born with an 'unbreakable' hide, you think yourselves superior. Unkillable. Allow me to show you they are nothing special."

His body did not change shape but the outer layer of skin morphed. It was a grotesque display of jagged spikes ripping through film with a brief spurt of blood. The blue liquid was slick across rows of flat spikes that sprouted across every inch of his form. The wounds closed as quickly as they appeared as the gray scales tightened against Veil. If there was surprise that the cut from Sariel remained, he did well not to show it.

The morphed changeling smiled widely. "Years of researching your body provided me with the secret to replicating your armor. You have nothing over me."

"You speak as if my elven mutations provide nothing," Sariel replied with careful words. Even now there was an opportunity to gather information from her captor.

"Aside from that weakened form, what else is there?"

The draconic elf couldn't help but laugh at how foolish they had been. All this time they believed Veil to be some mastermind with a grand plan. Or that Aeraza opened up avenues of research. So many different possibilities that perpetually ran through Sariel's mind stopped at that instant. Veil cared only for power. Aeraza was simply someone the changeling could not surpass and thus pledged fealty.

"Your intention was to simply weaken me," Sariel said while lightly curling their elven fingers.

"I had no reason to concern myself with you once I morphed you into such a state," Veil replied.

"Thus you threw me out." Sariel shook their head. "Doubtless believing that if we crossed paths I would be at your mercy."

"My beliefs are rooted in truth!"

Veil rushed forward while fusing his hands into a lance. By his estimates, Sariel couldn't produce a new weapon before being pierced through the heart. Whatever shame they'd wrought would disappear with an anticlimactic strike. That's what the dragon deserved after humiliating one of the demon king's confidants. Ideas of glory and his own army swirled in Veil's mind as the lance got within arm's reach of his target. Then all the momentum and force disappeared before a powerful impact pushed Veil back several feet.

Sariel hovered with their elven arm outstretched. Within their palm sat layers of sturdy wooden petals with a lotus growing from the center. Brown and green bark flowed outward like a river that clung to their skin. A pattern of scales matching the draconic ones in size and shape encompassed their entire body. The only difference was Sariel's face where they created a flat, full face helmet. Anyone else wearing the makeshift armor would feel weight akin to metal plating. Plant fibers tightly bound together within each scale to make them as strong as possible. None could feel the difference compared to a dragon's true hide. Its appearance gave Veil pause; exactly as Sariel intended.

"How could you produce magic from your elven half?" Veil asked with vitriol in every word.

"You simply forced a change in my shape. You gave me the appearance of a mutant elf," Sariel responded. "I have come to realize it was intentional in hopes of dragging me into despair." Calm coldness in their voice carried on the breeze and amplified, stunning nearby foes. "That was a failure. A misjudgment. For beneath this facade belies a dragon." With each word, branches and vines expanded Sariel's wingspan—casting a shadow over the land. "Every piece of me communes with nature," they declared as petals wafted off them towards the ground below.

Luck or coincidence carried them on paths that interfered with enemy vision. But it mattered not to Sariel. Their eyes were trained on the demon that stole over two centuries from them.

They bellowed, "I am the Sylvan Dragon and I will not succumb to you."

Veil unconsciously put up his arms with transformed shields. A wave of shame passed over his face before he forced it to neutrality. Even Sariel could commend the monster for remaining calm in an unexpected situation. Though outwardly, the dragon smirked at his reaction. Thankfully, the helmet provided a steely, unmoving mask of calm. The same could not be said for the changeling making great efforts to hide his emotion. Fake dragon-like scales did nothing to hide his fear.

CHAPTER SIXTY-ONE

Guiding Lights

Screeches of agony and fury rang out from all directions—friend and foe nigh indistinguishable. The demons had finally found their rhythm and retaliated against the Tetrian forces. Mutated demons stood alongside large cyclops and chimeras. Fear was obvious on the fiercest of fighters even while they pushed forward into the demons. Engagement slowed as the demons showed unexpected wits and abilities. If one was targeted, others would aid it and distract the Tetrian adversary. It was difficult to take down any beasts with two quick strikes before turning attention to another.

Thankfully, swaths of enemies crumbled to the might of a powerful owlbear. Avant empowered himself with an aura that sharpened his feathers before charging through monsters. A torrent of ferocity barreled into enemy reach before overpowering them. Talons and claws violently ripped small creatures in twain. His sharpened beak tore chunks out of any monster too large to easily defeat. If he became too overwhelmed, Avant shifted gravity to force the monsters to their knees. But slowed demons still had means of attack. Wounds marked the owlbear's hide from prolonged combat but he did not falter.

Similar could be said for the dwarf that watched over the battle. Size was of no consequence when pertaining to Vofric Starc. Even when everyone around him was in a frenzy, he did not hurry. Watchful eyes knew where to look and helped him arrive moments before aid was necessary. Deliberate steps accompanied powerful swings of his war-hammer. Where others dreamt of killing demons with one strike, Vofric had no need for wishes. The massive and unwavering arc of his weapon eradicated multiple enemies without effort. Larger beasts lost limbs when foolishly attempting to stop the holy warrior. Many of them died seeing the warm orange eyes angrily staring from under a weary gaze. Those that were stopped while harming Vofric's allies experienced the worst of his anger. A powerful jump sent him high enough to strike down on the head of the largest creature in a group. Once the impact reached the ground, a shockwave of light burst out and burned the enemies. An imprint was left on the crushed corpses in his path. But going for the far wall was fruitless as none of them had a chance against Aeraza and would simply hinder Aisha.

"Do not push towards the castle. Aim outward from our cluster and surround the enemy!" Vofric commanded.

Scattered acknowledgments could be heard amongst shifting metal. The nearest allies were Rusty's group—well versed in overpowering their foes. Tactical maneuvers combined with practiced abilities made it easy to gain ground. Soldiers twisted and forced their way into gaps in the enemy's defenses. Normally they would be in a weaker position but the situation was anything but. Golden weapons were gripped tightly in the hands of anyone near Vofric. It wasn't as powerful as blessing them entirely but this was already taking an intense amount of focus. None of the Tetrians dreamt of facing such unfortunate odds alone but were more than willing with magically blessed weapons. Fear didn't hinder them thanks to Avant's roars whipping them into a frenzy that would not be deterred by unknown concerns. Lifetimes of adventure provided awareness and focus even while taking hits from the enemy.

Unfortunately, magic wasn't enough for the Tetrian soldiers not to get overwhelmed. Some didn't get hit more than a few times before being torn from this realm. Others were able to retreat with cuts deep into their armor. While they couldn't be completely healed, enough could be remedied for them to re-enter the fray. Each fallen ally only drove the warriors to more anger. More rage at the unfairness of their situation. The only saving grace was the powerful leaders guiding them.

Soldiers with dexterous fighting styles followed Freckle and Spike's lead. Giant shadows stretching across the battlefield were their domain. Dashing between them made the hedgehog duo impossible to track. Demons didn't mind until they felt a small prick against their bodies. The precise strike left large gashes that ripped open vital muscle. A single step forward shifted the monsters' weight onto the wounded limb and sent them tumbling to the floor. Before they could rise again, Tetrian troops beset upon them like ravenous hyenas. Any enemy that crossed the shadowy assassins' paths was cut by a hurricane of blades before they vanished from sight.

Ferocity from captains' attacks ignited a flame that passed between soldiers. Each blaze empowered those nearby and themselves in turn. None would recall what individual thing drove them to fight with such fury. All that was clear was an ever-present hope of protecting their home and never facing a foe like this again. The wild abandon it wrought was rarely seen that few were fond of. The sentiment was shared by anyone who caught a glimpse of the Dawncaster commander. It was simultaneously inspiring and frightening to watch Rusty battle.

Waves of crimson ichor erupted from his blade and cascaded through enemies. Any blood that came in contact with his own was controllable. To maximize it, he allowed copious amounts to pour out of him and into the soil. Dirt and grime mixed with his life force as he wildly slashed apart any monster in his path. Fear had no place in his eyes even when facing the largest of foes.

A manticore breathed a plume of acid at the commander but was unsuccessful in harming him. Rusty slammed his sword into the ground and sprouted a thick wall of blood that protected nearby allies. Once the poison dissipated, he rushed through the shield and curved it down towards the beast's head. Blood plunged into its mouth while remaining liquid. Gags and choking were all the manticore managed as the entire pillar was forced into its body. The instant the wave was gone, Rusty barked something unintelligible. Jagged thorns forced their way violently out of the monster and returned to the red blade in the warrior's grip. He didn't so much as turn back to look at the beast he eviscerated.

As powerful as Rusty was, it was obvious his fighting style was taking a toll. Small cuts leaked as if blood was trying to escape his body. Attacks grew fiercer with each additional droplet but they were slow to recover. With each overpowering assault, Rusty pushed further into the enemy—isolating evermore. By the time his subordinates were aware of how much he'd weakened it was too late. Dozens of enemies surrounded the commander with no escape in sight. The smug look of victory on his face hid any fear underneath. Demons snarled and screeched as they rushed at him. Giant claws blotted out the sun over the commander's head but he refused to shut his eyes. Joining this battle meant facing death with his head held high.

The sight of a falling leader made others hesitate. They stood in stunned silence as the world seemed to slow around them. Defenseless observation left them open to most attacks. Those who recovered from the shock of Rusty being overpowered began defending their other allies. Shuddered breathing spread throughout the group as they got on the back foot. Thick clouds blocked the sun and assisted the demons in hiding the light. Even Rusty had trouble seeing anything past the upcoming darkness.

"This is a poor way to resign from your position," Prince Makani's voice rang out.

A silver orb launched from the crowd of Tetrian forces. It raced across the field and obscured the area around it. There was no doubt that it was targeting the demons currently bearing down on Rusty. The ball of moonlight collided with the nearest monster and disintegrated the point of contact. Forceful impacts ricocheted it between demons, burning off pieces and forcing them back. Only the commander, even battered and exhausted, noticed secondary bruises appearing near the monsters' burns.

When the orb finally stopped moving, its shadow could be seen. Albert, gauntlets raised, was delivering powerful open palmed strikes on anything within reach.

"Makani! Is it ready?" he yelled.

There was no verbal reply but it was clear the prince heard his friend. Slowly, the silver orb ascended and expanded. A larger demonic brute tried to swat it away and lost its arm for the trouble. The orb floated out of reach and only the commander and young brawler remained. Albert was acutely aware of how meek he looked next to the experienced warrior. That's why he wasn't surprised when a hobgoblin swung a heavy club at him. But Albert's eyes weren't on his opponent. They glowed emerald green while staring at the makeshift moon overhead. Without turning away, he blocked the hobgoblin but instead of retaliating with a blunt palm, he attacked with whetted white claws. Fur spread across the young adventurer's body as he transformed into his lycanthropic form.

"Everybody down!" he howled.

Only the two young adventurers knew it was an unnecessary declaration. But such a command often caused enemies to hesitate. Seconds were enough for the large orb to explode into rays of moonlight that traveled across the monstrous figures surrounding Rusty and Albert. More than a dozen creatures were instantly disintegrated as the light of the sun finally broke through. It made the werewolf look far less imposing but that was appreciated by allies who finally left their stupor. They tried to push through the crowd of monsters blocking them while Albert began tearing apart ones nearby. Prayers passed through grit teeth as they watched Rusty fail to raise his sword. An unshakable facade did little to hide his apparent exhaustion. Even the commander couldn't deny he needed aid if he was to keep fighting.

Spirits rose at the sound of a mighty roar traveling through the group of Dawncaster guards. Avant blasted a crowd of demons off the ground and rushed through. Atop him rode Vofric, masterfully batting away the levitating targets. Shuffled feet allowed the owlbear to skid to a stop while the paladin hopped down. A forceful palm strike against Rusty's back sent mana coursing through him. Golden light engulfed his form as wounds healed. While smaller cuts didn't seal completely, large ones did—seemingly self-inflicted. Life returned to Rusty's hazy eyes as he stared at his stout savior. Vofric did not look at his friend, ashamed of the anger he felt in such a dire situation.

"This is a deadly situation but you need not rush to the heavens. Be mindful and work with our many allies," the paladin commanded.

"I can—" Before Rusty could say more, Vofric interjected.

"My words are not a suggestion nor a request. This is an order from the captain you appointed."

Avant stood by Vofric's side, facing a fresh group of enemies mid-charge. Allies entered the open spaces created by the heroes' entrance. Teleportation placed Makani behind the dwarf while Albert stood opposite the owlbear. Before all the smoke vanished, Freckle and Spike appeared from within. They all awaited the Kingsguard commander.

Rusty shook his head, sighed, and lifted his greatsword. Golden light wrapped around every allies' weapon while blue energy engulfed their bodies. The frenzied defense of Tetria began anew.

428

CHAPTER SIXTY-TWO

Fire with Fire

Rage burned in Kargon and Elmud's eyes. Their simultaneous landings created a crater that pushed away nearby demons. Neither allowed themself to step out of the sizable arena as their limbs collided. Fists refined through grueling training retaliated against fierce swipes from devastating claws. Specks of blood riddled the ground but both fighters knew they had barely started. Had Elmud not pushed themself away from Kargon, the fight would have continued in relative silence save for their grunts of effort.

"You're much stronger than last time. But you're foolishly overconfident," Elmud groaned. "I did not prefer your silent hesitation but it carried an air of caution that you would be wise to heed."

"I'm not sure why you think I'm overconfident," Kargon replied. "I just invited you to battle with a smile."

As nonchalant as Kargon sounded, he couldn't keep anger off his face. The dichotomy of his words and actions clearly bothered Elmud and there was no reason to let the prick have ease of mind.

"With that little wave?" Elmud asked. "I don't buy it."

"Let me clarify: I don't think I'm overconfident." Kargon growled, "As my master would say: your loss is imminent."

Elmud took a heavy step to get within reach, projecting a right handed claw swipe. Rather than dodging, Kargon met it head on. The open handed strike was blocked by an equally powerful punch to its center. The half-elf's tightly clenched fist was as strained as the dragominn's rigid extremities. A small wave of fire burst forth from the impact. Both brawlers pushed forward in an attempt to win the power struggle. Elmud was more focused since Kargon couldn't help but think that Master Avant would be disappointed in him. Such an obvious attack could've been ducked past and retaliated against.

"Focus, boy!" a stern voice cawed from above.

Kargon didn't need to turn in order to recognize his master's voice. It was surprisingly level for someone fighting off half a dozen monsters by himself. Astral clones struck their targets with shining strikes. Other monks from the Sanctuary of Spiritual Combustion battled nearby. Some had succumbed to their wounds while others remained strong. None dared approach the fight between the prized disciple and his nemesis.

"Looks like you still need backup," Elmud grumbled.

They extended their free hand to the side and aimed at the nearest Tetrian monk. Fire raged inches from the dragominn's palm before launching outward.

"No!" Kargon grunted.

Pulling away from the clash forced Elmud forward. A left handed chop pushed their arm down and shifted the fireball's trajectory. With the strike's momentum, Kargon flipped and stuck his leg towards the flames. It was too late as the orb was quickly leaving his reach. With his back to Elmud, Kargon punched towards the projectile and extended a large flaming fist. It snuffed out the fireball instantly. Keeping his arm outstretched, the monk spun back and shrank the astral extension so the fist would collide with Elmud. They grunted lightly as the refined flames cracked scales on their forearm.

The dragominn smirked as he brushed away shattered pieces. "With backup and that technique it's no wonder you believe you can beat me. But delusion can only get you so far before it fails you."

Elmud stepped away from Kargon without bothering to get in a defensive stance. Instead, they patted distinct points on their arm and snickered before tracing a claw across the center of their face from above their left eye to below the right. It was immediately obvious to Kargon what his opponent was referencing. Myriad scars permanently marked his body from their last encounter.

But each warrior saw something different when looking at the monk. To Elmud, it was a sign that the adventurer was weak and easily defeated. Power was so prominent in the dragominn's attacks that not even a holy paladin could heal the wounds. Though there was some fact in their ideas, it did not phase Kargon. The scars represented his path to growth. They showed him previous shortcomings that could be outgrown. Without them he would not have become an equal of the heroes who stood by him.

But neither pride nor shame were prominent in Kargon's mind. Overwhelming rage pounded in his head. Without raising his guard, he stepped within inches of Elmud. However, neither moved to attack.

Lowering his goggles, Kargon forcefully scratched the scar on his face. "You're delusional if you think these mean anything. Had you not been so cocky I'd be dead by now. You scampered off and left me to heal. You had almost a year to find me and end my life. I was incapacitated. Yet you just let me be."

Elmud scoffed and a tuft of smoke escaped their snout. Neither could see their opponent past it at such close vicinity.

"It is my master's way to prepare a strong sacrifice on the path to domination," they said. "Make no mistake, I will kill you. You speak of the year I allowed you to train. Did you think I wasted it simply following orders?" Kargon had every intention to answer the rhetorical question but had no chance. "I researched your fighting style, Kargon. It confused me that you only used the most basic of techniques in Dawncaster. My conclusions were that you either failed to learn more or that you ran from your training."

"Both are cowardly options," Kargon replied with a hateful gaze.

"They suit you. Much like your combat style suited me better. I felt something... peculiar in that stance of yours I mimicked. Like I could rip out your heart without effort. Bestial beings equipped with natural tools meant for battle are the ones who should rely on barehanded combat. Not foolish humanoids with a death wish. Don't you agree?"

It took effort for Kargon to speak as his teeth were clenched so tightly it hurt his jaw. Anyone who used that technique properly could tear a heart out regardless of their race. It wasn't any different than the times that Kargon plunged his fist into monsters. By the time he could finally speak, there was no reason to mention any of that.

"I take it you've been practicing?" he asked.

"More than you ever have," the dragominn spat.

"Is it because you couldn't handle being burned?"

Elmud squinted and said, "You just overcame my resistance to fire. I can do the same to you."

With a sharp inhale they set their claws and feet ablaze. Flames trailed off shoulder blades where wings were hidden. Cracks along Elmud's body eked out embers as a roaring blaze shined under the scales. In response, Kargon slowly donned his goggles and pulled the straps to secure it. Sliding his right leg back lowered his stance. Not a single flame appeared on Kargon's form.

"You talk like you've won the fight," the half-elf grunted. "Who's the overconfident one?"

His opponent barked, "The one who can back it up!"

Elmud's attack was less projected and more precise. With the flames erupting from their limbs it was difficult to see the strikes. That was the case for anyone who glimpsed into the arena. Kargon, however, wore *Pyromanic* and magically modified eyes had no difficulty discerning the trajectory of fiery attacks. Focused movements kept him within reach but out of harm. He didn't bother to dodge the flames and simply absorbed them. As Elmud reached the end of their swing, a fist firmly slammed into their stomach. The attack was strong but a trained warrior didn't slow from such an impact. Kargon's rage-addled mind expected more of a reaction. It left him open to take the brunt of the next strike on his chest.

Neither separated—the dirt shifted as they buckled down. Punches scraped against claws like flint on steel. Sparks ignited between and encompassed them in flame. Without hesitation, Kargon engulfed his entire being and threw out the plan of toying with Elmud. The dragominn roared and released the flames trying to break free of their scales.

A crimson pyre burned in the middle of the battlefield with two dark spirits colliding within. No one could identify which was friend or foe as tails lashed out from both. Powerful attacks launched flaming blood across the ground. Super heated stone littered the arena like charcoal and further clouded any view of the battle. Tetrians and demons alike began using the inferno as a tool. Bodies were thrown into it and spontaneously combusted. The massive fire was not the creation of a single fighter and their brawl made it increasingly improbable to regulate.

The only solace Kargon had was that the flames that killed allies were not his alone. He couldn't turn away from the battle and intaking Elmud's fire wasn't an option during the onslaught. Any loss in intensity would result in more damage than either could afford. A single strike at the right location would put someone on the backfoot. Based on how ferociously Elmud attacked, it was clear they'd come to the same conclusion. Each strike cemented their resolve not to block. It wasn't a point of pride but self-preservation. Taking a head-on attack to a stationary limb introduced the possibility of breaking it. Whatever healer might help either of them was too far to assist. Pulling back to recover only opened each of them up for more attacks.

Such a cowardly tactic was unbecoming of the demon king's subordinate. A weak strategy that the Hero's right hand refused to humor. The dragominn's claw strikes grew in fervor, lashing out in hopes of a lucky grip. Ripping parts off a body would be easy with a solid grasp. Slipping through with minor cuts was all the monk could manage. Using his opponent's momentum as a weapon was simple. Tight punches reached towards his target but they dodged in kind. Scales tore and bruises sprinkled their body but it wasn't enough to slow Elmud down.

Master Avant allowed his clones to fight as he watched his disciple in shock. All their training and tactics were dismissed for a fiery fistfight. The control of flames was a point of pride for the elder but the accompanying attacks didn't sit right. Kargon was more than a punch drunk amateur. Years of training, no matter how impractical, had honed a powerful body. With a well-placed strike he should be able to force a change of pace. Instead he'd allowed Elmud to control the battle. Master Avant shook his head but hesitated to look away as realization dawned.

Kargon wasn't simply retaliating in a manner that suited Elmud. The fierce student was holding his ground. Planning wasn't his strong suit. But impulsiveness had given way to improved instincts. Ones that searched tirelessly for a moment to shift the battle in the monk's favor.

With a smirk, Master Avant turned away from the brawl. It was his duty to guide his student on the correct path. Scrutinizing his choices was unbecoming. Especially when the owlminn was hovering over a battlefield when he could be fighting. He dove back into war while wishing the firebrand luck. Little did he know his blessing would come to fruition shortly after.

"You. Will. Burn!" Elmud roared while stringing three swings together.

The effort of conversation gave Kargon room to breathe. Light shuffling of his feet got him out of arm's reach. As he slowed his escape, Elmud pressed forward. It was a second of difference but enough to matter. Kargon leapt upward, spun, and reverse roundhoused the dragominn's head. Scales shattered on the point of impact. The pressure cut apart the muscle underneath. Blood erupted from the wound as the monk landed.

"Make threats you can follow through on," he yelled back. "Something like; you will bleed!"

"You will!" Elmud roared and rushed forward.

A left swipe was easily backstepped. Instead of pulling the arm back, it was pushed forward to blind Kargon. The sensation of a blade cutting deep into his arm overtook him. The fighters separated long enough to assess their individual wounds. Blood dripped from the monk's left arm. Stinging pain unfamiliar to him burned within but he pushed it down. With focus Kargon raised his guard once more and rushed forward.

Deep indents in the dirt accommodated the footing of their creators. Rapid volleys flew between the warriors as their anger burned fiercer. Once again, they locked themselves in combat until an opening for change presented itself.

CHAPTER SIXTY-THREE

Fated Encounter

Lightning trailed from *Valefor*, slicing through the air on Aisha's dash glide Aeraza. He readily blocked with the legendary greatsword unsheathed from his back. Minutes passed as only the sounds of clashing blades could be heard between them. Neither made any headway during that time. Aisha was wary of using her empowered lightning slashes since Aeraza was clearly holding back. A single untoward attack invited danger. Yet, another part of the Hero knew she was safe—the demonic lord's demeanor made clear he had plans aside from battle.

Eventually, Aisha kicked the ground to separate from her enemy. Aeraza didn't follow, instead sheathing his weapon as their eyes met. No words were spoken until the Hero did the same.

The two figures stood only a few feet apart in an almost peaceful setting if not for the bloody war occurring around the spire. All of it the fault of a being hoping to conquer the realm. Aisha stood with her arms crossed, studying the demon across from her. It was infuriating that Aeraza stood with an almost friendly demeanor.

"That was quite an approach," he said. "You have trained your subordinates well for them to willingly sacrifice themselves to push you forward."

"They're my friends. And they won't have trouble dealing with your grunts," Aisha retorted.

A quizzical look appeared on the demon's face as he asked, "Why does your kind strive to consider everyone a 'friend?' Can they not simply be peons that provide a means to an end?"

Aisha wasn't sure a demon could understand. Every person on Vethyea experienced strife throughout their lifetime and crossed others who shared in their plight. The word used to describe such people didn't actually matter. Acquaintances, comrades, even strangers; anyone could help through hard times if they wanted. It just so happened that the same people helped Aisha repeatedly. The hardships they faced together made them more than friends. But any explanation felt like a lost cause considering the enemy.

"It's not how we operate," she replied.

"That is why you will not join me, correct? Because of this incessant need to empower the weaklings around you. Do you not understand how far above them you are?" Aeraza asked.

Even while keeping his usual placid face, there was a hint of genuine concern in his voice. He truly believed Aisha was wasting her potential

"Kharim made the same mistake. Gathering pests who hoped to prove something only for them to crumble under the pressure of a powerful opponent. Each one hindered him to the point of losing composure in battle. It's unbecoming of someone of his stature. Of yours."

Aisha remained silent. It intrigued her how obsessed Aeraza was with strength. Not the idea that others could be strong but that they wasted its presence by using it for others. For Aisha, power was meaningless if it wasn't used to improve the lives of those around her. If not for the needs of Tetria, Aisha would have remained a guard in Neves. In a truly peaceful world she would have spent her time running a shop with her family. There were a myriad of options to explore if adventuring wasn't required for peace. But part of her would always be thankful for being born in a time where she could help others with her natural abilities. That way others could live away from danger.

Aeraza glared at the distracted woman. "Is my conversation boring you, Aisha Ilphekiir?"

She replied with a shrug. "Honestly? It's nothing I haven't heard before. In fact, it confuses me how much you care about weak people. You seem to spend more time thinking about them than I do yet I spend more time helping them. Are you really so angry that they exist in a realm that you're not even part of?"

"It does when that same realm raises warriors like Kharim. If everyone were put in trials like him... This world would house the greatest army since the dawn of time."

"So, you'll kill off anyone who can't match up to him."

"It is possible for me to be disproven." Aeraza elaborated, "During the trials I introduce, individuals may grow in strength. They may overpower my threats. In those cases they will be invited to my ranks."

"You're not scared they'll target you," Aisha said confidently.

"Why should I be? Simply because they defeat my subordinates does not mean they can match me."

"Unless they reach Kharim's strength."

Aeraza shook his head. "We were quite evenly matched."

"Until your last battle," Aisha added. "I've seen the records and know how little you were able to do against the full might of the first Hero. All the pain and suffering you put Tetria through came back to bite you. And you could only get off a few hits."

Aeraza grunted without shifting his face. "Your kind would rewrite all of history if it suited your needs. Kharim may have defeated me but it was by the skin of his teeth. Do you think I would be capable of casting a curse in an overwhelming defeat? Our final confrontation nearly ended both our lives. I was shocked to hear he survived upon my return."

Aisha smirked as she uncrossed her arms, making sure to keep her left hand over *Valefor*. "That's what happens when you have friends to back you up. You simply had no one who wanted to save you."

A deep, guttural sigh came from the demon king's maw as he unsheathed his greatsword. Tilting his torso released the weapon from its metal bindings. With his right hand, he flipped it forward and planted the blade in the ground in front of him.

"Do not misunderstand my offer that you have repeatedly denied," he groaned. "You would be standing with the weaklings of this realm if not for the magical sword bequeathed to you. Even still, you are many leagues below Kharim in terms of power. The man was incapable of elemental magic and resorted to transforming *Valefor* into the shape of any weapon. It is beyond your capabilities."

Kharim's magic was the one thing Aisha never figured out and hoped it would aid her in some way. But transformation magic was rare and would have manifested long ago. Wallowing in it was pointless. The First Hero may have had unique magic but it had been replicated. Aisha had elemental mastery that was unmatched. Such a thought brought a smile to her face.

Aeraza tightly gripped his weapon as a constant wave of black ink poured from his armor. "Whatever you may believe—my weapon is beyond *Valefor's* capabilities. You chase after your land's Hero in hopes of matching him. I have long surpassed him."

Aisha shook her head at the battle hungry warrior. He was more frightening as an unknown threat. Whatever ideology or plan Aeraza might have had weighed on the mind of all Tetrians. But it was nothing special when stripped down to the core—the demon king sought to overpower others. There was no denying his strength but Aisha refused to cower to it.

Lightning crackled around her as mana poured into her magical eye. Flashes of purple electricity darted around her body and gathered near her hand before wreathing around *Valefor*. A luminous glow burst off the unsheathed blade.

"You lack the fear I saw in Spirefell. I commend you," Aeraza said as apathetically as always.

"Shove it," Aisha replied.

"I hope your strength poses any challenge to myself." Though he never acknowledged it, Aeraza was acutely aware of the exact words to twist emotions. It was the exact reason he had subordinates like Elmud and Veil. On one hand, they feared their lord, on the other, their mere existence infuriated Aeraza. That made it clear they could toy with any enemy they faced.

Aisha rushed forward and swung at Aeraza's chest. He masterfully pulled his weapon from the ground, blocking the attack. Repeated attacks clashed rhythmically. It felt obvious to the demon king that he outpaced the Hero. Shifting from defense, he stepped forward and swung his *Brachynox* in a vertical slice. Aisha exhaled softly as she sidestepped the blade. An instantaneous strike from *Valefor* collided with Aeraza's armor and left a thin cut on the pauldron. Swift maneuvers turned the blade and another swing struck squarely into the chainmail on the demon's elbow.

"You carry lightning on your blade," Aeraza muttered. "It is no wonder you have made headway in reaching Kharim's prowess."

Aisha ignored the conversation—focused on reaching the opening she found. This time when she extended her blade it was blocked by the greatsword. Both fighters separated but Aeraza landed first. The next attack was immediate but slow thanks to his weapon's size. Assuming dodging would be easy, Aisha left herself open to a strike on her right shoulder. Blood burst out of the sudden wound created by a longsword.

Aeraza stepped back and flourished the blade. Ink twirled around it before revealing the shape of a dagger. The demon reversed his grip while simultaneously changing his stance. Using his tail, he propelled forward and attempted to stab his opponent. One strike was blocked but the next landed. Lightning infused movements were needed to defend against each blistering demonic attack.

While Aeraza's swings could change in speed, his other movements remained steady. Only certain motions had any speed but they were nothing compared to the Hero's lightning infused dance between strikes. Some could be cleanly dodged and in turn provided an opening to retaliate. Aisha's attacks began tearing into the heavy armor of the demon king. His eyes twinkled with joy even while attempting to kill the half-elf. It wasn't until they split apart that she knew why.

Aeraza's dagger changed to a rapier that easily weaved into her range. With a flick of the wrist he struck her neck and pulled out a concealed necklace. Hanging on it was half of the Ring of Dominion. If not for a few trickles of blood, it would shine as brilliantly as the day it was found.

"The agreement was that we bring our halves," Aisha spat as she stepped back and stowed the ring. "Where's yours?"

"The agreement did not dictate we reveal them to each other," Aeraza replied candidly.

He got in close and Aisha held up her sword to block the rapier but miscalculated the necessary strength. *Brachynox* morphed mid-swing into its original form. The intense weight of the greatsword broke through Aisha's stance and allowed a deep cut into her arm. She quickly dashed back and examined the wound. Without hesitation she shocked the injury to force it closed. It wasn't perfect but it'd have to do.

Gritting her teeth, Aisha dashed into the demon's range. Even while her body was recovering it was possible to get an attack off. Aeraza confidently put up his guard, fully expecting to stop the Hero.

Suddenly, *Valefor* bypassed the larger weapon and cut a large piece off the demon king's armor. An emotion finally broke through his placid facade; shock. Instinctively, he studied the blade and quickly deduced what happened.

"You control its trajectory even at unprecedented speeds," Aeraza said. "My defense will be far less effective. Though my strength—"

"We're not equals," Aisha interjected. "I understand what you can do. There's no way you can win."

It was an exaggeration, plain and simple. Obviously Aeraza could win the fight. But Aisha cementing herself in the idea of victory was crucial. That was the only way to overcome the monster bearing down on her—on everyone. If Aisha couldn't defeat Aeraza, the lives around her were forfeit. With each passing minute the tides of battle shifted. No one knew when the winds would be in their favor. The only guarantee was that they were ever-changing.

CHAPTER SIXTY-FOUR

In Times of Need

Not a single member of the Tetrian army was unscathed. No amount of healing could close wounds wrought by the empowered demons. Thousands of monsters fell but more appeared to keep Tetria overwhelmed. Their sheer numbers couldn't be matched by the allied troops. A single soldier could defeat a dozen beasts while being wounded half as many times but it wasn't enough.

Small signs of effort sent ripples through the army. One soldier would do something unexpected that in turn inspired someone else. But the effects of such inspiration diminished based on who took action. Vofric was well aware of this fact and commanded his more powerful allies to split up within the army. It seemingly worked as larger groups of demons were eviscerated in multiple areas. Captains of different factions showed why they were revered. Amateur adventurers quickly learned from experienced counterparts to equalize the battle against powerful foes.

Vofric was well aware that spreading the troops would have negative consequences. They appeared quicker than anticipated when a small contingent of soldiers found themselves completely detached from the army. During the heat of battle they'd push deep into enemy territory. Each was heavily wounded but they continued to fight tooth and nail in hopes of rejoining the others. Even if they had a captain with them, it was wishful thinking. That didn't stop one from attempting to help.

The prince of Dawncaster teleported within the soldiers' ranks. Rays of light sprayed over them and killed the nearest enemies. Powerful winds whipped around the group and made a barrier that pushed back against the monsters' onslaught. It provided just enough room for the fighters to put strength into their attacks. Only one wave of strikes was possible before the demon's pushed past Makani's shield. Within seconds they were on the backfoot again.

"Albert! Makani needs you!" Vofric bellowed in a panic.

Without any signal, he ran to Avant and mounted the beast before they charged through the battlefield. Exhaustion weighed on their shoulders while focused on the distant friend. Attacks tore through Avant's reckless dash as he ignored enemies. It got noticeably to push through as a rain of quills flew past them. Dozens of blades launched off Spike's back as he rolled through the battlefield. The instant one slowed down he plunged his claws and teeth into them. Wild movements tore the creatures apart and created room for Avant to maneuver. As Vofric and his animal companions continued to press into the enemy, a silver blur arrived near Makani.

Massive werewolf claws covered in slick blood tore into the nearest demons. They hadn't fallen off the jagged bone before Albert targeted others. Ferocity of his caliber even frightened the hellish hordes. Gruff roars echoed as he searched inwardly for more power. No one else knew how glad Albert was for his years of vigilantism and training. If not for the ill-advised venture he would have succumbed to the beast in such a stressful situation. Instead, he could focus on protecting the soldiers nearby with his large frame. Blood and grime stuck to his fur but he'd long gotten over his own monstrous facade. It didn't even matter if the soldiers were scared as long as they were safe.

The path to the young adventurers grew perilous as monsters realized what Avant was racing towards. Thankfully, familiar shadows stalled the distracted creatures. Freckle's hair had grown in length and rigidity as she used her whole body as a weapon. Two smooth blades extended out of her palms and grew in length when plunged into her targets. Horrified gurgles were all the demons could muster as the mutant swords slowly pushed through their organs. With each movement, Freckle manipulated smoke into the demons' vision. Even her allies wouldn't see the short woman if not for the fact she was in front of them. With their united efforts, the path became more navigable.

For a member of the heroes' party to make a grand attempt at saving someone meant they were important. Waves of monsters raced toward the isolated soldiers and attacked wildly. Albert's defense could only handle so much with compounding wounds. Blasts of moonlight burned monsters apart but others would immediately take their place. The barrier of wind had long collapsed so Makani focused on attacks. Even those were being hindered by monsters capable of casting magic.

Fatigue was quickly overtaking the prince. Sweat dripped from his brow as he struggled to concentrate. Teleportation was no longer an option and he cursed himself for foolishly diving into the enemy. Even if he could leave, he wouldn't dare abandon his best friend or the troops.

"Prince Dicoris!" a soldier yelled out and leapt in front of him.

His vision was blocked as a long demonic claw pierced through the woman. In an instant, she went limp and dropped to the floor. Color drained from her face as blood quickly pooled at Makani's feet.

"No..."

The quiet mutter steeled the resolve of the remaining soldiers. They pulled Albert back to protect him from further harm. There was no opportunity for him or Makani to attack. Nearly a dozen panicked warriors came together to protect the young adventurers from any oncoming threat. Each only added seconds to the battle before their wounds were too much to bear. One by one, they fell at the Dawncaster elite's feet.

"Makani, we go down fighting, right?" Albert spat a wad of blood at the nearest enemy that just killed one of their allies. It took more strength than he expected to push his claws through it. Thankfully, a single strike was still enough to fell the demon.

A slow breath came from the prince's lips. "It is what Victor would want."

He mustered all his focus into *Lightbringer* and summoned dual beams of moonlight. One from the staff and another from his palm. Neither warrior faltered as monsters increased in number around them. Corpses kept piling up but the waves felt endless. A large fist got within inches of Makani's face but was stopped by Albert cutting it apart. It was clear to them the others wouldn't arrive in time. Not the ones they saw at least. Prayers could not be mustered nor a miracle summoned. All they could do was stall and hope something changed quickly. There wasn't much time left.

Protection came in the form of bloody spikes erupting from the ground inches away from the ring of Tetrian corpses. Drills of crimson eclipsed the monsters they tore apart. Large obelisks created a wall of death that bore through demons for hundreds of feet around. Within seconds, the monstrous encircling was replaced with grotesque structures of violence. They splashed to the ground, revealing Rusty hidden within as he stared sadly at his fallen comrades.

"Victor wouldn't want you to give up. But I'll be damned if he'd be okay with you dying," the commander said.

Rage burned in his eyes as he began sundering monsters with no remorse. Makani and Albert kept up their guard but quickly realized it was safer for them not to engage. Wild strikes from Rusty were unlikely to hurt them but he would be hindered if the younger men acted improperly. They couldn't help but smile seeing the mighty commander to one side of them and Vofric and Avant's group approaching the other. That was until they saw uncharacteristic fear on the paladin's face. Avant picked up speed as the dwarf roared.

"Protect yourselves!"

The spellcasting demons weren't near enough to be taken out by the spikes. Nothing ever stopped them from gathering mana into mounds of floating earth that molded into refined stone. Hundreds of hardened daggers empowered by a myriad of elements rained from the sky. Makani tried to manipulate the wind but failed. Albert stepped in front of his friend as a shield, unsure of what else to do. Their gazes turned towards a mighty Rusty as he turned back towards them and blitzed. The sky fell faster than he could travel. Only saving his young comrades mattered in that moment. Without hesitation he threw his bloody sword towards them and gathered every ounce of blood he could control.

The blade touched down near Albert before transforming into a massive disk of crystallized ichor. Any demon near the edge met with a violent spinning edge. Monstrous remains sprayed outward as the hail of daggers collided with the wall. Not a single projectile bypassed the structure, allowing Vofric time to arrive and begin healing the young adventurers. Everyone was rightfully stunned by the form of

Rusty's greatsword. As mana recovered and wounds closed, they scoured the crowd for the commander. The crimson disk turned back to liquid and drenched anyone nearby as the sword clattered to the ground. Kneeling on the other side was Rusty, staring blankly at the demon at his side. In its grasp was the warrior's amputated arm.

All the commander could manage was to turn slightly before collapsing onto his back. Avant leapt to his side and produced a wall of gravity surrounding their allies and pushing everything else away. While others focused on Makani and Albert, Vofric rushed to the dying commander, lifted him into his arms, and prepared to heal. With a slow, painful motion, Rusty shook his head to stop the paladin. Following that, he weakly tilted towards a stunned Albert and Makani. They were almost completely healed yet remained silent while walking to the commander they'd grown up respecting.

"This is how Victor would've felt if it'd been you," Rusty said and forced a smile.

Celebratory barks surrounded the group as demons continued to fight nearby. It wasn't enough to drown out the commander's words.

"Let me heal you," Vofric insisted.

"Won't work. Not after I threw away a blessed weapon," Rusty said while looking for his sword.

Albert dashed over and grabbed it without a second thought. The spiked hilt dug into his palm but the werewolf ignored the pain. Even in his bestial form it was troublesome to carry. To wield it so easily spoke volumes of the man who lay on the ground.

"You're cursed..." Albert whined as he placed the sword down next to Rusty.

"To lose friends, yeah." Rusty's voice grew softer with every word. "Accepted the sword to protect people. Think it did a good job?"

Makani shook his head. "You did a good job. The sword is but a tool. It would be worthless in the hands of someone less virtuous than you."

Rusty shut his eyes as tears flowed from them. "Then take it. Protect our people."

Makani and Albert stared at Rusty then each other. The prince planted a heavy hand on his best friend's shoulder to stop him from declining.

"It is his last request."

Albert nodded sadly. "Shouldn't you take it?"

"The Dicoris bloodline survives by their allies' swords. Will you honor Rusty and I by accepting his gift?" Makani asked.

Slowly, the young Greycastle nodded and kneeled next to the bloody weapon before placing a hand on the blade. "I will fight in your stead."

Rusty slowly tilted his head down. In reaction the sword liquefied and crawled up Albert's claws. At first all he could do was scream as pain overwhelmed him—like the sword was plunged deep into his body. Seconds felt like minutes when blood erupted from his fingertips and slowly crept along the claws. Finally he let out an ear piercing howl as the bequeathment ended. Bone white instruments were replaced with the metallic red of the sword that rested on the ground moments ago.

"At least I'll see Julian," Rusty said as he shut his eyes.

Vofric looked at his god-son then back to the commander who lay lifeless in his arms. An inkling of fear settled in the chests of every soldier nearby. Allowing such feelings would result in more losses and letting Rusty's sacrifice be in vain would be the greatest sin Vofric ever committed. A quiet prayer passed his lips as the commander was laid down.

A hand on Avant's head aided Vofric in rising to his feet. Large tears welled in the beast's eyes and blue energy swirled around him like a torrent while he wailed. Without a word or command Vofric stepped forward and unhooked his light hammer. Empowering weapons wasn't enough. Mana could be replenished but fully strengthening allies was an absolute necessity. It wouldn't bring Rusty back but would save all the lives he died for. They would be flooded with more power than they knew what to do with. Vofric's weapon's shape was lost in a burst of molten gold light. To his side stood the shadowy figures of Freckle and Spike. With conviction, Makani and Albert joined them, glaring at the demon toying with Rusty's arm.

"Captain Telos did not yield!" Vofric yelled. "He wished to protect Tetria so badly that he sacrificed himself. That wish has been bequeathed to us! Will we deny it?"

No one was sure if it was the shining light or deep voice of the hero. Maybe a calming spell was cast on them but that was doubtful. The cause didn't matter though. Every soldier who saw the ordeal had reignited vigor as they roared denial at Vofric's question.

"Let us give his spirit a proper send off! Eradicate the enemy!" the dwarf bellowed.

The soldiers put everything they had into acknowledging the command.

Vofric pulled back his light hammer and faced forward. "Glory to Tetria!"

The impact of his hammer against the war-hammer created a shockwave of light that vanquished dozens of surrounding enemies instantly. Golden light wreathed around every allied weapon and body it came in contact with. An unprecedented animalistic roar erupted from Avant and sent his mana in every direction. Blue light burned brightly in the eyes of the raging soldiers. Gravity shifted forward and forced the advance. For the first time since the beginning of the war, the demons hesitated. Watching droves vanish in holy light frightened them. Magically empowered soldiers had no mercy to show the frozen monsters. It was the first signal that Tetria would overcome their adversaries.

CHAPTER SIXTY-FIVE

A Dragon's Place

Fights moved like waves in an ocean of violence as tides shifted. Some Tetrians pushed forward while others were forced back. Unlike the slow ground based forces, airborne fighters moved all over the battlefield. It was possible to navigate even with many warriors in the sky. Most of them flew slightly above the primary battle but none reached the heights of Sariel and Veil.

Each time they engaged then retreated the battle moved higher. Their silhouettes could be glimpsed within clouds miles above Aeraza's castle. Demons didn't bother monitoring the mad scientist but Tetrian troops kept an eye out for their draconic ally. No one thought it was possible to help them but it would be foolish not to keep track just in case. Thankfully, a field of flowers and metallic scales marked the land wherever Sariel and Veil exchanged blows.

Naturally formed dragon scales were incredibly powerful. No more had been chipped since Sariel summoned the wooden armor. They made a point to block with it since it was more easily repaired. More surprising was that Veil's armor was as powerful as the true emerald hide. The amount of experimentation he had done to reach the high quality defense of a dragon made Sariel's spine shudder. Anger pounded in their head at remembering everything they endured. With every passing moment, the draconic elf's disgust grew. Their full-face helmet hid how they felt about the insect who'd stolen so much from so many races. Allowing it to show would be far too pleasing for Veil.

That couldn't be allowed to happen or he'd bask in the minor victory. Instead, Sariel sent the message by trying to rip the false scales from the demon's body.

With each failed attack, Sariel produced a different modification. Veil took it as a sign that the draconic elf could not create satisfactory weapons. Mockingly, he retaliated with weapons that rapidly transformed. Utilizing an open stance allowed Sariel to force the swings off course. Even if one did collide it only broke a few wooden scales which rapidly regrew. Unfortunately, powerful strikes opened wounds underneath which stained the scales red. But that kind of damage was beginning to appear on Veil as well.

Sariel's weapons grew barbs and dripped unknown ichors from porous thorns. Well placed attacks carved the changeling apart. unhealable wounds weighed heavy on his riddled body. Finally, he realized what the dragon's ever changing weapons were doing. Each transformation added higher densities of toxins and faster delivery systems.

Suddenly, a howl pierced through the battlefield so loudly that it reached the skybound warriors. Both hesitated long enough to catch a glimpse of the source. While Veil was focused on the blood soaked werewolf, Sariel's eye turned to the surrounding allies. Namely Vofric as he placed a fallen Rusty softly on the ground. A somber goodbye passed the dragon's mouth as they quickly turned back to Veil. The smarmy grin plastered on his face was infuriating.

"You have always been quite soft for a dragon," he said. "Your father never attacked settlements as your kind is wont to do. I am unsurprised that such an upbringing produced a weakling who dreamed of traveling. To meet humanoids on equal footing." He pointed towards Vofric's group and cackled, "Your weakness has resulted in the death of your precious allies. Their hearts waver with every loss. Wasting time attempting to defeat me will result in more deaths."

A familiar sound rang in Sariel's ears. Not loud enough for Veil to notice or unique enough to demand attention. Throughout their quest, the mutant elf had grown accustomed to whispered prayers spoken by a kindly dwarf. It was drowned out by peculiar wailing that Sariel identified as the owlbear who'd grown under the party's watchful eye. Part of the dragon wished to see what was going to happen.

However, there was no need to look back. A familiar sensation—one that followed Vofric and Avant's blessings—washed over the battlefield below. Powerful changes were guaranteed when that duo was enraged.

"A brief glimpse of my allies cannot inform you of their strength," Sariel explained. "They do not rely on me for protection but to fight as their equal. You are correct that I have failed them. By now you should have fallen and I have toyed with you for far too long."

Veil squinted at his adversary and spat at them. "You are nothing but a failed experiment. That is why you were abandoned."

"Both of those are the fault of the one conducting said experiments," Sariel replied readily. "You failed to completely morph me and opted to leave me mutated. You could not utilize magic tools made of my hide and discarded them. You failed to end my life and allowed me to wander aimlessly with lost memories."

Without showing any preparation, the dragon launched forward and stabbed a dagger into Veil's shoulder. He reached for the hilt but it quickly transformed into a small flower bulb before jamming under the quickly recovering scale.

"You lack foresight and reek of pride," Sariel declared.

"This coming from the fool who's attacks are being overpowered by my transformation. This was the only success your being wrought. Think carefully: would the Hero's party be any different without your presence?" Veil asked with a smirk.

An unabashed smile hid underneath Sariel's wooden mask. Memories flooded them even while crossing swords with the changeling. Insightful words from a small owlbear no one else could understand. Wise teachings from an ex-adventurer who was far too interested in other people's lives. Caring questions stemming from the curious mind of a small town warrior. Guidance from a woman wise beyond her years. Yet all of them had shortcomings for which they relied on a quiet mutant dragon who originally intended to separate from them.

"Your statements mark me as unintelligent yet you battle with a distracted mind," Veil barked. "Declarations regarding the insects beneath us split your attention. Time is wasted because you humor their needs. To even consider them while facing me is the epitome of having pride in your capabilities. That is the sin of all dragons."

"You are... correct," Sariel replied as they lunged forward again with two daggers. Both found targets on Veil's torso but he was able to retaliate with a morningstar against Sariel's leg. The wooden armor on their shin shattered and remained broken.

"Dragons are undeservedly proud creatures stemming simply from the circumstances they are born into." Sariel said while producing daggers at a rapid rate. Each one stabbed into Veil transformed and fused with him. In turn, he broke more wooden armor and began beating on the weak elven form underneath.

"However, my pride is different. It stems from the confidence friends place on me. Their hopes provide me with strength that I failed to utilize," Sariel barked as a heavy hit broke the armor on their torso. A retaliatory kick separated the fighters before the dragon shed the last of their wooden scales and mask.

"The people you consider insects have unique ideas that put your century-long experiments to shame. They risk themselves to push forward for even the slightest chance of overcoming hopeless odds," Sariel said with unabashed pride in Tetria. "That is where I defer from them—our battle is anything but hopeless. I learned from you to modify experiments but I will not give up until I achieve a satisfactory result."

Veil rolled his eyes and morphed his arms into two sickles. With his large webbed wings fluttering at high speed he resembled an insect far more than the people on the battlefield. The pattern in which he flitted through the sky was almost random. If not for Sariel's vision, he may have gotten the drop on them.

Closing the gap, Veil swiped at one arm. When it missed, he attacked with the other. It was too slow to connect. With a frustrated growl Veil attempted to strike again. This time he didn't move at all— his arms locked into place.

"It was foolish to allow my plants into your body," Sariel said.

"I... healed..." Veil said as his jaw tightened.

"Incorrect. I simply changed my bulbs to resemble your scales. Isn't it intriguing that my own resemble flora?" Sariel asked while nodding at her opponent's stabbed shoulder.

Cobalt flower petals forcibly pushed scales apart. They had the consistency of the layered armor Sariel had removed. Multi-layered flowers bloomed from every spot Veil invited attacks. Thorny vines rippled under the skin and burst outward. Poison tipped spikes froze the changeling completely. Once rapid wings slowed to the point that they provided no lift. Veil plummeted towards the battlefield, shutting his eyes in fear of the incoming impact. But no such thing happened. He watched as Sariel grabbed one wing to slowly place Veil on the ground.

Tetrian allies blocked any other demons from reaching the dragon. Nothing would pull their attention away from Veil as his facade completely slipped away. Apparent fear was written on his face as his body succumbed to the poison. Every scale slowly faded and only a gray featureless creature remained. The silver eyes that haunted Sariel for centuries stared at them in complete horror.

"Sariel, you were correct. I am a failure of a scientist. I can learn!" Veil shouted. "Allow me to speak with my master. We can come to an agreement."

"You have nothing to coerce myself nor my friends," Sariel said as they dismissed their wings.

"I can revert your form!" When Veil's declaration didn't elicit a reaction, he asked, "Do you not wish to shed this skin?"

Sariel scoffed while summoning an intricate arrow created with flora across Tetria. "Had you asked before, I may have agreed. Now I see it as a gift that allows me to walk alongside the people I adore."

Tears streaked Veil's face as he blubbered, "Keeping me as a prisoner makes you as monstrous as myself! Please, I will remove myself from this battle. You do not need to kill me."

"I will not keep you prisoner, Veil." Sariel's bow appeared in their left hand. "This is not removal or murder. You will provide nutrients to our world and be forgotten among the corpses of your brethren."

There wasn't time for a whimper before the arrow launched at Veil. Myriad hues of green swirled around the projectile as it drilled into the monster's chest. Flowers bloomed from the shaft on collision as nutrients from the dying changeling flooded into the roots. They ripped through Veil's limbs and dug into the ground causing flora to violently expand out of the lifeless container. An explosion of blood, guts, and petals shook the battlefield. Beauty overpowered gore in the brief moment a shower of flowers fell over the war.

Sariel took one last look at what little remained of their captor and summoned a fresh set of wooden armor. Only a few dozen Vethyeans saw the wide smile that appeared on the dragon's face. Others wouldn't believe it when spoken of in the future. Likely because it vanished moments later as Sariel returned to battle. Nevertheless, the legendary expression would never be forgotten by those who saw it.

453

CHAPTER SIXTY-SIX

Firebrand

No one dared approach the flaming arena surrounded by charred bones. The intense inferno was too much for humanoids and demons alike. Flames that broke away and licked the skin left burns on the recipient. Anyone who wasn't healed immediately felt excruciating pain that worsened if they didn't get away. It was the sole reason Kargon was thankful to be left alone in the battle. Unnecessary deaths would weigh on him even if the fire was controlled by Elmud.

By now the dragominn realized that flames had no effect on Kargon. Or at least that his body reacted differently to them. Scales across Elmud's body cracked and revealed burned skin underneath. Prolonged exposure to the monk's blaze caused Elmud's body to boil. Grotesque pustules of blood leaked over their metallic hide while the tar that lined their body melted. By some miracle it didn't completely come apart and allowed Elmud to continue their aggressive onslaught.

Scattered lines were carved all over Kargon's body. Each mark that remained from Spirefell guided the dragominn's attacks. Elmud took unhinged pleasure in reopening the wounds even if they weren't as deep as before. However, that wasn't enough to stop the monk's flurry of blow. If a claw so much as touched him, a solid punch or kick was delivered in response. Powerful impacts from the refined flame resulted in explosions that tore off scales with ease.

"You really are immune, aren't you?" Elmud spat as their claws left a small cut on Kargon's cheek. "Yet I'm considered a monster by lesser races. You can lap up my flames like a dog and I'm the problem."

As much as Kargon hated it; he understood Elmud. A young mind twisted the teachings of a frightened elder. He shuddered at the fact that they could have been allies if not for Master Avant's guidance. Guided exploration of aggressive abilities and trained self control kept Kargon grounded. Without fear of his powerful emotion it was possible to charge head first into anything.

Overwhelming rage within Kargon's mind was nowhere near as strangling as he once thought. Succumbing to the emotion allowed him to reach new heights of power. Instincts sharpened like a fine blade under the intense heat of his fury. There was nothing blind about the ferocity that dominated Kargon's being. There was a time it made him feel monstrous. Now, he realized it only made him more humanoid.

Elmud was more distracted by the flames surrounding them. They had whipped about wildly for however long the brawlers clashed without Kargon absorbing a single ember after the initial fireball. It was infuriating for Elmud to admit there was a silver lining—mana didn't need to be wasted on ineffective magic. Not to mention, there were things that could be deduced from how the monk was fighting.

With a powerful tail strike, Elmud whipped the ground and pulled themself back. Their flames dissipated as the gap widened. Kargon didn't completely dispel his infernal armor but lessened the intensity. They wrapped tightly over his body and kept him in the form of a dark silhouette.

"Humor me: how are you able to equip *Pyromanic*?," Elmud asked while stretching. "I have to assume you have fire giant blood. Based on the Artifact, your immunity, and that ever present anger." They studied Kargon's face but it was obvious he was too focused to talk. "It overtakes your mind and transforms you into a fighting machine. But I have to wonder; how much do you know about fire giants?"

The question bothered Kargon and he knew it was written on his face. It was something he wanted to learn about from his father but that meant putting it aside until after the quest. Lacking knowledge meant there were obvious weaknesses that the half-giant was unaware of. Nonstop encounters didn't give him time to even read up on common knowledge about his ancestors.

"Not as much as you'd like, I see," Elmud said with a wide grin.

Such an obvious shift made clear that the dragominn had a plan and Kargon rushed forward. There was a distinct slowness to his movements. An unfamiliarity surrounded him as the ever-present warmth in his body chilled. The sensation of cold air had always felt like a soft pressure that never overpowered the half-giant. Whatever was causing this reaction was wholly different from simple low temperatures.

Breathing felt unnatural and for the first time in his life, producing flames was near impossible. Attempts at creating powerful blazes were met with meek embers. Ice crystals stuck to his lips from a cold breath. The smallest movements became difficult as layers of frost appeared across his body.

The beads of Kargon's conduit glowed fiercely but nothing came of it. Mana was pouring into the bracelet but there was no blaze. Effort was met with nothingness as the temperature continued to drop around him. Losing heat was frightening for the ever-burning half-elf. He'd lived so long without the ability to use magic. But even without it he'd always felt the presence of heat within himself. All he could do now was hope that it hadn't been completely snuffed out. Wasting mana invited the unfortunate possibility. As much as Kargon hated it, he stopped trying to ignite and instead searched for the source of his predicament.

It took multiple seconds to turn towards the edge of the crater. Over the small ridge that surrounded the arena stood demons of different shapes and sizes. Mana radiating from them made clear why they were willing to approach the once burning pit. Air froze simply from their presence. In a wide scale battle they could easily manipulate the atmosphere and strengthen their allies. Now, their powerful magic was collectively focused onto a man who'd never felt the coldness of snow.

"Let me educate you about fire giants' greatest weakness. Your kind don't react well to ice attuned magic. Brighter you burn, the worse it feels," Elmud said as they picked at one of their burns. "You, my fiery adversary, are an inferno the likes of which even Master Aeraza has not seen."

They stepped forward, slowly raising an arm before cutting cleanly across Kargon's temple. Frozen air stung against his open wound and it couldn't be instantly cauterized like usual. The pain was still manageable, much to Elmud's pleasure. There was no reason to let their nemesis off easily when the time could be spent humiliating him. Kargon didn't let that get to him—focused more on getting back in the fight. Every moment that Elmud spent talking was one where the cold became easier to bear. Ignition wasn't possible while layered in frost but movement might be for someone who was half resistant to a fire giant's weakness.

"You're struggling a lot, aren't you?" Elmud laughed as Kargon strained to move. "Even if you could move, what good are you without fire?"

Kargon's silent rage was deafening as he focused on overpowering the frost. Insults had little effect with memories of training at the forefront of his mind. Master Avant drilled into his disciple that over reliance on magic was foolish. Battles demanded strong bodies and minds which he helped refine. Harsh lessons were burned into the disciple's core.

"It matters not if your flame is snuffed. Focus on the fire within," Master Avant had said.

Ice crunched as Kargon's fingers slowly curled into a fist. It was almost inaudible over the dying embers of the pit. Elmud swiped again and Kargon mustered the ability to twist his torso ever so slightly. Understandably, it was mistaken as a result of the dragominn's attack. Blood slowly trailed along the monk's body and he was delighted by the warmth. Elmud wiped their tail and knocked Kargon to the floor—scales leaving a deep gash on his shin. The only saving grace was that he fell forward and could soften the fall. Approaching footsteps pulled Kargon's attention upward.

"It suits you to crawl," Elmud said with a smug grin.

A slow, ragged breath passed Kargon's lips as agonizing frost overwhelmed him and he scoured his brain for a way to gather heat. Every second allowed for more motion but how many more he could survive were unknown. Nothing came to mind when considering his own abilities—ones he failed to recognize for years.

Other adventurers made clear to him that there were things only he could do. Infant Avant identified Kargon's ability to follow tactics. Vofric praised the younger man's willingness to face adversity head on. Focused observation was often a complaint from Sariel but they'd be the first to admit it's usefulness. Aisha even praised his impulsivity even when Kargon himself didn't care for it.

He would've kicked himself if possible as an obvious idea dawned. Strained grunts were all Kargon managed as he rose to his knees then pushed himself to his feet. Elmud was too taken aback to attack. Seeing the uncomfortable hesitation made Kargon crack up. For every part of his fighting style the dragominn copied, they failed to capture his reactivity. The bellowing laugh caused some of the demons to falter and Kargon felt the familiar sensation of heat on his skin.

Every normal plan had already been attempted. The actions his friends complimented were in full effect and couldn't be strengthened. However, Kargon missed something. Silence overtook him whenever on the backfoot. But instigation, arguments, and false confidence were where he shined—and they only worked because he never shut up.

"You complain... about my allies," Kargon said, cracking some of the frost near his jaw. "But I couldn't be beaten... without you calling... a small army."

Without intending to, he took a relaxed stance as ice slowly lost its hold. Thankfully, there was little difference in the amount of frost visible on him. The pain was still present but Kargon was sure he could fight with a little assistance.

"I am utilizing the tools my master provided!" Elmud argued.

"He thinks you're so weak... that you can't handle the Hero's 'lowly' friend? Aeraza must think highly of me," Kargon taunted.

In order to push someone over the edge it was necessary to target something they cared for. It wasn't hard to deduce after Kargon's years of studying people. He hated to admit he and Elmud were similar—partially due to the dragominn's obsession and partially due to coincidence.

"I think Aeraza and I could get along pretty well," Kargon said with a pondering tone. "I can be monstrous and wreak havoc."

Elmud spat. "He doesn't even know your name."

"I'm sure if I introduced myself he'd offer me a position by his side. Maybe even yours?" a genuine smile passed the half-elf's lips.

"Not on your life!" Elmud roared and swung at their foe.

As the claw drew near, Kargon leaned it and allowed it to hit his shoulder. The force allowed him to kick Elmud with minimal effort, pushing the dragominn aside. They rushed back in with wild abandon. Some attacks landed cleanly while others helped Kargon fight back. Each movement honed his senses and melted away the dull haze caused by magic frost. Unfortunately, motion made the pain of never-ending ice sharper.

Elmud pulled back and scoffed. "You speak so highly about yourself yet struggle to fight me."

"You talk like you've taken me down while actively being backed up by your lackeys," Kargon replied while pushing forward.

His right fist was cocked back while his left leg kicked the dragominn off balance. Though they quickly used their tail to get steady, it was impossible to dodge the follow-up strike. Even unempowered, the punch devastated Elmud's shoulder. Multiple scales shattered and jammed into Kargon's hand, leaving it a bloody mess. Elmud retaliated with a roundhouse which was met with a mirrored strike that pushed both fighters back.

Heavy breathing and strained grunts were the only sounds coming from the pit as each brawler used all their strength to attack. Any breaks one took to rest were abused by the other. Effortful retaliation could only minimize damage. Elmud's tail kept them standing if an attack from Kargon hit. Their immediate follow-up was to throw the monk back but he had enough time to find footing while the dragominn lumbered over. If they swung first, Kargon weaved into the attack and used it to empower his own. Repeated strikes to Elmud's torso left large dents in their armor which restricted their movements further.

Elmud ripped the clasps apart, letting the chestplate drop to the ground. Solidified black tar was pooled where their heart should be. Most peculiarly was the distinct flicker of fire within. Their scales rippled as they prepared to lunge.

"You're pretty vain for a power hungry dragominn," he said.

"What?" Elmud asked quizzically.

"I mean, those muscles are just for show, right? You can fly and use magic and work alongside the demon king. What's the point of all that?" Kargon replied while gesturing at his opponent's chest.

"It is simply a result of my training during the years I waited for Master Aeraza."

"Then they're definitely for show. I mean, otherwise you would've beaten me already."

"I am simply enjoying a battle as my master would."

Kargon scoffed, "Are you though? Are you enjoying all the broken scales and blood? Isn't it humiliating that you can't even overpower me when I have no access to magic? Hells, you've been training for over sixty years! I've done half as much yet I can match you. Why is that?"

The frustration in Elmud's eyes was a familiar look to Kargon. Many elders in Neves had that annoyance plastered on their face while talking to the young half-elf. Every question he asked was bothersome. No answer was necessary yet Elmud found themself considering how they ended up in the current predicament. Hesitation betrayed them further in confirming that Kargon was far stronger than anticipated. If not for an unprepared situation like Spirefell, they were almost evenly matched.

"In a single year you grew exponentially. How?" Elmud asked.

"I had help from those allies you hate so much. But you're the same, right? I mean, you escaped with help from your master and I'm pretty sure he's the reason you've got... whatever that is." Kargon pointed at his foe's heart.

"Help was not required."

"But you would have died without it."

"I had my own plans."

"Why not use those?"

Elmud sighed. "They were shifted at the request of Master Aeraza."

"So you weakened yourself for your ally."

"I was strong enough not to fail."

"We both know that's not true." Kargon snorted. "I mean, even if my party hadn't shown up, you would have failed. Once Makani got his hands on *Lightbringer* your plan was done for."

"He would not have had the chance if not for you."

"But you still would've failed."

"You don't have a clue what you're talking about," Elmud argued.

"I'm talking about how weak you are. Aeraza is probably ashamed that you're even near him."

Elmud paused and Kargon knew he'd struck the correct nerve with optimal pressure. It wasn't a harsh tone or accusatory language. Rather, the nearly nonchalant voice of the declaration triggered the dragominn.

"What about you?" Elmud asked while approaching Kargon. "Don't you bring shame upon the Hero?"

"I know I don't," Kargon replied.

"You fell by my hand in Spirefell," Elmud spat.

"Aisha doesn't resent me for it. Can you say the same about Aeraza when I beat you in Dawncaster?"

A flash of rage passed Elmud's face. Kargon remained unphased which infuriated the dragominn further. They planted their left foot with a heavy step and leaned towards it. The stance was familiar to Kargon as an attack he'd delivered hundreds of times.

Elmud pulled their right arm back and roared. "Enough! You know nothing of my master. I'm aware of what a failure your Hero is. I'll rip her heart out myself!" A massive plume of fire burst from their maw. It completely engulfed Kargon before he could respond and the dragominn plunged their claw into him. The familiar feeling of muscle parting as blood gushed out brought a smile to Elmud's face. It only remained until they failed to pull back—their arm stuck outstretched.

Kargon's talent for riling up his opponent didn't make him immune to it. With a single comment he reverted back to an enraged beast. Only that explained such a reckless response to Elmud's attack. The full force of the claw went directly into the monk's left palm. Flexing his muscles and using the dragominn's flames to cauterize the wounds locked them together.

"Before you lay a hand on her, finish dealing with me!" Kargon growled as dark flames burned wildly around him. The next attack was as projected as one could be. But there was no way for Elmud to dodge. A powerful flaming fist planted firmly against their face the force would've separated them if not for their bound limbs.

Frantically, the dragominn looked to the edge of the pit. Both fighter's realized that Kargon hadn't overpowered the magic on his own. True to form, he relied on the allies gathered around him. A quiet praise of thanks was all he said as demonic spellcasters fell at the hands of unidentified Tetrians.

It took more effort than ever to ignite but Kargon was too furious to care. Elmud's black flames morphed into the red hue that normally wreathed the monk. Pain tingled on his fingertips and the distinct scent of burning skin tickled his nose. *Pyromanic* allowed him to examine the origin of the smell—his own skin, blistering and peeling off.

"It won't stop," Elmud said with a weak smirk. "Now your magic is a detriment to your being."

Kargon stared at the dragominn who was failing to hide the fear in their eyes. "It might be." Kargon clenched his fist again. "You, on the other hand—my magic is definitely a detriment to your being."

Fire wreathed his body, welcoming the monk like a friend. Wounds began cauterizing and pain became more bearable. Rage boiled in Kargon's mind but his tone was eerily steady. Flames eked out of his mouth as he spoke. Elmud stumbled when their arm was pushed back by their captor forcefully stepping forward with his left foot. A steady breath caused embers to waft between the fighters. Kargon pulled back his right arm. If not for the raging flames, white knuckles would be evident.

"I won't give you the option to dodge," Kargon said. "And I won't tell you to pray. Just… grit your teeth."

It was clear to Elmud what was coming and they wanted no part of it. A sharp pain drilled into their tail as it was bound to the ground. Only an arrow shaft could be seen from the projectile running deep into the limb. The last option was to break Kargon's concentration somehow. But the dragominn was incapable of thinking as they studied the furious monk. Golden and blue light infused with the firebrand's inferno.

Elmud could only manage a laugh before the impact of Kargon's fist ripped through their body. Blood and tar morphed under the pressure of intense heat. Scales shattered and tore into the reanimated organ before bursting through the other side. The force was powerful enough to tear draconic claws from a humanoid palm. Enough for a half-elf's arm to plunge through his adversary's chest, keeping it aloft. A swift pull back separated the flaming warriors but only one remained upright. Kargon let out a slow breath and dismissed his flame. Allies surrounded him on all sides and nodded in approval. He did not reciprocate. For all the ways they deferred, Kargon understood Elmud's need for recognition. It was one thing the firebrand could give his fallen nemesis.

CHAPTER SIXTY-SEVEN

Fruition

Flashes of lightning illuminated inky black waves dancing on top of the spire overlooking the war. Sounds of scraping metal rang louder with each passing moment. Attacks went off course and shifted the landscape without regard for collateral damage. Tetrian and demonic forces alike were in danger of sudden slashes bisecting them. Massive portions of Mount Iana and Delras Range were destroyed and plummeted towards the land below.

Brachynox's size only mattered in regards to speed and getting past Aisha's guard. No matter what form it took, the strength remained even. If not for the Hero's masterful maneuvers, she would have been cut apart. Magical redirection allowed for swings that were impossible for others. Prolonged lightning infusion sped up her perception but Aeraza was still fast enough to make contact.

Cuts marked every piece of the adventurer's armor. Many were stained from wounds that were haphazardly sealed. If not for diligent training, the slick liquid would have made Aisha lose her grip. Instead, she focused on paying back her opponent. As powerful as Aeraza was, he wasn't impervious to wounds. At least not ones coming from the Hero's legendary weapon. Black ichor burst from his wounds but obsidian armor made it difficult to identify where attacks landed once the fighters separated.

These were not moments of respite since spells stopped either from recovering. A single chance to study their opponent would give the upper hand. Even Aisha's modified vision only confirmed Aeraza's attack patterns which were so powerful he didn't bother altering them. But even the demon king wasn't overconfident enough to battle without a plan. The ink changed shapes and rippled across the land for hundreds of feet centering around Aeraza. With a silent command, the malleable shapes solidified before lunging towards Aisha. Balls of electricity launched from the fingertips of her right hand, creating a protective field. Any creations that got too close were swiftly cut apart.

It was even clear to Aeraza that the Hero grew stronger with each clash as she was never on the backfoot. Reactive blocks transformed into serpent-like strikes that weaved around the demon king's relentless attacks. Aisha's movements became more refined while remaining nearly imperceptible. Every passing moment brought her closer to complete elemental attunement. Shockwaves traveled through every attack. Vibrations shook the ground with each lightning strike. Thunder boomed following every collision.

Aeraza did not waver as his opponent got the upperhand. Whatever damage Aisha dealt was healed within moments of creation. It was the same trick that allowed him to survive so many battles against Kharim. Though even Aeraza had to admit that Aisha fought with a peculiar ferocity. Unlike the First Hero, this one was desperate to succeed. Few things concerned her enough to hesitate. Bodily harm meant nothing in the face of her goals. After all, the demon king had to be stopped. On the off chance the Hero died—it would only serve as inspiration.

That's what made having a powerful combat partner so fun. Fighting someone on par with his killer would allow Aeraza to grow for the first time ever. With each bout he had more chances to learn from the warrior. Their deal was fresh in his mind—upon Aisha's loss she would become the demon king's combat partner. It was likely she assumed her life wasn't forfeit for that very reason. As if she needed to remain alive to become a servant of the demon. The mere notion was foolish.

"I wonder how much you will improve as a resurrected being," Aeraza said.

Aisha kept up her guard but didn't advance towards her opponent. Rapid lightning coursing through her body made it appear as a blur even while standing still.

"You must realize that in order to win yet keep you as a pet I do not need to hold back," Aeraza explained. "I can simply end your life then revivify you like my many underlings. It would make communicating with you less of a hassle." He looked past Aisha to the battlefield below with disgust. "Once I have dealt with you, no others would dare stand in my way. None can compare to your strength, after all."

With a curious tilt of her head, Aisha spent several seconds considering her reply. Toying with an opponent didn't suit her. But it was important to state facts as she identified them. No matter how far-fetched they may seem.

"You're not improving," she said plainly. "I'm not even sure you're stronger than you were five hundred years ago. Being so powerful made you stagnant. And that attitude of yours makes you complacent."

With a wary motion, Aisha raised her right hand to her face to examine it. Then she moved it to her side while looking at *Valefor*. The purple lightning streaked off everything around her at unprecedented speeds. Not a single bit of focus was used to empower her conduit. Mana flowed and manifested as easily as Aisha breathed. "You can't win so you're stalling. Or you're hoping to figure out some way past my defense." Not an inkling of fear presented itself in her eyes.

Aeraza shook his head and groaned. The unimpressed stare reminded the Hero of her early years. "I do not need further strength to defeat you, Aisha Ilphekiir. Growth can occur at a time when I do not have other matters to tend to. While I enjoy this battle, I must admit it is a hindrance towards my goals." Aeraza nodded towards the cliff and continued. "My army is thinning at a greater rate than I would like. This is only due to your subordinates assisting a large group of insects. I think it is about time I thin the herd and guide my troops to conquering Tetria."

"That involves you overpowering me. You'll need time to kill me even at full strength. By then, I think my allies can take out the strongest of your troops. Who knows, maybe they already have?" Aisha retorted.

There wasn't a shred of doubt in her voice. While she didn't like to assume things, Aisha believed explicitly that her friends could overcome anything. It was clear that confidence alone was enough to aggravate Aeraza.

His stoic face briefly revealed obvious annoyance. "I cannot deny that I feel more confidence in your subordinates' combat abilities than my own. "However, Elmud and Veil had a capacity for violence far beyond single combat."

"I knew Veil's experiments had to be for you but didn't realize the Dawncaster attack provided anything," Aisha said.

"You are far too obvious about your need to gather information," Aeraza sighed. "Once I've humored you, I expect regret to follow. Let me begin with what you're sure of. Veil's experiments were indeed to assist me upon my return."

Black ink that had pooled out slowly receded into the demon king. Upon completely disappearing, a shockwave of energy burst forth. It wasn't strong enough to physically affect the Hero but it didn't get past her notice. Something was coming and she prepared for it without taking a step towards Aeraza. The wheels were in motion—there was no stopping that.

"There are innumerable races capable of transformation. From mighty titans to weak mimics; they are able to shift forms in incomprehensible ways," Aeraza explained. "That remains the case for many people in this realm. It is not so for those privy to Veil's research."

"He did research outside the explicit goal of hunting magic items," Aisha said candidly.

"Those lacking your wisdom could figure that out. Yes, centuries were spent solving what allowed creatures to transform freely. Magic and nature bound together in ways that were inexplicable. While I am not one to indulge in brutish practices, I cannot deny their results. Hundreds of thousands of lives were sacrificed and eventually the ability to introduce transformation to any race's capabilities was no longer a dream."

Loud grinding echoed from the demon king's castle as the ground buckled beneath it. Half the spire Aisha and Aeraza fought atop crumbled as the fortress plummeted to the ground. Hundreds of Tetrians and demons perished under the building. Metallic clanging reverberated behind the walls as hidden gears activated. Familiar squelches like the sound of uncovered muscles slowly grew in volume and frequency. The demon king stepped to the side so his fortress was directly behind him. He wouldn't allow the Hero to ignore what was coming.

Past the condescending figure was the familiar sight of black ink. An unprecedented volume poured out of the bending joints of the castle. Purple, bloody muscle and viscera expanded under the stone walls, increasing the building's size. Four bulging trunks raised the massive structure higher. Each sprouted upwards from the base before bending down halfway like those of an arthropod. The ends were flat like an elephant's feet but a single appendage eclipsed multiple of the large animal in size. Giant spires on two sides of the central pillar erupted into muscular arms ending at meaty hands with three towering fingers. What were once walls were now armor plating on the grotesque beast.

A bellowing roar burst from the final intact piece of the stronghold. The central spire shattered for a featureless head to erupt from. Jagged teeth lined the giant maw that wrapped almost completely around the creature's face. All the remaining violet skin opened wide to reveal hundreds of massive insectoid eyes. Each one moved individually as they flitted about in search of prey.

It took everything for Aisha not to freeze at the sight of the gargantuan beast. The lightning and vibrations around her masked fearful shaking. With every fiber, she focused on calming her nerves. The fight wasn't over and Aeraza's expression made clear that he wasn't finished yet.

"Atlas is quite magnificent, isn't he? Veil allowed the mixture of organic and mechanical beings," Aeraza explained. "Such a pained form excuses its habit of running rampant. However, Elmud helped control that infuriating problem. You are familiar with the *Lightbringer*. Do you recall its use in Dawncaster?"

"The light shield. It blocked magic but didn't do much against physical entities," Aisha replied as her nerves slowly calmed.

"Full marks. That shield naturally encompasses the wielder. With the use of certain tools, it can be amplified. What if the magic that is modified is not from an Artifact but from one's self?" Aeraza asked and held up his gauntlet to reveal engravings lined with silver. Ink endlessly flowed along the embellishments and over the demon king's body. Similar, thicker lines squirmed over the entirety of Atlas as his frantic motions slowed. Each eye turned in a wave—all focusing on the minuscule being of lightning.

"My growth in strength needn't be a surprise to you or myself. Well-laid plans always come to fruition." Aeraza flourished his sword nonchalantly. "This will eradicate your lands. It will show the vast difference in your strongest warriors and my most mindless of servants. Every waking moment left for Tetria will be drowned in horror—especially once I wield the Ring of Dominion."

Saliva dripped from the giant's mouth as his hunger for battle grew. Quivering muscles wriggled under tight skin when Atlas finally moved. Hundreds of feet were crossed in one step for it to stand directly next to the cliff. As high as the landmass was, the monster's torso rose above it. It inhaled slowly in unison with Aeraza.

"You take great pride in that speed. Why wouldn't you?" he asked while flexing his fingers to test control of the demon. "It allows for weaving through any attack; including those made by *Brachynox's* true form. However, those attacks are on a much smaller scale than Atlas. How will you defend yourself from it?"

Ink flowed rapidly around his unmoving body. Atlas's muscles bulged as it reared back a giant right fist. The swing traveled much faster than a creature of such size should be capable of. Pressure equivalent to a falling meteor accompanied the incoming strike. Aisha stared at the monster, completely frozen. There had to be a way to dodge the strike. Obviously redirecting it wouldn't be possible. The difference in size would require her to fight with a different style. Slow, heavily empowered strikes could possibly wound the behemoth. There was even a chance to cut through the entire arm—granted it would take more than one attack.

Even with her faster mental processing, there wasn't enough time to think of a complete plan. Not to mention that Aeraza wouldn't allow Aisha to respond without interference. Trying to defeat either of them while the other was present was simply impossible. The massive appendage grew ever closer but Aisha found herself unable to act. All she could do was stare as it slowly traveled closer.

Pressure from Atlas's attack was overwhelming but Aisha suddenly felt calm. While the arm was still a ways away, she felt a wave of heat on her back. There was no way to describe the sensation as anything except comforting—though the blaze was surely full of fury. One that steeled Aisha's eyes as she turned her focus back to

Aeraza.

It was clear that her next action would trigger a response. There was too little time to consider how the demon king might react. But the Hero didn't work on assumptions. With unabashed confidence she stared at Aeraza—no hint of fear in her eyes even under Atlas's threat.

Finally, the demon king's facade cracked completely and twisted into boiling anger. There wasn't a hint of hesitation on Aisha's face. Atlas was nowhere on her mind. The giant wasn't her problem to deal with.

CHAPTER SIXTY-EIGHT

Burnout

Every warrior, regardless of allegiance, paused when the castle fell. The ground shook violently and upon seeing the grotesque transformation, many opted to turn away. Some wished with all their being they were imagining it while others knew they had no chance against whatever the structure turned into. Winning the battle against the enemy was crucial if they hoped to assist with the massive homunculus.

Such ideas weren't welcome in the mind of Kargon Meliamne. Since defeating Elmud, the monk had focused on killing any demon within reach. Every movement resulted in a monster's death. Cauterized wounds burned painfully with each ignition. The mutated flames were slowly turning back to normal but some aftereffects overstayed their welcome. For every moment the half-elf was ablaze, more skin peeled and bubbled on his right arm. Avoidance caused him to rely on his left side.

That was until he saw the demonic castle's panels shift. It was a mere second before the first grinding stones but he couldn't ignore the squirming black ink. That was enough for him to break into a sprint towards the rocky spire at the center of Tetria. Flaming explosions from his feet sent him sailing over opponents. Instead of aiming to kill, he focused on traversing the battlefield. Attacks levied against him were tools to cross over larger spaces. However, the enemy grew smarter with each of his attacks. They purposely dispersed to force

Kargon to push farther. At first it was a blessing as he soared over hundreds of monsters. But then attacks struck him upon landing and hindered him from advancing.

Kargon focused on protecting himself and killed any demons that got close. Those surrounding him moved slowly with coordinated steps—attacking with simultaneous efforts. The monk's focus was split the moment he could see the distant spire. Legs just came out of the castle base and lifted it up. Aisha might be strong enough to handle it alone but not while also fighting Aeraza. There wasn't a doubt in Kargon's mind that he could distract the behemoth. How he'd do it was still anyone's idea but the least he could do was try.

The onslaught of attacks pounding on him needed to be stopped. Endless attacks meant some were bound to get through. Especially since the defense of a complete ignition was unwise as the battle was nowhere near complete. Frustration and anger clouded Kargon's mind as weaklings were able to land easily avoidable hits. Unhealable bruises spread across his body from repeated strikes. Adrenaline kept him going but with no end in sight it felt daunting. Nevertheless, he wouldn't succumb to doubts. All he had to do was hold out until an opening presented itself.

It came in the form of a curmudgeon owlminn crashing down on top of a demon. Silver astral spirits rained from the sky and mimicked their creator. Half a dozen monsters were cut apart by talons or smashed by the end of a staff. Master Avant himself landed directly next to his student and blasted away three nearby enemies with an astral fist.

"I've found him!" he cawed loud enough to be heard over the commotion of battle then turned to his disciple. "Rest for a moment and gather your strength."

"I need to stop that thing," Kargon replied.

"We are well aware of what your goal is. Allow us to carve a path."

Master Avant seemed almost relaxed as he swatted away his foes. More astral spirits emerged with each strike and attacked other monsters. It was more effective than Kargon alone but not enough to clear the way. But the master wasn't one to lie; nor did he ever refer to his spirits as "we."

Monsters behind them were flung skyward before a beam of moonlight pierced them. Corpses crashed to the ground around charging Tetrian soldiers guided by Makani. Bloody spikes and waves tore through enemies that targeted the small contingent. Crimson claws protruded from Albert's hand and summoned forth magic once controlled by Rusty. Deaths were a given during war but the unknown loss of a friend weighed on Kargon. It made it more crucial that he reach Aisha before she got overwhelmed.

It took a few seconds for Kargon to mentally map a path before he rushed past his master. The elder sighed and took the sky to keep an eye on his student. Only seconds passed before his aerial view was needed. Demons made way for larger allies who eclipsed the fiery monk even while airborne. They hindered him with no effort but couldn't attack thanks to a flood of shadows that surrounded Kargon. Lumbering movements turned completely rigid as the mist crawled upwards. Black quills appeared for split seconds before vanishing just as quickly. Blood and viscera exploded forth as targets fell to the ground. Some could still move but the halfling had already distanced herself further into the crowd. Kargon stepped forward to kill the dying monsters but was stopped by Spike's sharpened blades. Swiftly weaving through the crumbled demons sliced away their last bit of life. The large hedgehog made a point of ending one monster before dashing to the next. As the smoke moved further forward, a large quill planted in the ground presented itself—eclipsing Freckle in size.

"Your master says those should be a good starting point," she said from within the magical fog.

Kargon looked between the thin platform and his hovering master who tilted his head towards the slim rods. Raised platforms would let him launch over the larger monsters. It was all the master could think of on short notice to help his disciple. One who happily took the gift and pressed forward.

The spire remained distant and quills quickly ran dry due to Kargon's speed. Thankfully, monsters couldn't mess up his path again since silver projections kept them at bay. Kargon couldn't help but question why his master didn't drop to the battle and help. But that didn't matter as much as figuring out how to get to the top of the spire. A launch from Vofric's war-hammer might work but he wasn't around. Not to mention, he'd be left completely vulnerable afterward. Such a risk wasn't worth an easy ascent. If all else failed, Kargon would climb the rock face. Enough momentum would make it possible to get halfway up before needing to do the hard work.

High pitched whistling pulled Kargon from his reverie. Crashing down in front of him was a being clad in unrecognizable mahogany armor. A rain of arrows followed, piercing through over a dozen surrounding monsters. Any that missed ricocheted off the ground and collided with further enemies. Familiar green scales on the left half of the bow-wielding warrior's body brought a smile to Kargon's face. With a slight turn, Sariel nodded at something behind their fiery friend.

Intense pressure from an incoming creature would send chills down the spine of anyone unfamiliar with it. Instead, Kargon's smile grew wider as an owlbear mounted dwarf rushed past him. An ear-piercing roar came from deep within Avant. Gravity surged and sent any creature deemed an enemy far away from the group. Once the area was clear, Vofric dismounted and ran to Kargon. A golden glowing palm struck Kargon's chest—washing away pain and exhaustion. As much as it was appreciated, he had to stop the paladin from using his remaining mana. Golden light couldn't hide how tired Vofric was from the lengthy battle.

"Just heal some of my internal injuries," Kargon insisted. "You need your energy."

"You must get to Aisha. The healthier you are, the better." Vofric's eyes were trained on the monk's burned right arm. Skin up to his wrist was peeled away and muscle was beginning to char. Healing could only do so much given the power of Kargon's magic. Vofric sighed softly as he rebuilt the monk's body. "I sense a diminishing curse."

"A parting gift from Elmud," Kargon replied.

"I can slow the burns but if you are not careful, you will lose your right arm."

"If I hold back, I'll lose Aisha."

The conviction in Kargon's voice normally impressed Vofric but now it sent a chill down his spine. Unfortunately, it wasn't possible to argue so he focused on healing what he could without expending the last of his mana.

"Sariel, I like the new look," Kargon said casually.

The dragon scoffed. "You needn't compliment me to ask a favor. And no, I do not see a clear path ahead."

"Likewise," Master Avant said, landing near the group.

Avant barked something and tilted his head. It took a moment of consideration before Sariel translated. "He believes it may be possible to spread out the enemy so you can press forward. However, there is no need."

"I'm not going to let Aisha face that thing alone!" Kargon yelled while pointing at the transforming demon. By now it had revealed muscular arms and the central tower was fiercely shaking.

"Obviously, Kargon. Give me a moment," Sariel said and stepped away. They knelt down and studied something in the dirt.

"We must remain here to assist the Tetrian troops," Vofric explained. "But we'd be damned to let you press forward without us by your side."

Kargon patted the dwarf thankfully. "I'm still not sure how to stop that thing."

Avant trilled and nudged his master. The monk knelt down to meet his familiar's gaze. Chirps and soft coos ill-fit the battlefield but their message was surprisingly clear to the panicking firebrand.

"Doing what feels right seems like solid advice but I don't know how much a punch will help," Kargon said as he rose to his feet and tightened his arm wraps. "Doesn't mean I won't try it." Approaching Sariel, he asked, "Find what you were looking for?"

They grunted and gestured for him to stay back. Lightly planting their claw on the ground, they summoned roots that rapidly grew towards the sky. Emerald energy guided them towards the spire. The massive bridge didn't reach the cliff face but easily crossed the remaining battlefield. It reminded Kargon of fleeing Balur.

"The climb looks to be unavoidable," Sariel groaned.

"This'll help plenty," Kargon said and stepped onto the bent trunk.

Sariel stepped back to join Vofric and Avant as they looked towards the departing monk.

"Hold on, Kargon," Master Avant barked, stepping past the party and towards his student. "It's rude to ignore allies who came to send you off. I didn't follow you simply because your friends required a beacon."

Kargon blushed, "Sorry. I—"

"I am aware of what is on your mind. Lest we forget you are the pupil." The master took a deep breath and continued. "My prized pupil. Take this with you." He shoved the bo staff in his grip at Kargon.

The younger monk hesitated. "I'm not very good with weapons. Are you sure?"

Master Avant flicked his wrist, shrinking the weapon to fit in his palm. He stepped closer to Kargon and tugged at the sash on the younger man's hip. A small loop in the knot was loosened to fit the rod before being pulled taut again.

"It will amplify your astral magic. I am not foolish enough to expect your battle tactics to change," the master said.

"But don't you need this? How are you going to keep fighting?" Kargon protested.

Master Avant pulled a small rod from his hip and flipped it like a coin. In mid air, it grew into a bo staff which landed back in his hand. "Do you take me for a fool who would leave himself unarmed?" he asked with a smirk.

Kargon would've defended himself if not for the earth shattering screech erupting from the homunculus as it finished transforming. All its flitting eyes searched for a target. Everyone on the battlefield heard the scream—Kargon heard the following one. A collective shout that pushed him to move.

"Go!"

Kargon sprinted at a speed he'd never produced in his lifetime. It might not match Aisha but few could hope to catch the monk. Burning footprints marked the path as he dashed across. The fury of the small infernos set pieces of the path ablaze. Part of Kargon felt guilty for destroying his friend's gift. But Sariel wouldn't care as long as he reached their leader. Blue light glowed in Kargon's eyes as he narrowed his focus. Gold energy trailed off him with every empowered step.

It wouldn't be long until he reached the spire and needed to ascend. There was literally no turning back with the pyre chasing him. But instead of focusing on the wall, his eyes were focused on the lumbering monster. Hundreds of eyes were bearing down on the Hero Kargon loved. Killing intent was a norm in their lives but the otherworldly hunger of the giant was daunting. The only way to turn that attention to him was a display of power. Such an idea felt foolish and impossible.

But Aisha could do the impossible. She was facing Aeraza and based on her stance, she was holding her own. This behemoth was the demon king's attempt at showing a difference in followers. Such a thought infuriated Kargon beyond reasoning. No one had the right to insult Aisha's beliefs. One she was so confident in that she left her allies in charge of leading the charge into a war. That kind of trust couldn't be disproven, not even by a giant.

The word stuck in Kargon's mind as the end of the vines drew close. There was technically more than one giant on the battlefield—less than one more to be exact. But Kargon wielded their power just as well. Rage boiled in his blood since childhood. But that was all he knew of the race. What mattered more than being the son of a fire giant and elf was being the son of Zigon and Velana. They sacrificed everything for love. It wouldn't do for their son to do any less.

A sensation of pressure called from the miniature staff Master Avant provided. Twinges of pain trickled up Kargon's arm but a golden glow kept them at bay. It wasn't going to stop the accursed flames from Elmud but they would be slowed. Faint embers trailed off the firebrand's entire body; growing with each step. He clenched his fists and visualized a far greater inferno than Master Avant had never seen.

With a mighty leap, Kargon escaped the burning bridge—magnificent flames wreathing his body. Expansion was almost instant but how far the limbs went was unbelievable. Legs that towered into the sky stood over demons that once looked down on the monk. Hitting the ground sent a flaming shockwave across the field. Arms made of fire stretched for hundreds of feet. Anything nearby felt the temperature rise as the form settled. Atop a blazing torso rested an infernal head with a flaming eye wrap that resembled the warrior within. Floating in place of a brain was Kargon with glowing eyes that gathered vision from the form he manifested. The fire licking the remnants of the bridge were sucked into the flaming astral giant and created a sash similar to the one his master provided.

If any part of the form surprised Kargon, he hid it well. The monk didn't question why he could stand within his flames. There was no worry as the flesh on his right arm bubbled once again. The titan across the spire sent a massive fist slowly towards Aisha. Kargon put out his left hand and blocked the strike. Both giants turned to make eye contact. One remained emotionless, a husk to be controlled. The other, burned bright with rage.

CHAPTER SIXTY-NINE

The Hero and Right Hand

"It must sting to see your doomsday monster get stopped by someone you deem weak," Aisha taunted.

Kargon's flaming giant form delivered a powerful punch to Atlas's face. The sight of a half-elf manifesting such a powerful ability was unprecedented. For it to be on par with the demon king's creation was beyond belief. Such an obvious opponent made it impossible for Atlas to follow his master's orders. The Hero remained in the beast's sight but was difficult to attack with the inferno protecting her. Flames of such caliber needed to be snuffed before engaging anyone else. Kargon capitalized on Atlas's distracted mind with two quick jabs and a straight.

Embers showered the smaller beings but Aisha felt no need to avoid it. Sparks of lightning caught the falling flames in a loving caress. Similarly, Aeraza's thin black tendrils swatted away the cinders.

The ground shook with each impact between the goliaths. However, only Atlas retained visible damage from each strike. Attacks against Kargon's astral form manifested as bruises on his real body. Any problems it might be causing for the monk were completely ignored. Instead, he continued to throw haymaker after haymaker in hopes of breaking the shell around his opponent.

There was no more chatter from the demon king. Any words would be inevitably drowned out by the thundering bludgeons overhead. Aisha didn't hesitate while trying to think of a plan with unknown variables. Nothing could pull her attention from Aeraza even if he hoped it would. Kargon's presence made it feel like any situation would be handled regardless of the unforeseen.

Lightning danced along *Valefor* as Aisha swung it to her left. Anyone else in such a stance would be defenseless but her speed bypassed such a flaw. One step forward balanced her—the next made her vanish into a sprint. Only Aeraza could keep track of the speedster and blocked the incoming attack. As the swords clashed, Aisha redirected her blade for a follow up. Rapid attacks struck the demon king from every angle. It was as though the adventurer was dancing around her adversary without a care. Openings that she couldn't see before became clear. It especially helped that the earth shaking fight overhead hindered Aeraza.

It wasn't that the demon king couldn't keep his footing. Rather, he wasn't expecting Atlas's arms to repeatedly land nearby. The massive slabs blocked Aeraza's movements while simultaneously improving Aisha's due to Kargon's input. Learning to fight in a new form was easier for him than for Atlas. Every clash resulted in one of its arms planted firmly on the cliff. Deep divots formed in the land and forced the smaller beings aside. Aeraza tracked Aisha but wasn't prepared for her nimble maneuvers. Leaping off the large arm, she spun, kicked the demon king's head, landed into a crouch and slashed through the armor on his legs.

Aeraza groaned and lifted his sword high over his head. With a fierce chop it cut into the ground. Aisha dodged it without issue. Rushing forward, Aeraza grabbed her by the neck. Even while choking for air, the Hero didn't falter. A heavy kick planted against her opponent's chest as she tried to separate from him.

Before it could connect, Aeraza slammed the warrior headfirst into the ground. Blood burst from a gash on Aisha's head as the monster pulled her back up. When she swung *Valefor,* Aeraza caught it and glared at the sword. The moment his eyes turned from Aisha, she screamed. Lightning erupted from her mouth and bore into Aeraza's face before exploding—forcing him to release the adventurer. But blindness didn't stop him from swinging *Brachynox* which hit Aisha's right arm and forced her back. Lightning could only seal edges of the cut as blood poured out but she didn't waver.

"Well-laid plans might come to fruition but that doesn't mean they can't be messed with," she said as blood trickled from her lip.

"Contingencies exist for this very reason," Aeraza growled.

"You have a contingency for a flaming giant? Because let me tell you, even I didn't know Kargon could do that."

"I'll simply take him under my control with the Ring of Dominion."

It was infuriating to see a slight upward curl to Aeraza's lips as he looked over Kargon's astral form. Aisha would be damned if the demon king had the chance to engage with anyone else. This spire would be his grave.

Sparks flew as their blades collided once again. They were too fast to see but it didn't matter as Kargon's eyes never left Atlas. The lumbering monster wasn't much for hand to hand combat but its many eyes blasted a random assortment of spells. Only a handful affected the flaming behemoth. Over time, Atlas deduced which ones were effective and solely used those. Each portion of the magical form that was torn away quickly recovered at the expense of mana and more burns across Kargon's right arm. Worse yet were the few eyes looking at the monk's real body. Blasts of ice pierced through the flaming shield—frozen beams cutting against his skin. The sharp decline in temperature caused a forceful reaction that reopened old wounds. Nevertheless, Kargon didn't falter. Blood poured from massive burns across Atlas's body. Shattered plates were jammed into its muscles and further hindered its movement.

Suddenly, Atlas stood straight and all its eyes looked at the astral giant's chest. Hesitantly, Kargon looked down, realizing that his magical form was the only thing protecting other Tetrians from the titanic demon. Familiar high pitched humming radiated in unison from hundreds of deep black eyes. Based on the different spells that had already been used it was hard to discern what the sound entailed. Mana collected near Atlas's many eyes as small beams fired from them and collided with the fire giant's torso. They dispersed upon collision but got more intense with every passing second.

Kargon lunged forward and planted his astral right hand on the monster's head. Lasers fired moments before contact. The fiery giant blocked most of the magical beams and Kargon screamed in pain. He was too slow to block the next attack—a single massive laser. It easily destroyed a portion of the fiery arm and collided with the battlefield below. The beam was persistent and Kargon's only choice was to force the monster's head to look elsewhere. It took all his effort but to push it back as the magical attack ripped through his arm. The dark laser cut across the crowd below; killing over one hundred Tetrian soldiers in an instant.

For a short moment, the monk hesitated. Eviscerated corpses littered the ground marked by the Atlas's beam. Fear was evident in the eyes of survivors below. Yet they grit their teeth and carried on. Tears didn't flow from sorrowful faces. Fierce attacks were all they could use to release their anger. Rage was all that kept them sane as the blood of allies poured over them.

Kargon swore at himself for forgetting what he was here for. The astral giant bellowed and fire erupted from its maw. A surge of flames regenerated his left astral arm moments before it grabbed Atlas's face and slammed it down against the spire, crumbling down to the battlefield. Balled fists rose up and pounded against the monster's head and body. Viscous purple blood mixed with thick black ink as they burst from wounds and pooled on the land. Eyes popped like bubbles under the intense heat and pressure. Flames erupted outward each time a fist crushed parts of the beast. Atlas flailed its arms to beat the overpowering astral being. Each wild impact shook Kargon's head. Bruises quickly formed all over his body but that wasn't enough to stop him. Even Aeraza was stunned at the furious display from the firebrand.

"What an unbecoming display," he said plainly while examining the dark pool of splashing across the spire and below.

"It's what's needed to protect everyone. You wouldn't understand," Aisha replied, noticing lightning dancing on the rippling blood.

"It's a waste of strength."

"It's more strength than you could muster."

Those words struck a chord in Aeraza that Aisha hadn't expected. Another shift of *Brachynox* returned it back to greatsword form. Heavy footsteps carried the demon king forward. They were so slow and deliberate that it felt like he was asking Aisha to retaliate. It was obviously a setup. But not reacting meant taking the brunt of his attack. Playing into the trap was awful but the best option.

The collision of swords sent both of them backwards. Aeraza allowed the momentum to carry his weapon high over his head. At its peak, he dropped it. A forceful step forward pushed the adventurer back and blinded her to the next transformation. There was no chance to figure out its form as she had to block one powerful punch and dodge another. Both thick arms easily blinded Aisha and allowed the demon king to strike.

Brachynox had taken the form of a dagger and fallen into Aeraza's waiting tail. It weaved around his shoulder and blade stabbed directly into the Hero's prosthetic eye before slashing downward along her scar. Almost instantly, the lightning around her vanished. There were no minute vibrations blurring her movements. The air escaped Aisha as pain surged through her eye.

Aeraza pushed the adventurer back while retrieving his dagger and roared. "You dare lecture me about strength?! You waste what little you have on weaklings!" His weapon transformed to its original form. "Kharim was more skilled than you without elemental attunement! Both magic and martial prowess were his to command! You pale in comparison to the point that you can't even face me alone!" He pointed the sword at Aisha's bleeding eye socket where the broken prosthetic remained dormant. "You rely on the weapon of a dead man without knowing its true power! You require a crutch just to imitate his strength!"

Silence invited Aeraza to keep speaking but it seemed he'd run out of words. There wasn't an inkling of fear as Aisha stood in the presence of the beast baring its fangs at her. Before he could take another step, thunder boomed overhead.

Clouds gathered as Aisha raised her sword forward to match Aeraza. Heavy thunderclaps pounded in unison with Kargon's beating of Atlas. Static in the air raised Aisha's hair as her temper flared. Finally, a bolt of lightning streaked down and collided with her blade. Silver light was nowhere to be seen as violet bursts of electricity completely encompassed the Hero and her weapon.

"I should thank you, Aeraza," Aisha said with light flashing in her single working eye. "Up until now, I wasn't fighting on Kharim's scale; not really. But facing you—here—that's something he could do. Fighting you on even footing allowed him to master *Valefor*. I should've realized I could do the same." She shook her head and smirked. "I'm the chosen one, after all."

CHAPTER SEVENTY

Ring Out

Purple lightning on par with Void Storms signaled the final shift of what would be known as Tetria's Defense. Tetrians and demons alike feared the battle overhead. Not only was a giant furiously pounding another to death but the very skies were shaking with each clash between the Hero and demon king. The frequency of metallic clanging rose with every passing moment. Lightning fast cuts surrounded Aeraza before he could react. Some landed while others were blocked by a constantly shifting *Brachynox*.

"You truly are a worthy opponent, Aisha Ilphekiir. Though your growth only puts you on par with Kharim. I do not foresee my defeat," he said.

Aisha kicked off his chest and made space before responding. "He was enough to defeat you. And with how obsessed you are, I have a feeling you haven't grown very much past the person who lost five centuries ago."

"That sharp wit of yours is definitely different from his. All he spoke of were ideologies and the good of the world."

"He understood his duty better than someone forced into it," Aisha replied through grit teeth. "That choice led to him allowing you to curse our world. I have the weight of that curse on my shoulders. It won't happen again."

"You'll do much worse than letting me return to this realm. Have you forgotten that only I know where both halves of the Ring of

Dominion are?"

Aisha tried to examine her opponent but he rushed forward. Their weapons clashed as the dance started anew. Both of them could only see immediately in front of them. They, however, were not the only ones on that spire. Blood evaporated off the thick arm of the astral giant as Atlas breathed his last. Rage of unprecedented caliber had overtaken Kargon's mind upon seeing so many comrades die in an instant. Guts dripped off fiery fists as they pulled away from shattered stone.

Kargon rose to his feet to watch for an opening in the clash between legends. Aisha and Aeraza both moved too quickly to see when attacking. But moments of conversation made them visible. Every part of Aeraza looked out of place in this realm. Horned beings were commonplace yet his looked like they didn't belong to him. They violently tore through his forehead before curling to his back. Hair spiraled around each and jewels were strung along them like the walls of Edthecridalyrth's cave. It looked so gaudy and yet Kargon couldn't take his eyes off one of the rings.

The astral face didn't improve Kargon's vision but the shining accessory looked peculiar. It shouldn't have fit over the horns but they had been shaved down to accommodate it. Looking closer revealed that the spots where ornaments were attached were wounded. It could have been because of Aisha but these weren't battle scars. They appeared to be piercings forced onto the cranial appendages with no time to heal. Looking between the many rings and chains pulled Kargon back to the shining piece. He was sure it was incomplete—like half of it was missing.

As the warriors reengaged, they vanished but Kargon kept his eyes peeled. The more he looked at the ring the more sure he became. Now it was only a matter of retrieving it. The astral form was too slow to grab such a small item. Even if he tried, Aeraza would likely cut the giant apart. The best option was to steal the ring up close. Though their natural difference in height would make that a challenge. But with Aisha pulling the demon king's attention it might be possible to sneak the ring away.

The bigger issue was Kargon's astral creation. As powerful and useful as it was, there was no precise way to battle small foes. He wasn't even sure how he was completely still while floating inside.

With the fierce movements of the giant, he should be moving too. Thankfully, Aeraza wasn't focused on the astral being towering above him. Splitting his attention wasn't possible if he wanted to defend against Aisha. That was the only reason Kargon attempted to learn about his form. Meditation was the best option but it had to be fast.

Flaming fingers curled and he felt the sensation on an unmoving hand. Demons below struck his giant legs which, proportionally, tickled his real ones. The head of the giant was like a gelatinous cube and Kargon needed only will his body to move. It couldn't pass the neck but every part of the head was possible. It dawned on the monk that his flames always had the capacity to change their density. The astral giant was created from unleashing all the mana he had. There was no reason to assume it operated any differently.

Two giant arms planted on the diminished spire as Kargon leaned forward. Another clash ended and he watched Aeraza shift in place. This time Aisha engaged first. The giant reared its head back, carrying Kargon with it. Eventually, the fighters separated but no movement occurred from the flaming behemoth. The sword wielders clashed many times while the burning monk waited in his awkward stance. Finally, he saw exactly what he was waiting for.

Aeraza's lip moved ever so slightly. Most people would assume it was to breathe but Kargon knew words were coming. The giant violently rocked its head forward like a headbutt. At the instant it had the most speed, all density vanished and launched its creator through its forehead.

Sharp senses caused Aeraza to look up. The plummeting firebrand was too slow to land a hit on the demon king's torso. It would be a foolish attempt if that was Kargon's goal. As his target stepped forward to dodge, Kargon struck the horns. Pain surged through his right fist and he finally saw the decrepit, charred black husk where his muscular arm once was. Vofric's warning rang in his mind as he ignited once again and shattered the end of Aeraza's horn. With a well timed kick, Kargon never landed, instead dodging an incoming strike and retaliating with a left-handed punch.

The display did little to amuse the demon king and he slammed Kargon's face into the dirt. Claws dug into the monk's head then lifted him from the ground. Arm outstretched, Aeraza held the interloper at eye level then stared daggers at Aisha. Kargon pushed through the pain to turn towards his counterpart. A warrior looked back without betraying a hint of emotion to her opponent.

Kargon saw a twinkle in the fierce swordswoman's eye. Questions were racing through Aisha's head as to why her best friend would interfere in such a way. Even with all the doubts in her mind, not once did she question Kargon's faith in her abilities.

"You shattered my horn even upon missing an attack," Aeraza said. "I commend you."

"Th...anks!" Kargon choked out. Blood dripped from his forehead into his eyes.

"That does not mean I forgive this intrusion. I despise interruptions.

Kargon grinned widely. "You're really... going... to hate this!"

Mustering every ounce of strength left, he flung his decrepit arm up. Uncurling the blackened fist was excruciating. Chunks of flesh peeled off and showered the ground like burnt wood. Amongst the flying blood and gore was the shining half of the Ring of Dominion which Aisha caught out of the air with her free right hand. Aeraza turned sharply to feel his horn and it became clear what the monk had done. With a fierce swing, he threw Kargon across the spire. The sound of bones cracking rang in the air as he collided with a fallen piece of Atlas's armor. It was close enough for Kargon to keep watch on the battle through bleary eyes and a fading consciousness.

Aisha furiously tore her own half of the ring off her neck. Without hesitation she fused both pieces together and raised it up. Eyes of two wounded warriors met through the small circle.

"It would be foolish to use it against me," Aeraza said. "Don't be rash as your kind are wont to be."

With a smooth motion, Aisha moved the ring into her palm and squeezed it. "I won't deny that my kind are rash. One of them let you talk until you were able to cast a curse. According to my mentors, you need to be approaching death for that to work," Aisha replied confidently. "But it's not just Kharim. Barbatos left tools of mass chaos around as a contingency plan. All they did was lock them in magic boxes as if their enemies couldn't break in."

"You are wise beyond measure, Aisha Ilphekiir. Come, let us continue this battle."

"Hold on," Aisha interjected. "I didn't deny that I was rash. If this ring exists, you will use it. It doesn't matter if I win or lose. Tetria... All of Vethyea will be unrecognizable the moment you get your hands on it."

Aeraza's eyes widened. "You can't mean—"

"I said you're never coming back. I mean to end you and any hopes of you returning, right here."

Aisha threw the ring only inches in front of her. The world around Aeraza slowed to a crawl as his tail propelled him forward. Overshooting was fine as long as the ring was in his possession. It was so close to his fingers.

Then the lightning struck.

Faster than even the mental processing of a demon lord. *Valefor* cut down on the ring with enough force to shatter the metal. A clean split could have been possible but invited too many unknowns. The Hero intended to end any hopes of using the Ring of Dominion ever again.

"You fool!" Aeraza roared and swung his sword at a clear opening. The force tore apart the nearby landscape. It wasn't the strength he normally used. But to Aisha it represented a last resort.

Deliberate steps quickly brought her closer to *Brachynox*. Measured focus let her see its shifting form before the change was complete. Thunder clapped as she brought her blade into the mess of malleable metal. Violent shattering rang out across the battlefield at an unprecedented volume. It sounded unlike anything the thousands of warriors—allies and enemies both—had ever heard. The two legendary blades didn't clash; one of them weaved into the magical body of the other. Pieces of *Brachynox* blasted away. Before Aeraza had the chance to figure out what happened, Aisha struck again. Not once, or twice but an onslaught equal to a lightning storm. The final attack launched the demon king backwards. All that remained in his hand was a tattered hilt with flecks of black steel.

CHAPTER SEVENTY-ONE

As Legend Foretold

No one except for Kargon, Aisha, and Aeraza saw *Brachynox* shatter yet every demon on the battlefield froze momentarily. It wasn't more than a second—moments every warrior of Tetria would remember well. Blades tasted victory. Hearts pounded with hope as monsters fell. The shifted tide would be heard with roars that hungered to end Tetria's Defense. It wasn't lost on Aisha as she slowly stepped towards Aeraza, staring in shock. Confidence washed away as the Nevesi Hero marched forward.

There were no condescending remarks or witty replies between the fighters. A five hundred year old mask of serenity was torn away. The demon king scrambled for a way to fight back. Broken weaponry would do no good and his legendary sword was no better than a branch. It was tossed aside as the monster leveraged his size. Towering a few heads over Aisha wasn't enough to scare her. Armored claws did little when used by an untrained fighter.

No mercy existed in Aisha as the weak demon attempted to retaliate. It was so pathetic that she didn't bother to use her lightning speed. Their difference in strength needed to be ingrained in Aeraza— even if only for the last minute of his life. A simple side step dodged the claws before they were met with a blade. *Valefor* cleanly cut through the limbs and blood burst from the wounds. With a slow turn, the demon tried to slam his tail into the Hero. Without dodging, she lopped the appendage off.

"You will never be enough!" Aeraza screeched as Aisha bisected his left arm. "There are unknowable threats in this realm because of your kind's intermingling!"

Slashed tendons forced him to his knees. The thick pool of ink and blood splashed across Aisha's grim face while her enemy flailed wildly. Emotion was unnoticeable in her eyes. Others would believe it was a Hero's drive to save the world. Kargon knew it was the will to finally end the curse hoisted on her shoulders.

Aeraza roared. "I will—"

"Enough!" Aisha screamed and sliced across the demon's mouth.

Bones cracked under *Valefor's* powerful strikes. White specks sprayed the ground as Aeraza's jaw was torn from his head. The fleshy tongue that carried multiple lifetimes of confidence and insults flopped to the floor. Whines were all the demon king could muster while kneeling in his pile of failure. Even on the precipice of victory, there was no joy in Aisha's face. Violence of this degree wasn't her preference but it sent a clear message to Aeraza. To anyone who might dare attack her realm—there was no mercy here.

Aisha held her sword next to the demon's neck and said, "I told you how this would end."

Aeraza did not shut his eyes. A brief moment of stoicism was all he managed when an untraceable strike rended his head from his body. The pool of blood had barely rippled before the demon king's body began to disintegrate. It wasn't like when Elmud disappeared in Dawncaster. There were no flakes carried on the wind. The presence of his spirit couldn't be felt. Rather, every single part of him burned away into nothingness.

It didn't take long for other demons to follow suit—dissipating in the middle of combat. Disintegrated corpses no longer demanded space on the land they destroyed.

At first the Tetrians were hesitant. They continued to attack the thinning hordes. Even when they were all gone, the soldiers searched for someone to fight. A sudden howl from Albert garnered the attention of every remaining ally. Makani stood with his hand on the werewolf's shoulder. Winds picked up and carried through the valley. The sensation was enough to confirm what everyone was sure of. Yet they couldn't help but wait for the future king of Dawncaster to utter the words.

"Tetria…" Makani paused to clear his throat. "We are victorious!"

It wouldn't surprise Kargon if the entire continent shook from the army's cheer. He wished to scream with them but only managed to hack out some blood. For some reason that satisfied him. To know that he'd helped to bring about Aeraza's end. Aisha's dumb childhood best friend ended up being her ace. It wouldn't surprise Kargon if she had always known that would be his role. Every fiber of his being wanted to ask her. Talk to her. Spend more time with her. But the fading adrenaline made him aware of what his body went through. Mutilation and burns sent searing pain through his body. Deep cuts and bruises covered every part of him. Tears rolled down his face, mixing with blood and dirt. Not even an ember would appear in his limp hand.

A fuzzy silhouette approached and held Kargon tightly. Even without his vision it was clear who it was. Firm body with a soft touch always meant it was Aisha. She'd hate how ready Kargon was to die in her arms. Moments before his consciousness could fade, a surge of energy engulfed him. His eyes shot open as golden light wreathed his previously damaged body.

"One more, Avant!" Vofric bellowed with both his hands on the half-elf's chest.

Master Avant was pouring a potion into the dwarf's mouth as both of them stood over Kargon along with Sariel and Avant. Sweat poured off Vofric's brow as his usually neatly tied dreadlocks loosely hung around his head. Soft smiles began appearing on faces as Kargon made eye contact with each of them. Wounds closed and bones reformed at a speed that eclipsed uncomfortable and was downright painful. But complaining about it at this moment was a terrible idea.

"I think… I'm good, Vofric," Kargon said as he caught his breath. "Aisha's face has a deep cut. Might wanna heal that."

"I'll be fine," Aisha said softly, gripping Kargon tightly. "Head wounds just bleed a lot."

"That doesn't make me feel any better."

Vofric shifted one of his hands and tapped Aisha's shoulder. Healing both fighters was no issue now that the battle was over.

"There will be scarring for both of you," he explained. "And I will need multiple appointments to heal that arm, Kargon."

The monk looked at the burnt husk quizzically. "I won't lose it?"

Sariel snorted. "Would you prefer that over a momentary loss of function?"

"No! I just... I thought it was done for."

Aisha snickered and asked sweetly. "Were you ready to lose it just for me?"

Kargon was dumbfounded to see the woman he loved express herself so innocently after the ordeal she went through. Even he was having trouble grounding himself after fighting Elmud and Atlas. But every passing moment surrounded by friends made it easier to calm down.

"It was the only plan I could think of. Couldn't have done it without Master Avant's staff," he replied.

The master was playfully tussling Avant's head and said, "I promised to get you back to Aisha. There was no limit on how many times I would accommodate the request."

"You have a peculiar delivery system," Sariel said.

Avant chirped to express agreement.

"Taze and the staff might be odd choices but they were perfectly suited to my protege," the master replied and turned to Kargon. "Aren't I correct?"

Kargon nodded slowly. The pain was finally subsiding and he found it awkward to stay caressed in Aisha's arms. They hesitantly stared at each other as the healing finished. Vofric's mana ran dry and he pulled himself up. Without effort, Aisha rose to her feet and assisted Kargon in doing the same. Flashes of pain trickled in his right arm as wind touched the healing burns. Implications of a swift recovery were highly exaggerated.

Aisha almost walked away but Vofric stopped her. A glance passed between them before the dwarf tilted his head back. Reddened cheeks appeared on the swordswoman's face.

"After all you've done, this preamble is unnecessary." the dwarf rolled his eyes and nudged his young companion.

Returning to the group, Aisha extended her right hand. When Kargon hesitated to take it, Sariel slapped his back. It was far from playful and forced the monk to catch himself in his beloved's hand.

"Does your monastery teach this kind of behavior?" Vofric chided Master Avant.

"Is it not common in such places?" Sariel asked.

The owlminn groaned. "Some monasteries do not support overt displays of affection but the Sanctuary of Spiritual Combustion has no such beliefs. My pupil is simply, excuse my language, romantically challenged."

Sariel and Vofric smirked at each other before the latter replied, "We're well aware."

It took everything for Kargon not to react as his face reddened, matching the hue on Aisha's. They looked towards the battlefield and stepped forward. Avant walked on his master's right, providing much needed support with his lack of balance. Next to the owlbear was his namesake. On Aisha's left was Vofric along with Sariel who rested a hand on the dwarf's shoulder. As they appeared over the edge of the cliff, the Tetrian army cheered once again.

Howls and roars sounded from thousands of soldiers. The loudest was Albert, who clapped like a madman while slowly transforming back to human form. Even Makani didn't remain cordial as he hollered happily at the sight of his friends. Freckle made eye contact with Sariel and they both smiled widely. A hyperactive yip from Spike was reciprocated by Avant as he hopped in place. With his size, it shook the ground nearby and almost knocked Kargon over. Vofric looked over the crowd and found various captains gathered together. It seemed they were already planning next steps.

"We lost many allies," he said softly. "I pray they find peace in their next life. Hopefully their families are taken care of."

"With connections like ours it will be possible to find them and make sure of it," Sariel responded.

Avant grumbled softly while nudging lightly against Kargon's wounded arm.

He ignored the pain to comfort his familiar and said, "We'll help as many animals as we can. I'll make sure of it."

"Your lives grow ever busier," Master Avant pointed out.

"That's how it is for adventurers. One quest ends and we look for new ones." Aisha replied.

The group stared at the army a little longer, trying to ignore all the work they had to complete. Even so, all of them wore smiles. Serenity washed over them as the sun approached the horizon and moonlight showered Tetria. Kargon clenched his right fist and winced. This was no dream or waking nightmare. It was over thanks to his best friend drawing a sword from stone.

CHAPTER SEVENTY-TWO

Epilogue

Commands and shouts echoed in the halls as vendors scrambled to make sure everything was prepared. Velana's quiet calmness was gone as she barked orders to the workers. Even Zigon couldn't calm her down and instead tried to leverage his build to aid in last minute setup. Both were clad in crimson ensembles with black jewelry that symbolized their connection to the guests of honor. With them was Marniese, stressed that decorations weren't perfectly set as guests began pouring into the wedding hall. A violet dress hugged her form with a sheer shawl on her shoulders. Jewelry matching Velana and Zigon hung from her ears. The town of Neves had seen larger crowds throughout its history but this was the first time people were invited directly by the Heroes of Tetria.

Neves had gone through many changes since the beginning of the Hero's quest. The biggest was a banquet hall Quintin oversaw in hopes of holding a celebration to honor his old friends. Intricate pieces created by Petla's skilled hand hung along the walls. Catering was provided by a high-strung Bennett as he spent almost a week preparing for the single event. They employed the aid of the Tenrok family, who had shifted to the town after Wolden fell apart. Melinda and Margaret studied the list of guests to make sure only those invited could enter the hall. Anyone who tried to force their way had to deal with the mighty orc, Pavrin. Though most interlopers stopped trying upon seeing the first guests arrive.

King Nasim, Queen Lyra, and their retainer Victor casually spoke to members of Barbatos. Exploits during Tetria's Defense had quickly spread around the world and many were getting employment opportunities on other continents. Amongst them was the vigilante once known as Palehound. Albert and Makani were ushering people to their seats like they hadn't been bequeathed the will of the Kingsguard commander. Others were shocked trying to think of how Greycastle market could function while Mia and Louise were here, entertaining local children. Though, it had to be easier with the natural charms of Avant and Spike.

Near the front door was Freckle Kiraan, openly talking about how she assisted the heroes in Shusyoun. The scholars would be livid if they heard her but clearly that didn't matter. If they wanted to challenge Freckle they would have to contend with the elderly elf who accompanied her. Few recognized the man known simply as Ed, yet he demanded respect. Taze walked through the crowd and offered petals for people to toss at the newlyweds. The person who garnered the most attention was an owlminn monk adorned in a pristine robe. Whispers about Master Avant spread through the room as he stood statuesque at the end of the aisle, waiting for the guests of honor.

Nearly an hour passed as hundreds of guests mingled in their seats. At the front were Velana, Zigon, and Marniese surrounded by their children's closest allies. Everyone else filled whatever seats they could find. Once the noise settled down, Avant walked through the aisle and took his place right of the officiant. They chirped in unison to calm the room. Next, Sariel and Vofric walked in. A fitted emerald suit and cape was adorned by the dragon. While Vofric still resembled a man of the cloth, he had received new clothes from Melinda and her family. The adventurers each stood on one side of Master Avant with space left for Kargon and Aisha.

First to enter was the fiery monk. His right arm was mostly healed but remained in a sling to deter from moving it. As was customary for Nevesi grooms, he wore an all black fitted suit. The flat colors only made his hair look all the brighter. Nerves challenged him to stay back but that wasn't enough to stop him from pressing forward. Hundreds of eyes watched as he overthought every step that carried him to the altar. He settled into place between Avant and Sariel. They both looked far more comfortable in their outfits than the man who hated sleeves. It brought a smile to Kargon when he noticed the new outfit on Vofric. The dwarf shot a smirk to his younger companion before they all turned towards the door.

Kargon couldn't recall what music played when Aisha appeared. Clearly it was pleasant as some eyes were drawn to Margaret's skilled fingers flitting across the grand piano. Velana and Marniese had said something about the woman's expertise. The firebrand only heard his heartbeat in his ears as the woman he loved stepped through the gate. Aisha was clad in a strapless black gown that trailed behind her. It was far from anything she'd wear to a battlefield. A crown of flowers laid softly on her head, complimenting her horns and bringing color to the dark curls underneath. Unlike Kargon, she walked with confidence. Clearly the years of being adored had paid off. Years old scars marked her upper torso and demanded reverence. As Aisha got close to the altar, a smirk appeared on her face. No one but her party and Master Avant could see it. She couldn't help it upon noticing Kargon's stunned expression.

"Are you really that shocked by the dress?" Aisha asked.

Kargon shook his head quickly and replied, "No! I, um, thought you'd skip the party like usual."

"Kargon, I invited you to this one. It'd be bad manners if I didn't show up."

"It wouldn't do to put out all the people you personally invited," Vofric added.

"People who await a ceremony," Sariel said. "Are you prepared?"

Pristine white chains rested in Sariel and Vofric's hands. They protected them since the day it was known the half-elves would wed. Aisha and Kargon's eyes met and a silent conversation passed in an instant. They smiled then nodded to Master Avant. Only those present heard what was said between the lovers.

***

Sariel stood back and admired their handiwork. Days had passed since the wedding. With express permission they created a gift for the entire party—though it was being presented quite late. Sariel managed to finish with minutes to spare before the others arrived. All the guests had left and only Zigon, Velana, and Marniese remained to see off the group. The first to arrive were Vofric and Avant with the majority of their supplies. An audible gasp passed the dwarf's lips as he stared at the carriage in front of him.

"You truly crafted this without any assistance? I'm impressed," he complimented.

"The wagon was meant for Kargon and Aisha to admire," Sariel said. "I believed the driver's seat would be more to your liking."

Vofric's eyes went wide and he dashed to the front of the carriage. The sight of familiar mechanisms lining the seat brought a smile to his face. From a cursory glance they looked more advanced than the party's old vehicle.

"I presume Taze had a hand in this," he said.

Avant cooed in reply while climbing into the covered wagon.

Sariel translated. "It is Taze's idea of a wedding gift. And I am not so proud to think I could build it myself."

"Those two really didn't need to request goods for our party." Vofric shook his head and sighed. "Where, praytell, are the newlyweds?"

"We're here!" Aisha yelled from afar.

The beautiful gown was a distant memory as she had donned new armor. Behind her was Kargon, doing slow exercises with his right arm before putting it back in the sling. A smile on his face turned to shock as he took in the carriage. Their parents trailed behind with surprise at the armored warriors who, up until recently, looked like average villagers.

"This is a beautiful construction, Sariel," Marniese said and squeezed the dragon's arm. "Well done."

Velana approached Vofric and looked over his armor. "Your holy presence is strong regardless of your clothing. I imagine it's rather forceful atop a steed like Avant. Do be soft with him. He is but a child."

"I'm aware, Velana. Worry not. Your son and grandson are safe with us," the dwarf replied.

"And my daughter-in-law?"

Sariel chimed in and said, "We will protect her if the moment ever comes to pass. Though, Kargon will be leading the charge so you need not worry."

"Take care of each other," Zigon said softly and ruffled his son's head. "Help people."

Even a short meeting resulted in tearful goodbyes from the adventurers. Eventually, however, they needed to depart. A wide grin appeared on Vofric's face the instant he started the engine. Smooth rhythms rocked the carriage as the motor puttered to life. A slow roll carried them out of town and back on the road. Exhaustion was still evident as Kargon sat down and promptly fell asleep. Without hesitation or shame, Aisha leaned into him and followed suit. Avant readily laid down near their legs and provided a soft cover. An unfiltered smile stretched across Sariel's face as they glimpsed a sparkle under the half-elves' armor. Each wore a thin white necklace, binding them together wherever their life of adventure led.

Acknowledgments

The Hero's Right Hand could have never happened without my closest and oldest friend introducing me to Dungeons and Dragons several years ago. I find myself debating how to refer to you, Sparrow. You've got myriad names like the old gods but for me you're always Boss. My obsession with a right-hand man wouldn't have existed without you and I owe you more than I can put to words. You deserve the world.

I have to also thank Jesse and Hamza for being friends, party members, and siblings I could rely on throughout my life. I don't know what a fair weather friend is because of you. Parts of our little four man crew are sprinkled throughout Kargon's party and I know you know it.

Thanks to Lucas and Nate who convinced me to write a web novel. It built my consistent habit of writing every day without worry. It pushed past my editing roadblock and silenced the perfectionist that every creator grapples with. My life as an author has been irrevocably changed by our friendship.

This story wouldn't have been possible without my own Master Avant; my big brother, Anurag. You came up with stories off the cuff to entertain me as a kid. You made me a hero alongside you even when I was a brat. Whatever events have ever separated us, I know our bond is unbreakable. I hope to leave you speechless as I carve my path and know I'll always have you in my corner.

Finally, thank you to my wonderful spouse, Robyn.

You full well know Aisha wouldn't exist as she is without you. You inspire me and drive me to be better than I believe myself to be. I would be stuck wondering if scenes were too corny to include if you hadn't guided me. Thank you for being my first reader, editor, supporter, and best friend. I'm excited to see your story unfold for the rest of my life.

about the author

Bhav Das-Romain is a non-binary Indian obsessed with all things fantasy. Escaping to distant worlds has been his favorite pastime since childhood. Video games are his go-to time sink and his greatest pride is his action figure collection. He lives in Madison, WI with his spouse who feeds his fantastical ideas. Coffee and chai flow through his veins. If he could be anything else, he'd be a bear.